THE WAY TO WITCH FARM

MARY TREPANIER

Published by Cwtch Press, Redmond, WA 98052

Cover design by Mariah Sinclair

E-book ISBN: 978-1-947234-31-4

Print ISBN: 978-1-947234-32-1

10 9 8 7 6 5 4 3 2 1

Trigger Warning: Graphically violent scenes in this book might be disturbing to some. The material is not appropriate for people under age 18.

THE WAY TO WITCH FARM

Tales of the End Times Book 3

MARY TREPANIER

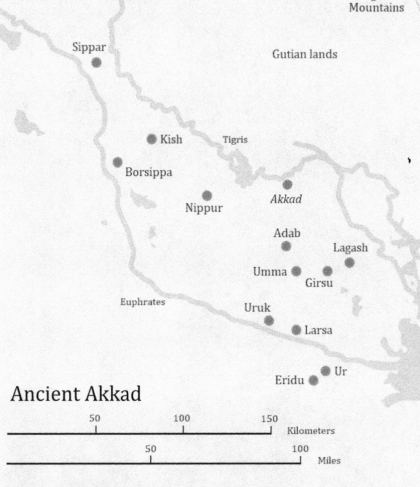

Zagros Mountains

Sippar

Gutian lands

Kish

Tigris

Borsippa

Nippur

Akkad

Adab

Lagash

Umma

Girsu

Euphrates

Uruk

Larsa

Eridu

Ur

Ancient Akkad

50   100   150   Kilometers

50   100   Miles

The site of Akkad hasn't been located in modern times.
Some think it lay on the Tigris River.

Chapter 1

The path lay a skein of mud, overarched by trees in a green hollow. Moss sat to either side, bright yellow-green. After the end of the world, the new beginning was quieter.

But it was laced with birdsong—robins' liquid insistence, flat chickadee music. A crow, far away, complained about something, almost barking.

People were here too, as if part of the woodland, reading books among the trees. Nearby, Joanie sensed a lake or pond. The cool air hinted at water.

This was Seattle, but in some future.

The scene changed, to somewhere distant from the central city. Her view stepped backward, and she saw a vista of the new world. A hill of grass rose under an overcast sky, among the ruins of foundations. This was twenty, maybe fifty years in the future.

The day was warm, the sun hiding, the clouds milky. It felt like early fall.

A house stood nearby, between two low hills, single-level

and earth-sheltered, with open sliding glass doors. It housed a collective, loosely woven people who were friends and friendly; everyone knew each other and how they fit together. It was familial but not only family.

She walked in and people greeted her, hugged her. There was something to plan, a meeting to have.

Before she found out what, she woke up.

The coven Joanie belonged to had combined their summer solstice ritual with another's. They'd slept over for dream incubation, to find a true dream. They focused on calling in a healed future world.

The friends' covenstead was outside town, down hairpin-turn roads draped with cedars, near the National Forest. They'd slept in a yurt at the border of a meadow. The house was set among gardens, one of herbs and vegetables, another full of daisies beside a huge white-flowering mock orange. A green-house nestled nearby. Lanterns, now dark, stood along the path from the house to the yurt, which crossed a bridge over a brook. Maybe that was why Joanie had sensed water. The yurt path and meadow edges were lined with purple and white foxgloves.

But with all the meditation and the ritual setup they'd done, this dream might tell the future.

She sat up in her sleeping bag. She was the first to wake; Cleo, her girlfriend, curled beside her, was still asleep. Out the window, tinged with dawn, a few clouds bathed in rose light. She found her fleece boots, threw a sweatshirt over her night-gown, and made her way to the main house.

Nora, the priestess of the other coven, owned the house. She was an early riser, so in the terracotta-tiled kitchen Joanie found a full pot of coffee. Nora wasn't there—probably working in her gardens. She ran a small farm with help from live-in coven members. In the adjoining dining room, on the long formal table, candlesticks sat wreathed with fern leaves for the holiday. Joanie filled a mug and took a seat. She sipped the coffee, and warmth came into her.

Humans had predicted the end of the world for at least two thousand years. But now pole ice was melting, forests were burning, and each month was the hottest of its name. Oligarchs bought islands and built compounds. The rest descended into chaos. She woke up mornings facing a state falling into fascism. It had happened so quickly.

But giving into despair seemed like the best way to ensure the worst future. Today, here, now, it was a beautiful morning. The dream said there might be a future worth hoping for.

"Hey, Joanie." As she'd stared out the condensation-hazed window at the pink light, someone had come in. It was Gus.

They eyed each other. Only six months before, Gus had broken off a relationship with a man who'd turned out to be a white supremacist. At the same time, Gus had started dating her friend, now-covenmate Alyssa. Good had triumphed over evil in Gus's heart (so Joanie would put it), but she wondered if it would stick.

Yet Gus and Alyssa were engaged, living together, and Joanie was polite. She'd made mistakes herself. Not too long ago, she'd gotten rid of a sugar daddy who'd nearly killed her.

"Hi." She breathed in the scent of coffee, elixir of life. "How're you doing?"

"Glad to be done with finals." Gus was a biology undergrad, just finished with his junior year. Joanie was only a couple years older than Gus, and by happenstance of schooling only a year ahead in college. He still seemed young and unformed to her.

"What next, do you think?"

"Thinking about graduate school," he said. "I need to decide."

"Same." In effect, she'd decided for the coming year already by not applying to grad schools. She no longer wanted what she used to—get a master's, help create a new economy.

She wanted to get back to whoring. It was a talent wrested from a background that could have shamed her from sex entirely. For her, it wasn't just about money but her calling, wrapped up with her devotion to the love goddess Inanna.

But that path meant an identity outside the professional world. She wasn't sure semi-outlaw status was what she wanted.

She'd also applied for local business jobs. She was good at statistics, which helped. One of her professors had recommended a university position, pushing her to apply to grad school the following year: "You have a talent for economics. Don't waste it."

But the university job wouldn't pay much more than she made now as a barista. She supplemented that with posting pictures on a subscription fans page, but she only made enough for the occasional dinner out. In her post-sugar-daddy time, she'd already accrued plenty of student debt.

Above all, she needed money—a lot more than she was making. Right now, she was running to stay in place. So much of the future was uncertain, not just hers but her whole generation's. She needed stable finances and to pay off her loans. She'd grown up poor, watched her mother lose her house. Debt to her was anathema.

Working in business, over time, with luck even quickly, she could pay everything off—without the complications of whoring, which was at best only semi-legal.

"Mmm." Gus took a sip of his own coffee, yawning. "Did you dream?"

"I did. And you?"

"I did too. Want to talk about our dreams?"

She wrinkled her nose. "Let's wait for the next part of the ritual, in the yurt." She leaned to catch sight of the kitchen clock. "It's in about an hour, after breakfast."

Chapter 2

*I*n the heavens appeared no throne or torches, but a wave of green-golden light, a dancing fire. Puabi-Ekur knew they were with Hekate.

From a half-sleep they were drawn up and out quickly, without friction, easily as thought, to this fire the color of new grass. The Lady spoke without sound.

"You are with me on the plane of becoming."

Though Puabi-Ekur was an incubus-succubus in Hekate's service, they had no idea what that meant.

"Only watch."

They stepped out, away, down, to a place between planets. From high above, they watched as sunlight poured across the globe of the Earth, which turned faster and faster, till it was a blur, years passing. A blackout.

"Do they all die?"

"Watch."

They dove further inward and downward to the surface.

Blackberry grew over a rubble of ruins, with stands of violet fireweed. It was daytime, warm and overcast. Grey cloud hung over a hill of waving grass.

In the distance, someone played a panpipe, flubbing notes. Slowly, a cart pulled by a small horse or pony toiled along uneven ground up the hill. Two people led it, a silver-haired woman with black eyes and a young man with tight-curled black hair, his lips to the pipe. An olive-drab canvas tarp covered the back of the wooden-sided cart. The young man beamed at his companion and tried again.

At the front of the cart sat a wooden bench with cushions. On the bench, a young woman lay asleep, her body curled around a baby, wrapped into her shawl. A red curl had escaped her braid and lay against her cheek.

Puabi-Ekur focused on the older woman.

Those black, black eyes.

She is my Joanie.

The young man played a rill, and another, then started a simple melody, breathy and slow. The same notes repeated again and again. Finally Joanie said, "Stop."

The young man pulled the pipes from his lips and looked at her, his own liquid black eyes conveying deep hurt. Then he burst out laughing.

"If you insist. But it passes the time." At the top of the hill, the pony stopped to crop grass. "Caesar says we should take a break."

Where were they going; what were they doing?

"Wait and watch," Hekate spoke—not a voice but a sonorous sound, reverberating through Puabi-Ekur.

"We should try to get there by dark," Joanie-of-the-future said.

"We've only got a couple hours' walk."

"It depends on what's between us and there. And what's there."

"There haven't been any reports of raiding for a while."

"Just because the raiders are lying low doesn't mean they've disappeared."

"We've got nothing to steal."

"Cornmeal, bread, dried fruit—it's not nothing. We're safer traveling in daytime. I don't want to get there after dark."

Her companion turned to squint toward the cloud-covered sun. "Not likely. Give us a few minutes. I'm hungry."

Foraging in the wagon, he found a ragged blue-and-green plaid blanket and a cloth bag. He shook out the blanket and threw it on the grass, adjusting it so it lay flat, and from the bag unpacked some coarse bread, dried fruit, and meat jerky, a rough picnic.

"Do you have any dandelion tea left?" From the wagon bed Joanie produced a stoppered glass bottle and two cups. "Do you think we should wake Tamsin?"

"If you do, you'll wake the baby. Let them sleep."

"Maybe we should start a fire."

"No. I don't want to be here that long."

She watched him a few moments as he shifted restlessly from one foot to the other, then sat. They ate in silence, sipping the dandelion tea. The panpipe lay abandoned at a corner of the blanket.

With a rustle, footsteps approached.

"Shit," the young man said.

Joanie-of-the-future eyed him. "It's okay, Tracy. But let's pack up." They shoved the food and blanket in the wagon. Tracy picked up Caesar's halter, began leading, Joanie taking the other side.

Up the hill from behind the wagon came two burly young

men in riot gear, one with a US flag wound around his neck like a scarf, flapping behind him. Picking up on the energy around them, Puabi-Ekur understood this gave away their allegiances. Only raiders, fascists, and fascist fellow travelers carried US flags, though in the Salish Sea Federation (also known as Cascadia) everyone was a US citizen.

The wagon had no distinguishing markers, but not posting anything spoke, too.

"Hello there." The one without a flag, a muscular young man with close-trimmed blond hair, stepped forward. "We'd like to inspect the wagon."

Of course he had no right to. His friend circled the wagon, taking a moment to look over the sleeping Tamsin, and returned.

Stopping the wagon, Tracy and Joanie traded a glance.

"Are you from around here?" Joanie asked. "We're friends of the Aaronsens. If there's trouble, they stand behind us." As she spoke, she stepped over to Tracy's side of the wagon, and Tracy moved forward—not menacingly, but with interest. He didn't look like someone who would step down from a fight.

"We don't have anything of value," she continued. "Some food. We can give you cornmeal if you need it."

The man draped in the flag laughed. "Cornmeal! We don't need cornmeal, lady." He looked as if he was about to step forward, but his companion caught him by the arm and whispered in his ear a moment. Flag Guy frowned, flicked a glance at Joanie and then Tracy, and spat.

"We don't want your fucking food."

He pushed past Tracy and Joanie and started down the other side of the hill, his blond friend trailing him.

Tracy and Joanie watched them go.

"Let's give them some time to get ahead of us," Joanie said.

"Do you think they'll ambush us?"

"I don't think so. They seemed to know who the Aaronsens were."

"That type is generally cowards. I could have taken them both. I'm pretty sure of that."

"Better you don't have to."

Rustling in the wagon. Tamsin sat up, carefully, not to disturb the baby. "Did I miss something?"

"Only Joanie holding off two raiders."

Joanie-of-the-future laughed. "With the power of a magical name." Tamsin raised a red eyebrow. "Aaronsen."

Hekate swept Puabi-Ekur away.

It was only one future, Puabi-Ekur knew. There are many futures.

The flickering yellow green, like fire, like aurora borealis—you could lose yourself watching it.

"Puabi-Ekur." The Lady's voice rang deep, bell-toned. It went through them.

No token appeared this time, no information at all, just the knowledge borne on sound that here was their mission: something to do with Joanie, something to do with the time ahead.

"But Lady—what can I do about the future?"

No answer, just the hissing of the flame that was not a flame.

Chapter 3

$\mathcal{S}$lowly, the two covens and friends gathered in the yurt, yawning and sipping coffee in morning shadow. About twenty witches seated themselves on a set of mats and big pillows, a few older ones taking folding chairs. Nora and Hannah, who'd put the ritual together, sat up front.

They set the space, calling in a circle in Hannah's tradition's way. Nora added, "We're grateful to do this ritual here, on land that is traditionally Snoqualmie tribal land."

Over time, cobbling it from books and experience, Hannah and Nora had put together a dream analysis practice. For each dream, the dreamer gave a framing, then people in the circle called out pieces that might be precognitive and symbols and images that showed a theme. Then the group brought interpretation to a close, and the dreamer decided on a next step.

After Joanie told about her dream, Gus spoke up.

He wasn't part of Hannah's coven, but came as a friend. As Joanie was, a lot of the coven members were on the fence about him, particularly Joanie's girlfriend Cleo. As he spoke, Cleo tensed beside her. Cleo tossed one of the ends of the sash tied around her demi-Afro over her shoulder, impatiently.

"What would you name this dream?" someone called out.

"I guess I'd call it 'The Camp.'"

Gus sat across the circle from Joanie, next to Alyssa. Pale, slender, blonde Alyssa at least looked healthier now than when Joanie met her, when Alyssa was walking the street, a life she was glad to be done with.

Gus sat forward, his elbows on his knees, gazing at the yurt's wood-laminate flooring.

"It's one of the most vivid dreams I've ever had. When it starts out, I'm in a dark place, on a pallet, tons of people around me. A baby's crying somewhere. It's the middle of the night. Someone comes in to wake me, and they see I'm already awake."

He looked up, across the yurt, straight at Joanie.

"It's you, Joanie."

She felt called out in some unnamable way. For thinking ill of him? She had reason to.

"You say, 'We're breaking out tonight.'"

He continued. Several people related to the coven were in the camp: Gus, Joanie, Alyssa, Cleo, also Hannah but in the medical tent, down with the flu as hundreds of people were. She'd made them agree to leave her. The others followed Joanie.

"You'd called in a favor to break us out."

She understood him. She'd used her skill as a whore.

In his dream, outside the tent lay deep night, blue-black sky poured full of full moon light. They had to be far away from any city, in Eastern Washington he thought, because you could see stars as well. The camp was so large it had gotten hard for the militias staffing it to control—they'd rounded up too many people too quickly.

Guards patrolled the edge, with a no-pass zone between two quickly erected concrete walls topped with barbed wire. Joanie led the group to a guard—a handsome man with a close-trimmed black beard. Stepping up, she gave the man a deep kiss, grinding her pelvis against his.

She gestured, and the other five came out from behind her.

"These are my friends. Just lead us out of the camp, out of sight. We'll do the rest." He took them first to a small concrete hut whose tin roof flatly reflected moonlight, along whose inside wall, sat a set of olive-drab cloth packs.

"Then we were out, on the road, walking away." Theirs was a long walk, up through the Cascades, but all of them were in good health.

"That's where the dream ended."

Silence fell for a few moments, then several people talked over each other.

"One at a time, y'all," Hannah said. She was a big woman, head shaved except for a topknot dyed hot-pink. She'd come by her Southern accent honestly, growing up in Atlanta.

Kevin was the one who summed it up for the group: "I feel as if this is a true, precognitive dream. But if so, it's a pretty scary one."

Nora leaned forward. She was a tall, hatchet-faced woman, long hair streaked with grey bound up in braids.

"What next steps do you want to take for this dream?"

"Don't know. Write about it some, maybe, see where that leads me." He looked across at Joanie. "Be nice to Joanie."

"You'd better," Cleo muttered. When Gus had flirted with white supremacism, hers had been one of the strongest voices calling him out.

"That was an intense one," Nora said. "Let's ground." She led the group in a grounding as a tree, roots in the rich earth, top in the stars.

Nudged by Gus, Alyssa spoke up next.

In the last six months, Alyssa had become both a witch of the coven and a devotee of Hekate. Her former wardrobe, heavy on pale pink and blue, had changed to dark reds, purples, and blacks. She'd stepped up in the coven as a visionary.

"What would you call this dream?" someone asked.

"'The Deer and the Goddess.'"

A shaft of light struck a gold highlight from her blonde hair. So fair, she was almost transparent, her angelic, pale skin set against a fuzzy sweater the color of pomegranate juice.

"The beginning was like a vision I had last year. The goddess brought me to a cave covered in ancient paintings of animals. An altar at the back held a giant deer skull, crying tears of blood. When I came up to the deer skull, it nodded to me. As if my task was done."

She and Gus exchanged a glance. Joanie understood. Alyssa's part in helping Gus save himself from white suprema-cists was done.

"The next part was set on this property, except there was a tiny cabin back in the woods."

Nora broke protocol to speak: "There really is a cabin there."

Alyssa's wide blue eyes shifted to gaze at her. "I didn't know. Anyway, in the cabin, there was a shrine in the corner, with a small goddess statue. I sat down in front of it and lit a candle. I could see the goddess's face move as she spoke. She said the dark time we've seen coming has begun. It's going to be both easier and harder than we imagine it. But those who follow the green path will be on the right trail."

She looked down at her scrunched-up toes, nails painted black.

"And then what happened?"

"That's the end. I'm open to feedback."

"If it were my dream, I'd wonder—what's the green path?" someone asked.

"For me, it's a Native American prophecy," Alyssa said. "Winona LaDuke talks about it. It's specifically shared with non-natives. We get to choose between two paths, one well-worn but scorched and one that's green."

Joanie raised her hand, and at Nora's nod, spoke. "These dreams don't really read as dreams for me, but visions. The deer is telling you one task is ended. The spirit in the cabin is telling you about the future."

A few others offered interpretations. Nora let the group speak, then said, "You didn't know there was a cabin on this property."

Alyssa shook her head.

"My former husband and I built the tiny houses here. The biggest is that cabin. I put a shrine in there to honor the spirits of the land. Then someone came to live it."

"Who is she?" Alyssa asked.

"We don't know, really. She's an earth spirit, definitely here before us. Some people have seen her as a bear." Nora lived abutting a wilderness area, and deer and bear were frequent visitors. "As we've started working together, she's taken the coven under her protection. We call her Dea, for goddess."

Kevin frowned. "She's just some random spirit? How do you know she's a good one?"

Nora turned a forbidding gaze on him. "I know she's good because her help to me has been good. She helped bring my daughter into the world. She's also helped others in the coven."

"For me," another woman of Nora's coven said, "she's always brought good luck."

Hannah laughed. "Don't go disrespecting your coven's patron goddess, Kevin."

Kevin looked down, face surly.

Bars of golden sunlight fell across the grass in the late afternoon, lighting the yurt interior by reflection. Hannah and Nora sat at the apex of the circle as the other witches collected, seating themselves on mats, pillows, chairs, some yawning. They'd been up late, the previous night, solstice eve, drumming by the firepit. Then came a midmorning ritual, now this closing one, as the day's rays grew long.

Over the weekend, each person had created an image to symbolize their next actions based on their dreams—of cloth, cardboard, paint, embroidery thread, or twine, or some combination of these. They'd brought these charms, and now they would charge them with energy.

In the center of the room stood an altar, its cloth green velvet, machine-embroidered in black with Celtic knotwork. It held a number of candles, a statue of Diana and of Pan, and purple and white foxgloves picked from the meadow.

Hannah and Nora rose, the group following them. They cut the circle, called in the goddess and god, and as they did at midsummer called the fey kingdom, a broad term for their tradition that included ghosts and spirits, not just nature sprites. As they called in the fey, Joanie caught a sense of a bear goddess—Dea, the goddess Alyssa had met.

"We'll raise energy for our charms by toning," Nora said. "To do that, let's go around the circle and each choose one or two words to symbolize what we took from our dreams this weekend to help create a better future. I'll start." She paused, took a breath. "Focus."

"Energy."

"Right action."

"Witnessing."

"The green path."

The circle wound around to Joanie.

It had taken her a while to bring together meaning from her dreams. The best she'd come up with was this: "Community."

As she gazed around the circle, as she thought about Firebird House, it felt right to her. How else would they create the future?

With their words, the circle began to tone. Each sang their word on a note; the notes harmonized, were dissonant, and harmonized again, free-form, and rose. At the climax, they sent the energy with a shout, their group magic toward a healed world. She could almost see the energy, an iridescent golden ray shooting from the yurt.

Chapter 4

From the ether, Puabi-Ekur watched this new goddess, this Dea.

She didn't seem new to Puabi-Ekur, but old, one of the early goddesses who strode out of the Ice Age. They saw a bear goddess, connected with a people who hunted bear and revered them. Such people had lived all over the earth. A strong protectress, she was a guardian of the portal between life and death. Natural that she'd appear now at summer equinox, the time of the foxglove, the height of power for a winter-sleeping bear goddess.

What did Dea have to do with Puabi-Ekur's quest?

Puabi-Ekur saw again the green-gold flame, the field of becoming, the color of spring turning to summer.

After the confrontation with the raiders, it took a couple of hours for the cart to reach its destination, the Aaronsens' house.

Their path lay through ruins and broken foundations, half-walls grown up with brush, shattered corners of nameless buildings sheltering wildflowers. Sometimes the cart followed a dirt road, sometimes a few feet of old asphalt from a former street. Grass grew over and around these ruins, but native plants had also come back, salal and deer fern, in some places small groves of Douglas fir or cedar.

Once the raiders were gone, they saw no one. After the skirmishes and wildfires had died down, after the decimated regional governments partnered with the NGOs on serious cleanup, after it became clear the intentional communities and extended families would survive while the oligarchs died in their towers, there weren't many people left. A virulent strain of flu mutated and mutated again, along with other viruses, burning through the shocked and stressed populace. By the end of the final pandemic, the Salish Sea Federation had a third of the population that the same combined territory of Washington, Oregon, and Northern California had held in 2025.

In the warm, overcast afternoon there rose chants of birdsong. Tamsin and the baby went back to sleep. The pony picked his way forward, stopping sometimes to forage. Joanie-of-the-future let him eat a bit for his trouble but kept a sharp eye on the westering sun.

As the rays grew long and golden, the cart rolled past the first of extensive gardens. Soon to either side they found orchards, apples tiny on their branches, plums nearly ripe. A light wire fence with an occasional stylized A posted made it clear these were Aaronsen gardens, but there was no guard here. Knowing she would be freely given it, Joanie reached out, picked a plum, and ate it, juice dribbling down her chin. They turned a corner, and, facing them between two low hills, stood an earth-sheltered house, single-level but large. Its front sliding-glass doors stood open.

"Here we are," Tracy said, and picking up his panpipe played an introductory rill.

It produced a wary young man—tall, wiry, with black hair cropped close to his head. He wore olive-drab fatigues, sunglasses, and a rifle.

Joanie nodded at the gun. "That's new, Isaac. I though you all were committed pacifists?"

"Except for self-defense. There's been an uptick in raiders lately. But this is ninety-seven percent for show."

"We met a couple raiders on the road," Tracy put in. "Wearing riot gear and the American flag. But Joanie invoked the name of Aaronsen, and they ran away."

"That's good," Isaac said equably. "You looking to spend the night?"

"Yes. And do some trading."

Isaac cracked a smile. "I was hoping so. Let's get you settled, then I'll call Old Josh." There were two Joshua Aaronsens, father and son, and at some point someone had nicknamed the father Old Josh.

The Aaronsen Family Collective fell between the categories of intentional community and extended family. If the Aaronsen Family Collective were a tree, the main trunk and the biggest branches were all Aaronsens. But then there were partners, with polyamorous other partners, and children and adopted children, and co-living friends—smaller branches—and tons of mycelial connections to dozens of other small and large communities, the interconnected network that was the fabric of the Salish Sea Federation.

Joanie and Tracy's small collective, originally built around an interconnected set of covens, was known as Witch Farm. They had a series of gardens and a henhouse; Tracy and a few others kept bees; one witch had a greenhouse where she grew tea, though not enough for trade. Their witch gardens produced medicinal tinctures and infusions, and they traded their most popular items under their medicinal label.

Isaac directed Joanie and Tracy to bring the pony into the small stable. They unharnessed him, currycombed him, gave him a bit of hay. Then Isaac led them all into the house, down a long, narrow dark hallway, white-painted stucco, hung with pictures of the collective. He pointed them at a room. "That do?"

"Sure."

"You want to wash up before dinner?"

As Witch Farm did, the Aaronsens had a well and gravity-fed water, with a solar hot water heater.

"Yes, please."

"I'll get you some towels."

There were two separate communal showers, men's and women's, and a couple separate ones for people who wanted privacy. They'd taken the cart for a week on a trading round, and to bring Tamsin and baby for a wellness check at the doctor's. It had been that long since Joanie had taken more than a sponge bath.

She relaxed under the hot water, let herself go.

It had been a week, too, since she'd felt fully safe.

She loved and trusted Tracy, who was a good fighter. She herself was a pretty good shot, if it came to that. There was a shotgun behind the cab of the cart.

But any time you went beyond Witch Farm's fences, you were in wilderness. There was law, organized along tribal lines —there was a conscious effort, in the new world, to return to indigenous thinking.

But over thousands of square miles of land, there was very little policing. And though the pandemics had eliminated a lot of oligarchs who'd thought they could make themselves immune—and some had been eliminated by their security forces—there were still raiders, petty thieves, and grifters.

So, in the wilderness, Joanie was always just a little tense. Here, behind the Aaronsen's walls, with their network of ally-ships, she felt safe. Perhaps even safer than at Witch Farm.

She let the hot water run through her hair, lathered up, and rinsed off, doing her best to release all thought.

An hour or so later, she pushed back her plate after a heaping portion of plum cobbler. The main room of Center House was big and low-slung, with oil-lamp chandeliers and a hardwood floor covered with multiple throw rugs, one over the other. A small fire burned in a woodstove; the early-autumn night had gone chilly.

"What have you got to show me?" Josh asked.

In no hurry, Joanie unearthed wares from her burlap side-bag. She left the honey and beeswax but got out two mason jars. They were both labeled Witch Farm Medicinals, one Lavender Tincture, the other Rosemary Tincture. To call these "tinctures" was a sleight of hand to keep what remained of federal law at bay. In the early twenty-first century, they would have been called infused vodkas.

Old Josh was a big man, muscular, roughly Joanie's age, with a shock of pepper-and-salt hair tied back in a leather thong. "You know, it's good to see you again, Joanie."

She saw herself in his eyes.

Her hair was now silver, her neck creased. But war, illness, and hard work had left her a slender form, and people guessed her age ten or even twenty years less than it was. Her looks were an asset, a tradeable, in these times, as they always had been.

"You too, Josh."

Witch Farm also ran a brothel. Or, from another angle, as Cleo said, they threw a great party.

The Aaronsen Collective's tradeables were food, and education—how to organize and run an organic farm, in these days, on the border of the Salish Sea. They ran pay-as-you-can workshops and working internships. Like Witch Farm, they had a spiritual bent—Josh's daughter Freida, a rabbi, ran services and a series of outreach programs.

With a heavy movement, Josh stood, headed for the rambling kitchen, after a few moments returned with two cordial glasses. Joanie wondered how these had survived destruction. He twisted open the rosemary vodka, poured them each a shot, and nudged hers across the table to her.

"The plums are excellent this year," he said. The plums were flourishing in the Northwest's new warmer weather—more like California had been, back before. "Also our lemons."

"Lemons sound great." Witch Farm ran a small bar on weekends—lemon worked for drink garnishes. "Do you have any late potatoes or turnips? We can use some to supplement our stock." Potatoes made the base of their vodka.

The haggling continued, a quarter-hour, a half-hour. Under the conversation, two people maneuvered to see if they were going to bed together.

As a lover, Joanie had Cleo. Joanie also still had a few clients—older men who didn't want a younger woman in bed, who wanted conversation and comfort more than acrobatics. Josh fell into a category between client and friend.

"So, a case, half rosemary and half lavender vodka—"

"Tincture, please." She laughed.

"Tincture, for two twenty-pound bags of potatoes, fifty lemons, fifty plums, and two dozen of the special tomatoes."

"That should do it."

Drawing over a jar of walnut ink, Josh scratched the numbers into his account book using a quill pen made from a feather from one of his collective's geese. She pulled her own account book from her ancient canvas bag. She'd transfer her numbers to the computer when she got back to the farm. Between the chances of theft and inclement weather, the risk wasn't worth it to carry a laptop.

She caught his dark eyes on her. Still a handsome man, he was about her age, she thought, pushing sixty. If that could be imagined. She didn't feel it, except sometimes on a creaky morning.

He put out his arm, as a gesture, and she came and sat in his lap.

"What would you say, Joanie, about tonight?"

She kissed him, long and slow, with a kindling of desire. "What would you say about another bag of potatoes?"

Chapter 5

*F*or her midsummer charm, Joanie had used "community" to sum up what it meant. Her witch circle reflected community back to her. But how to draw the pieces together, she didn't know.

Since midsummer, she'd realized she was swimming in debt. She'd sent dozens of résumés and had a couple interviews. If she kept trying, she'd find an entry-level business job—bank teller, accounting assistant, something like that. She'd lost all her professional outfits when she left her sugar daddy, so she'd gone shopping. You had to spend money to make money. But it made her feel more poor.

At the same time, Inanna called her.

Meanwhile, the world was falling apart. The neo-Nazis had backed off a little, for now. They'd stopped trying to protest on Capitol Hill and moved to outlying districts. But climate change, if anything, was getting worse faster than predicted. The oligarchs had built their castles and were planning to pull up the drawbridges.

It was late, after a closing shift at the coffee shop. Upstairs in her room at Firebird House, Cleo worked on her thesis. Sitting on her bed, she tapped at her computer, breaking off to sort notes. Light reflected, glittering from the gilt-threaded sari tented above her and from orange and magenta pillows sewn with mirrors.

Joanie entered; they traded a quick kiss.

"How is it going?" Joanie asked.

"So-so." Sighing, Cleo sat back and rolled her head on her shoulders, stretching her neck.

Her thesis was about perception and creation of race identity for people with mixed Black and Indigenous heritage, a background she had herself. She'd taken a second extension to finish it. Her own mixed heritage came from her father, a musician who'd left Cleo's mother when she was four and who'd bounced into and out of her life since. Her research had included interviews with her grandmother and great-aunt, which raised painful memories. Some days, she revised the same page over and over.

"Oh, baby." Joanie sat down beside Cleo, put her arms around her. "Same old same old?"

Cleo burrowed into her arms and nodded.

"Maybe look up that therapist we talked about?"

A growling sound. "Don't have time for that nonsense."

"Cleo, sweetheart. Are you sure you're not just playing the strong Black woman?"

"Shut up, white girl."

Joanie hugged her hard. "Please think about it."

After a few moments, Cleo released herself. "I'd better get back to it."

"Need food or tea or anything?"

"No, thanks."

Climbing off the bed, Joanie shut the door gently and went downstairs.

A curtain separated Joanie's bedroom from the rest of the basement. Sitting down on her bed covered with the quilt her aunt had made her, Joanie lit Inanna's coral-pink candle on her desk. Breathing deeply, eyes closed, she relaxed into trance.

Instead of the goddess, Puabi-Ekur appeared. They greeted each other.

Joanie jumped into it. "This world. It's a mess." Puabi-Ekur made an affirmative noise. "I have to get off my ass and act. But how?"

"Follow your calling."

"What does that mean?"

"You know."

Sex work, work for Inanna, but work with the aim of healing and love. She could do sacred whoring, call it somatic bodywork if she wanted to make it a career. For that, she'd need to go back to school for some kind of method—massage, therapy. But even semi-legal professional sex work was iffy now.

She thought of Hannah, her high priestess, talking last Samhain: "You know pagans and witches are crap with money. There must be something you can do in finance to help. Having a couple strings to your bow's not a bad thing."

"I want both," she said now to Puabi-Ekur. "I want an independent life and I want to do my heart's calling." She knew so many people trying to monetize their spirituality, and it didn't work well. "What I want isn't a pile of cash but to be free of debt. And I want community, and to clean up some of this mess if I can."

"What do you desire most?"

"I want to start the Inanna circles again, but for the ritual of it, not the sex work. Though for sex work, I have a few clients I could check with if I want extra cash." She contemplated this. "I want a day job too. Do accounting or something in finance for a while as an employee, then branch out on my own."

Hekate had told her to listen to her high priestess, who'd suggested that.

Great. Three different life plans. She could definitely go three directions at once.

Hours daily, she searched online, putting in more résumés and applications. She got a phone interview. The job paid barely enough to justify leaving the coffee shop—a data entry job "with possibility for advancement." A week after the phone screen, she followed up. Her lack of enthusiasm must have shone through, because the job was filled.

For an accounting assistant interview, she took the bus downtown, among shining buildings and construction dust. She thought she'd nailed it, but the company never called back. For another accounting assistantship, at a food brokerage, she took the ferry to one of the islands to interview. She thought she had that one, but no.

She sent more résumés. She applied for an accounting assistant position at a trucking firm, south of downtown, and got an interview. As soon as she walked in and met the dough-faced, hostile receptionist, she knew she'd never be a fit.

Part of her feared she'd never find anything. At the turn of the month, her student loans ate more cash.

Late one afternoon, she got back from the coffee shop, hot and sweaty from a frustrating shift. Her phone rang as she brushed past the curtain to her room. She'd started working with a couple of job recruiters, and the caller was her favorite one. She picked up.

"Hi, Joanie, I have something for you, at the Gunnar Group —it's a financial planning company downtown." It was an entry level position, not a bad one, but not in the profession she wanted.

"I was hoping more for an accounting assistant or something like that."

"I understand, but I'd give this one a try. It's a great job to move into the financial industry, which was one of your possibilities. It's not sales but admin support. And did I say—this one is well-paid." She named the figure.

If Joanie got this job, even during training she'd make half again as much as at the coffee shop. In about a year or so, she could erase her student debt.

Into Joanie's pause, the recruiter added, "It's always easier to find a job if you have one in a related industry. I think you'll really like the woman who's the primary contact."

Putting in her job application online, Joanie had a flash of panic when she saw that it said that "all applicants are subject to extremely thorough background checks." But Joanie had met the conditions of her probation for prostitution, and her criminal record had been expunged.

A few days later, she got a call back. They wanted her to come in for an interview.

For an outfit, she chose a new dark maroon pencil skirt, a white oxford shirt, black pumps, and a black blazer. She polished her nails to match the skirt. She was ready.

It was on a Wednesday morning, ten a.m. She burned

incense for Hermes, lord of commerce—the day belonged to him. She hopped a bus downtown.

Stepping off, she oriented herself. Ahead lay the building, all shining windows and steel. She entered and crossed the marble-floored entry, heels tapping. The elevator came, wood-paneled inside.

No matter what happened, she'd be done with this soon.

The wall behind the reception desk was painted cobalt blue, with the company logo stenciled on it. She announced herself to the receptionist, who offered her coffee and water as she waited.

After a few moments, her mouth dry, Joanie got a glass of water. She reminded herself she was good at interviewing.

Then a woman appeared in front of her, tall, with a long reddish-blonde bob. "I'm Monica. It'll just be me today—Jack had a conflict."

Jack Gunnar was one of the principals of the company. Joanie had researched Jack and the company—the firm was well-regarded. She hadn't looked up this woman. Her heart pumped faster.

Monica led her across a sunny, wide-open office full of bright colors, cobalt blue, burnt-orange, and chartreuse against white. Monica had an office along one wall, with a blond wood desk and a big window with a view across the city. Joanie took the cobalt-upholstered guest chair.

"Tell me a little bit about yourself and why you're interested in this job."

Joanie turned on her high-wattage smile and answered. She enjoyed the performance of interviewing. She'd learned how to do patter as a whore.

"I see you've been a student. You didn't have any business internships?"

"This last bit, besides school, I've been making coffee. I became a manager four months ago." Her recent résumé only went back a year—she'd padded it with early jobs, like working as an office assistant when her mother ran a salon. "I took some time off to concentrate on my studies."

Monica met her eyes.

I was a whore, okay?

A moment passed, then Monica went on.

The job would mostly be support, a little sales but not cold calling; she'd make appointments and do some follow-up, after being trained.

"You'd be supporting Jack, Don, and me," Monica said. "Mostly Don and me."

Monica finished, answered a few questions from Joanie, then stood. Joanie followed; they shook hands.

"I have a few other folks to interview, but we'll contact you either way next week. If you go forward, the next step is an interview with Jack. Don's out on paternity leave." Monica smiled. "I think you're in the running."

It made Joanie's heart lift.

At the very least, she'd had a good interview for a job in a field she had the background for. If she got it, she could use the cash.

She'd liked Monica. The cobalt blue office wall, the bright colors, the shining building—she could see working there. Unlike the coffee shop, it was a job where she could get a modicum of respect and use her brain. She liked that.

Chapter 6

The tent sat at the edge of a desert flat, behind it a hill of brush. Wind had come up during the night, and everything was covered with a fine layer of brown dust. The sun was just rising, gold-red, floating above the horizon on a rim of gold. An outcropping of palms stood silhouetted against the light.

Ekur woke suddenly, body tense, as he had for so many days. Every moment, he had decisions to make, military strikes to plan and perform against the desert raider, Gutium, who had brought war to the people of Uruk, spilling blood on the city's white terraces.

On some level, he was surprised not to have been shaken from his sleep.

Slowly he relaxed among the blankets.

He'd forgotten—the campaign was won. The forces of Uruk had conquered. Gutium's army was broken and routed, many dead, many fled, many rounded up as prisoners, future slaves. The Gutian king himself was slain, although so had been the king of Uruk.

Ekur sat up, rolling his shoulders, which hurt—many days
of spear-fighting did that. So too did a long gash on his thigh,
sewn up and healing but still painful. The eldest son of a noble
house, he'd recently been promoted to general. He'd led his
men into battle in his chariot and had fought among them.
Many good men had fallen to spear, axe, and mace, lying in
their blood in the dust. His troops were bringing home what
bodies they could for burial, wrapped in reed matting.

Cross-legged, he sat amid a mess of blankets on a mat on
the floor—it was an active campaign, little splendor to it.
Though his hangings were embroidered red and blue, and he
had a small shrine to Inanna as goddess of war in one corner.
Her image, cut of alabaster, was painted in bright colors, and a
necklace he'd plundered coiled before her.

He tented his hands, sitting fingers to forehead. His head
was pounding. Last night, he and his captains had celebrated,
drinking beer.

"Eannatum," he called, "bring me some water."

He fell back on the bed.

Tan light filtered through scraped skins of the tent. Through
the tent opening, a breeze brought the scent of burning juniper
wood and dust.

Eannatum came in quietly. He'd seen some fighting as well,
but mostly he functioned as Ekur's aide-de-camp.

Helpful Eannatum. Slender, brown, lissome Eannatum.

Eannatum brought a jar of water and a smaller cup—field
ware, coarse terracotta.

"Here, sir." Sitting on the edge of the camp bed, setting
down the jar and cup, he brushed a curl of Ekur's long, waving
black hair back from his forehead.

Sitting up, Ekur gulped the water. Then he took Eannatum's

hand and kissed it, watching Eannatum's face as he mouthed his palm. Eannatum closed his eyes. His lips fell open.

That mouth, lush as a fig. Ekur pulled Eannatum toward him and kissed his mouth, hard, biting. Eannatum broke the kiss and gave him a sidelong glance.

"Should I close the tent flap?"

"Yes."

No hangover could compete with the spell of Eannatum's beauty.

Young and pliable, though so were most of the camp prostitutes. And his wife. Though his wife was far away, and all that was complicated.

Eannatum wasn't complicated. Or, if he was, he hadn't let on.

"Take your clothes off."

Eannatum slipped his long kilt off. Fair, even brown skin, unblemished, like a ripe piece of fruit. Ekur stood and took his hips in his hands, from behind, reached around to Eannatum's straining penis.

They crumpled to the floor, and Ekur was on him, slicking onto himself a mouthful of spit thrust inside him, both groaning and straining. As Ekur came so did Eannatum, filling Ekur's palm, spilling out onto the sheets.

Rough and quick. The whole thing had taken five minutes. It was plenty. It was perfect. They lay together, Ekur still on top, panting and sweating.

Today they continued their march back to Uruk.

In Uruk, what would happen to this?

Ekur rolled off; Eannatum shifted onto his back, eyes shut facing the tent ceiling.

Close and hot, the space smelled sweetly of sex.

Ekur watched Eannatum's face. His brown-purple lids lay like the petals of a flower, precious and trembling.

Chapter 7

The day of the second interview was hot. It was a Monday, no one's favorite day, an eleven-o'clock interview, and she had to work afterward.

Before she left, she said goodbye to Cleo, bringing her coffee.

"I like the place. At the same time, I'm not sure I want this," she told her. "It would be full-on capitalism. I'd be in the financial industry. Creating wealth for people, if that's what you want to call it."

Cleo eyed her over the cup brim.

"It's capitalism either way, whether you're at a coffee shop or a financial planning firm. And you're still a worker, not a capitalist."

"But the one place, people at least get coffee out of it. The other place, I play with money and try to get fees. A lot is tax avoidance. I'd be in the belly of the beast."

"Learn a few things to take down the oligarchs."

"I suppose."

"From a pragmatic point of view—you'd be making significantly more money, and you'd be able to start paying down your student debt. We fight capitalism, yes, but we still have to live in it." Cleo thoughtfully tapped her coffee cup, held in both hands. "You're going to get this. I feel like it'll be a turning point."

"I hope so."

Still, she stood next to Cleo, wanting something... more? else?

Setting down her cup, Cleo patted her arm. "It will be fine, honey. You'll get the job. If you hate it, you can quit. They love you at the coffee shop—they'd take you back. Give me a kiss before you go."

Joanie breathed in the sandalwood smell of her girl, the smell of home. It gave her strength.

The interview went by in fifteen minutes. Jack asked the same questions as Monica, though not as many. A square-built man in his forties or fifties, going bald with a half-ring of hair left, he shook her hand at the end. "We have one other candidate doing a second interview. We'll let you know by middle of next week."

She wanted the money and the respect. At least the financial industry would expect a minimum of intelligence. Not so for being a barista, at least not from the customers.

She was sweating by the time she got to the coffee shop and went in the bathroom to wash. Even in coffee garb, she looked good today. She had her brunette hair up against the heat. A little light shadow accentuated her ink-spot eyes.

When she'd first discovered the coffee shop, she'd liked it because it was off the beaten path, because it served coffee better than generic, and because the baristas left her alone. When her sugar daddy relationship tanked, it was easy enough to get a job. Whoring was a great preparation for customer service.

Now she'd fallen a little in love with the place. It made her happy to come here—the play of shadows and light, the chocolate-brown walls. Above all she loved her savvy, cheerful co-workers. She'd miss it if she left.

At the counter now stood a middle-aged blonde woman in sunglasses, an orange designer bag hanging off one arm. She looked at Joanie over the top of her glasses. "Do you still have that Kenyan variety you had a couple of weeks ago?"

"No, I'm sorry, we're out."

"Are you sure? Could you look and see?"

"Ma'am, I'm sure." The woman stared at her. Joanie saw that nothing would do except that she walk into the back room, stand there a few moments, then return. "I can look, though." She did the exercise, trying to keep her patience. Three people stood in line behind the woman.

Back at the counter, she said, "Sorry, ma'am. We expect to get another Kenyan soon, though it may not be that one."

The woman continued to stare at her over her glasses.

"I was told you'd have it." No one at the shop would have said that. "That's the kind I want, and I want it today." She hitched her bag onto her shoulder, glaring.

"I'm sorry, we just don't have it."

"Can I speak to your manager?"

"Ma'am, I am the manager."

"I see." The woman stared at her another moment, snorted, then turned, deliberately swinging her bag. It connected with a hand-made coffee cup, for sale on a stand. The cup fell and shattered as the woman stomped out.

The other barista rolled her eyes and went for a broom.

Working in financial services suddenly had more appeal.

Joanie got the call at the end of the week after her second interview. Monica said, "Come in Wednesday."

She arranged time to give notice; she needed to break it to the coffee shop owners gently. She was one of their favorite employees. She didn't want to do anything to ruin that, in case she wanted to return.

The first day at the new place, fifteen minutes early, she sat in the lobby with its cobalt-blue wall and prominent logo. Despite her ambivalence, excitement bubbled up in her.

Monica came to meet her, with a dazzling smile. "Let me introduce you around."

Sunlight spilled down onto the blond wood floor. Joanie smelled cinnamon tea. She shook hands and tried to remember names.

Then Monica sat her down in her sunny office. The view today was full of cranes; across the street, a new building was going up. Employment papers dealt with, Monica gave her the lay of the land.

The firm had been built off the two principals' advisee lists, though Monica now had her own list too. "We need an assistant now. Over time, if it works, we'd love for you to take on some of Don's list and move into planning."

Jack had the best list, centered on a few large families. Don had a larger number of customers, many in the technical sector. Monica's list was more up-and-comers, and she was working to grow it.

"It means I'm out a lot. The person you'll see the most of is Don. For now, I'll get you set up. We have a ton of admin work to get through. We just switched sales systems and have some cleanup to do." She looked at Joanie, her head tilted. "You're going to want to work toward your Certified Financial Planner certificate, which will help you move up."

"Of course." It made sense, and it had never crossed her mind. She had the uncomfortable feeling Monica could read her thoughts.

"You'll get the hang of things soon."

The day was a sunny haze. For lunch, she got a too-expensive sandwich at a nearby deli.

Chapter 8

The army bivouacked among dusty palms, which shaded them from the noon sun. Eannatum brought Ekur thick Sumerian beer, drunk with a long straw, and he kissed the boy offhandedly on the cheek. His captains glanced over, but none of them cared; it was customary to take lovers in the field. Ekur chewed dry bread and talked over the past campaign with his captains, in leisurely fashion, for pleasure more than anything else.

The problem was, they were returning to the city.

Theirs was a great victory, and the spoils would win Ekur many things. He could build onto his house and adorn it; he could endow the temples and give entertainments. As a general, he could use his contacts to become an administrator if he wished. And he did so wish, because that was the way to power and also to best serve Uruk—Uruk of the high temples and white terraces, which he loved. His children too could win high places, if he himself did not fall.

His wife would love that he had advanced her in the world.

He loved Irkalla as best he could. A beauty like a fruitful

palm, slender-hipped but ripe. In the first years of their marriage, they'd had much pleasure.

But she didn't love him. She didn't know how; she wasn't made like that. She loved frivolity, parties, imported wine, spangles, dresses that showed off her body, and impressing men. He didn't begrudge her these things, though she thought he did.

What he regretted was that she regarded him now as a necessary nuisance, and even more that she regarded their children so. He could find other love; he had. He gave the children everything he could; he loved them dearly. But as a commander or administrator, he would often have to be away.

The children had to rely on nursemaids for love, in the day to day. He wouldn't have minded Irkalla had lovers, if she'd made time for the children.

Then there was Eannatum.

It was usual to have a lover in the field, but when they returned to Uruk everyone returned to the grind-mill of their former lives. Eannatum, the young aide-de-camp, could be swept into Ekur's administration as a high-level clerk with expectations of advancement. Maybe they could meet for quick fucks at midday. Eventually Eannatum would have his own wife and household. He too was a young nobleman of Sumer, though his family was of lower rank, with connections to the eastern mountain folk.

Was that acceptable? Was this just sex?

It was not unheard of for men to live together, in Uruk. It needn't even cost a man honors.

But to divorce Irkalla would hurt their standing, both for Irkalla and for him. She'd be touchy even about an affair, if she learned of it, if it were in the city, if it weren't enclosed in the box of war and set aside. She could make trouble with her well-placed father, who had the king's ear.

If he saw Eannatum in the city, Irkalla would find out.

Why was he wasting time, then, eating bread and talking?

He yawned and stretched. A palm frond waved, casting its shadow across his face. A dry breeze touched his face, smelling of dust.

"I think we should take an hour or so break, under this hot sun."

The army was in no hurry. Best to take a leisurely pace and spare the men.

"Eannatum, bring some more of that beer into my tent."

Then he was kissing Eannatum's mouth, tasting of beer, and Eannatum was sucking him, to their muffled cries of pleasure.

Ekur vowed to take as long as possible returning to Uruk.

Chapter 9

*P*uabi-Ekur woke from the memory as from a dream. These dreams and visions Hekate sent were puzzles, which solved to tasks for them as a spirit in Hekate's service.

More than two and a half millennia ago, they had been Ekur, a general of Uruk in Inanna's service. The next step, perhaps, was obeisance to Inanna.

And to Ereshkigal, her sister, the goddess of hell.

The staircase spiraled downward, carved through living rock. Every few yards, inset lanterns shone. The deeper the stairs went, the simpler the lanterns were, going from metal to fired clay to chunks of stone. Then there were no more lanterns, the only light a faint red glow from below.

Puabi-Ekur traveled downward embodied as Puabi. Their long, crimped brunette hair fell over small breasts high on a slender, wide-hipped frame. Centuries before Ekur had lived,

Puabi had been a dancer of Inanna. As was traditional, Puabi-Ekur had let go their clothing and jewelry to the gatekeepers above. They wore their naked beauty proudly.

The final gate, basalt bound with silver, stood open, torches flaring to either side. In the forecourt of the Great Below, the walls receded into darkness.

At one end of the space sat a huge throne, basalt inset with black chalcedony. The throne was empty. The forecourt was also empty. Perhaps the dead had business elsewhere.

Puabi-Ekur prostrated themself before the throne and settled in to wait.

It had been some time since Puabi-Ekur had spoken to Ereshkigal. They'd been busy shepherding the boy Gus. But now Max, his hot but despicable boyfriend, was out of his life, and perhaps Gus could be left alone for a while.

In the dark space, a voice echoed: "My altars have been empty. No sweet incense have you burned for me."

"Lady, I will change that."

"You have not prostrated yourself to me. You have not given yourself to me in the night."

"Lady, I will change that."

"You have not performed my rituals. You have not sung my songs."

"Lady, I will change that."

"Do you know the story of how Enlil, god of storms, brought his wrath upon Sumer and Akkad?"

"Lady, I have knowledge of it, but remind me."

In a moonlike light with no apparent source, Puabi-Ekur could now see the Lady on her throne. She appeared as a Sumerian queen, brown-skinned, with a tiered skirt and crimped black hair under a conical headdress of silver bones.

Rimmed with kohl, her eyes burned bright red, signaling her displeasure with Puabi-Ekur.

"Let me quote you 'The Curse of Akkad':

For the first time since cities were built and founded,

The great agricultural tracts produced no grain,

The inundated tracts produced no fish,

The irrigated orchards produced neither syrup nor wine,

The gathered clouds did not rain, the masgurum did not grow....

He who slept on the roof, died on the roof.

He who slept in the house, had no burial.

People were flailing at themselves from hunger.

"Is Enlil angry?"

"Many the gods of earth are angry. They have been for decades, even centuries. Humans have fallen out of alignment with holy things. Surely you know this."

"Yes, I know, my lady."

"You know too the gods' wrath will return. It has been written by your prophets, your scientists."

"Yes, my lady."

"What are you, Puabi-Ekur, going to do about it?"

Me?

At least Puabi-Ekur could give one answer.

"My lady, I have been given a task by the Lady Hekate." The two goddesses were close enough to have been syncretized in ancient Greek curse tablets.

"So you have."

"My lady, I trust you and the Lady Hekate will lead me in the things I am to do."

The burning of the eyes had dimmed. Perhaps they were mollifying the goddess.

"How can we instruct you if you will not come before our altars?"

"My lady, I will rectify my omissions."

"See that you do. But in the meantime, I have a task for you." She lounged in her throne, slipping down a little. "Come here, Puabi-Ekur, you succubus of legendary powers. Prove yourself again to me."

She hiked her skirt. Puabi-Ekur positioned herself between the goddess's legs and licked.

Having paid homage in hell, they ascended into heaven.

They found the path easily, rising through the ether like smoke. They'd been dedicated to Inanna for more than three millennia.

At their destination, a swath of stars rolled in all directions, blazing suns of emerald, gold, white, and fiery red. Among them sat a golden throne, inset with lapis lazuli, carnelian, and crystal. Before it a golden brazier burned frankincense and rose petals, wafting perfume into nonair.

Again, Puabi-Ekur prostrated themself and waited.

After some time, the Lady Inanna flickered into place on her throne. Like her sister, she wore the outfit of a Sumerian queen, a tiered linen robe with a conical golden crown. Her huge black eyes were ringed in kohl.

"Well, little Puabi-Ekur, I could say what my sister said. Where have been my offerings? Where have been my obeisances?"

Puabi-Ekur hung their head.

"It is as she said—we need you to stay in touch, or we cannot instruct or help you. We are coming into another narrow time, and it is well in such times to maintain one's allyships."

"Yes, Lady Inanna."

"However, the Lady Ereshkigal and I have been your patronesses for millennia. We are not going to drop you now. You have a new deity to pay fealty to, however, or at least to get to know."

"My lady?"

"Your Joanie, and your boy Gus, came together with their coven to perform dream incubation. And in that incubation, young Alyssa received a vision, of a goddess they call Dea, who has a shrine on the priestess Nora's land."

"Yes, my lady?" All this was true—but what was the point?

"Your humans, Joanie and Gus, are bound in place and time. And the goddess of that place is Dea."

"Yes, my lady?"

"Introduce yourself."

They were tempted to ask how, but Inanna and Ereshkigal had already been forthcoming, for deities. As Puabi-Ekur made a last genuflection, throne and goddess disappeared, leaving Puabi-Ekur among the blazing stars.

Chapter 10

*a*s summer gilded the city, Cleo stayed heads-down on her master's thesis much of the time. If she could tease out these particular racial problems on paper, maybe that would help change the world.

Joanie was getting adjusted at work. The company had switched sales software systems, which had proved more complex than they'd hoped. For her first task, she kept busy at cleanup and troubleshooting. Also, as they could, Monica and another admin trained her. But they could only make so much time for her, and she was still getting to know the other office staff. She missed the camaraderie of the coffee shop.

One morning, just past first light, feeling sleepy and wistful, she went in for coffee before work. So early, the space was quiet, idle rays of sun falling across the charcoal-grey concrete floor. A few customers sat in the booths, intent on laptops.

Alyssa was on shift. After taking Joanie's order, she glanced to either side, then pulled something out from under the counter.

"Check this out. It was taped to a Black Lives Matter poster in someone's yard."

Alyssa pushed a flyer over the counter to Joanie. She went to community college in the city center—that must have been where she found it.

Joanie scanned it in a blur: a nasty caricature, the n-word, a demand for law and order—code for racism.

She looked up at Alyssa. "Are you surprised? I mean, we just had a run-in with white supremacists the end of last year."

"No. It just shouldn't be like this."

Joanie wondered what Alyssa's boyfriend thought of her opinion—Gus. He was the one who'd been caught up with the racists last year.

Alyssa caught her gaze. "Even Gus would agree with that."

"Really?" A switch flipped in Joanie. "I'd like to see him prove it. Cleo and I were talking about going to the next alt-right protest in Seattle to counter-protest it. Maybe you and Gus can come."

"Maybe."

Chapter 11

The pony cart and drivers returned to Witch Farm in early twilight. The east still reflected pink from the west, a tinge of green in the darkening blue behind.

The farm centered on a rambling three-storied house, which sagged a bit in places, porches held up by square red-painted wooden posts. The house's facade showed black-brown wood topped by a weather-beaten red metal roof. From corners and edges, banners fluttered and wind chimes called in the breeze.

Several smaller outbuildings, even closer to collapse, were also propped by strategic posts. Cleo and Joanie lived atop of one of these; the main house was for people who had children and held the kitchen.

Joanie brought Caesar the pony to the small shed that served as a stable, as Tracy and Tamsin took the baby up to their room. They'd encountered no danger returning from the Aaronsens' place. No people, no animals—as much as raiders, travelers feared roaming wild dogs.

Just as she had when they made it to the Aaronsens', Joanie

found herself relaxing. She didn't spin when footsteps approached, and when arms came around her she relaxed further, because they were Cleo's.

"Baby, it's good to have you home," Cleo said in a low voice. "I always worry, when you're out wandering around."

"It's necessary."

"You're in time for group supper. Do you want to talk, or wash up first?"

"Wash up, I think." It had been a long, hot journey.

"All right."

After a quick rinse at the communal shower, Joanie went up to their narrow room, whose entryway was a maze of load-bearing posts. Cleo had decorated as she always did, ceiling hung with red silk, wide bed deep in mirror-sewn pillows. It smelled like incense. Joanie breathed in deeply.

Home.

She let herself fall back onto the bed, looking up at the silver-threaded silk above her, still holding a hint of sunset in its folds.

The raiders weren't as bad now as they had been during and just after the set of skirmishes now called the Salish War. Right-wing militias had taken over swaths of what was now the Salish Sea Federation, especially to the east, across the Cascade Mountains. They'd set up internment camps to hold their enemies, which fell to protests backed by a series of legal challenges by the attenuated but still present US government. As foreseen long ago, Joanie and some others had briefly been in one till they escaped.

But as the Aaronsens had reported, there'd been a rise in raider activity lately. Enough to worry you, if you were a worrying soul.

Supper was casual, semi-vegan: lentil soup with carrots,

homemade bread, and a salad. Oil lamps and beeswax candles lit the low-ceilinged room, and a woodstove banished a seeping chill. Filmy reclaimed-polyester curtains were tied back to show twilight over Witch Farm's gardens. Nearest on the flagged patio lay containers of herbs—rosemary, sage, thyme—and a few apple trees marked the edge of the orchard.

Cleo claimed the spot next to Joanie, but they didn't talk much till dessert, fresh peaches from the greenhouse. "Have you heard from Clayton?" Cleo asked.

"Not over the last bit." Most adults in the household had cell phones, though access to repair was harder than in the past.

Clayton, another sometime-partner of Joanie's, had done much of the systems planning when they built the farm out from the original main house. He'd set up their wireless computer network and the biodiesel-fueled generator that provided backup for their solar panels. The consortium that maintained the internet was one thing that hadn't changed drastically.

As many Witch Farm residents did, he worked in the core city weekdays and came back to the farm on weekends. Getting back from the core part of Seattle city took half a day now, with the crumbled infrastructure. But in Seattle core, if you wanted, you could find most things privileged urbanites of 2025 had, though with more effort or credit.

In Seattle core, too, Clayton could occasionally meet his daughter. Otherwise she shunned him and the farm. She had taken another side and called herself a patriot, one of the white racialists who lived in their own enclaves and traded mostly with each other. Joanie blamed Candy's stance on a husband she'd met at just the wrong time.

You can't save everyone, she thought.

Or, more properly, you couldn't save anyone at all. They had to save themselves.

"Another peach?" Cleo asked.

"I'll split one with you."

Twilight darkened to night, blue with just a tinge of orange in the west.

Full and happy, she let herself sink into the smell of woodsmoke floating from the kitchen, the taste of peaches in her mouth.

Puabi-Ekur watched this. It was one of many futures. Why were they seeing this one?

Perhaps it was the best one possible. Joanie was still alive and happy. It looked as if the rape of the world might have abated.

Yet still remained the threat of racial violence.

Humans stayed human, after all.

Chapter 12

$\mathcal{E}$kur's men came into the land of the two rivers, the Tigris and Euphrates. In early autumn, it was still hot, but not the burning heat of summer; even so, they marched morning and evening and took a break midday. They traveled oasis to oasis, led by the king in his gilded war-chariot, pulled by half-wild asses. Ekur also had a war-chariot, but coming homeward he marched with his men.

If Ekur could have stopped time, could have laid hands on it and broken its back like a rat's, he would have done it.

Instead, his midday breaks got longer. Instead of being first in place, waiting for the rest of the army, now he was last. Instead of being always clear-eyed and level-headed, he had beer brought to his tent.

Eannatum was there, his shadow, always.

No words had been spoken between them. But Eannatum knew how it would be in the days to come.

There came the last midday before they entered Uruk. The army had been dispersing to its parent cities, Uruk in the south near the end of the list. In the shadowy tent interior, light filtered tan through the hides. On the incense coals, Ekur put frankincense, pungent and spicy, for Inanna, lady of war and love. Eannatum tied the tent door shut behind him and lit one of the oil lamps.

Ekur stood to meet him and embraced him. In the heat, Eannatum wore no cloak, only a long kilt decorated with fringe. Ekur's palms cupped the slender shoulders, smooth brown skin covered with fine hair. He laid a kiss on Eannatum's shoulder, and Eannatum sighed.

Ekur kissed his full lips, his liquid mouth. Eannatum had been chewing thyme, and his breath was sweet. Kissing, they lay down in Ekur's blankets.

Eannatum brushed Ekur's curling dark hair out of his face, let it fall, and picked it up again. "Have I told you your hair is beautiful? See how it shines in the lamplight." Letting it fall again, a wave of darkness, he stroked it.

Ekur grabbed his hand and kissed it, lips to the palm. "You are too kind to me."

"What does that mean, too kind?"

"Every day, you're thoughtful and patient, doing all this busy work, this scribe work. Looking after me, picking up after me."

"It's needful. You've done your share."

"Coming to my bed at night, leaving before dawn, so nothing gets in the way of our duties."

"I won't have it said I undermined your leadership."

Ekur wrapped himself around Eannatum, kissing and biting at random, beginning to work the long kilt down off his hips.

"I'm grateful. More than grateful."

"Yes," Eannatum whispered.

There was no more talking. Eannatum pulled off Ekur's

long kilt, mouthed his cock. Ekur was instantly hard. "Don't finish me. I want to be inside you."

"I want you inside me."

Sweat rose in the heat. Ekur slicked himself with sesame oil stolen from the lamp, and slipped inside him. They both groaned. With the rhythm of their rocking, the feeling grew. The slap of skin against skin, faster and faster.

The scent of frankincense, the pop as a spark burst off the coal.

The dam broke. Ekur cried out. Eannatum did too, a moment later, Ekur stroking his cock, milking the last drops as he shuddered.

They flattened onto the linen sheets, flung across the matting bed. Their rough breathing quieted. Ekur wiped his hand. Curling around Eannatum, he held him as if he were precious, which he was.

"I wish this could continue," Ekur said. "Forever. A lifetime."

"We can see each other in Uruk. We can find a way. It's not that hard."

"But I want—" how to put this—"I want you officially. It can be done."

Eannatum gave a small smile. "Ekur, you are a dreamer. Why is it so necessary? It will only cause trouble. Your wife—"

"Demons take my wife. She doesn't love me."

"She does in her way."

"You don't have to live with her."

Eannatum looked over his shoulder, a flash of dark brown eyes. "I do, in my way. It's best I believe positive things of her."

"Believe what you want to."

Eannatum roused himself, crossed the tent, and got the jug of beer. "We have a little time left. Have something to drink."

The Sumerian beer was so thick it was almost chewy. He set

it down; they drank it from the jug with long reed straws to avoid the bitter dregs.

They drank. Ekur got up, replenished the incense, which crackled on the burner, and returned, sitting down wrapped himself around Eannatum. He couldn't lose contact with Eannatum's flesh, not now, not so close to the city, where everything was going to change.

"You want to see me when we return to Uruk, then," Eannatum said.

"Of course."

"I wasn't sure." Many such connections ended when a campaign did. "That will anger Irkalla if she finds out. She will make life hard for us."

"Let her."

Eannatum groaned. "Ekur, she will make life hard for *me*. You've established yourself; you've won your battles. I'm a subaltern. I can't afford for her to figure out some way to hurt me."

"Mmm." Mostly Ekur just wanted to feel Eannatum's soft skin, smell his sweat, breathe in the scent of sex like honey cake. Almost he was ready for more. But he needed to listen. "You're saying you want to keep this quiet, to protect yourself."

"I would like that, yes. And to keep my parents happy."

"And your future betrothed."

Eannatum glanced over his shoulder again. "And my future betrothed. Ekur, I just want to have a life, as you already do. You have your wife; you have your children. Please don't begrudge me mine."

"I begrudge you nothing."

"I will find time for you. I swear it. If that is your desire."

How could that be a question?

But Ekur saw it, as Eannatum laid it out. Eannatum was

twenty. Ekur was twelve years older; he'd married the woman his parents had found him and fathered children. He'd made his mark as a general and could move to administration now. Eannatum was just beginning his own such trek and needed to avoid interference. Would he, Ekur, have thrown away his career for love? Probably not.

"I would never stand in your way," he told Eannatum.

But from his further perspective, Ekur saw things Eannatum did not.

He stroked the downy brown skin, the fine hairs burned blond by the sun, kissed the shoulder, bit it gently.

If Eannatum was lucky, he would make a good relationship with his betrothed, create a household, have fine children. But this was not lightning from heaven, desire like being drunk, not how he'd felt for Eannatum from first he saw him. That kind of feeling—Ekur had had it a handful of times in his life, mostly for men.

Now, in his middle thirties, life yielding his desires in many ways, he wanted to share it with someone who didn't look past him when he came to view, someone who wasn't Irkalla.

Eannatum wouldn't know till later how rarely lightning struck.

"Let it be as you desire," said Ekur, who wasn't about to lose him. Gently, he took Eannatum by his shoulders and turned him so they sat face to face. Kissing him, he took his penis in his hand.

Through the green fire, through the plane of becoming, Puabi-Ekur had seen the future. But also there arose now this distant past, this life as Ekur.

Puabi-Ekur considered the tale Ereshkigal had quoted, the Curse of Akkad. Now, as then, the gods of earth were angry. Their vengeance would return. But not for retribution; it was cause and effect. The gods were only protecting the natural order—they were the natural order.

And yet, what Puabi-Ekur saw was themself happy. Or as happy as humans were in this world.

Chapter 13

On an icy day in the past December, Gus had spent a morning with a lawyer, dropping more money than he had to write a statement against Odin's Hunt, the Northern pagan group with white-supremacist leanings.

He still missed Max, his former boyfriend, his link to the Hunt. Tall, muscular, hot, a convincing top, Max had introduced his politics slowly. Gus had been naive, or blinded by lust. Or both.

The lawyer had suggested taking a quarter off, but Gus didn't have a job or money, except student loans and a small college stipend from his parents. He couldn't expect more—his mom had been angry enough about what he'd spent on the lawyer. And there was no way he was going back to live with his parents. Nothing was worth that.

After the holidays, Gus took precautions. He changed his phone number and disappeared from social media. He gave up his apartment and moved into Alyssa's tiny room in Hannah's house—Hannah knew the story and supported him. He was waiting till another student moved out to get his own space there.

So far, he hadn't heard again from Odin's Hunt. Maybe he'd covered his tracks well enough.

Now Alyssa came into their tiny room, barely enough to hold a double bed and desk. Above the desk, shelves were built into the wall; one held a shared personal altar. Perched on the desk chair, Gus focused on a burning blue-black candle, part of his tiny shrine to Odin. When Alyssa came in, he started.

"Sorry to disturb you."

"I was done." He blew out the candle. "What's up?"

"Joanie suggested I show you this." She put a piece of paper on the desk in front of him.

Ugly picture, ugly words. A racial slur. He knew the type of people it came from. "My friend found it taped to a Black Lives Matter poster in someone's yard. She and some other people were going around the neighborhood taking them down. I brought it in to work and showed it to Joanie."

She paused. "And?"

"Joanie wants us to come counter-protest the alt-right thing, by the community college, end of next week."

A loyalty test. It was bound to come at some point.

"Against the people I'm trying to hide from?"

Alyssa wrapped her arms around his neck, bit his ear gently.

She'd changed in the last few months. When he'd met her, she was pretty, pliable, soft-spoken, dressed usually in pink. Maybe now she was finding her anger. A good thing for her, not necessarily good for their relationship.

"Do you want to keep hiding?"

She said it with no edge, but he knew what she meant.

"Maybe I do. Maybe I don't want to get doxxed, or swatted. That'd hurt everyone here, too."

He'd never known someone who was swatted—the SWAT team sent to their house with a report of someone armed and dangerous—but he did have troll friends who'd doxxed or gotten doxxed, personal information posted so enemies could torment them. The Hunt was capable of that and more. When Gus's boyfriend thought he'd sold them out, he'd pushed Gus off a mountain.

"I suppose. But, look, when you grew up, when you read about the world—did you read *The Diary of Anne Frank*?"

He nodded; he'd had to read it in school.

"Didn't you wonder what those times were like, and why people went along with what they did?"

"Sure."

"These are those times again, right? Some of these guys are flat-out Nazis. You know that better than anyone." Their eyes met. He made no sign. "So which side are you on, Gus?"

Did she want him killed?

She was right, though.

He didn't like to be pushed. He'd gotten enough of that at his parents' house. He didn't plan to give in—not now, anyway.

"My own side." He got up, shouldered past her, and left the house, slamming the door behind him.

Chapter 14

The army came into Uruk through the great mud-brick north gate, thicker than a man's height, taller than three men. Banners flew from battlements atop colossal mud-brick walls, painted blue and decorated with gilt processionals. Above the gate had been carven images of Inanna and of Anu, her grandfather, who co-owned the city. At the middle of the day, the sun stood at its height, who was Utu, Inanna's brother.

Ekur marched at the head of his several hundred men, midway in the huge throng. They trod the processional way, a long slope of mud-brick cobbles. Through the arch he saw the ziggurat, product of a recent king. The army marched into the city to the sound of shouts, the clash of cymbals, the high skirling of reed pipes; this cacophonous music got louder as they passed through the gate.

The central square was too small to contain them; they halted to stand in ranks along the processional way. Far away, at a dais, the king began a speech. Ekur sweated in his leather cloak, sewn with bits of metal as armor. No beer till later, but the taverns would be full to bursting tonight.

Ekur would be expected to go home to Irkalla. He longed to embrace his children, to sleep in his own bed.

Now the army was dismissed, each troop in formation rolling off to a different quarter of the city. He stood up before his men and let them go with words of praise. They sang their troop chant; it was done.

He watched his men march away.

Surrounded by droves of people, there was no one close, no one he could talk to.

A leather sole rasped on the sand. Eannatum stood next to him. His subaltern, after all, had to support him with any last details.

Ekur embraced him.

"Tonight, the Lion's Head Tavern?" Eannatum said in his ear. The men would be drinking there.

"I'm not sure." He had no idea what Irkalla would want. His parents would also be at his home to greet him. Irkalla might have invited her father and all their friends, the house full of people for a party. Or she might have some new lover and want him gone.

"Please come. Come late if you need to. I can find a place for us to go."

When they lay together in the tent, Eannatum had sounded so reasonable, describing the life he wanted, of which Ekur could only be a minor part. Now his voice had a catch in it.

"I will if I can." In a whisper, a thing he hadn't said before: "I love you."

The dark-brown eyes, like those of a beautiful bull-calf, caught his.

"I love you too."

Still in his battle-dress and armored cloak, Ekur walked across the city to the house of his family. Waiting at the top of the front steps, Irkalla met him in a tiered dress of fine embroidered linen and elaborate gilt earrings, such as the wife of a general might wear. His son and daughter threw themselves at him, hugging his knees. "Daddy, Daddy!"

With tears of joy, he kissed them over and over.

Irkalla was all gaiety, fed him beer and sweetmeats and roast fowl in a pie. Both their families were there, full of laughter, embracing and kissing him. But Irkalla's kiss was tepid, and her eyes slid past him.

There was some man in the picture, somewhere. It was her nature.

By law and custom, she was on shaky ground. A Sumerian man had the right to take a concubine. Women did not have the reciprocal right to take lovers, though many did. Ekur wouldn't have cared, if there were room for him and the children too.

He saw the children to bed, lingering in the doorway to watch them in soft lamplight, till the nursemaid shooed him away. "Their father may be back, but they still need their sleep."

He returned to the roof-courtyard, encircled with potted pomegranates. It was cool up here, the sun long set. Irkalla leaned back in her chair, a jar of wine beside her on the painted table. Behind her stood a pair of oil lamp torchieres, moths batting at the light. The evening star shone in the west, the star of Inanna.

He took a cup of wine. Because it was needful, because in his heart he was fond of her, he kissed Irkalla's cheek.

A glance fell from her dark eye, almost hostile.

"Oh, Ekur. It's been *such* a long day."

He had still hoped, but his hope died.

"Then you won't mind if I go meet my men later."

Her look gauged him. Just because she took a lover didn't mean he could. She wasn't so much jealous as possessive—she wanted her husband in his place.

But he had long practice, and he passed her test.

"Here, he's here!"

"Lord Ekur, sir. We're over here."

In one of the streets of the lower town stood the Lion's Head, traditional tavern of the Ninth, the brigade he'd led. He waded through the place, nudging men out of the way; it was packed.

The long, low room had whitewashed mud-brick walls, smudged, with occasional graffiti. It opened to a wide porch, where his men were sitting. Torches and fire baskets lit the room and porch, casting a warm glow on low wooden benches and tables full of men, most out of battle dress, wearing long kilts and blanket-shawls or cloaks. It stank of beer and a bit of sweat. The room was full of men, with a few women, tavern servers and a coterie of whores—ordinary whores, not priestesses.

The sound was deafening: shouting, laughing. In a far corner, men sang a drinking song, tune wobbling.

The men of the Ninth made a space for him beside Eannatum, who within all this was a dark warm silence, a depth in the space. The men accepted their relationship since Ekur never showed favoritism. "More beer!"

Next to him, Eannatum hiccupped. Ekur laughed at him. "You're drunk."

"I should hope so. I've had enough. I wasn't sure you'd come."

"I couldn't know for certain."

Eannatum's eyes were like dark agates. Ekur's glance touched Eannatum's long straight nose, his full lips. Longing poured through him.

He wished they were in his tent, or a bedroom high above the city, night-blooming jasmine trained on the balcony wall. He'd known a courtesan who'd had that, long ago. Most things felt like long ago, even the campaign, though it was barely a week behind him.

Between Eannatum and him there lay a quiet, but not a separation: a quiet that prepared for darkness.

Ekur got drunk quickly. They sang the brigade song. A lazy moon watched them, lying on its back. The tavern emptied, and the night air grew cooler. The men of the Ninth slipped away one by one, to homes and wives or concubines.

"They're not going to close till dawn," Ekur commented, drinking through the long straw, focusing on that, arm around Eannatum. "They'll make a moon's worth of silver tonight."

"They rent rooms here too. I secured one," Eannatum said.

Ekur let slip his straw and turned toward Eannatum, eyebrows raised.

"I didn't mean to presume. But I wanted the option." Eannatum was an expert at planning things.

"I see."

"I meant no harm."

"I didn't think you meant harm."

A breath of night air crossed the porch.

"Are you going home to Irkalla tonight?"

Eannatum and Irkalla were distant cousins. Irkalla had

looked after Eannatum when he was small. He knew her nature.

"Tonight, I can do as I wish."

They exchanged a glance. The torches were burning low, but still a reflected blaze leaped from Eannatum's eyes.

In the whitewashed room lay a simple wooden bed with linen sheets; one lamp lit, the scent of sesame lamp oil floated. A window sat open to the moon. Well after midnight, the raucous parties of the army's homecoming had quieted to night-sounds. In the distance, a nightjar called.

The innkeeper's servant closed the door. Eannatum stepped forward, and Ekur took him in his arms.

They stood quiet a moment while the world dropped away, as if they were on a high hill in moonlight looking over valleys.

They kissed. Ekur took Eannatum's face in his hands, pulled him closer as if he could climb inside him, kissing and kissing. Eannatum's hands went to his waist, undid his long kilt, which fell to the mud-brick floor. Ekur stepped him backward to the bed, pulled off his kilt, lay skin to skin.

"Fuck me," Eannatum whispered.

"Not yet."

He smoothed his hands over Eannatum's body, brown skin newly shaven, in a light sweat, slick as butter. Lamplight made him shine. Ekur tweaked his nipple. Eannatum moaned.

So much beauty here, like riches.

Eannatum's cock stood and Ekur put his hand on it, skin slipping over the engorged shaft. He bent to put his mouth on it, licked it, teasing. Eannatum moaned and wriggled. "Please."

"Roll over."

Grabbing some lamp oil, Ekur coated himself, began nudging himself against Eannatum. Eannatum threw his head back, eyes shut.

Ekur rammed in, and Eannatum cried out.

He rode him, watching. Eannatum put his hand to himself, and Ekur moved it, replacing it with his own hand. He held himself back, watching Eannatum, riding him. Eannatum's shut-eyed face, turned to the side, had a searching look.

Eannatum moaned, again, again, gave a final cry, and shuddered, coming. Ekur let himself go and came a moment later, collapsing on top of him.

The sound of their breathing fell into silence. A night bird called again, far away. Ekur blew out the lamp and let moonlight fill the room.

What he'd had with Irkalla had died. This was what he wanted.

Their host had left a jug, and Eannatum reached for that and the long reed straw, began sucking down beer.

He knew what Eannatum was thinking; he thought it too.

It hung in the air until Eannatum said, "What now?"

Who could know? "Now we begin again."

Eannatum had been so certain they'd find a way. He didn't sound certain now.

"We'll figure out how to see each other," Ekur said. It was clear Irkalla's mind was elsewhere.

"I have to keep it from my parents. They won't care what happened on campaign, but they won't want me distracted while I make my career and take a wife."

"I understand." Ekur placed his own straw and sipped the warm beer. "My father is finding a place for me in administration. If you like, I can find you one too."

Chapter 15

*I*t's not a good enough answer, to say you're on your own side, Gus."

Gus and Alyssa lay staring up at the ceiling from the bed in their room, the space above them hazed with smoke from weed and incense. A couple of candles flickered. Alyssa had picked up the conversation as if they'd never stopped.

With Alyssa's shift to goth clothing something had shifted in her personality, revealing a bedrock layer Gus hadn't seen before. It took adjusting to. But he didn't want to lose her.

"There's a time when not acting gives the wrong people power."

He hated being pushed. But she was right. Much as he hated giving in.

"Yes, okay, sure, whatever. Where did you put the pipe?"

Sitting up, she handed it to him from the desk. If he caught the ghost of a smile on her face, he kept it to himself.

A sunny July day, it was hot for Seattle. In the high blue sky, clouds floated like mounds of bubbles. Joanie, Alyssa, and Gus met at Firebird House, in the University District. They bussed over to the park on Capitol Hill, in the center of the city by the reservoir. The park was full of Frisbee players, dogs, runners, people on blankets reading, variegated spots of color on green —a typical summer day.

Joanie saw no sign of either protest or counter-protest. She checked her phone again for the location.

"I think it's over here."

They rounded the reservoir, and there they were.

At the south end stood a small stone building, elaborated with nineteen-twenties-style scrolls and Ionian columns, which probably held equipment. A chain and padlock shut its blue-painted door. In front of this building stood maybe fifteen protestors, blending into a crowd of onlookers behind. Across the building, spanning the whole thing, hung a red-white-and-blue banner with an airbrushed eagle and the words "Keep America American," tagged with the name of the organizing group, the Washington State Patriots.

A handful of men stood in front of the building and banner. Joanie scanned them. One white man, bulked up, with a chestnut beard, wore a dark-green t-shirt with camo pants. A shorter one, with a buzzcut and dad jeans, stood out for his t-shirt emblazoned with a huge American flag.

Unexpectedly, with them was a Latino-looking man, skinny, wearing wraparound sunglasses, and another man who looked African-American, a powerlifter by his arms, in a camo jacket over a black t-shirt and jeans. The powerlifter bent over a portable loudspeaker setup. From the hand of the man with the chestnut beard hung a bullhorn, Joanie guessed connected to the speakers. In front of the men stood a few galvanized-steel crowd-control barriers.

And in front of these barriers stood at least three times as many bemused, vaguely hostile Seattleites, many young and alternative: black-clad or rainbowed, dreadlocked, shaved. Up by the barriers ranged a few all in black, with bandanas over their faces, Antifa—mostly small-built young women.

"This is Antifa?" Alyssa said, surprised.

"Sure. One version of it."

"Respect." Alyssa watched them with interest.

Joanie wasn't ready to fight, herself, even to protect the rest of them. Though she might throw glitter and run away; she had some glitter. Mostly she was here to laugh in the alt-right's face. All of her anti-authoritarian bent came out for this. To razz them, she had a noisemaker left over from someone's birthday party. She wore street clothes, black t-shirt and black jeans, and her witch pentacle necklace.

Alyssa and Gus had brought nothing. Gus faced the alt-right brunch frowning furiously, arms crossed across his chest.

"What?" Joanie asked.

"I'm just paranoid I'm going to see someone I know."

"Relax—it can't be that small a world. Can it?"

Gus rolled his eyes.

"You can take off if you want to. No one's making you stay."

Alyssa flicked Gus a glance.

"I'm staying," he said.

As an answer, Alyssa clasped her hands in his folded elbow, leaning into him.

The bullhorn came online with a furious blast of feedback. They all jumped. Chestnut Beard yelled into the bullhorn. Joanie took a step back, reflexively. It was so loud.

"Hey you!" Red face, wide mouth. "Don't you love your

country? We've got to rise up to protect it—protect the core of what we believe."

She tooted her shiny plastic noisemaker. Its flat brassy sound broke up the loudspeaker. Next to her appeared a man all in white, wearing a red bandana, carrying a drum around his neck. Nodding at her, he started banging it.

"Nazis go home!" yelled a woman beside her, and others took up the chant: "Nazis go home!"

Amid the noise from the anti-fascist side, snippets blared from the alt-right bullhorn, a kind of word salad: "—not Nazis, American patriots, trying to support our president. Make American great again. And to do that, we can't be overwhelmed by illegal immigrants—"

An opposing chant rose from the counter-protestors: "Say it loud, say it clear! Refugees are welcome here!"

After a quarter-hour or so, a contingent of bicycle cops showed up, in shorts and bulletproof vests. They stayed behind the crowd-control barriers, some milling, some straddling their bikes, looking around, a few talking into walkie-talkies.

"Say it loud, say it clear! Refugees are welcome here!"

Their shouting drowned out, the alt-right put on neo-Nazi speed-metal. Joanie kept blowing her noisemaker. Gus and Alyssa chanted.

Buzzcut Dad-Jeans approached Joanie. "What's that there?" he asked, pointing to her pentacle. "Are you a Satanist?" She laughed. "A witch?"

She shook her head. Everyone the alt-right engaged just got into a shouting match. The older man next to her stepped up, inches from Dad-Jeans' face. "You know, I have relatives who died at Auschwitz. I couldn't rest if I didn't stand up to you. This is exactly what happened in Germany—you and your leader, that clown. Everyone laughed at Hitler, too."

Dad-Jeans moved on to him: "We're not neo-Nazis; we're good Americans. We have nothing against legal immigration—why should we?"

"I didn't say anything about immigration."

Conversations went in circles, with the backdrop of the music's racing drums and shrieks. Joanie couldn't understand the lyrics. She kept tooting her horn. Beside her, Alyssa chanted, "Say it loud, say it clear! Refugees are welcome here!"

Joanie noticed a few newcomers on the alt-right side; a tan blonde woman at whom someone shouted, "Go home, Nazi Barbie!" A larger geek-type guy wandered up, in a peach polo shirt, with a feed-cap with Navy on the band. She glanced around for Gus; he was shouting at the skinny guy in wrap-around glasses, who seemed to be trying to get Gus to hit him. A cop loomed at the crowd's edge.

Meeting Joanie's glance, Alyssa moved over and took Gus's elbow. He backed off, came away under shade of the maple trees beyond the reservoir. It was a known tactic of the alt-right to taunt anti-fascists into starting fights.

Then, suddenly, the loudspeaker stopped, the cops turned the crowd-control barriers, and the alt-right group was on the move. A middle-aged man with a professional look, who had helped organize the counter-protest, waved them into a huddle.

"This was billed as a march, so I guess they're finally going to start marching. We need to follow them, but leave some space between us. My guess is the cops will enforce that."

The alt-right group moved quickly; the powerlifter packed up the loudspeaker with practiced speed. "They're going to head for Broadway," the organizer yelled. The counter-protestors followed.

Out of the overhang of the big-leaf maples, they went into glittering sunlight. Joanie slid on her sunglasses. She had to jog to keep up with the group, pausing a moment to let Gus and Alyssa catch her. "Broadway?" Gus asked.

"Yeah," Joanie said. In a couple blocks, they were there, poised on the corner. "Catch that light!"

When they were across the street, the cops blocked them. They wanted to keep the two groups of protestors on opposite sides of the street. The alt-righters raised their own chant: "Make America great again!"

Seattle's Broadway neighborhood, bemused and confused, studied the tight group of obvious strangers—no one wore red, white, and blue on Broadway—packed around with cops.

"Nazis go home!" shouted an Antifa girl beside Joanie, and Joanie picked it up. "Nazis go home!"

They came even with the alt-right group. Then it dove downhill, toward downtown. "Where are they going?" Gus asked Joanie.

"I have no idea. I guess we should cross the street." After a tense moment confronting the cops, they went around them, crossing at the far corner.

Joanie saw the Antifa girl again. "Now what?" she asked her.

"Down here."

The alt-right bunch had dropped downhill a block. Now they were surrounded on all sides by a police cordon. They moved slower as a line of cars drove past, blocking them.

Confused, hot, and tense, Joanie, Alyssa, and Guy paused on a street corner, cut off by the police. A black-clad man with close-cropped red hair and a black bandana over his face stepped up to Gus, who embraced him.

"Come meet my friends. Alyssa, Joanie, this is Pete."

Joanie had heard the name. "Hi."

"Good to see you come out," Pete said, not focusing on Gus, and it clicked into place who he was: an Antifa guy whom Gus had clashed with, in the time of Gus's dalliance with Odin's Hunt.

"But look," Pete said, nodding toward the alt-right.

The group had changed, milling behind their police—maybe three police officers for every alt-right protestor. A few had dropped away; a few had joined. One man, brown-bearded, had pushed to the center of the group, a big man with shoulders all muscle, built like a bear.

"Bruni," Gus breathed.

"You know him?" Joanie asked.

"Yes. He's part of Odin's Hunt." Quickly, unobtrusively, he slid to stand behind Alyssa.

Pete glanced at him. "They must know you changed sides."

"They're moving again," Joanie said.

Surrounded by police, the alt-right protestors were walking and chanting. "Make America great again!"

"Nazis go home!" Joanie yelled. "Nazis go home!"

Bystanders took it up. The alt-righters looked confused and distracted. Rounding a corner, they went back to Broadway. Police continued to keep the two groups separate.

"They're heading back to the park," Gus said.

They took a narrow feeder street back, between a low concrete wall at the park's edge and a brick building. The alt-right bunched together. The cops had thinned out and hadn't kept up with them. The two groups were suddenly face to face.

Bruni leaned in toward Gus.

"I see you've switched sides," he said.

Pete came up to stand shoulder to shoulder with Gus. "So did Max, Bruni. He used to stand with us."

Bruni ignored Pete. "We know what you did, Gus. You betrayed us."

"I did the right thing."

"We know where you live."

"Don't be too sure about that." He'd moved to make sure they couldn't find him.

"Don't be too sure we don't."

Watching Bruni's face, Joanie thought, *They don't know now. But they may find out.*

Pete turned to Gus. "He's trying to trick you into fighting. Let's get away from here." He grabbed Gus's arm and pulled him backward, toward the park, into the green shade. Alyssa and Joanie followed.

"We know who you are," Bruni roared like a cornered bear. Then a couple of cops, catching up finally, stepped between him and Gus. The alt-right group continued forward. With a last angry glance at Gus, Bruni went with them.

"Stay here a moment," Alyssa said, holding Gus's other arm. She drew him to sit on the low concrete wall. Gus was breathing hard.

"I knew that was going to happen." He glared at Joanie.

Pete stood with them too. "Don't take them too seriously. They'll say anything to get you to fight them in front of the cops. Which would get you thrown in jail."

The alt-right group returned to their perch by the small stone building. For a few minutes, they stood talking, then headed for the edge of the park, an exit south.

"They're calling it a day," Pete said. "I think the counter-protest was successful."

They stared at him. It hadn't felt successful.

"We had at least twice as many people on our side. They ran off with their tail between their legs."

But it felt like a nonending. Joanie stood by the concrete wall in the shade of the maple trees, letting a breeze cool the sweat along her hairline. What next?

Maybe it was hers to take the initiative. "Let's go get a beer. Pete, you want to come with us?"

Pulling down his bandanna, he smiled at her. She saw herself reflected in his eyes: slender, dark, with eyeliner-drawn eyes and brunette hair, black clothes, silver pentacle. And an anti-fascist.

"Sure. A pleasure."

She saw then how going out with him, with Gus and Alyssa, would form two couples. She didn't know if she liked that. She was off boys right now, except for her long-distance partner Clayton, who was in California working on his engineering master's.

But, too late. She'd asked.

Chapter 16

*T*he neighborhood dive bars had vanished, so they settled for a cocktail lounge. Not far from the park, it gaped as cavernous as a beer hall but with bright-orange-painted walls. Given the opportunity, Joanie ordered a craft cocktail with sage-infused vodka. Just the one. She remembered the days when, as a working prostitute, she'd been able to afford as many as she wanted.

Alyssa sat by Gus, so Joanie sat down next to Pete, who eyed her with curiosity.

"I know Gus a little. But not anyone else here."

He'd ordered a middle-of-the-road beer, a pilsner, a good choice with the July heat.

Alyssa leaned forward. "I met Gus at the coffee shop where I work."

Gus cleared his throat and put his hand over hers, possessively. "We're engaged."

Pete gave him a long look. Pete had known Gus as Max's boyfriend.

"Three cheers for bisexual visibility," Joanie said. She lifted her glass, and everyone clinked it with theirs.

Pete turned his smile on her.

She swallowed. It took courage to out her job self to this Antifa boy. "I have an entry-level business job at a financial firm. I'm not proud of it. It's pure capitalism. But my real trade is sex work. And I'm a pansexual, polyamorous, kinky cis femme, and a witch."

"I just joined her coven," Alyssa said, bouncing in her seat with excitement.

"There's a lot of overlap between magical groups and Antifa," Pete said. "We have a couple of Thelemites who usually show up, and some Satanists. Some witches too, none today." He tilted his head and looked at Joanie. "I did sex work for a while, when I was in my teens. Gay for pay. It's not really my thing, but I miss the money."

Gus stared at him a moment, then dropped his eyes.

"The world's oldest profession," Joanie said. Everyone clinked glasses again.

"I feel left out," Gus said.

Joanie laughed. "You could make some money if you wanted. Though I wouldn't say now was a great time to start, with the current laws."

Gus turned to Pete. "How serious do you think Bruni was about his threat?" He leaned across the wooden table. "I told the police about what they got up to—that's what he meant."

Pete locked eyes with him.

"Maybe serious. Maybe not. We should talk."

"We should."

"Not here and now."

"No."

After that, talk turned to sex work, trading stories. Pete's past wasn't that much different from Joanie's or Alyssa's. In his teens, he'd been homeless a while and ended up hustling on the street. He'd managed to make enough money to find somewhere to live. Later, he had a brief career in gay porn, before he started college.

"Now I'm just a boring student."

"What in?"

"Working on a master's in political science."

"I wonder if you can get extra credit for hands-on experience?" Joanie asked, thinking of the march just past.

Pete grinned. "Or combine my skills and become a Senate page?"

"There you go." Against her will, Joanie was starting to like him.

Not too long after, Gus and Alyssa had to leave. Both headed for the bathroom. Leaning over the table, Pete asked, "Mind if I call you?"

"Not at all."

He handed her his phone, and she typed in her number.

Chapter 17

*T*he setting sun floated on the horizon, a liquid drop halved by the blue-grey silhouette of a flat-topped building. The bulk of the temple complex lay behind them; ahead was a residential quarter of surrounding Uruk.

Ekur turned away from the window. At the end of an afternoon before the New Year high holy days, almost all of the scribes and administrators had disappeared, leaving him and Eannatum.

His whole life had become a search for scraps of time and space. But here, Inanna—goddess of love—had found him what he needed.

Across the wide, low-ceilinged, whitewashed room, Eannatum bent over his clay tablet. Ekur pitched his voice to carry. "You can stop now."

"Let me just finish this account."

"You are too good." He came up behind the boy and stroked his long dark hair. "Too good."

Eannatum leaned back, pressing his head against his hand, rolling his shoulders. Almost he purred like a cat.

It had been four months since they'd come home from war. Ekur had entered the Inanna temple's administration; through his connections, he got a coveted post running the administration of tithes. He was proving himself, working long hours, leaving his brother to run the family estate—his father was old and grey, and they let him sit in the sun.

He let Irkalla do what she wanted.

He'd rented a small room above a tavern, a short walk from his office in the temple complex. Some nights, he worked late and had to stay over. Past midnight, thieves could be out, and the house he shared with Irkalla was a long walk away.

Eannatum worked late a lot too.

At night, the small room was lit by a cheap pair of lamps. To begin with, it held silence; then it filled with whispers, gasps, Eannatum's voice crying out. Then silence fell once more.

Irkalla would find out soon enough. If she were going to make herself happy, though, Ekur would do the same.

But he couldn't work late every night, and he didn't. He loved his children, even when they complained or told staggering lies. One night Dildala, all sweetness and huge brown eyes, claimed her favorite doll had told her to run naked around the central courtyard.

One twilight a few weeks later, his son Henbur met him on the house's front steps. Ekur exchanged a significant glance with the nursemaid, standing behind the boy, then focused on Henbur. "Yes?"

Henbur looked up, his face streaked with tears and dirt. "Daddy, in the courtyard—it was all Dildala's fault."

Behind him, the nursemaid cleared her throat. "Henbur, we

talked about this. You can't blame your sister. She was playing in another room."

"I was trying out my slingshot—" something he'd been forbidden to do in the courtyard— "and I broke one of the palm pots."

"Just the lip off it, my lord," the nursemaid put in. "But we agreed he should tell you."

"Nurse says you work hard to get us nice things and I shouldn't break them."

"Well, Henbur, I have to agree." Henbur's lower lip wobbled, and a tear dripped down his cheek. "Are you sorry for what you did?" Henbur nodded vigorously. Ekur reached out and patted his head. "You're forgiven. Just don't let it happen again."

Henbur turned and ran back up the steps and away. The nursemaid followed.

At dinner in the formal dining room, Ekur noticed Irkalla was quiet, as if a weight had been set on top of her. He guessed some kind of talking-to was coming. He focused on his food. The main dish was grilled carp, lettuce with watercress alongside, and fig pudding for dessert.

After the children went to bed, he met Irkalla in the roof courtyard. Full night had fallen; a breeze moved the cooling air, making the flames of the standing oil lamps flutter. The serving girl set out a small jug of beer on a side table, with the usual long reed straw. Irkalla got wine imported from the Zagros mountains, which she preferred.

She let the silence last till the girl was gone. Then she leaned forward, torchlight golden on her face.

"I understand now about you working so late."

A shiver crossed Ekur's flesh. He took a steadying draw off his beer.

"I'm new to the administration of tithes. I have to prove myself."

He knew she was seeing someone.

"If that's what you call it. My father might have an opinion about all this *work* of yours."

She was such a hypocrite.

"What is it you want, Irkalla?" Ekur gestured across the courtyard. "Everything here, is it not of the best? Do you not have all the things you desire?" The standing lamps, painted and inlaid, cast light on banks of flowers, now day lilies, refreshed every season. Her imported wine was the finest on the market. "All these things have a cost."

She pounded her fist on the side table, making the jugs jump.

"It's not about *things*—I need you to respect me!"

"How am I disrespectful?"

But he knew the answer. He wasn't the adoring husband of her dreams—he had his own life.

"You promised my father when you married me you'd treat me well."

Her high-ranking father, who doted on her, had been the king's advisor and still had influence. She saw he was listening.

"He takes an interest, and he likes me to be happy."

This wasn't what he wanted. He wanted peace. "Irkalla—"

Leaping up, she grabbed her wine. "Find somewhere else to sleep tonight!"

Striding past him, she clattered down the steps in her hard-soled sandals.

Chapter 18

*P*uabi-Ekur tracked Joanie and Gus as they protested, watched the memories rise from Ekur, noted the scenes of the future. They saw no pattern yet. But they'd gotten a rare direct instruction from their deities: seek out the goddess called Dea.

Puabi-Ekur started with their beloved Joanie, their strongest connection in this space-time. They found her asleep in the arms of her lover, Cleo. Joanie's coven leader was Hannah—a strong, warm presence, a Southern girl. Hannah had known Nora a long time. Puabi-Ekur saw earlier in their lives the two women had jockeyed for power. That had passed, but on the astral it showed as a swirl of energy, clotted and bound up.

Puabi-Ekur traced the strands to Nora's house. At the edge of the wide green lawn, now in July the foxgloves dropped their flowers. Back in the woods lay the tiny cabin with its corner shrine and small, homemade goddess statue.

They turned an astral corner, to meet a blast of strength. A wall frightening and spangly, like a shield made of night sky.

They bounced back.

They weren't trying to intrude. They'd been sent on a mission. But deities could be touchy, particularly age-old deities with few followers.

"Greetings, spirit of this place, Lady Dea," they said without sound.

The spirit surrounded them energetically, inspecting them.

"What are you doing here?"

"I was sent by the deities Inanna and Ereshkigal."

"Doesn't matter who sent you. Why are you here?"

"They want me to introduce myself because my people have to do with your people. I'm connected to three humans who have visited your land." Puabi-Ekur sent images: dark Joanie of the black eyes, sandy-blond Gus, pale blonde Alyssa. "There is a connection here for them and for me, some way forward."

"Mmm, I see, introduce."

"I am Puabi-Ekur, incubus-succubus in Hekate's service." Most spirits knew of Hekate, who in her way ruled all spirits, demons to angels.

"No... introduce." Dea wanted more.

Puabi-Ekur went a little deeper, imparting themself as a series of images: Puabi, the dancer, in silver spangles before the Sumerian nobility; Ekur, a general in his metal-plated war cloak, an administrator in a long Sumerian robe; Maelan, the Briton warrior, with long golden-red hair. They showed their connection with Ereshkigal, Inanna, Hekate, their fealties and allegiances.

As part, wound in, inescapable: Long they'd floated outside forward-moving time, and now some impulse propelled them forward—a thing they almost didn't want.

And what were they now, in their essence? They hadn't considered it till now. A protector spirit for their people, perhaps.

It had been a long time since Puabi-Ekur had introduced themselves to a new spirit. One could be as alone as one wanted, on the astral.

"And yourself?"

Dark and old, this goddess had been attached to this place many years. Recently this land had been wild and free, humans travelers on it, salmon-fishers with winter and summer camps. Long before, she'd come down from the north. She had a connection with bears.

A spirit of initiation and challenge, a protector of certain clans, she found herself at length in a quiet space, without humans except the friendly ghosts. She still aligned to her spot, this edge of the woods on a ridge, over a valley of fir and cedar.

Then Nora and her husband had appeared. The cabin was built, and Dea came to live in it.

"So this is who we are."

Both spirits had chosen a place with humanity, and their people were becoming connected, perhaps over time allies.

Having introduced themselves, they went their separate ways.

Puabi-Ekur had spent centuries drifting. They'd visited men, visited women, taking semen from one, impregnating another, doing the work of an incubus-succubus. From another point of view, they'd continued the weave of life, mixing bloodlines that otherwise wouldn't be mixed. They brought a little chaos, a little change.

Ancient Sumer, and even early Akkad, had been an open place; sexuality of all kinds was accepted. Since then, things had ebbed and flowed. Sometimes Puabi-Ekur found themselves exorcised by priest or shaman. Sometimes those whom they visited appreciated a beautiful stranger in their dreams. This time around, that boy Clayton, Joanie's now, had called them: "I wish someone would take over my body and run my life," he'd said, over and over again, not knowing he was calling someone in.

Puabi-Ekur had recognized why they might be here when they saw Joanie.

Confronted with the task of going forward, Puabi-Ekur was inclined to curl up in the current moment—to bask in Joanie's essence, to watch the world with curiosity. They would answer any call to protect her, of course. They would even protect Gus, who annoyed them, perhaps because he was male.

Puabi-Ekur had been male plenty of times. All that testosterone, all that fighting, the male prerogative. The battles of General Ekur. Planning. Killing people for territory. At the time, in that life, it had been important. But what stayed with them was love.

But here, now—through the spirit realms close to and far from earth, resonances rippled from change. The Anthropocene, the humans called it.

Puabi-Ekur had been human once. Humans had helped ruin the climate of Sumer. Where humans traveled, deforestation and ruination of land followed. Perhaps Enlil had cursed ancient Akkad. But first they had cursed themselves.

For the first time since cities were built and founded,

The great agricultural tracts produced no grain,

The inundated tracts produced no fish,

The irrigated orchards produced neither syrup nor wine,

The gathered clouds did not rain, the masgurum did not grow....

He who slept on the roof, died on the roof.

He who slept in the house, had no burial.

People were flailing at themselves from hunger.

Now humans had dominion over and were laying waste to the entire earth. The earth's living systems returned a response. The temperature and the seas were rising.

Seeing their task, Puabi-Ekur shuddered in their essence.

They didn't have to buddy up with other spirits, but alliances were the only thing that might work. Human-tied spirits would share the fate of humans, or at least be first to take in the refugees as hordes of the dead entered the spirit world.

How could they, and Dea, and spirits like them, help guide their humans through these changes?

It was enough to drive a spirit out of time to go haunt the past of ancient Sumer. At least that story was over, and there had been something like a happy ending—humanity had continued.

Chapter 19

𝓛 ate July turned to August; days waned and grew golden. One hot afternoon, Joanie went to grab a sandwich from a nearby deli. Standing on the street corner, waiting for the light, she smelled woodsmoke. Haze covered the sky. On her phone she found the news item: fires in Eastern Washington. Forests across the mountains were burning, animals running, people in danger.

The next few days, the smoke was bad. When she had to walk outside, she wore a mask.

It was eeriest at night. At the top of the house, she leaned out a gable window as the moon topped the trees, red as a portent. It sparked a body-level fear.

End times.

At work, she was still learning the ropes. Cleo was busy and tired; her energy went into her thesis struggle. Pete had called Joanie, they'd made plans, then at the last minute she'd had to cancel—a summer cold, not good for a first date. She'd meant to call back.

When she'd checked in with Puabi-Ekur, they'd said to follow her calling—her work for the goddess.

Getting the job was not enough. She needed to move in the rest of her life too.

That weekend, she drew up a list of people to help with Inanna shrines and thought about shrine dates. And she texted Pete.

<Sorry not to get back to you sooner. Want to try again?>

He didn't reply that day, nor the one after.

Retreating from Joanie into the ether, into the time between, floating in the universe like dust, Puabi-Ekur contemplated. Now and again they saw the green flame of the plane of becoming.

I need to move too.

They'd made obeisances to Inanna and Ereshkigal. They'd seen glimpses of the future world and memories of the past; they'd met Dea. They knew their role, as protector. Responding to cries for help, that was obvious. How else could they be of service?

Service was an odd idea for an incubus-succubus, whose task for centuries had been trading body fluids and complicating lives. Not only was it a task, it was a pleasure, entering bodies and feeling the rich density of human life, with none of the downsides. Except racking up karma.

Now Puabi-Ekur was called to do more. They could backslide, but the cost would be greater now.

The enemy was different now too. If their enemies were djinni, they weren't the same kind. That pathetic Bruni was only human.

The enemy facing Puabi-Ekur now was more a whirling maelstrom, a dense wall of cloud made of something like metal shavings. Materializing out of that, the oligarchs advanced with their knives. The bullies were less frightening than the cold ones, there to count their riches. The fabric of their worldview threatened like a wall of cold steel wool, behind it the sound of a mechanism crunching.

But Puabi-Ekur had allies.

They began to see where a nature goddess fit in.

Chapter 20

In the whitewashed room, one lamp lit against the night, Ekur and Eannatum lay on the narrow bed talking.

Eannatum's parents considered it a blessing he'd had a relationship with his commander during the Gutium war. It had gotten Eannatum his administrative posting, a clear step up in the world. But they'd always assumed their son would have his own wife, household, and family. Now it was time to put away the things of a young subaltern, just as he'd put away a young man's drinking and whoring, time to find a wife and start a household.

But he hadn't stopped spending time with Ekur. Ekur paid his cook and servants a bit extra to learn when Irkalla planned to go out. He had to promise not to say where he learned it—his staff was on his side, but they had to stay on good terms with Irkalla, who did the hiring and firing.

Eannatum lay staring at the ceiling. Ekur beside him gazed at his lover's face.

"My parents want what's best for me. And they want me to carry on our family line."

So had Ekur's parents. "I understand. But I don't want to lose this."

"Neither do I."

"How does your family see this working?"

"My parents are seeking a wife for me, and I am to review the candidates."

"It is something that could take considerable time, such review."

"It could."

But it wouldn't take forever.

Ekur settled back onto the bed. A little circle of lamplight enclosed Eannatum and himself—a bound, a protective circle. Like the circle of their love.

He felt Eannatum watching him. "It needn't be sudden," Eannatum said. "I'm sure we can figure something out."

The young were always sure things were manageable. Or else nothing could be managed and the only solution was double suicide.

Ekur wanted neither of those, instead more of what they'd had: beautiful afternoons, beautiful evenings, interesting work that wasn't overtaxing. He wanted to build on that, make a home with Eannatum, declare this love the center of his life.

But apparently his wish would never come true.

Here he was, getting dramatic.

"Oh, Ekur." By the lamp, a moth sizzled as it went into the flame. "Don't be sad. There is an answer here, I'm sure of it. I'll find some girl who will give me the space to have what I want. All my parents really care about is having grandchildren. That, at least, I'm sure I can make happen."

Ekur eyed him. "You think so?"

A small smile played about Eannatum's mouth. "You're questioning my manhood?"

Their eyes met in accord.

"I think I should check your manhood." Lifting the sheet, Ekur reached for his cock. Under his hand, it grew hard.

In late spring, the sun baked Uruk. Outside at midday, flat white heat slammed down. Administrators took breaks midday, which meant Ekur worked late, Eannatum also. It made sense to sleep in the rented room. Irkalla stayed out often herself. Ekur relaxed a little.

He and Eannatum were fast asleep in the first breath of night air when a pounding on the door woke them.

"Open up!"

They sprang from bed. Ekur grabbed his knife; Eannatum scrabbled for his. When Eannatum nodded, Ekur stepped to the door, unlocked, pushed it open.

There stood Irkalla. Beside her were two men in town-guard uniforms, with spears. A third man held a torch, flickering in light breeze. Her father must have gotten her the guards.

"I caught you!" she cried. "You've been lying this whole time, Ekur. You're coming home."

A guard gestured at Eannatum. "What about him?"

She glared at the younger man. "He can stay the night if he likes. I'm sure his parents would *love* that."

A piece fell into place for Ekur: Irkalla had told Eannatum's parents they'd kept up their relationship.

He and she took a long walk under a chip of waning moon, the sound of the guards' boots behind them. He bided his time.

Long ago, when they'd first married, he'd thought he was in

love with her. It was the first time he'd had regular sex. She wanted it as much as he did. Six times their wedding night, five times the night after. Then later, on the dining table, to the maid's chagrin; on the stairs with Irkalla humping herself upward like a cat in heat, moaning.

He remembered the first time he realized this largesse wasn't just for him.

Till recently they'd been friends, of a sort, co-parents; he still cared about her. They'd had sex sometimes, when they slept in the same bed. He'd thought he'd learned to manage her.

When they got home, the manservant met them in the doorway.

"*You* can go to bed," Irkalla told him. "You too," she told the guards. She and Ekur went through the dark entryway to the central courtyard, lit now by a handful of lamps.

In the center, they stopped and stared at each other, a foot apart. Side-light threw dramatic shadows. Potted palms' leaves shifted in a night breeze.

"Where am I supposed to sleep? Last time we fought I wasn't supposed to stay here."

"I want you here, as my husband. I want you in my bed."

"Really?" He stared at her, and she had to look away. He was tempted to take her up on the offer. He could push her into angry, stupid sex—he knew her. "I can sleep on the roof. But tell me, what do you want from this?"

Having played punisher, she switched to child. She pouted.

"I don't like people making fun of me behind my back. A young man his age should be looking for a wife."

"He is looking for a wife."

"Break it off, or I swear I'll make sure no girl in Uruk will have him!"

Eannatum had predicted this.

Ekur clenched his fists, letting his nails bite into his palms, so he didn't hit her.

At the temple, midday the next day, Eannatum asked to talk.

The heat was blinding, but Ekur found a courtyard open to temple staff, not often used. It was built around a tamarisk, all wispy grey-green leaves, a now-dry basin set around its roots. Four stone benches sat arranged around the tree, and at the edges of the courtyard pots of seasonal flowers interspersed with mint, which gave off scent when brushed. They sat on one of the benches.

"I can't do this anymore," Eannatum said.

Tears rose behind Ekur's eyelids. "I can see that."

"My parents are past middle age. I'm their oldest son. They have expectations. And they love me."

"I know."

"There's a path I'm supposed to take. I didn't want to do it this way, but I don't want to hurt them. If Irkalla makes good on her threats, they'll never understand."

A tear rolled down Ekur's cheek.

"We have to break it off. A clean cut is easiest."

"People say that kind of thing."

"Please don't make this harder."

They embraced. The scent of Eannatum, light sweat and the thyme he chewed, enveloped Ekur.

He sat back from the hug. He had to ask. "Can we have one last night?"

Eannatum closed his eyes in pain. "Who knows who's

watching?" The breeze whispered, bringing scents of thyme and mint. "I'm going to see about getting transferred."

"Don't do that."

"We have to see less of each other. The temptation will be too great."

"I beg you, don't."

"Ekur, please don't stand in my way." Eannatum stood. "I have to go."

Ekur took Eannatum's arm, tugged gently. "Stay just a little longer."

"You're making it harder." Eannatum pulled away. "Goodbye."

In three long strides, he was across the courtyard, through the archway, gone.

Chapter 21

$\mathcal{F}$alling into the rhythm of the job, Joanie continued to stop by the coffee shop now and again, to say hi to Alyssa and check email away from her sometimes-dark basement.

Her workday started at nine a.m., downtown, the epicenter of rush hour. She learned to be early. They'd finished her training and the sales system switch, and the job now was mostly admin work. She also took part in client meet-and-greets. Sometimes that was just carrying in coffee. Often she took basic information in a first interview, and she set new clients up with their portals and did troubleshooting.

In early August, she met Don.

His self-presentation was business basic, chinos and blue shirts, sports jackets, on presentation days a repp tie, but everything was premium brand. Blond hair in a conservative fade, a ready smile. He wore a woody cologne that smelled good, nothing bargain-basement.

The key was the narrow blue eyes, which flicked from one

place to another, always looking for something—a score, maybe, or a way out.

A hustler, a sales guy, he reminded her why she'd never meant to be part of this industry. Still, she was here now and needed at least to give it a fair try, especially given the money. She'd just started to pay down her loans.

He breezed in at nine-thirty on a Monday morning and swung by her cubicle.

"So you're the new girl." She stood, and they shook hands. He gave a hearty handshake, a little hard, but she gave it back— just another male dominance game. "You did good work checking our system transfer. That's awesome! I'll have some stuff for you soon."

Then he strode away to his own office.

He was a hard worker, she had to give him that. But he was massively behind on all his admin work that wasn't client-facing, and he gave it all to her with a smile and a cup of coffee. The coffee was a nice touch.

"Get through that this week, and I'll start giving you things that are more interesting."

"This week? I'm finishing a portal setup for Monica, besides some other things."

"As soon as you can." He gave her a broad smile. He was used to bowling women over. He wasn't remotely her type. But she needed to stay in good with him, so she smiled back.

Later in the day, she checked in with Monica. Nearing the end of summer, they'd had no significant rain yet, but out Monica's window the day was overcast. Crows spun in an arc and settled on a far roof. Joanie spun a little in her cobalt-blue-upholstered chair.

"He's not supposed to dump all his admin work on you. We have a couple other assistants."

"I can do it. He said he was going to give me some more interesting work later."

"As long as he's supporting you." She gazed at Joanie, who stopped spinning her chair. "You're a hard worker, good with clients, smart. I think you can go far here, if you want to. I'd suggest you start studying for your CFP. We might be able to help fund the training. Once you have that, we can make you a paraplanner and you can work toward managing your own accounts."

Joanie hadn't decided if she was staying, but she wasn't naive enough to say that.

Puabi-Ekur watched her with the same frustration their goddesses had felt with them.

Joanie was heading into the cloud of metal shavings, the inimical energy now Puabi-Ekur's opponent. The not-caring, the money-pushing. This Don had the feel of the new djinni, like a wall of bundled razor-wire.

Puabi-Ekur could almost hear their cruel, metallic laughter. It refined into an electronic buzzing, as near overhead power lines.

Short for time, Joanie wasn't meditating or reading Tarot. There was no way for Puabi-Ekur to step in and warn her.

She was in danger, and was heading into worse, and she didn't know.

This is why spirits knocked things off shelves and cabinets to get attention—a bit like giant housecats.

Chapter 22

*a*fter nearly a week, Pete texted Joanie back.

<Sure. When's good?>

They settled on a Tuesday evening, drinks and dinner, at a place a little more intimate than the orange-painted cavern on Capitol Hill. They picked a restaurant near both of them that served pan-Asian food and cocktails.

A date. It had been a long time since Joanie had been on a date that wasn't a for-hire client appointment. And Pete had been up-front about asking, too. Confidence was sexy.

He had to be a little queer, or queer-positive, if he'd been gay for pay—right? He must be somewhat down for sex work, if he'd done it himself? She hoped, too, he wasn't a hardcore atheist. Because she was definitely a witch.

She wasn't sure what she wanted from this date. At minimum, she enjoyed his company, and she wouldn't mind getting laid. But she'd be okay if it were more.

She took a Lyft down, getting the driver to drop her a half-block away from the restaurant so she could scope it out. Its wood pillars stood set among bushes and trees; in front sat black wrought-iron tables. The sun was out, westering, early evening. A morning of rain had contained the fires for now. Haze still hung in the air, with a scent of smoke.

She saw Pete at an outdoor table before he saw her. Nervous, she backed behind a tree. She'd dressed up but not too up, flowered sundress and light sweater, espadrilles, new-painted toenails, dark hair up and wispy. She wore sunglasses so she could hide a little, and light makeup. The flowers on her sundress were purple and green on black; for anyone who knew, they were belladonna.

If she wanted to, she could stop traffic. She could also put this power away. But a boy like Pete could see, perhaps, past the shiny façade. Did she want that?

This might be just anxiety talking.

She stepped into view and officially saw him. Entering through the restaurant, she told the hostess with a high-wattage smile, "I'm meeting a friend."

She alighted beside him. She could tell she'd played it right. He seemed a little stunned.

"Well, hi," he said. "You look lovely."

He himself didn't look a lot different than the last time she'd seen him. Guys could get away with so much. Black jeans, a black t-shirt, a dark maroon shirt hanging loose, unbuttoned. All a bit dark for a fair, freckled redhead.

"Thanks." She pulled out a chair and sat. The waitress appeared. Pete had a beer in front of him; she ordered a gin drink with lime.

She wasn't worried. She could get back home—that wasn't an issue. He could be dangerous, maybe; she'd taken that from Gus's stories. But he wouldn't be dangerous to her.

But did she like him?

She didn't not like him. With her, with guys, that was rare. It had been a while since she'd met anyone new, of any gender, she might consider. She was restless, primed to take a chance, sexually, emotionally. Energy came off her like heat, pheromones mixing with her perfume, night-blooming jasmine.

It was still early evening. The last yellow light was fading, hiding behind the hill up to the University District, leaving a warm glow and purple shadows.

The warm light tinged his blue eyes a little green. They met hers.

A moment, a breath.

She wanted to set dinner and conversation aside, and just go to bed with him, find out about him that way. But he didn't know her. Suggesting sex so fast might spook him.

"How goes the world of Antifa?"

"That's not what I spend all day doing. I go to rallies and so on, but I have a regular life too."

"Mmm. And what does that look like?"

"Study, mostly, right now. I'm back in school, working on my political science master's. What about you?"

"Working at the financial management firm, mostly."

"I thought you were all about the sex work?"

She shrugged. "There's legal downsides to doing it for a main gig. I have to be part of what you call regular life myself. But what I want to do is more spiritually oriented."

"You said you were a witch—something about that? Witchcraft seems very fashionable these days. Everyone's got their crystals and sage."

She was a little offended, but she could tell that, beneath it all, he was asking a question.

"Not witchcraft, or not as such. Not magic, or not much, more ritual. My main goddess is Inanna. Some people call her the patroness of sacred whores. Some people think there was no such thing as sacred whoredom, of course."

He grimaced. "I know a little bit about that, but tell me more."

She did, sketching in the idea of the sacred whore as a sexual healer, watching his face. He seemed open to the idea.

He'd had his own experience of whoring. He'd been a street hustler. There might be trauma there; she didn't want to pressure him.

Between them hovered possibility, one moment bright, the next fading. She didn't know if she wanted this flame to burn, but she wanted to be the one to decide if it went out.

"I don't mean to be hostile," he said. "I'm a little sensitive on the subject of spirituality. My parents are pretty religious."

"Mine too. Or at least my mother is."

Over dinner, they traded Christian-parent war stories. She elided a few things, but he seemed able to read between the lines.

He leaned forward, elbows on the table, beer under his hanging hands. The sun had set now, the west stained pink, fading to lavender then an even blue. The air was still warm as bathwater. A cool breeze snaked through it.

"My dad's father was a preacher, and my dad believed sparing the rod spoiled the child. He took it very literally, like with a switch or a paddle."

His tone was joking, so she laughed, though clearly the memory was painful. "Did he realize he was raising a young anarchist?"

"I've never been able to figure it out. Even when I was very young, like five or six, I thought that kind of punishment was ludicrous. It didn't teach respect. I didn't respect my father, and neither did anyone else. He was a drunk." He stared into his own beer a moment.

"Yeah, there's alcoholism in my family too. My dad left when I was two—my mother raised me on her own."

He glanced up toward her.

"You had a stepfather?"

"She had boyfriends. She's considering getting married now, I guess. I don't hear from her much."

"I don't talk to my parents much either. Though they're still together. I don't know why. My dad likes to get drunk and call me the young Communist."

She reached out, put her hand over his; she couldn't help it. "I'm sorry."

He laughed, a short bark. "I didn't mean to come here and make you feel sorry for me. I don't know why I'm talking about this."

She took her hand back. "I don't feel sorry for you. If we're going to get to know each other, we talk about our pasts, right? It seems like we have some things in common."

The light had faded from the sky. Their waitress stopped by and lit the candle that sat between them. Joanie looked down at the last of her soup, a few noodles in broth.

"Tell me how you got into Antifa."

"That part is easy."

"How do you mean?"

"I'm basically an anarcho-communist. I also have some background in fighting—I trained for a while as a boxer and then studied kung fu. When it became clear some of the local marches needed people to stand between the protestors and right-wing assholes, it seemed like my job to step up."

"And you know Gus—how?" She'd heard Gus's version but wanted to hear his.

"I met him first when he was hanging out with Max. You know the story—they left this rotting goat's head at my friend Rob's. So when we found them on the street, we were ready to dispense justice. But one of my pals was potentially going to really hurt Gus, which was the wrong thing, since he was clearly at most an accomplice. For me, Antifa is about protecting people. So when I saw Gus again, I took him for a beer."

He took a big swallow of the beer he had, finishing his pint.

There was more to the story. Gus had ended up giving a statement to the police, because an Odin's Hunt ritual had left Rob dead.

"I agree, I think we have to keep reaching out," Joanie said. She'd long since finished her own gin, though now she wished she'd ordered another drink. "So many people on the right just get this misinformation."

"You consider yourself a leftist?"

"Yes. When I was going to go for my economics master's, I wanted to reform the economy. In part to help figure out how economics can help address climate change. By the time I realized that wasn't going to be discussed in any depth in our econ department, I'd already set my course of study. Now I have to figure out what to do with my degree."

"I understand. On the flip side, feeling the way I do, for me the big question is what am I doing in a master's program? Hiding, probably." He met her eyes. "Sorry, I don't mean to be so negative." He eyed his empty beer. The waitress had stopped by already once, to see if they needed the check, though they'd shooed her away. It was time to make a decision.

"Maybe it wasn't such a good idea," he said, "us going on this date. I guess I'm feeling darker than I thought. Not great company."

"I don't mind. I like to hear you talk about what you care about."

A breath of cool air twined around her. She folded her arms and rubbed her shoulders, ribbed light cotton under her fingers.

It was her call, her decision, and the time was now.

"I wouldn't mind keeping talking, and I don't mind if the talk's a little serious. Anyone intelligent is a little prone to dark moods now, right? We could get a glass of wine or something."

"You could come to my place. It's not huge, but my roommate's in Portland. We'll have the place to ourselves."

"Sounds better than mine. I just have part of a daylight basement." And her girlfriend lived in the house. Though Cleo was okay with this date, Joanie didn't want to rub her nose in it.

They paid, waited outside for their Lyft. The evening lay blue, with a light haze and a smell of smoke. Only a few of the brightest stars pierced through. The moon would rise later. She wondered if it would shine red tonight.

In the dark back of the car, Pete was silent, and so was she. She didn't doubt her decision, but she didn't want to talk in front of the stranger who was driving.

To maintain some kind of contact, she reached out and rubbed his knee. He put his hand over hers, warm.

There was something here. She didn't know what yet.

It was only a handful of blocks, but traffic was stop and go. Red lights flared against darkness, the black silhouettes of buildings against the nearly black sky.

Her relationship with men was more complicated than hers with women. With women, she'd see a pretty girl across the room and be smitten. The hard part was getting close.

With men, often she was too close to begin with. She'd hooked up first with Clayton for money, back in her escort service days. It had been random chance—and the help of Puabi-Ekur, she'd come to realize—they'd proved so compatible in bed. And Clayton was a good person, what her mother would call a gentleman.

Now he was far away, and she rarely missed him—sometimes when she heard his voice, she remembered. What sustained things between them was that he was in love with her. She'd been happy when he started to date. She cared for him, but she had no idea where things would go.

Whom she missed, acutely, was Cleo, but she also understood Cleo's need for focus.

"Here." They stopped in front of a set of grey buildings near fraternity row, newer construction, the outer walls matte and boring. She barely got a look before they went inside.

They climbed a staircase, along the hallway found the door of the apartment. Its interior was equally boring, tan wall-to-wall carpeting and off-white-painted walls. On a leatherette couch lay a crocheted blanket, purple and gold, university colors. She guessed someone's mother or aunt had made it. Otherwise the only bright spot was a Dropkick Murphys banner, a black, white, and green pirate emblem.

"Celtic punk?" she asked—a description of the music.

"Down to the stout. I mean, I have a couple of bottles of stout. You said wine, though. My roommate might have some. Or there's the end of a bottle of whiskey."

"I'd take whiskey. No need to steal from your roommate."

"I'd pay him back." He was busy banging through the kitchen cupboards. Through the open arch, the kitchen though basic was clean, with off-white tiles and walnut-finish cupboards. "I'm not finding wine, though. Whiskey it is."

He set the whiskey on a low table in front of the leatherette couch. There was an overhead light by the door, but not in the main living room; he turned on the floor lamp.

"I wonder if we have any music in common?" he asked.

"I like the Dropkick Murphys just fine." She nodded at the poster. "But it's not great background for a conversation."

"I have a playlist that's Celtic. Nothing too cheesy."

He went to a small Bluetooth stereo setup in the corner, on the shelf of a bookcase. Slipping off her espadrilles, she tucked her feet under her, watching him.

His close-cropped hair shone copper in the light. He had a narrow frame, wiry, but with muscles. Tension or anger thrummed in him, like a high-pitched sound ringing just out of audible range. She herself had a lot of anger. Or so she'd been told, over time, by friends, partners, therapists.

He glanced at her a moment, then turned back to the stereo. His eyes were pretty, under an underhung brow and dark blue, so they weren't the first thing you noticed about him.

The music came up, and he adjusted the volume. A fiddle mourned. Returning to the kitchen, he brought out a couple of jam jars. "I hope you don't mind. We don't have a lot of glassware."

"I don't care." He poured them each a finger of whiskey. She took a sip. "If you had your perfect world, what would happen next?" He stared at her, and she saw with the break in conversation he wasn't sure what she meant. "I mean, if you could wave your wand, as an anarcho-communist, what would the world look like tomorrow?"

He grinned. "You want me to talk for half an hour? Or three?"

"Give me the nutshell."

He settled into a corner of the couch, facing her, half a foot away. "Obviously we'd have more direct democracy. Live collectively, vote on more in smaller groups. Workers would own the means of production. We'd grow our own food and make our own things where possible, have a gift economy and systems of social exchange otherwise."

"It's not unlike the Firebird House ethos."

"Ah, you live in a community house. I was part of one, before I moved in here. But it broke up."

"They do." There had been turnover at Firebird House, too. "We do Forum to help build more transparent communication. I think community living takes inner work as well as outer work. But it can be hard, for sure. Luckily we have a few people really committed to both supporting the community and sharing power."

He took another sip of whiskey.

"We have a lot in common. I was kind of surprised when you showed up in a sundress. My last girlfriend wouldn't have worn a dress if you paid her."

Joanie raised an eyebrow. "I might. I've done a lot of things for money. It doesn't mean I'm a huge fan of capitalism. But I have to live here and now."

"Poor choice of words on my part."

She was getting tired of his backhanded jabs, which she read as some underlying anger at women. She set down her jam jar.

"You don't like that I wear dresses, and you don't like I'm a witch. I'm not your last girlfriend. You sure you want to be on a date with me? I can go home."

"Hey." He sat forward. "I'm sorry. I'm just in a weird mood today, and I couldn't tell you why. When I saw you—I hadn't realized—Jesus, you're a stunningly beautiful girl, Joanie, and I guess when I first met you, you were dressed down, and..." He sighed. "This is me, not you. I like you. I like you a lot. I'm sorry."

"I didn't dress to seize the means of production. I'm on a date."

Radical honesty. It was a catch-phrase some of the Firebird House folks used. She didn't use the phrase or attempt the action often, but she was ready to now.

"Look." Reaching across, she grabbed his knee. "I came here because I like you, and I don't care if you're feeling down. Not that I want you to be, but if you're there, you're there." In the music, voices sang something tragic in Gaelic. "But I'm not going to take it on. If you need to be alone with your bad mood, I'm fine with that."

Leaning forward, she gazed into the dark blue eyes.

"But like I say, I came here because I like you, and I want to have sex with you. Is that something you want? To have sex with me?"

His mouth dropped open a moment, and then he laughed.

"Why yes, it is. As a matter of fact."

She slid forward along the couch, so they were inches away from each other, close enough to kiss. He smelled sweet, of whiskey.

"Can we get there from here? Or are you in too bad a mood?"

He stared. His eyes were a midnight slate blue, full of pupil. "Are you joking?"

"No."

"Well, then, yes. We can get there from here."

She leaned in to kiss him. He tasted like whiskey. He pulled her onto his lap and kissed her back, deeply, stroking her hair; pulling the clasp out of her hair and letting it fall, a dark curtain, running his fingers through it. "Pretty hair."

He pulled her tight against him, so she straddled him; pressing against her, the erection in his jeans was hard as rebar. For a moment, she wondered how long it had been for him. She rode him, kissing him, as he continued to draw his fingers through her hair. Then taking her by the waist he flipped her so she was beneath him, jostling the table so their glasses clinked, pressing hard against her—her panties were so wet—kissed her, biting a little, not enough to leave marks, her mouth, her cheek, her neck; he slid down the straps of her sundress and released her breasts, kissing and biting her nipples.

"Harder," she whispered.

He bit harder, and something inside her broke open and ran, like the skin of a fruit bursting. She connected with his energy, a jolt like she'd never felt before.

She had to have him inside her.

"Fuck, fuck, fuck. Do you have a condom."

"Not here. Come with me."

He stood, took her hand, pulled her up, led her, pushing open the door to his bedroom; she got an impression of shadows, darkness. He slung her onto the bed and she laughed. He scrabbled in the drawer. She pulled off her dress and panties, pushed down the blanket, found the sheets. Then he was on top of her. He was unzipping himself, shucking his clothing.

There. He was planted; he moved inside her, stroking her hair. A band of light from the living room fell across the bed. For all his earlier tension, this link had a deep sweetness; the room lay hushed, filled with a holiness.

Fleetingly, a look on his face said he took this much more seriously than she did.

She got caught up in the rush of it; it had been a while for her too. Ah, the beauty of it, a scent of sweat, the rising feeling;

it was she who couldn't keep it together and she came, hard, shuddering, and then he did.

He lay on top of her, and she cradled him in her arms.

After a few moments, he came to. "I'm crushing you."

"No." But he rolled off, pulled her into his armpit. He took off the condom, pitched it, and lay back down as he'd been.

She drew her fingers over his chest. He was slim, fit, not overly muscular; if she had a type, for guys, he was it. "How long has it been?"

A flash of white side-eye in darkness. "Long enough. Nearly a year."

"Since your girlfriend?"

"Mmm-hmm."

"It's been a while for me too. My girlfriend's working on her thesis. She gets caught up in it."

"You said you were poly?"

"Yeah, she knows I'm out with you. I think it's a load off her mind, honestly."

He laughed. "I can't see it being such a hardship, having sex with a girl like you."

There it was again, some resentment she didn't understand. "What do you mean, a girl like me?"

"A woman, I should say. A beautiful, smart, together woman, with the world in the palm of her hand."

She half-laughed. "I'm glad I give that impression. But that's not me."

"How isn't it?" He sat up on one elbow. "I mean, I'm not stupid, I get there's a lot of ways being a woman in this world has its problems. I like to think of myself as an ally, though in the end it's not me who decides that. But you could have anything you wanted."

The idea was so foreign to her that it gave her pause.

"What do you mean?

"You have all the things. Intelligence, beauty."

"You're funny. You don't have those things yourself?"

"I don't know about beauty."

"You were desirable enough to be a porn star, right?"

"That was mostly being in the right place at the right time."

"Au contraire." She stroked her finger down the length of his penis, which shivered.

He had a lovely cock, at least to her taste, almost too big if anything. She would think guys would like it also, but she didn't say that.

"Besides, I don't like guys, or not more than enough for that... I can get hard, but who I want to spend intimate time with is a woman."

"I hear you there."

He sat up on one elbow. "Then why are you in bed with me?"

She laughed. "Because I want to be. I'm pansexual, I'm not kidding about that. I like guys too. And I'm picky, I mean, I choose quickly, but... why do you ask?"

"You're too beautiful for me."

He seemed to mean this. "You're flattering me, I suppose, but I don't get it." She sat up. "It's nice to be considered good-looking, but it gets me attention I don't want. So, yeah, I dress down plenty. But for a date... I like you, and you'll just have to get used to it. Unless you don't want to see me again."

"I didn't say that."

All right, then, she thought, *stop talking.*

Leaning over, she gave him a lingering kiss, his response heartfelt. She took his shoulders in her hands, pushed him down onto the bed, straddled him; taking his face in her hands, she leaned over, kissing him, leaning so her breasts just touched him, nipples to smooth skin. He groaned. Reaching behind her, she found him beginning to get hard. Sliding down, she sucked till he had a full erection.

The problem with a big cock—it didn't fit into the mouth as well. However, she was a pro.

"Condoms in that drawer?" He nodded. She slid one on and mounted him.

This time could be drawn-out, languid, and she could drive; she positioned herself so each stroke hit her G-spot. Slow, slow. She didn't always like guys, but she liked cock. She rode facing him, slow, watching his face; his eyes were shut and he looked reverent.

She could get used to this.

She loved Cleo, but right now Cleo had no time for her.

She hoped it wasn't a problem this boy wasn't seeing anyone else.

His hands came up; she took them in hers to brace herself. Speeding up her rhythm, she watched his face. His mouth fell open. Then he sat up and put his arms around her.

They sat in embrace and watched each other in the shadowy light. She still thrust against him, and he met her. She could have brought herself off, but she wanted to see how it played out. So it built and built, exquisite, almost painful pleasure.

"I have to—I'm not—"

"It's fine, it's fine."

A few more slow, long thrusts and he came, and surprisingly she did too, not as intense a peak but a long, slow resonance. They embraced. She smelled again her own perfume, night-blooming jasmine.

Chapter 23

*T*here was something here. She didn't know what yet.

They sat wrapped in each other's arms, she on his lap, sitting across each other scissor-fashion. Their breathing quieted. His eyes were shut but hers were open, watching his face.

Among shadows, a band of light from the living room fell across the worn wooden floor and onto his coverlet, onto her thigh. Under his delicate eyelids, lavender in the light, his eyes moved as he thought. The resonance ebbed, leaving her warm and sleepy.

His eyes opened; his gaze searched her face. She didn't know what for.

This is my work, she thought, *sexual healing.*

It wasn't just work, but her calling.

He closed his eyes again and kissed her. She met and returned it, exploring. Every human was a new world.

He moved, and she let herself fall back onto the bed, hair shaken across the pillows, confident in her nakedness. Sitting cross-legged on the bed, he stared at her and shook his head. "Such a beautiful girl."

"You're pretty gorgeous yourself, you boy. And you have one of the world's great cocks."

He rolled his eyes. "My small bit of fame." He took off the condom, sliding off the bed, and threw it in the trash. She didn't move to get up yet.

"Not small."

He eyed her. "I'm told I rank well by my fan club."

He probably meant it literally.

He pulled on his underwear and jeans and strolled into the other room. From there, he called, "You know, we didn't even finish the whiskey."

She checked her phone. They'd started the evening early, and now it was only nine o'clock.

Throwing on her sundress, she followed. "We can't have that."

They sipped, golden warming liquid. She didn't want to get too tipsy. She wasn't going to stay; she had work in the morning. "I'm curious about anarcho-communism."

"Sure. Like what kind of thing?"

"I'd love a reading list, if you've got one."

"There's one I like online; let me point you to it." They exchanged email addresses and he sent a link. He told her about some authors he liked. She downed her last bit of whiskey.

"Should we make plans?"

"Definitely. If you want to."

"I do."

They called up calendars on their phones. As he entered information, she looked around the room. A few candles would help. She wondered what the roommate was like.

Though the room felt empty, unfinished, as so many guys' rooms did, still it held possibility, as if the fabric of the universe might be open here. As if this space and person offered something to be curious about.

They both stood, and he took her in his arms.

The sex had opened a door between them, and she sensed again his energy, which had come to her as a jolt before. Now it was warm and steady.

Standing on tiptoes, taking his face in her hands, she kissed him deeply, dropping artifice and just being, between them a fluid space.

She realized he frightened her, not because of the anarchism but because he was a serious boy. A doorway open on darkness, a possibility that might lead to joy or pain.

She'd wanted to have sex with someone new; she'd not really planned on feelings.

But in the kiss, she rose to the challenge. Unlike many boys, he met her energetically.

He broke the kiss, staring at her, then shook his head.

"Goodnight."

When she got home, she went upstairs to talk to Cleo.

"How was it?" Tonight Cleo sat at her desk, tucked into a corner beside her bedroom door, her laptop open and a pile of books next to her.

"Surprisingly good. Though he's got some resentment around women. It's something to watch out for. But we had a lot of connection."

"Come give me a hug."

She did. Her beautiful girl smelled like sandalwood, her

usual perfume. She folded into her arms Cleo's long slim form, in a bright-colored nightgown, orange and magenta.

"Did you fuck him?"

"Yeah."

"I figured." Cleo laughed. "You smell... hmm, not fishy, kind of sweaty. Besides all the jasmine."

"You have the best nose!"

"Come snuggle with me, I'm at a good stopping place. Tell me how it went." Cleo locked her laptop, and they went into her room. Lighting a candle, she pushed down the coverlet, slid in, and drew Joanie into her arms.

Joanie knew the answer, but she had to ask: "Before I get into it—are you okay with it? Like really okay?"

"I am. I don't think some random white boy can mess with what we've got."

"Okay."

"So tell me."

Halfway to falling asleep, Joanie told the story of her night bit by bit, with long drowsy pauses. Candlelight flickered on gilt thread and bits of mirror in the throw pillows and the sari hung overhead.

"He's going to send you a reading list? My kind of boy."

"Yeah, I liked that part."

"So you think you'll see him again?"

"I think so."

"I like that he was in a community house before. Did he say the name? No? Find out when you get a chance, we can do some research on him."

"Mmm." Joanie was three-quarters asleep. "Can I sleep with you tonight? I don't know if I can make it downstairs."

Cleo raised an eyebrow. "Do you need to set your alarm?"

"No..." and Joanie fell asleep.

Chapter 24

$\mathcal{E}$kur and Eannatum still worked together. Eannatum's transfer had yet to come through—Ekur had done his best to prevent it. He'd argued Eannatum's work was essential. In the meantime, they were very careful with each other, very correct.

Put it all in the box of war and forget about it.

There was a lot of work, and Eannatum was an excellent aide. Ekur stayed nights at their rental room—his rental room —often. Alone.

Things with Irkalla had changed; he couldn't imagine sleeping with her. He'd accepted her nature long ago, but now she'd threatened his future.

As part of Ekur's job, he had to entertain, take outings and bring his family, go to other people's parties. For all these, he had to have his wife at his side.

He realized how much their earlier relationship had

depended on a certain balance. One of two sisters close in age, Irkalla had a bone-deep sense of rivalry. This rivalry she played out with Ekur.

She was winning now. She wasn't a good winner.

Toward the end of spring, a high administrator showed off his wealth at a party. It was hard to get into the several-storied house, so many people were invited. On the gravel terrace outside, torchlight glittered off headdresses and jewelry—crystal, amethyst, gold. On the front steps, Ekur waited for the crush to pass; he wasn't in a hurry.

Inside, he saw Irkalla, with a girlfriend. "Oh, *there* you are, Ekur. Nintuda, you've met my husband, Ekur?" Gazing at Ekur, she leaned toward Nintuda. "I told you about Ekur's little folly? But he's done now." Nintuda simpered.

At a servant's call, they went into the main dining room: a sit-down meal for fifty, with gold plates. Ekur was seated across from Irkalla, whose dinner partners at left and right were men her own age, ten years younger than him. Ekur had to be polite to the women to either side, so he barely heard Irkalla's conversation. But her dinner partners gave him disgusted looks.

After the meal, he didn't stay. He made his goodbyes, brushed his lips across Irkalla's cheek, went out through the big double doors.

It was walking distance home, the moon nearly full. He didn't bother with a torch-bearer, stepped down the low steps onto the terrace. A weight lifted.

Running footsteps crossed the gravel behind him.

Turning, he got a punch in the face. The momentum threw him to the ground.

He leaped up.

One of Irkalla's dinner partners, Anbu, stood there, angry

face wadded in a knot. A huge man, all muscles, he looked ready to murder.

A chill ran down the back of Ekur's neck. Had his luck run out?

"What in seven hells was that?"

"That's for Irkalla, who you dishonored." Anbu danced back and forth, fists air-punching. Around the two, servants gathered.

This fool could kill him.

"Go back inside, Anbu, and don't meddle in something you don't understand."

Anbu struck out. Ekur stepped neatly out of the way. Anbu staggered, almost fell. Spinning around, he yelled, "Fight me like a man!"

He leaped forward, as if to grab Ekur by the shoulders. He connected for a moment, then Ekur slipped his grasp.

"A man doesn't fight a boy." Especially a boy twice his size. "Go back inside."

Servants milled, not knowing what to do.

"You don't deserve her!"

Anbu grabbed him again, threw him to the ground, and jumped on top of him. Ekur twisted, close to throwing him off, but Anbu landed a punch. Ekur managed to turn so it glanced off, to avoid having his nose broken.

Anbu swung back to punch again. Ekur kneed him in the groin. As Anbu folded, he pushed himself away, skin ripping on the gravel.

He leaped to his feet. Did he need to run? Anbu scrabbled upright.

A high-ranked servant stepped forward. "Lords, please, we can't have fighting here."

"I'm defending the Lady Irkalla!"

Emboldened, the other servants surrounded them. "Please come inside, my lord."

Anbu scowled at Ekur. But the moment had passed. Anbu let himself be led away.

Ekur rubbed his cheek. It was going to bruise.

"Please don't skip our after-work get-togethers," Ekur's supervisor told Ekur. "It says the wrong thing." These were loose gatherings, nothing formal, in the administration common area. Servants brought in dark thick ale, dates, flatbread, chickpea spread.

Ekur made sure not to sit with Eannatum, but of course he ran into him when he went to grab a bowl of dates.

"Come talk to me," Eannatum said. "Just for a few moments."

Ekur let the younger man draw him onto a balcony. The setting sun poured peach-colored light across the city, flying birds silhouetted against it.

"How are you?" he asked. He could hardly bear to look at Eannatum—slender, brown, muscular in his young man's long kilt. None of that was for him anymore.

"My parents have started introducing me to suitable young women."

"Are any of them worth your time?"

"I don't want it. I can't make the best of it, as my cousin said I should. I want to be with you."

Ekur's heart beat in his throat.

Nirah, Irkalla's father, a widower, lived semi-retired. He spent most of his time on his estate, though he still had dealings in the city. Ekur stopped by his younger daughter's household, where he stayed in town, but for Ekur he was always out.

Finally, not telling anyone he was going—Irkalla had spent the night at "a friend's"—one sunrise Ekur saddled his riding donkey and left the city. The deep blue of the sky turned grey as dawn birds called. Willows drooped leaves into the canals. Nirah's estate wasn't far, but Ekur took his time.

Along a lane through a field of barley, green and rippling under the wind, he rode past some out-buildings to a long farmhouse, flat-roofed, white-plastered in the town style. He swung off his donkey, called a groom to take care of him. At the carven wooden door, he knocked.

A grey-haired womanservant opened it. "Lord Ekur, we didn't expect you. The master—"

From the house interior, a voice said, "Now, Gemakala, I want to make sure they move that brush pile today." The older man shambled into view from a dark passageway, scratching the back of his head, clearly just dressed. Looking up, he saw Ekur.

For a moment, his face went blank. Then it settled into a grim smile.

"Ah, Lord Ekur. I wondered if I might see you. Gemakala, could you find Lord Ekur a seat in the courtyard, and maybe some beer? Unless it's too early for you."

"Not at all." Nirah would want beer. Ekur intended to drink slowly.

In the courtyard, a few chairs sat by a wooden table, behind them a grapevine trained on a trellis. While he waited, Ekur amused himself by taking not the best-padded chair, probably Nirah's, but the one positioned best against the moving sun.

The old woman brought beer, and at his request also well-water.

When Nirah reappeared, he'd changed into an administrator's long robe. Ekur wore a warrior's kilt. The robe didn't intimidate him; he wore one daily.

"Lord Ekur, I suppose you've come to talk to me about your marriage."

"Not so much about my marriage, Lord Nirah, but about your daughter."

"Ah, yes, the Lady Irkalla. You were lucky with her." From the beer-jug with its two straws, Nirah took a long draw. "Still a beauty, too, after two children."

"She is that," Ekur said. "I see your barley's doing well this year, Lord Nirah."

They sidetracked into barley farming, in which the old man was an expert. Ekur wanted him a bit drunk before he made his points.

"You can call me Nirah, son."

Nirah had half-drained the jug and was smiling lazily. The sun had crept across the lap of his robe, but he hadn't shifted positions yet.

He cleared his throat. "Ekur, my daughter tells me you've been sleeping with your former subaltern. Of course you're your own man, but it's important to me my daughter's happy."

"Irkalla didn't tell you I've set my relationship with Eannatum aside? I thought you talked fairly often." Nirah made a noncommittal noise. "Has she told you about her own affair?"

"An affair? My Irkalla?" Nirah narrowed his eyes.

"She stays out all night two or three nights a week. Sometimes, when I work late, she brings him home, or so the servants tell me."

"My Irkalla? Never. A flirtation, maybe."

"She's had lovers throughout our relationship. Ask around —you can find the truth."

"Irkalla's always loved outings and parties. Of course if you treat her badly, she'll avoid you."

"Nirah, I've been patient. But I won't be her stooge."

"I don't believe Irkalla would do anything so foolish." My daughter wouldn't get caught, Nirah's face said.

"She has."

Nirah smiled, his face in the wall's shadow. The smile didn't reach his eyes.

"Prove it."

"I can do that."

"Have a care how, son. If you're wrong, I'm bound to support her. Even if that means her and the children moving back to our family house."

Chapter 25

*W*itch Farm always helped the Aaronsens with their tree-planting drives. Western red cedar had been the mainstay of Salish Sea peoples for centuries. But in the waves of fires, Western Washington was swept by flame. In the waves of human die-offs, from flu and other illnesses, no one planted trees.

Where it was wet enough cedar thrived still, a mother tree for shelter, clothing, medicine, incense, food preparation. Early spring was the best time to plant it, but you could also plant it in early fall. The Aaronsens did both.

A few weeks into autumn, Joanie, Cleo, Tracy, and a couple of the younger witches hitched up the pony cart, threw in medicinal tinctures for trade, and headed toward the Aaronsens. It would be a several-day trip, with camping equipment to stay over. Some of the young ones brought drums, Tracy his fiddle. With a few of the extended Aaronsen clan, they planned to play music till dawn.

Warm under a blue sky crossed with bands of cirrus, the

uneven landscape lay green, with yellow from big-leaf maples starting to turn. The pony, who considered himself an adventure pony, snuffed the air and shook his mane, and set out almost at a trot. "Whoa, there, Caesar," Cleo said, because the walkers had to keep up, and the pony decided a walk was fine.

A mile or two into the journey, Tracy sidled up to Joanie, who sat with arm tucked into Cleo's as Cleo drove the pony. "I have a new tune for you." He played it, a simple air, vaguely Celtic.

"Reminds me of someone I used to know, who loved Celtic music," Joanie said.

Cleo traded a look with her.

Tracy looked from face to face. "I feel as if there's a story here."

Puabi-Ekur watched. Something was rising, like a fish surfacing from deep water.

That night, around the fire, Tracy played his tune and a few more on fiddle. Others played guitar for singalongs. A young Aaronsen gifted with a voice sang folk songs to make you shiver. The drummers took over, and the young ones danced, lit red and black against the flames.

Around her arose the new world. Much had fallen apart since she was young, but much had come together.

She rarely missed creature comforts, except the ability to have a stinging hot shower at any time. And a few foods—it was hard to find good chocolate or coffee. She missed the former plentitude of coffee shops in Seattle. Her learnings at her own shop had helped her build her distillery business.

More than anything, she missed the people she had lost.

Chapter 26

It was a night Irkalla expected Ekur to be gone, the dark of the moon. He often still worked late—he needed to, and he didn't want to see Irkalla.

He had a temple guard walk him home, late, carrying a torch. In among the silent houses, black buildings against black sky, an owl hooted. The late-night prostitutes were out, one girl suppressing a yawn against the back of her hand. He eyed her, wanting to laugh. Misreading him, she pulled her breast from her robe, held it toward him in the goddess's famous gesture. He shook his head and went on.

The servants had told him who Irkalla's lover was. The cook and maidservants were happy to tell about her lover's visits.

Did he care?

For a long time he'd been fond of her, as of some wayward child. Was that even true now?

Again an owl hooted.

Entering the house, he nodded to the manservant at the bottom of the stairs. He went up to the master bedroom.

It lay dark; he left it dark, crossing to lean against the low clothes-chest that stood by the wall. His dagger lay on the chest behind him, but he didn't think he'd need it.

After a time, below, the house door banged open. He guessed whoever opened it was drunk. Her voice filtered up to him, laughing. "Come upstairs, come upstairs!"

"No, sweetness, I feel bad about that. Let's not do that again." A man's voice.

"Not do what?"

"Not have sex in your marriage bed." Ekur had to applaud the man's taste.

"Oh, *Shulgi*—you're silly."

This confirmed what Ekur had suspected. The Sumerian nobility was too small for him not to know her lover, and Irkalla was too status-conscious to have a serious affair outside the nobility. Ekur had gathered from the servants this was serious; she saw Shulgi a lot.

Feet stumbled up the stairs: the light slap of sandals, the heavier tread of boots, as she closed in the chiming of her earrings. The room door flew open.

In her hand she carried a lamp, lighting her face from below. The man was a shadow behind her. She gave a strangled scream.

"Ekur! I didn't expect you."

"Obviously."

"But I—" She turned. "Shulgi, you'd better go."

Shulgi looked from her face to Ekur's.

"Very well," he said. He moved to embrace her, thought better of it, and fled down the stairs. The outer door opened and shut.

Ekur and Irkalla were alone.

The single lamp with its scent of sesame oil cast its light

across the room, throwing long shadows. They stared at each other.

He'd thought he'd have a sense of victory, the pride of the hunter who'd caught his prey. But mostly he was sad. He'd never wanted to prevent her from having what she wanted.

"The game's up, darling," he said.

Her mouth twisted. "Don't pretend you're not still seeing Eannatum."

He stood.

She faced him defiantly, half in lamplight, half in shadow, in the middle of their bedroom. Between them lay their marriage bed, made up with a light wool blanket, under it fine linen sheets.

"Do you honestly care who I see?"

He saw doubt flicker across her face. She didn't care; she just had the habit of trying to smash anything in her way. Like a two-year-old.

"Do what you like. *I'm* going to my sister's house, and I'm taking the children."

Chapter 27

idmorning, under the bright blue skies of near-summer, Ekur crossed a broad sand-strewn courtyard surrounded by palm trees. A light wind shuffled the leaves as he walked up the shallow steps to the main administration building.

It had been two weeks since Irkalla had moved to her sister's. In the meantime, he'd made inquiries and made sure Irkalla's friends knew what had happened. A divorce would be ugly. The ugliness would cost both sides, but Sumerian law favored the husband.

Now Ekur's chief, the head administrator, had called him into his office, which on one side fronted on a roomful of scribes and on the other had a line of windows overlooking the city, white and sand-colored towers interspersed with painted, inlaid walls. The streets flowed with people in multicolored dress, Sumerians, Akkadians, foreigners. One man walked his pet antelope on a leash. Besides himself, the office was empty, so he took the visitor's chair, facing the handsome desk of inlaid wood.

Across the room, a set of small stone sculptures sat along the top of a chest. One caught his eye, a man with wide ivory eyes inset with lapis lazuli, his mouth in a wide smile. The man looked happy and a little foolish.

Ekur contemplated the statue.

The world had something against happiness. It thought of happy men as fools, or cowards: men content at home, who didn't go out to wage war.

The empire of Akkad was always seething with war; now was simply a break in the fighting. He had been lucky to leap from generalship to administration, with the aid of his father. That didn't mean he'd never lead men to war again.

A shadow fell across the doorway, and his boss entered.

"You sent for me?"

Sitting, his supervisor pushed across the desk a baked clay tablet. "I have an opportunity for you."

Ekur's stomach dropped. He did his best to smile. "Excellent." He stared at the tablet a moment but didn't pick it up.

Striving for calm, he stared at the inlay along the edge of the desk, light and dark narrow triangles of contrasting colored wood inlaid in even medium-polished cypress wood.

His boss tapped the tablet with a stylus. "The city of Akkad has need of additional high-level administrators. The chief administrator there sent to us and asked if there was anyone I could recommend. He wants only my top men. I thought of you."

Ekur stared for a moment, then collected himself.

"Tell me more."

"You'd need to move there for at least a year. Obviously it would take you away from your family, so you'd be compensated accordingly. Arrangements could be made as well to house your family in Akkad, at a reduced rate, or if not you would get a smaller house in the palace district free of charge. You could also take a certain number of staff. I thought of you because one of the placements Akkad wants to make is an administrator of tithes." His chief was watching his face closely. "Think it over, don't make a hasty decision. But I need to know by moon-day next."

"I'll need to think about it. Check with my family."

Though this move to the capital would be a rise in station, he couldn't help wondering if he were being kicked upstairs. He believed his work had been exemplary. But perhaps his supervisor had heard rumors of unrest in his household.

Or perhaps this had been Nirah's work. Perhaps Nirah had seen the lay of the land and decided to get Ekur out of town. His boyfriend too, if need be. Because if Irkalla didn't see her danger, Nirah did.

His chief said, "This has nothing to do with wanting to get rid of you. I'd much rather keep you, so please, say the word if you want to stay. I just owe it to Akkad to offer my best people. They're overwhelmed tallying the spoils of war."

He rose, and Ekur rose with him, picking up the tablet.

"That covers the details. Give it some thought and get back to me on moon-day."

Chapter 28

*P*leading a headache, Ekur left early that afternoon, wandering like a sleepwalker as long blue shadows fell along the thoroughfares. The streets were full, but he walked as if he were alone. Once he almost stumbled straight into a man leading a donkey laden with panniers of grain.

He stopped in the tavern below his rented room, where he'd been spending a lot of time. The barkeep settled him in a corner of the tavern porch, sheltered by the leaves of a couple of palms.

There, at the close of afternoon, a breeze barely moved the air. The green scent of just-watered plants rose from nearby. A lattice of palm-leaf shadows crossed rays of sunlight.

He must have dozed off, because Eannatum was shaking him. He'd told him they needed to talk.

"I heard you left early. Are you ill?"

"No."

"The barman says dinner's made. I'll ask to have it brought out."

They ate, lentil stew seasoned with garlic and sprinkled

with goat cheese, barley bread and oil to the side. Ekur told Eannatum about his conversation with his supervisor.

Eannatum stared.

"But that's a significant promotion. Aren't you pleased?"

"I'm not sure how I feel about leaving town." He watched Eannatum's face.

It struck him: He couldn't do this without Eannatum. Though maybe he would have to.

"I can take what administrative staff I like, up to ten people. Of course you'd be my first choice, and not just because I love you—you're my right-hand man. Would you consider going?"

Eannatum drew a mouthful of beer through his straw. "I'd have to think. My parents might not like it, but then again they might." Ripples of controversy had reached them; the Uruk gentry was not large.

You're a grown man, Ekur thought. *You don't have to do what your parents tell you.*

"What do *you* want?" Ekur asked.

"I told you. I want to be with you. Let me think."

The next evening, Ekur went to eat dinner at what he couldn't help thinking of as home. Irkalla had agreed to meet him, with the children, since they needed to talk.

As he walked there through the twilight, images of the house slipped through his mind: the tall front steps, the painted doorway, the dining room with its high-backed inlaid-wood chairs the children struggled with, a gift from Irkalla's parents at their wedding. He had built this house, with his brother's and cousins' help, just before he and Irkalla were married.

He saw again her bright embroidered clothing, her shining

eyes when he dropped the veil over her head, signifying she was now his wife. Long ago.

Mounting the steps, he opened the front door.

"Daddy! Daddy!" Henbur came running and threw himself at him. "Fix my toy sword! Dildala broke it."

"Did not!" Dildala wrapped herself around his knees.

"Mamma says I can't beat Dildala up when she makes me angry."

"She's right, darling."

"Can I have a tame gazelle? I know how to get one."

As Cook made dinner, the family gathered on the roof terrace. Ekur fixed the pommel of Henbur's toy wooden sword, binding it with twine and then, for decoration, red-dyed cord.

"Can you carve it to make it sharp, Daddy?"

"No, darling, it's just a practice sword." He patted Henbur's shoulder. "Soon enough you'll have a real one."

Irkalla had already started the wine and looked at him waspishly over the edge of her cup. Of course he meant that soon Henbur would be a man, not that he'd give his son something dangerous.

The servant called them for dinner. Along the steps, the lamps in their wall sconces gave a glow of warmth. He held Dildala's hand in his. Irkalla glanced sideways, frowning. She was jealous of his relationship with the children.

Entering the formal dining room, which Irkalla insisted on using, he took his place at the head of the table. Dinner was three courses: chickpea stew, lettuce with early radishes, roast mutton. Irkalla again and again beckoned the servant to fill her winecup; the servant stalled. She was more irritable when she'd been drinking.

Sweet date tarts came for dessert. He could not wait to leave. Something about this space always made him feel trapped. In part, it was the long narrow room itself. With the door shut, the only outlet was high windows on one side. He blamed himself; he'd designed it. The air seemed hot. He wriggled his shoulders in his robe, which seemed tight, tamping down the desire to bolt.

The children ate silently. Irkalla spun the wine in her cup, watching it like a child fascinated with a toy. "How is work?"

"Busy. I have some news for you later." Her dark eyes flickered his way, rested on him a moment—almost curiously—then moved away. He guessed she was thinking of Shulgi.

The nursemaid appeared in the doorway. He followed her and the children to the children's room. He tucked Henbur in and told little Dildala another installment in their tale of a princess from the mountains, who had a magic gazelle who could talk and fly. Henbur's bright dark eyes, still open, said he was listening, though he never admitted an interest in "girl stuff."

"And then the gazelle went to sleep in her little bed, right next to the princess's. It's time to go to sleep."

"Good night, Daddy."

He folded the light blanket up to her chin. Her eyes shut, her lashes fringed on her flushed cheeks, breathing heavy, almost snoring. He kissed her on the forehead.

Climbing the stairs to the rooftop terrace, he paused a moment. Though it was late spring, the air was heavy, muggy. On the roof, he found a clear night, stars sparkling beyond the city's haze, a little chilly. He'd brought a light cloak and threw it on. In her chair, Irkalla was wrapped up as if for winter. A brazier was lit. The servants had planted striped squill-flowers in the terracotta basins, the shut blooms pale against the night.

Irkalla took her cup from the low table with the jingle of bracelets. "You said you had news?"

He told her about the proposed transfer.

"That's *quite* a promotion. It would be good for the children." Their eyes met. "Not now, perhaps. You'd see them less. But over time. You'd be rising in the administration—you could become one of the empire's top men."

A smile lay on her painted lips. She was trying to be pleasant.

Her father must have explained how it had to be.

"Akkad isn't that far," he said. "I could come back a few days at a time." With just him on a donkey, traveling back would take less than a day. On the initial journey of two days, he'd bring staff, servants, and household goods by ox-train. "I might take the children for a few days when I visit."

"That could work. I could send the nursemaid along."

His going to Akkad would open up time she could spend with Shulgi—he could read that on her, as if it passed in cuneiform across her forehead.

"I'll do it, then."

He had to, whatever Eannatum decided.

Suddenly he was done with her, done with this evening, ready to go. He leaned, touched her cheek with his lips, and left for his room at the tavern.

Chapter 29

$\mathcal{P}$ ete's roommate had extended his visit to Portland, and Pete offered to make Joanie dinner. She found herself looking forward to it more than she expected.

She'd done her best to pick apart his issue with her. A lot was about her looks, and whether she dressed like a girl. Yet she'd always been proudly femme. She wasn't going to be shamed out of dressing up, or dressing like a witch.

So: black, black, and more black. Witchy. Knee-high boots, not too high a platform because she had to walk. A long black skirt, a long dark-grey floaty t-shirt over, silver jewelry. No bra, subtle nipple. Or not so subtle. He'd have to deal.

Did she even want a boy? Part of her regarded them as not fully human. And yet, this one, the energy that poured off him was intoxicating.

She appraised herself in the full-length mirror in the bathroom.

She looked great. She looked hot.

It was still warm weather, but she had a lightweight duster

she could throw over her outfit to tone it down, so she didn't get harassed on her way across the University District.

At the end of August, the truce with the eastern fires held; though she could still smell smoke, the haze wasn't overpowering. Healthy people were okay to walk.

In golden hazy light, the sun floated among a raft of clouds behind her. Crossing the University District toward frat row, she swung into the grocery, got a bottle of wine, then dove into long tree-lined streets. They met her with green scent, a whiff of flowers as she passed an armful of red dahlias, then black-eyed Susans in someone's planter. Pink roses like small scented pillows climbed a trellis. She stopped and put her face in them.

Almost she wanted to turn around and not go on this date, keep everything in suspense. She loved that breath, that moment before you entered a relationship. Poly friends of hers favored the term "relationship escalator"—the corollary was, you could step off, not do marriage, two children, and a picket fence. Yet you still had to solve the problems of sex and living with people, even if you solved those by having neither.

She buzzed his apartment and he let her in; she entered, pulling off her duster. "Where should I put this?"

"Over the back of the couch is fine." He looked her up and down. "You look amazing."

He was in all black, which brought out the paleness of his skin. His hair gleamed red as a copper penny. "At least we match today."

She hoped he'd kiss her, but after a nod he backed away toward the kitchen. "I've got to keep an eye on the food."

She followed, leaned against the wall watching him cook. He had a bunch of ingredients in a frying pan, various bottles around him: sesame oil, vinegar, chili sauce.

"Smells heavenly."

"Just stir-fry. Sorry, I meant to do something a bit more special, but I ended up staying late talking to a student."

"I'm fine with stir-fry." She pulled the bag off her wine, set it on the counter next to his stove. "I brought this."

He glanced up. "Corkscrew's in there." She rummaged a bit, found it and jam jars, and poured them both wine. "Thanks." He took a sip.

He still hadn't connected with her, and she wondered if the second date was a bad idea.

"It's ready." He plated it up. "Let's eat in the living room." Setting the plates down on the low table, he settled on the couch, and she sat next to him.

He thrummed with tension. Was something wrong? He wolfed his food as if he hadn't eaten in days. She finished, set her plate aside, and took a sip of wine.

Then she leaned in toward him, watching him, and kissed him. He kissed back, carefully, holding himself back. She drew away again.

Maybe he'd been burned his last relationship, or sometime in the past?

"Talk to me. What's up? You seem nervous," she said.

"I am."

"What is it?"

"Same stuff, also just stress." He flashed a glance at her. "A friend of mine's been getting death threats. I think it's okay now, but it's been pretty stressful."

"What's the deal? If you want to tell me."

"Hmm." He glanced outside, a long narrow window the couch faced. Between black-leaved trees, an even blue sky spread. "Do you want to go for a walk?"

"Sure."

He took his phone out of his pocket, turned its power off, and pulling a small bag out of his backpack, put it in that.

"What's that?"

"Faraday bag. Prevents wireless communication."

He was afraid of being traced or recorded by his phone.

"Maybe I'm being paranoid, but—yeah. Could you?" She took her own phone out of her purse and slid it into the same bag. "We can take them, if you want."

"I won't need mine." She swallowed hard. "But first, I have a request."

He looked at her, a real look, perhaps the first one their whole visit. His dark blue eyes were full of pupil. He wasn't just nervous, he was terrified, but she got it wasn't about her.

"Can I have a proper kiss?"

A half-smile flitted across his face, and he kissed her.

Searching, questioning, she met him, and fire leaped. She realized how much she'd wanted this, without letting herself know she did. She climbed into his lap and kissed him deeper, petting his shoulders and back, wrapping her arms around him. He was hard below her.

It was all she could do not to cup his erection, pull him out and have him, but he'd asked to walk and she didn't want to be disrespectful.

She paused, and in her pause he sat up—she'd half pushed him down.

"Let's walk and talk. I'll be a lot better if I can get this off my mind."

Outside, he turned northward. "Mind if we go to the park?"

"Fine with me."

She took his hand, and smiling he folded her in, close to him, falling into step with her.

"It's a group close to Gus's former friends. These groups metastasize constantly."

"Do you think they're serious about going after him?"

"Probably somewhat, but if he's dropped off social media and moved, that may be enough to throw them off track."

He fell silent. "So what about your friend?"

"It started off with the usual garbage fire on Twitter. Hate speech, literally Nazi stuff. He took exception, and it escalated. People showed up at his apartment in the middle of the night to threaten him."

"What happened?"

"Some neighbors intervened. One called the police, who sent the Nazis home."

"That's all they did?"

They'd entered the park and walked under dark trees, a margin of sky above. Through the park ran a ravine, the air heavy and humid from the water close by.

"They took the point of view it wasn't clear who had started it. I think he's going to need to move. I've started to be more careful around this stuff myself. I don't do social media under my own name. I go masked to rallies. I try not to talk about sensitive stuff around my phone—ninety percent of the alt-right are morons, but ten percent are actually capable of, for example, hacking your phone."

"I've known a few people who've gotten harassed. Not to that extent. That sucks."

"Yeah. He may need to couch surf a while at my place. Which is also stressing me out, but that's my problem."

The path lay dark among alder, big leaf maple, and fir. She stopped, and he stopped with her. Catching his arm, she drew him to her and hugged him. Through her ran a desire to draw his pain out of him.

"Just be still," she whispered. "Be quiet."

In the silence, light wind rose, shaking the trees.

"Let it go. Imagine yourself connected to the earth, and let it go into the earth."

He sighed deeply, closing his eyes, took a number of deep breaths.

"Is this witchcraft?"

"Yes."

Opening his eyes, he took her face in his hands, and kissed her, softly, then more deeply. She thought of the creek hidden in the ravine.

The walk back to his place was nearly silent.

"Is there anything more that's bothering you?"

He reached out and caught her hand. "I'm just preoccupied. I'm glad you're here, though."

"You seem to have some compunctions about my being a witch. What's up with that?"

"It's just not part of my world-view. As I say, my parents were religious. I regard myself as an atheist."

"Well, I'm not." That left the conversation at an impasse. They walked in silence, still holding hands.

She tried again. "I guess for me, I haven't believed in the Christian god my mother does for a long time. But I've always had a sense of other things in the world besides ourselves—ghosts, spirits. And learning to work with my own energy and with other people's has been good."

"I'm not hardline. I went through a religious phase when I was in my early teens. But that kind of fundamentalist Christianity leaves me cold. I'm not a hardcore materialist, though. The world's too large and strange a place." He grinned. "I'm a Celt, after all."

They stood now outside his apartment house, under tall

shadowing maples. Darkness had fallen, to a clear night with a breeze, just a bit of haze. Still the air smelled of smoke.

"Are you sure you want company?"

"I do. If you'll stay. We still have that wine. I got some ice cream for dessert. I'm not sure it will go with the wine."

They ate ice cream. "Tell me about your witch practice."

She talked about how the coven worked with the wheel of the year. "From the bird's-eye view, a lot is Celtic or English-based. We're pretty flexible, though. Some of us are basically Greek devotionalists, dedicated to Hekate."

"And where do you fall?"

"I work with Hekate, but more with Inanna. She's the patroness of sacred whores, as I said, bringing the love of the goddess to humans."

"But you said you're not focusing on sex work now?"

"With the newer laws, it's too easy to get caught up in the human trafficking thing. Of course there's human trafficking, of course that's bad, but most of what people like me do is far from that."

"You're preaching to the choir."

"So, I have my financial services job. It's not what I wanted, but it pays half again as much as the coffee shop."

A wave of shame washed over her. She closed her eyes a moment.

"When I figured out the economics I wanted to learn wasn't offered at the university, I thought I'd move to accounting. But I'd have to go to school again. In the meantime, I have student loans."

He was studying her.

"It seems to me both of us have done a lot of things to survive. Some of them similar. If I understand you, you'd like to bring to the world sex-positive ritual and sex work that benefits everyone. Is that fair?"

"Yes."

"We're still here in late-stage capitalism. It hasn't gone away while we've been talking."

"No." It was the same thing Cleo had said.

"You feel bad about it, though. Especially talking to an anarcho-communist."

"I do."

"Well, two things. One, if you think studying for a master's in political science is the anarcho-communist paradise, think again. Most of our internships are in the legislature, not a hotbed of anarchism. Two, there may be a lot you can learn in financial services to help subvert the capitalist system. Where better?"

"I suppose you're right."

"You have chocolate on your lip." He reached out and wiped it with his thumb.

She caught his thumb in her mouth and sucked it, watching his face. His expression didn't change, but he flushed, hot blood filling his skin.

"Come here, you." He drew her forward and kissed her.

She climbed again in his lap and kissed him everywhere, his face, his chin, his neck, landing on his mouth. He drew her rump forward so she rode the bulge in his jeans.

He drew her top off and mouthed her breasts. "Bite me," she said, and he did, and lust flooded through her. She'd been thinking of going slowly, trying new things, but all that disappeared. Reaching under her, she unbuckled his jeans, put her hand around his cock, slid her hand up and down. Standing, she pulled him into the bedroom by his cock.

Part of her wanted to prove her prowess as a cocksucker, but even more she wanted him inside her.

She met his eyes, which were full of pupil, his mouth half-open, mad with lust. She grabbed a condom, slid it on, and, pushing him down on the bed, mounted him.

Chapter 30

*a*fter Ekur agreed to go to Akkad, it took a couple of weeks to pack and settle details.

Eannatum took this time to think. He wanted to live up to his parents' dreams. Someone like Ekur hadn't been part of those, though going into administration in Akkad would raise Eannatum's status.

Three days before Ekur started off, at the end of the work-day, he drew Eannatum aside onto the common-area balcony. The year was edging into summer; they'd worked till late twilight. Sunset bled across the west, rose-color reflected on city walls.

He gestured to a small wooden table and chairs. "Come, sit. If you come with me to Akkad, you can't leave like a thief in the night. You need to plan and pack."

Eannatum glowered.

"I decided. I'm going. All right?"

As if Ekur already knew.

"Are you?"

Eannatum leaped up in frustration. "Of course I'm going. Didn't I say I wanted to be with you?"

He walked to the balcony balustrade, stared at the city a moment, walked back, and sat down.

Almost Ekur's mouth dropped open.

When were you going to tell me?

"How did you persuade your parents?"

"They understand this is good for my career. A man can marry later in life. They don't like it, but I forced their hand."

Clearly, he didn't want to talk about it.

Ekur's own parents had come to understand his problems with Irkalla. But he'd been dutiful and only stepped out after two children, except occasionally with prostitutes. His parents thought of his relationship with Eannatum as an oddity, one they could overlook for this rise in status.

Against the darkening sky, swallows swooped after insects.

"I'm sorry. This last week has not been easy. My mother cried a lot. She thought I liked the last girl."

Ekur half-smiled. "Did you?"

"Not to marry." He met Ekur's eyes. "I don't want some girl in my bed. I want you."

Drawing his chair around the table, he put his arms around Ekur and kissed him.

Something deep in Ekur relaxed. It had been so long.

"I want to come with you to Akkad. I can marry. Or not. My parents have two other sons to carry on the line. If we do well in Akkad, and we will, there will be plenty of wealth for everyone. My younger brother loves the farm as much as I do. He can have the land. I want you." Eannatum let out a long breath. "I thought ours was just a wartime romance. That's not so."

He sat up, pushing his hand through his long dark hair.

Reaching out, Ekur stroked his beautiful mane and his smooth back. Eannatum was naked to the waist, still just in his long fringed kilt though the air grew chilly.

"I didn't expect it. But what I want most, here and now, is you."

They met in a kiss, exploratory, full of desire.

Ekur wrapped himself around Eannatum, hugging him into his body.

The scent of him was green like thyme, a little sour with sweat, entirely sexy. He nuzzled his warm, smooth skin.

"I want you to have everything you want. Marry, have children. Later, if you want to. My children make me very happy. Have your farm. We could farm together."

"Maybe. Right now, let's just go to Akkad. But before that—" he kissed him, drew back, nipped him, kissed him again. "Let's go to your tavern room."

~

In darkness, it was as if they hadn't stopped, except hotter, more intense. Their bodies remembered. Again and again. Eannatum didn't even try going back home that night.

~

Then they were off for Akkad city, a two-day journey, with an ox-train and eight assistants besides Eannatum.

It was a reprieve, a gift of the gods, what Ekur had wanted. Yet he was sad to leave Uruk. He would miss his city as he went among strangers. He would miss his children.

Another wistfulness traveled with him like swamp mist,

though he tried to shut it away. It was an illusion; what he wanted had been gone a long time.

The image of a good marriage was so Sumerian. Sumerians loved a garden, barley bread and beer, and an armful of children. The point of marriage was children, but the ideal was family happiness. But whatever he'd had once with Irkalla was gone.

He had to face toward Akkad.

Over three generations, the cultures of Sumer and Akkad had merged. The Akkadians might call Inanna Ishtar, but they still worshipped her. An Akkadian princess had been Inanna's high priestess, two generations ago, and there were still Akkadians serving Inanna at the highest level in Uruk.

Likewise, a boy from Uruk, city of Inanna, could make good in the imperial city of Akkad. Ekur had passable Akkadian, necessary for a general and administrator. He hoped his work would speak for him.

And Eannatum's work, for Eannatum. In Akkad, Ekur had heard, some looked down on a man who received another man in sex. He didn't want Eannatum to be held in anything less than respect. He wanted Eannatum to have his desires, too—children, if he wanted them. A farm. But Ekur's supervisor had thought this would be a clear advance for them both.

He could always go back if he failed. Now, he would go forward.

They traveled the well-irrigated land between the two rivers, cut by canals. Drivers led the slow oxen, drivers who knew their foibles and how to wheedle them across the bridges. He rode alongside the wagon-train on a donkey, Eannatum with him or doubling back to gossip with the other assistants.

His heart rose at the flight of the ibis from the wetlands, at ducks gabbling at sunset among the reeds. The small caravan took a long midday break the first day, then traveled a half-hour after sundown, lit by a waxing moon. They stopped on the road between cities, paying farmers to let them put up tents in a fallow field. As they made camp, servants set cook-fires. The smoke of burning juniper rose.

As Ekur entered his tent, a grey lizard ran over his foot and away into darkness. The shadowy tent was dressed with embroidered red and blue hangings, a small alabaster Inanna enshrined in one corner.

The servants had unrolled their bedroll, and Eannatum lay on it. He threw himself down beside him.

Without words, they returned to the conversation they'd begun again above the tavern.

After another night in the countryside, they entered the city of Akkad midmorning on Inanna-day, as deemed auspicious by the camp astrologer. With ten Sumerian administrators traveling together, of course there was an astrologer, a priest of the Inanna temple.

Though it was a warm day, they wore all their finest official gear. The retainers sported thick felted capes and the leaders each a kaunakes, a long kilt in an ancient style with tufts of wool sewn on. Ekur wore his own kaunakes and heavy gold jewelry of state, and the pointed helmet-hat spoke to his warrior background, though far more modest than a ruler's would be.

Uruk was dedicated to its lady, Inanna, and the height of Uruk was Inanna's temple. Akkad elevated the king above all. The palace stood at the top of the low hill that was the height of the city, and the administration Ekur would join was that of the palace.

He'd have to get used to that.

In the day to day, administration was administration.

The city they approached was surrounded by a monumental wall, even more imposing than Uruk's. Like Uruk's, it held a high frieze of processionals, but these showed processions to the king. They'd put the king in the place Uruk would put Inanna.

By moving to Akkad, he would change his culture. It was a chance, a possibility. He'd mostly thought of it as advancement —he hadn't much considered how it would be to be surrounded always by Akkadians. He'd be at the beating heart of empire, where decisions were made, but also part of empire's everlasting war. Would he become more hard-edged, more warlike, less a son of Inanna?

He would always be Inanna's in his heart.

The column moved forward. The day was inching toward midday, the sun warm. He sweated under his kaunakes. The city crept closer, visible in the distance, tan mud-brick against a blue sky with high clouds. Around a last bend, they saw the final wide canal that served for irrigation, a waterway, and defensive purposes. Past it over a bridge stood the huge gate, three stories tall.

The gate's crown was painted lapis-blue, and on it long-horned bulls pulled a chariot, a fanciful thing. The king in it, at the center, wore the high-stacked helmet-crown. The image of the king was bland, faceless, stern—not a portrait.

They crossed the bridge and passed through the gate. A small waiting group of greeters perked up to see the first guards and then Ekur, mounted for show on a half-onager, a tall half-wild ass. It was important he'd once been a general. All forms of state and rank must be brought forward now as he entered Akkad.

He stood with his palms clenched on the reins.

The first greeter stepped forward, bowing his head. "Every welcome, Lord Ekur, to the city of Akkad. A thousand thanks for coming to our aid."

He dismounted.

Chapter 31

*T*he weather cooled, at the cusp of fall, beginning-of-school time, bringing with it wistfulness. Maybe Joanie should try for that master's.

But not right now.

One late afternoon, she got a text from Pete: <I've had a day. Want to go out, blow off some steam?>

She had no plans. Though she didn't necessarily want Pete to know she was available to him. But she hated that kind of game.

<Meet you at your place at 7?>

<Sure>

As she walked across the University District, a new cool moved in the air. The first yellow leaves, falling, skittered on the sidewalks. At Pete's, she buzzed the doorbell, climbed the stairs. He opened the door to her.

A beat, while they stared at each other. Then they were on each other, flame to flame. Some barrier was gone for him. Grabbing her, he dragged her in, letting the door shut pushed her up the wall, kissing her, mouthing her, mauling her breasts with his hands.

Sliding out, she grabbed him by the belt and towed him to the bedroom. She'd planned something more complex, but right now, she just wanted to fuck.

Unbuckling him, pushing his jeans down, she couldn't help taking him in her mouth—mouth and hand, he was too big for just her mouth—pushing him on the bed, straddling him, sucking.

Then she sat up.

"You don't mind if we fuck first and eat later, do you?"

He laughed. She pulled off her panties. Grabbing and sliding on a condom, she mounted him; he took her hands in his, and she rode him.

"I'm not going to last—"

"I don't care."

But she beat him, coming, a cascade, and then he came himself. She fell down on top of him; he pulled her to him. She lay flat, breathing heavily. He was too.

He laughed.

"Hello, Joanie. It's nice to see you."

"It's nice to see you too." She rolled off, not wanting to constrict his breathing. A boxy room, all shadow, almost empty except for a bookshelf, dresser, and clothes basket. On the wall hung one piece of art, an impressionist print of a factory.

Some block between them had moved.

"I think you're the horniest girl I've ever been with."

"I'm not always like this. I'm just not seeing anyone else. Except for Cleo, and all of her energy is going into her thesis."

"I'm not complaining." Reaching over, he pulled her into an embrace.

She eyed him sideways. "Don't get too used to it. It goes in waves, you know?"

"I don't have some list of expectations."

"I do kind of expect dinner, myself."

"Let's go."

Between quarters, he was living off his savings, and she was chronically stretched, so they went for pizza. As they crossed the U District, sunset smudged orange on the horizon, striped with velvet purple. At a build-your-own pie place, they split a veggie pizza.

"I'm hungrier than I thought." She was inhaling it.

"I always eat too fast. I have five brothers and sisters. If you wanted enough to eat in my family, you ate fast."

"I see." She reached over, ran her hand over his buzzcut red hair, pulled back leaning on the table edge. She sighed with something like contentment. "Well, so far this evening we've satisfied our needs very quickly. Maybe we can slow down now."

"What do you want to do next?"

"I don't know. Go to your place. Talk a little more. Get to know each other better."

"I got a little more whiskey. If you'd like to drink whiskey."

Chapter 32

*J*oanie had done good work making it through Don's backlog, and he'd taken notice. He sent her a meeting. It had to mean she was getting more tasks.

The following afternoon, they met. Don's office was along the same wall as Monica's, a bit bigger. Through his window, cranes worked at a new skyscraper.

"Monica's been talking to you about your future here."

"Yes. She wants me to get my CFP and move into a para-planner role."

He gave her an assessing look. "We might be able to get you into that sooner rather than later. I have a financial instrument, a tax-relief plan, which I'm trying to get into the hands of a particular client. If I succeed with your help, I'll make sure you're on your way up in this company."

"Let me know what you need from me."

The sky-blue eyes were blank, impossible to read.

In the background sounded a high-pitched whine, almost a

buzzing. She wondered if there were something failing in his laptop.

"I'll draw up the initial papers. I'd appreciate it if you'd read them over and let me know any questions you have. Then I'd like you to go to the client meetings with me."

Across the street, a crane arm moved, carrying a load, and lowered it into place.

With a little cash in hand, Joanie took Cleo to their favorite pho place in the University District. Stepping into the space, she took in the familiar green-brown walls, the scent of hot broth and cilantro.

Back home, up in Cleo's room, Joanie tossed her lover down among the glinting pillows. Surrendering to Joanie's mouth, Cleo threw her head back with a cascade of shimmers. In glimpses, Joanie drank in her soft shut eyelids, her orchid mouth, the musky scent of her mixed with sandalwood.

In the morning, Cleo woke her, sliding out of bed. They met in a kiss. "I have to get to work," Cleo whispered. She'd had a heart-to-heart with her advisor and saw a way forward on her thesis, but it involved a recast and full revision. "You go back to sleep."

But Joanie had to go to work. She pined for a day together, at least a morning, leisurely coffee, out to breakfast at a diner, something.

The next day, Joanie returned to Don's admin work, odds and ends of nasty detail. She powered through on coffee, for lunch took her sandwich to the building's roof court, among potted juniper bushes. A breeze tossed a bank of pansies.

On a whim, she texted Pete.

<You busy tonight?>

<I have some grading, not a huge amount>

<Dinner?>

At this point, "dinner" seemed like code for "sex." But they would eat.

<Sure>

Without dwelling on it, she noticed they were both easily available to each other.

They made plans to go back to the Asian fusion place. She arrived early. Propane heaters burned on the outdoor patio, elements coal-red against the gathering dark.

In the cobalt-blue evening, a deep, almost brown orange wash of sunset spread across the west. The trees silhouetted against it recalled Halloween.

This was their fourth date, if these were dates. Was this becoming a relationship? Neither of them had touched on that. Her body was having a conversation of its own, liquid between her thighs, pheromones to add to jasmine perfume.

Something about the newness of their connection brought up a sense of challenge, even fear, fight or flight added to sex. Perhaps she was hard-wired to conflate these things.

This date, she was determined to take it more slowly. They shared a bowl of hot and sour soup, then entrees.

Full night had fallen. A scent of leaf decay floated on the air, almost like woodsmoke.

"Tell me about your last girlfriend."

He took a long sip of the porter he was drinking. A passing car flashed headlights across his face; in the sudden blank white light, he looked like a death's-head.

"We met at a march. She knew some Antifa friends of mine. We started dating. She wasn't very comfortable with my bisexuality, or my having had sex on camera. She was—I guess you'd call it demisexual."

"Mmm." That would be a bad fit.

"She came from a Catholic background, and though she'd left the church, she hadn't entirely left it. She had a connection with the Christian God, also witchy leanings."

That might explain why he'd been touchy about Joanie's witchery.

"We both of us cared a lot about the anti-fascist work. But it was easy to fall into this position where I was the aggressive guy and she was the retreating girl. She wasn't comfortable with poly. Her understanding was based on a pretty ordinary cis het sexuality."

"I've had some bad luck dealing with folks who weren't queer. Most queer folks have had to interrogate their sexuality. Which makes everything look different."

"Yes."

"I can see how my witchy stuff bugs you."

"Yes, and your practice is different. That stuff for her entered the realm of superstition, and the conversation would stop. You seem more flexible."

"How did you break it off?"

"She did. We talked. She felt pressured for sex, whether I said anything or not. And I'd had a more dysfunctional child-hood. My moods could be dark in ways she didn't understand."

"Who made the decision?"

"She did. We're still friends, of a sort. Though it's awkward."

"That was some time ago?"

"Almost a year now."

It was in the air, so she spoke. "For me, I'm not in any hurry to define this relationship."

He stared a moment at his pint glass, then took another mouthful of porter. "You're just looking to have a good time?"

That bitterness again. She pressed her lips together.

"I'm open to this becoming whatever it wants to become."

He stared at her. Light from their table candle illumined his face from below, with faint red glow from the heater. His eyes were in shadow.

"So am I."

The Lyft dropped them in front of his anonymous grey apartment building, gilded now by street light. Wind shook the limbs of the trees beside it; dead leaves rained down, dancing.

Up the stairs, he let them into the apartment and flicked on the light, bringing the harsh glare of the overhead.

"Is your roommate still not back?"

"I think he's going to move to Portland, though he hasn't said so. So far, he's still paying rent."

A little sweaty, he smelled like pine. Maybe he wore cologne, though she hadn't seen evidence of it. He took her hand. She dropped her jacket; they went to the bedroom.

They sat on the bed. A ray of light fell from the main room.

"We've moved quickly these past few times," he said. "Let me make love to you."

"All right."

He drew her forward, kissing her, and slid her t-shirt and bra off. Kissing her, little by little, biting gently, till her nipples hurt with desire.

"Can't we—"

"No." He slipped off her long skirt, with it her underwear.

Sliding down, he teased her with his tongue till she wriggled. But she understood what he wanted, and she was curious.

The feeling rose, wave after wave, an ocean encroaching on

the beach. In glances, he watched her face, pushing his fingers into her. Shutting her eyes, she gave in to the overwhelm.

A burst of white light, and she called out, pressing his head to stay in place. The reverberation, the retreating pleasure; she let go. He slid up and took her in his arms.

Half-asleep, she woke with his cock nudging her. Reaching back, she took it in her hand, worked him a few moments, then pushing him onto his back she leaned down and took him in her mouth.

"I thought—"

She lifted her head. "Turnabout is fair play."

She wanted to show her skill. But almost too quickly he came, filling her mouth, grunting, twitching, eyes shut hard. The warm wave of energy flowed over her, and she basked in it.

"You're good at that."

"Thanks."

"A lot of girls aren't. I've gotten a bit gun-shy. Do you want— would you spend the night, tonight?"

"I don't have a change of clothes. These aren't really work clothes."

"Okay."

"I'd like to, though. If I gave it an extra half-hour in the morning, I think I could swing it."

She snuggled against him, watching the room's shadows. The dappled colors of the print on the wall, of the factory, in the half-light showed grey.

Energy made its long withdrawal, the ocean sliding away. But somewhere at the base of it, at a center far away, something changed. A spark cast itself through him. His cock twitched against her thigh.

She put her hand on him and stroked; under her hand he

came alive again. He had as much sex drive as she did, even more perhaps.

No wonder his vanilla girl had found him too much.

Slowly stroking, she whispered, "Shall I climb on top?"

"Yes."

She took him inside her. She was determined to slow this down, draw this out.

The window in the main room was cracked open. A mutter of talk rose from people passing, which gave way to a low whisper of wind and the smoky smell of leaves. In the room swirled a rising energy between her and Pete. Rising like the wind that traveled outside restlessly, circling the block, whispering among the houses, ascending to the clouds, higher, all these things connected.

Suddenly she was certain: if there were other lives, she'd known him before.

She caught a flash of an ancient cave, flickers of firelight illuminating paintings, figures dancing. He was present with her in old darkness.

"I feel like I've known you before. Very long ago. Honestly, I'm seeing a Paleolithic cave—"

After a moment: "I think yes. But ssh."

They finished in silence. All the time she felt the height and width of the cave around her, its ceiling over her head, felt his energy from long ago, almost smelled the smoke of the fire.

Puabi-Ekur watched.

Why had they not foreseen the advent of this Pete? Or maybe they had—the feeling of something rising from dark water.

They sensed he came from a different thread than Puabi-Ekur, some other life weave. Many people and spirits drew together now as human and earth systems roiled. Alliances were crucial in creating the best possible future.

But who was this boy?

Clayton, at least to begin with, had made himself a puppet. Cleo was a queen, but wasn't Puabi-Ekur's concern. Gus was Puabi-Ekur's former lover, and though there was anger there, there was also caring. Gus, at least for now, was traveling the right direction.

Puabi-Ekur had wanted Joanie to notice the world of the unseen. Her connection with this boy Pete had brought in spirit, a wave from long ago—a golden time, not perfect, but a time when humans were aligned with the rest of the world.

Such an ancient line to the past. Perhaps Puabi-Ekur's lives stretched back that far, but they did not recall.

They saw, however, what this path pointed to—one of the early goddesses who strode out of the Ice Age, connected with a tribe who hunted deer and bear, who had for millennia lived in a different way in the world. Dea.

Puabi-Ekur stepped out, and out, and out, to the wave of green-golden light, the fire dancing.

Diving back, they followed the strands to the tiny cabin with its corner shrine and the goddess there. Without words, they found a level, connected, seeing.

Puabi-Ekur had not been an earth-spirit as such for millennia, and when they were, it was a spirit of the desert wind. Since then, Puabi-Ekur had wound in and around human lives, and taken on human lives as well: in countryside, in city, going here and there like wind.

Dea was a spirit of a hillside whose climate was close to

rainforest. Dea had crossed the land-bridge before there were cities, and for millennia she'd been right here.

They both were touchy, spiky, and protective, but now they were allied. As were their people. One of these people perhaps being Pete.

But if Puabi-Ekur's deities had sent them to Dea—what were they supposed to learn? Not to become rooted—that was not their nature.

Perhaps it was about what they both faced.

Chapter 33

*C*ome have some whiskey. If you want."

He'd pushed himself out of bed, heading for the bathroom, now was rummaging in his kitchen.

"Bring it in here. Please. I don't want to put clothes on."

"You don't have to." Returning, he opened a dresser drawer, found her a t-shirt, plain black. She pulled it over her head in case the roommate turned up. Tight on him, it was loose on her. It just skimmed her ass.

"Cute." In the main room, he turned on the floor lamp, but she shook her head.

"I want to get you some candles, or maybe a smaller lamp. The light in here—it's kind of awful."

"You're right, though it's not something I think about."

He brought her a jam jar with a finger of whiskey, and one for himself. She sipped. Warmth and sweetness. She was tempted to simply relax. But she had to speak.

"Speaking of gods and spirits, you said you saw the cave too."

He looked at her, his eyes wide.

"I did. It sounds like I saw the same thing you did."

"It reminds me of a vision Alyssa had, some time ago, that's become a reference point." It had come up in the June dream-work: a cave covered in ancient animal paintings, at its back an altar with a giant deer skull. Alyssa's dream said she'd finished her work there. But the cave might still be a place to return to.

Joanie continued, "I feel like in this time, as everything seems to be falling apart, we need to reach backward as well as forward for models. We can't return to a life as hunter-gatherers, but maybe we can learn from earlier systems. The Saturnian golden age, if you like."

"I hear what you're saying."

"But you don't agree."

"The spiritual take makes me uncomfortable."

"But you saw it too. And you've also said you're a Celt, and open to the otherworld." She put her arms around him, kissed his cheek. "It's not a thing that happens much to me, this combination of spirituality and sexuality. I don't want to push you, but I'd lying if I didn't say I wanted to explore it."

He wrapped his arms around her, put his face against her neck. Hiding below her chin, he said, "This spirituality is very different from what I grew up with. But it still touches some painful things for me. Let's go slowly."

"I don't mind that."

He drew her closer still, his energy a wave of pure terror.

The rainforest hillside, the ancient cave—Dea had a foothold in both these strands, Puabi-Ekur saw.

In their own way, in their different flow of time, the spirits connected, interpenetrated, seeking to understand.

It was a time of earth-change, a time of challenge. As in the past.

They had a warning for their people, and Puabi-Ekur had seen their enemy: the wall of metal shavings.

But even more than Puabi-Ekur, Dea saw there was no fighting this enemy head-on.

She too stepped up, and up, outside time as it presented itself, an arrow pointing one way. As she did, she illuminated changes, points along the arrow's flight. From a forest draped with fern where humans revered cedars as the tree of life, to the coming of people who made settled towns, with different crops and animals, without an understanding of the land so braided with its people.

The forest shrank, the weather changed, and the wall of razor-wire encroached.

This was an enemy to fight sideways, choosing the few who would listen, choosing the spots they might have best effect.

Chapter 34

$\mathcal{E}$kur's first weeks in Akkad passed in a whirlwind. At the palace, he met his workforce and started learning the work. Palace people had found him a house, but he had to furnish it, find servants, and fill the larder. All this he did with a language barrier. He knew administrative terms, but at home he was frustrated by the simplest things—what to call salad ingredients or linens. Luckily Eannatum could help.

In structure, the house was much like his in Uruk. Its central courtyard they filled with potted palms and geraniums. They shared the master bedroom, which had a small balcony overhung with roof.

Eannatum found servants who didn't blink at having two masters. Their cook-housekeeper kept referring to them as "you boys." But she had such a way with food no one corrected her, and she brewed her own beer. Her daughters acted as maids.

A month into their stay, Ekur found himself beginning to relax.

"Let's take a ride into the country," Eannatum said. "There's a hostelry where we could spend the night. There's little huts among palm trees, by a couple of small lakes. You can swim in one and fish the other. You deserve a little time to rest."

"I should go see the children."

"Not without proper notice to Irkalla, or she'll throw a fit."

"There's last quarter's barley inventory."

"You work too much. Take some time off, with me."

Eannatum made a kissing mouth at him, and he laughed. Eannatum missed his trips to his family's farm, where he always had some project going: a hybrid chickpea, a stronger strain of beans.

In red-tinged morning light, before the sun got hot, they rode northeast, each on his own donkey. Ekur dressed down, in a light robe and sandals; Eannatum had found them broad sunhats.

Among hazy green fields, oxen and donkeys grazed; farmers worked routing water through irrigation canals. By midday, they made it to the hostelry, found their hut, whitewashed mudbrick. Outside, the hostelry cooked grilled lamb on spits. They lunched outside at a table under a woven-reed awning.

Ekur stretched. "I feel lazy. I want to lie down."

In the brown shadows of the hut, the open window faced one small lake. On the shore, an ibis posed, then dove for a fish. Ekur threw himself on the bed.

"I'll go find some beer and then join you."

Ekur fell into a half-sleep, drowsy. Then Eannatum was next to him, kissing him lightly, and though he thought he was too tired that proved untrue.

Engorged under his lover's hand, his lover's mouth on him, his on his lover. Then with no haste he entered: that moment of connection, blessed by Inanna, holy. Afterward they slept.

Eannatum roused him for supper. "They're serving wild-fowl pie. They're famous for it."

In the brown-purple twilight, oil lamps cast a warm glow across the tables under the awning. Wild-fowl pie appeared, with some kind of spice he couldn't name, also a salad and dark-brown barley beer. "They have a northern wine that comes highly recommended." He had that afterward, sweet and dense.

"They also have a kind of barleywine they make in the far south."

"Maybe tomorrow. I'm content with the wine."

The next morning, they went fishing for carp—or rather Eannatum did. Ekur lazed on the bank on a blanket and kept the fish-basket closed.

"If we get enough, they'll make traditional fish stew," Eannatum said.

They took a full basket back to the outdoor cook-shed, an open built-up hearth under a reed awning. The cooks received it smiling, promising fish stew in the afternoon. "And perhaps some of that barleywine you're famous for," Eannatum suggested.

One of the cooks looked troubled. "I'm not sure, my lord. I can ask the master."

The host came to the hearth, all smiles. "I'm so sorry, my lords. My source for barleywine has dried up."

"Can you tell us why?" Ekur asked.

"It's a southern recipe, and my brewer requires a particular strain of barley from the far south. But there's drought in that region, so they no longer export it."

Ekur frowned to himself. "We'll have more of the beer, then."

The host bowed his head and retreated, and the cooks took the fish for the stew. A little breeze circled the hearth with its banked fire.

"You're angry at yourself for not knowing, aren't you?"

"I should know these basic facts. It's my job."

They ate then ambled back on their donkeys, road dappled with palm-leaf shadows. All the way, Ekur wondered about the drought.

The south, the hottest part of the empire, tended to feel the effects of less rainfall first. But they had years of grain stores.

As Ekur began the workweek, he checked the barley inventories for the previous year, which said the same thing. Barley production for the southern part of the empire had been cut in half, wheat as well. The people survived off stores but couldn't export to the rest of the empire. The tablets told a story of barren fields invaded by desert sand, farmers barely subsisting, men and women traveling to the city for work.

He saw a matter for concern, but nothing the empire hadn't dealt with before.

Late that first day, he visited the office of his supervisor, a high lord of Akkad surprisingly pleasant to a foreigner. He took Ekur's report.

"We see this every ten years or so. For now, we monitor the situation. Is it only Ur and Eridu?"

"Yes. Not yet Uruk. Should we transfer stores from one of the other cities?"

Lord Sharru looked down his aquiline nose. "That wouldn't gain us any friends. Let's save that for when there's real distress."

Ekur imagined the farmer with sand drifting across his fields, the irrigation canals overwhelmed and useless. There was real distress already. But he kept his mouth shut.

Chapter 35

That evening Gus and Alyssa spent studying. In his last year of his biology degree, he had his hardest classes, and she was working on her transfer degree.

They still shared the same room, since they were broke. He was going to spend every night wrapped around Alyssa anyway.

At three a.m., the dead of night, the air split with a sound of shattering. Slivers, splinters, chunks of glass sprang outward, some onto the bed.

Shocked awake, Gus yelped and sat up, upper arm blazing with pain, bleeding. A shard of glass stuck out of it.

"What the fuck?"

"What was that?!" Alyssa squealed.

His eyes took it in, in streetlight glare, blue-white. His heart thumped in his chest.

"I don't know. Stay still. Let me check it out."

He slid off the bed. Over the trash barrel, he pulled out the glass, and grabbing a tissue, used it to stanch the wound.

This was crazy.

He was glad he'd slept nearer the window. The bed sat in the corner, headboard to the window's wall. Only a little glass had fallen there, and only on him.

He switched on the light. In the middle of the pile of glass shards lay a rock. Wrapped around the rock was a piece of cloth that held writing.

"Omigod, Gus. Omigod."

He found his slippers, past the bed end where there was much less glass. He shook them out, picked them over, put them on. Gingerly, crunching lightly, he went to the rock, picked it up.

He knew what the writing would say before he read it.

"We know where you live."

He knew who it was from. His whole body flushed with rage.

He looked up to see Hannah standing in the doorway.

"It's come to that, has it? I'll call the police."

"Do that. Though I wonder if it will do any good." What he wanted was to punch someone.

"We need to get it on record. We use the tools we have."

Alyssa crept over. "Omigod, Gus, your arm." It dripped blood.

Call made, Hannah pulled Gus into her room. Under her desk lamp, she examined his arm. "A puncture wound. We'd better take you to the ER."

"I'll do it," Alyssa said. "Can I borrow your car?"

"No, not yet," Gus said.

"But Gus—"

"I won't die of a puncture wound. I want to wait till the

police get here. I need to tell them my background with Odin's Hunt."

The other two housemates poked their heads into Hannah's room. "What's going on?" The other three filled them in. "Anything we can do to help?"

"Not really," Hannah said. "We can't clean up till after the police come. You'd better just go back to bed."

In the kitchen, she made tea. The three shared it in the living room, below the Celtic-knot hanging, one lamp throwing light.

"I can't believe this," Alyssa said.

"I can," Gus said.

"Fuck those guys. I want to go after them. I want to hurt them."

"Me too, but not here, not now."

About four a.m., a policeman showed up. He took notes and a number of photographs, crossing the room to the crunch of slivered glass, which glittered in the street light. Gus filled him in on the background.

"You sent in your statement about Odin's Hunt last December? Can I get the name of the detective working on the case?" Gus gave it to him, though nothing had come of that so far. "I'd recommend putting up some video cameras for the future."

"Thanks for the suggestion," Hannah said.

The door shut behind him.

"Like we can afford that," Gus said. His arm was hurting; he wouldn't sleep the rest of the night.

Hannah shrugged. "I'll suggest it to the landlady. It's not that expensive. Maybe we can all go in on it."

"Now let's get to the ER," Alyssa said.

A little woozy in the middle of the night, they headed over.

The doctor gave Gus a couple of stitches and some antibiotics and sent him home. They were up cleaning the room till dawn.

In the morning, Hannah called a war council: the housemates, Joanie, Cleo, and a couple other coven people. Before Gus set out for class, he swung by her room, where she was busy texting everyone.

"We should add Pete," Gus said. "He was part of the march, and he knows Odin's Hunt. He'll have good ideas."

Hannah looked at him over her glasses. "Pete who's dating Joanie now? As long as it's not awkward for Cleo."

"Could you ask Joanie?"

"I can do that."

Chapter 36

*J*oanie got Hannah's text on break. She'd been wondering since the march in July, a couple months now, when the white supremacists would catch up with Gus. She called Cleo.

"All right, I'll meet your white boy. He knows where we stand, yes?"

"Yes. And he's not a run-of-the-mill white boy."

"I hope not."

"If he's an asshole, I will call him out."

Cleo laughed. "I'd come just to see that."

Then Joanie texted Pete, who answered: <I think I can. I might run late. Send me the address separately.>

They were using a safe texting app, but Pete still used extra caution. She appreciated that.

She added: <Cleo will be there. I can introduce you>

<OK>

~

At seven p.m., the sun had dipped below the horizon; the west lay blue-green. Joanie and Cleo arrived at Hannah's bungalow as a breeze shifted the branches of the sheltering trees. The trellis beside the door stood full of yellow roses tipped with pink.

"Is your boy going to be here ahead of us?" Cleo asked.

"He said he'd run late."

Cleo glowered.

Cleo and Joanie had been here dozens of times for rituals and Inanna shrines. It was their home turf. Joanie caught her hand and squeezed it.

It was kind of cute to see her tough girl worried about a boy.

In the living room, Hannah had taken a corner of the big couch under the Celtic hanging. From the table by her elbow, a cup of chai tea wafted spice. Cleo sat down next to her on a folding chair.

"Do you want some tea?" Joanie asked.

"Sure." Joanie went to the kitchen for tea for them both.

"Gus, could you get Alyssa?" Hannah asked. Alyssa had wanted to study up to the last minute.

A knock came at the front door. Joanie leaped to answer.

It was Pete. Her anxiety burst into excitement to see him. Also she wanted him to meet Cleo, though she didn't know how it would go.

He looked beautiful, edible, all in black, t-shirt showing off his toned arms. Facing away from the living room, hidden, she bit him lightly on the shoulder.

She whispered in his ear, "Thanks for coming. I wish we didn't have to do this. I wish I could be fucking you instead."

"I wish that too. But here we are." He glanced around the room. "Introduce me, will you?"

She led him in. "Here's Pete, for those who haven't met

him." She drew him toward Cleo. "Cleo, Pete. Pete, my partner Cleo."

Cleo stood and took his hand in her own, shaking it firmly, looking into his face.

"Are you a Molotov cocktail kind of anarchist?"

"Depends on the situation."

Cleo flashed a half-smile. "We should talk." She turned toward Hannah. "Let's get started."

Hannah gave a progress report, ending, "The landlady's going to send someone to fix the window over the next few days. In the meantime, it's boarded up. I told her we suspected some white supremacists one housemate confronted at a march. She was supportive."

"She was?" Gus asked.

"Half her family's Jewish."

In the talk, two camps emerged. Hannah and Alyssa wanted Gus to stay and the household to stand and fight. Gus wanted to move out to protect them.

In the end, Pete broke the deadlock with a suggestion. "My roommate just told me he's moving to Portland. We could kill two birds with one stone and have Gus move in."

He glanced around the room. "But how did Odin's Hunt find out where Gus lives, and how are we going to prevent the same thing from happening again?"

"I'll just have no social media presence whatsoever," Gus said. "Watch who I associate with, who follows me home. If anyone."

"Do you want to be silenced?" Hannah said.

"Social media isn't important to me. I wouldn't let it stop me marching."

They broke up with some decisions made. Gus would move in with Pete. Alyssa would then trade and take a basement room. Either way, Hannah would price a video camera system and see if the landlady would cover it or split it with the household. And Gus and Pete would find out the current activities of Odin's Hunt.

On the way out, Pete stopped at Cleo's chair. "I'm glad we met. You're working on your thesis? I'm going to start mine soon."

"I'm almost finished with this latest draft."

"I didn't know you were so close," Joanie said. "That's kind of exciting."

"I haven't wanted to talk about it too much." Cleo eyed Pete. "Do you have a topic yet?"

"I'm still narrowing it down. Good luck."

"Good luck yourself." After a pause, Cleo reached out, and they hugged.

Pete and Joanie were falling into a rhythm, especially since Cleo was laboring to bring the end of her revised thesis together. In the mornings, Joanie found her hunched over her desk, tapping at the keyboard.

Gus began moving his things into Pete's.

"We should throw a housewarming party," Joanie said to Pete on her next visit.

"A party—I don't know."

"Just something small. You could meet the rest of the coven. And Nora's coven, the Silver Branch. I think they used to do more Celtic work than they do now." She watched his face, which was careful. "Think about it, anyway."

a few days later, Gus dropped his last box for the night in his new room and shut the door behind him.

"Thanks again for giving me a place."

Pete sat on the leatherette couch scrolling through social media on his phone, a beer on the table. Behind him, the Dropkick Murphys banner shone green.

"I need a roommate. And I think even Odin's Hunt will think twice before taking us both on. Want some stout?"

Gus retrieved a bottle and sat at the end of the couch.

"We told Hannah and the coven we'd figure out what Odin's Hunt is up to. How do you propose to do that?"

Pete shut off his phone, standing up went to his room and tossed it on his bed, shut the door, and returned. Gus's was buried somewhere in his room.

"Mostly online, I think." Pete threw himself back on the couch. "They know us too well for us to do it in person. What I want to know is, why throw a rock through your window? What are they afraid of?"

"They know I told the police about their shit. At least, I think that's what Bruni meant in July."

They stared at each other.

Gus had never told Pete the whole story of Max's ritual manhunt that ended in Rob's death. Would it do any good to do that? Or would it just put Pete in danger?

"I've known Max a long time," Pete said, as if answering Gus's thought. "When I first met him, he was an anarchist. I think he ended up thinking the movement was too soft for him."

"Sounds like Max."

"You know something Odin's Hunt doesn't want you to. I've watched Max's—I wouldn't call it progress. His fall into Nazi bullshit. I can guess the kind of thing that happened. But that's why they're afraid of you."

Elbows on the back of the couch, he leaned back, watching Gus. "They're trying to frighten you into shutting up. Maybe the answer is to do the opposite of shutting up. Whatever that is."

Everything snapped into focus for Gus.

"Yes."

Gus got an appointment midday, between two classes. He strolled through the downtown entryway, twelve feet high and paved in marble, sat in the law office reception lobby hung with nature photographs. After a few minutes, his lawyer waved him into her office.

"What can I do for you today?"

"I wanted to check in. We wrote that statement and sent it." In the end, they'd sent the statement to both the Thurston County Sheriff's Department, which had jurisdiction where

Odin's Hunt had their land, and the Seattle Police Department, because most of the Hunt were from Seattle. "I know detectives contacted you. Has anything happened since?"

"I would have let you know if it did."

"Last week Odin's Hunt threw a rock through my window. Or, at least, I'd bet it was them." He told her the story.

She sat in silence a moment, tapping her lips with her pen.

"I think getting a video camera is a good plan. And moving. Are you sure you don't want to take time off and move away for a while?" He shook his head. "I'll call the police and the sheriff's department. But it's unlikely they'll comment on an ongoing investigation."

"Could I hire a private detective?"

"You could. I have a handful I like and trust. Want me to send you some names?"

"How much do they cost?"

"It ranges. Maybe fifty an hour for background research online. More to stake out your former friends."

It was less than she charged. But he didn't even have enough to cover this appointment—he'd need his mother to pay. He couldn't afford more.

"Not right now, thanks. Let me know if you hear anything."

Chapter 38

"I still think you should throw a party."

Joanie and Pete were at his apartment; Gus was spending the night with Alyssa. Joanie had bought a number of big soy-wax candles for the living room and bedroom. Between the floor lamp and the candles, the living room lighting was almost how she wanted it: warm, gentle, flickering.

"Nothing to conflict with our Samhain. But something small? Halloween themed? C'mon, it'd be fun."

He took a sip of his beer—she'd brought harvest ale. "I don't throw parties."

"I throw parties. I'm good at it. We could do something chill. Just a drop-by thing."

"I'm broke."

"But I have money. Some money, anyway. You know—it's not my revolution if I can't dance." She'd gotten her business job to pay down student loans, but she didn't want to live on peanut butter.

"Fair enough."

It wasn't quite a yes, but she didn't want to push further.

"While I'm telling you what to do—we've been having a lot of fairly vanilla sex. Maybe let's try something else tonight. I don't want to get stuck in a rut."

Reaching down, he stroked her labia through her panties. "There are good ruts. Very good ruts."

She almost gave in, but she moved his hand. "You don't get out of it that easily, freaky boy. I want to see your porn."

"Trust me, it's not artistic. I'm not sure I can find most of it."

"Just one or two, to give me the flavor."

They set up in the bedroom, streaming using his laptop. He found three. In all, he played the top, though in one he got fucked as well.

"Omigod, that's incredibly hot. Was that at all fun for you? I would die to peg you."

He gave her a sideways look. "If you want to, let's do it. I don't have any toys here, though."

"I came prepared." She'd stuffed a bunch of toys in a messenger bag, wrapped in plastic bags to keep things discreet. He laughed out loud.

"You win. But I should at least take a shower."

"Let's share it."

Hot water, lavender soap, his fingers on her. "You're trying to make me come before I fuck you. That's totally cheating."

Wearing towels, they went into the bedroom, sat kissing. Releasing her towel, she slipped down, mouthed him. "I want to fuck you."

"Okay."

Something in his tone made her stop.

"Are you not okay with this?"

"It's something you want."

"I don't want you to just endure it." She pulled down

coverlet and sheet and got under them. "Come snuggle with me."

He slid in, and she wrapped herself around him, big spoon to his little spoon. "What is it?"

"I haven't taken it in the ass with a girl before. The videos came from right after my hustler days. Another way to make cash."

"So five or six years ago."

"For me, all that is about that time. I guess I still have some shame about it. I probably shouldn't, but I do."

"You haven't had kinky sex with a girl in all that time?"

"Only as a top. I didn't bottom."

"It's not required. I don't have any great need." She hugged him.

"I meant what I said, I want to try it. But it won't necessarily be easy."

"What would help? Should we set the scene somehow?"

"I'm fine, or as fine as I'm going to be. Let's just get on with it."

She didn't like her partner approaching sex like a dose of medicine. On the other hand, she'd often approached sex pragmatically, as a job. He got to choose.

With his help, she pushed one of the towels under him. She got out lube and harness, climbed into the harness, and tightened it.

"Let's just make out a while first." Coming up behind him lying on the bed, she stroked his now-soft cock, kissing, licking, biting him. His hard-on returned.

She rolled him onto his back, his knees bent to his chest. "Stroke yourself." He did. Lubing him, she placed the head of her silicone cock at his asshole, nudged him gently.

"Meet my eyes." He held her gaze as, bit by bit, she pushed the length of the cock into him.

"Touch yourself. I want to fuck you while you come."

He nodded, mouth softly open, saying nothing.

In the shadows, striped with light, she pushed in and in, gently, rocking. His eyes never left hers. He rubbed himself in bursts.

He closed his eyes. "I'm close."

"Come for me."

He cried out, and came onto his stomach. In the light she barely saw it, just a slick of reflection.

They sat there a few moments, the only sound their breathing.

Slowly, gently she pulled out, stood and stepped out of the harness, and going to the bathroom cleaned up. He joined her.

Full night outside, a ray of moonlight.

"That seemed to work?"

"It worked."

Moving away from the sink, she came to lean in the open doorway. "Partly it's purely physical."

He flushed the toilet, washed his hands. "Yes."

There was still something dark and distant in his eyes.

"Come lie down and tell me how it was for you."

They lay down again, spooning as they had.

"The feeling is its own thing. There's something of submission in it."

"Yes, I get that."

"It was hot. But I can't help having echoes and overtones. Of course it's different. It's you."

They drifted to sleep.

~

In the middle of the night, she started awake, knowing Pete was awake in her arms.

"What is it?" she whispered.

"Nothing. I'm just scared."

"Scared of what?"

"This. You. Connecting with you."

At least he knew enough to say so. "What in particular scares you?"

"I feel like I'm already closer to you than I ever was to my ex."

"Isn't that a good thing?"

"Sure."

But she could finish his sentence: Sure, but the closer they are, the more it hurts when they betray you.

"Have a little faith," she whispered.

He was silent, and after a while she fell back to sleep.

After some revisions, Don sent the papers he'd mentioned for Joanie to go over. He was helping a business self-insure to save taxes. Jack would check the legalities with the help of their contract lawyer.

The initial meeting would be with the financial manager. Don stopped by to fill Joanie in. "You saw the email? Eleven a.m., Wednesday next week. It's downtown; we'll walk over."

In the meantime, Joanie planned the Halloween party. Or tried to—her guests were hard to pin down. Hannah had to plan for Samhain, and Alyssa had a shift till eight on party night. Back at Firebird House, Joanie checked in with Cleo, again huddled at her desk. She carried her a cup of tea.

"I guess I can come to your party for a while."

"There'll be food. You have to eat."

"I'm getting so close. I want to give my advisor a copy by the end of the month."

Joanie bit her tongue.

Usually Joanie was easygoing about this kind of thing. Something small might be fine too. But this time it frustrated her. Part of it was she knew she was supposed to be putting on parties, but different ones, for the goddess Inanna.

What was it Hannah always said? "The right witches show up for ritual." So too, thought Joanie, with a party, in its way a type of ritual: wild magic, mixing people from different places, different strands.

Puabi-Ekur, onlooking, thought: *Not unlike the work of an incubus.*

Chapter 39

*J*oanie hadn't gotten a chance to talk much to Cleo for several days, so she leapt at the chance to make her dinner. She concocted a variation on beans and rice, which for Cleo was comfort food.

They ate in bed in Cleo's room for privacy. Gilt and mirrors on the pillows shimmered.

"I wonder if I haven't picked up a boy who's damaged goods. We're all damaged goods, but some more than others. I want someone to mess around with, not to nurse."

Cleo slurped a spoonful of beans.

"Seems like he's trying to be honest with you. It's rare for a guy to be willing to talk about his vulnerability, in my experience."

Joanie stirred her bowl and took a bite. "True."

"You could take it as a gift and see what comes of it."

She gave Cleo a quick sideways glance.

This was the most complimentary she'd ever heard Cleo about someone male.

"You like him, don't you?"

"He seems woke, for a white guy. I have to like that. He's not trying to run away with you, which I also like. You're happier with him around. I'd give him a chance, Joanie."

These were words she'd never expected to hear from Cleo.

Mid-October gave them high blue skies, a flurry of falling leaves. When Joanie walked to Pete's, the line of birches along the street stood golden, like walking through sunlight.

She amused herself by bringing Pete decorative gourds for his apartment. He rolled his eyes. He'd sworn he'd invite his Antifa friends to the party, but she wasn't going to bet on it.

She backed off for now trying new things, but even in simpler sex there were moments. Once again they came to the Paleolithic cave.

In his room afterward, one candle lit, buttery light waved on the wall. She lay curled against his side, waves of orgasm retreating.

"I saw that cave again," she whispered.

"I did too."

"I think we should follow up with meditation one day. Maybe with magic."

"If it's something you want."

She placed her hand on his chest, just for the pleasure of feeling his breath make his ribs rise and fall.

"You should come to Samhain and get a taste of our ritual."

"I can do that."

She lay back.

"I'm just afraid everything about me is hard for you."

He picked up her hand and kissed her palm. "What's hard here is worth it to me."

Don and she took the first of the meetings with Walker Nelson Hospitality, the company he was working to self-insure. The company ran a group of boutique hotels, one in downtown Seattle, where the meeting was held.

They crossed downtown on foot. Don was better dressed than usual, in a navy three-piece suit with a striped-silk repp tie and a pocket square to match. Joanie had also taken care with her outfit, a subdued grey pencil skirt, white draped blouse, a multicolored scarf tied at her neck. Mirrored in a window, the look was complete Capitalist Girl.

Middle of the week, midday, the core city was full of people on early lunch breaks, with the occasional bike-courier. In the shadow of a building, someone hunkered over a backpack.

Joanie caught his gaze. His eyes were empty and lost, his face rough with greying stubble and tanned from living on the street.

There but for a few lucky breaks went Joanie herself. And here she was playing Capitalist Girl.

Shame washed over her. She blinked and shook herself.

Ordinarily she might stop and give him money. But she had to keep going.

They entered the hotel lobby, between flanking ceiling-high palms in multicolored pots. It had an Art Deco touch, with paintings of bathers. "The meeting rooms are on the second floor," Don told her, taking her by the elbow and directing her toward the elevators.

They found the small meeting room, dominated by another painting of bathers, walls a neutral beige except for one that was exposed brick. Walker Nelson's financial manager met them there—a grey man in a grey suit.

Standing, he shook hands with both Don and Joanie. "I looked over everything you sent. I just had a few questions to ask."

"Sure thing. Joanie, do you mind taking notes?" Don was a stickler for written notes—he said he had no memory.

"Of course." She got out her laptop. The questions got technical fast.

In her mind's eye, the homeless man still stared at her.

Could she justify propping up capitalism?

But she needed the money.

Chapter 40

*B*ack in Akkad, Ekur continued digging for information on the drought. Eridu and Ur had been hit hard. They had less than a year's worth of stores before they'd need to import food.

The other southern cities also suffered. Over the last year, Lagash had produced less barley than usual and in particular less wheat, a more sensitive crop; so too had Ekur's own Uruk. The dry weather had also hit fruit, dates, and fish-farms, which in turn affected taxes paid.

In another late-afternoon meeting, he brought this before his supervisor, Lord Sharru.

Across rays of gilded light, a breeze that was almost cool floated through the high window. Though wood was dear in Akkad, Sharru had a fine, polished desk, dark wood inlaid with lighter. Ekur laid his research across this table, a set of tablets.

"I think it's becoming a regional problem."

Lord Sharru studied, trading one tablet for another with a scrape.

"I see what you mean, Ekur. Good work." He sat back in his chair, the leather creaking. "But I still do not believe it is necessary to offer Eridu and Ur relief. Not yet."

Ekur's stomach sank.

Later might be too late.

Maybe it was merely he was from the south and grew up with tales of drought. Maybe he saw a hint of the future.

"What I'm interested in now is last month's tithes," Sharru said. "It would be useful to have the tallies in the next day or so."

"I should go south," Ekur told Eannatum. "I want to see my children. And I want to visit the areas affected by the drought. It will be hitting Uruk by now."

"I should come with you to see my parents. Especially since they've stopped lining up potential brides-to-be."

Since they weren't moving their whole household, getting to Uruk took only half a day. In the chill of early morning, they saddled a pair of half-wild onagers, riding asses.

As they came closer to Uruk, they noticed the changes, perhaps because they were already aware. Ekur stopped as they went along to check on farms they passed. His official robe and his manner gained him entrance.

"I've lost three-quarters of my arable land, my lord, because I don't get enough water to irrigate," one farmer said. He pointed to the nearby irrigation canal. "I could manage if I got water even three or four days a week, but I only get it two." A line of palms provided a windbreak; reeds lined the irrigation canal. "Can you take our news to Akkad?"

"Of course."

"The king is a good man. The king and the gods, they will make it rain."

A dry wind whispered among the reeds.

Chapter 41

*L*ooking back, Puabi-Ekur saw where Akkad had left the path. Perhaps if they as Ekur had pushed harder, or others had listened, they could have changed Akkad's fate. It was not enough to do your best, to try—in some things, you had to succeed.

Here and now, Puabi-Ekur saw what Dea showed them, the wall of razor-wire encroaching. This enemy they had to fight sideways, not head-on, choosing allies.

But they had to fight. They had to do their utmost to see Joanie stayed on her best path. Perhaps this time they could make it right.

There were other gods of the land, other potential spirit-allies. The cave-dream reached back into the past. But such a past was not so very long ago, to spirits, and its gods could be called forward.

The second meeting was planned for the same hotel. Joanie wore the outfit she had to her first interview. It was an excuse to wear the dark maroon skirt, which she was fond of.

"I'm hoping this one will be short," Don said as they took the elevator down from their own office. "The financial manager has signed off. This is the opportunity for the CEO to take a look."

They met in the same meeting room, all in neutral tones: black-varnished table, grey drapes, cream-colored wall. The bathers on the painting draped over each other, little detail to their bodies.

The financial manager was there, greeted them both. "Mark will be along in just a few minutes." He meant Mark Walker, the company CEO. Finding a seat, Joanie got out her laptop.

"No notes this time, if you don't mind," the financial manager said, still smiling.

Joanie glanced across at Don. He nodded. "That's fine. I can catch the important things."

Five minutes, ten minutes passed. At the corner of the room sat a drip-coffee urn and water pitcher in the corner, with cups and glasses. Joanie went and got herself water, bringing Don a glass too. The financial manager already had one.

The door opened, and the CEO, Mark, entered. Joanie glanced over him: still-abundant grey hair, square jaw, body muscular. Sea-blue eyes. "Hello, Don." Stepping forward, he shook Don's hand.

Don stepped back, ceding space. "This is my assistant, Joan."

Surprised, Joanie stepped forward. He gave her a quick handshake, firm; he didn't try to crush her fingers.

As Don had predicted, the meeting was short. Mark

scanned the papers, asked a few questions, and insisted on a couple of minor changes. "It seems in order, overall."

He leaned across the table. "You're sure this will work for our purposes."

"Tax laws change constantly," Don said. "But given that, this should be fairly watertight."

Mark gazed at him a moment, then at his financial manager, who nodded. Then for the space of a few breaths he gave Joanie an assessing look. She didn't know how to read it. "Make the changes we discussed, then we can meet and finalize things."

They stepped outside, returning from the meeting. The day had turned unseasonably warm, almost summer; when the wind fell still, Joanie's black blazer felt hot. But mostly it was autumn-windy. A gust buffeted her then turned away, howling down a narrow street between tall buildings.

On a plane beyond the weather, there was a feeling—what?

As if she approached an inimical metal barrier, like a wall of steel wool. Or sharper, like balled-up barbed wire. She paused at a light, trying to get a feel for what it was, but it eluded her.

It had a sound, too, an electric buzzing in the air, like you heard near overhead power lines.

She'd expected a slow afternoon at work. She focused on following up a thorny portal problem. She also had admin work to do. When she saw Don heading her way, she assumed he wanted to talk about that.

"Got a second to talk?" He gestured toward his office.

She blinked a moment, because he usually dropped off his orders and walked away, but she followed him. He shut the door behind her.

"Thanks for your help on the Walker Nelson thing."

"Help? I did nothing."

"You did enough. If all goes well, I think there's going to be one more meeting, where they sign the papers. Either way, I think you and I are a good combo, and I'd like to get you permanently on my team, particularly to focus on that account. It's important. As part of that, I'd like to make you a paraplanner right away and give you a twenty-five percent raise."

Her mouth dropped open a moment until she consciously shut it.

"Don't answer right away. Monica's going to want to talk to you, and I need you to make your decision after that conversation. Let's dot the i's and cross the t's. Okay?"

"Sure."

He grinned. "Bet you thought I was going to load you up with a bunch more work, huh?"

"Kind of, yeah."

If she were a golden retriever, he would have scratched behind her ears. "Nah. It's not that at all."

Chapter 42

*T*hat evening, she managed to skate out of work a little early to finish party setup. At least Pete had promised a few of his friends would show up. She'd met Pete's best friend, Dave, but only in passing.

As she got off the bus, the wind tried to pull her scarf off. It ran laughing, throwing leaves, small sticks, bits of fir branch. Part of her just wanted to run away with it, to run away from this version of the earth. She could live in the Ravenna Ravine with the squirrels and raccoons.

Though she couldn't help being curious about Don's offer. Twenty-five percent more a paycheck. She could pay off her student loans early. She could have savings again.

But something here was fishy. She did good work, but she was still new.

Don made it sound as if Monica was a hurdle. She was inclined to like and trust Monica. If she were a hurdle, there might be a problem.

At Pete's apartment, everything sparkled—she was impressed. "Gus did the kitchen. Great roommate so far."

Gus half-smiled, uncomfortable, whether with the praise or with the party upcoming it was hard to tell. "Pete did the dishes."

"And swept." He grinned, full of himself for some reason. She kissed him lightly, saving her lipstick. She'd gone costume-lite, wearing sequined cat ears, a tight black leotard, and a black velvet skirt. Finding a jam jar, she poured herself some red wine.

"We're pretty much ready. Should we put on the music? Maybe the chill but upbeat playlist." Pete nodded. Gus shrugged. She started it.

The music had been the hardest. Pete was all about punk and Celtic. Gus leaned toward industrial and electronic. They met in the middle over punk and industrial, but a soundtrack like that would drive half the party out the door, particularly the older witches. Compromising, they got Alyssa to choose. Alyssa liked dance music; Joanie trusted Gus to weed out what no one else could stand.

"Okay, it's time," Joanie said. "And we're done. Of course no one's here."

"Very Seattle," Pete said.

"Alyssa won't show up till at least nine," Gus said and retreated to his room.

Joanie curled up in a corner of the couch. Pete grabbed a Scotch ale out of the fridge and flopped down beside her.

"How are you and Gus getting on?"

"Fine. He's pretty much an introvert, and he spends most of the time at Alyssa's. He's also pretty clean. All in all, he's the perfect roommate."

She eyed the shut door. "And the political stuff?"

He slid down on the couch, throwing an arm over her. "I understand he went to his lawyer, who said there wasn't much to do on the Odin's Hunt front. He's lying low, which is a smart thing to do."

"I'm sorry I haven't made it to any marches lately."

"Don't be. You had conflicts. I'm sure you'd be out if there were, say, a general strike." He stroked her leg. "I'm tempted to drag you into the bedroom."

"It's a sure way to get people to show up."

"Mmm." Pushing himself up to sitting, he gave her a long kiss.

"You're wearing lipstick now."

"It's a party, after all."

A buzz sounded, someone downstairs—Alyssa. "I got off work early!"

A little later, Hannah showed up. "I brought pinot grigio, just in case."

Joanie took the bottle. "Let's get this in the refrigerator."

In the main room, they'd switched to the party mix, and Alyssa was trying to get Gus to dance. "Just stand opposite me and sway." Eyes three-quarters shut with the desire not to do this, Gus complied. "Was that so hard?"

Watching this, Hannah commented, "Back in my day, we had the pogo."

"The pogo?" asked Joanie.

"Just jump straight up and down."

"Very punk," Pete observed.

"It's nice to see you, Pete! Gimme some sugar."

Pete looked blank. "She means give her a hug." He did.

"We're putting coats in Gus's room." Joanie led Hannah in there. Shadows, a bed lumpy with jackets and bags. "I meant to ask, is it okay if I bring Pete to Samhain? He'll participate and be respectful."

"Sure, if that's true. I like him so far. I like those red-haired boys."

Joanie laughed. "Don't steal him away, Hannah."

"I thought you were poly?"

"Okay, fine. We can share."

Just then there was another buzz, and Joanie let in Nora and a couple of the Silver Branch coveners. Tailgating them was Dave, Pete's friend.

Nora gave Hannah a hug. Pete gestured from Joanie to Dave. "You've met, right?"

"Just in passing." Tall, a little heavyset, he had a mane of dark hair and a short-trimmed beard. They exchanged hellos.

"I've known Dave since we were in middle school."

Joanie gave Dave a hostess smile. "You'll have to tell me everything Pete doesn't want me to know."

Dave smirked. "Have you heard about our experiments with black powder?"

The door buzzed again, but Pete dealt with it.

The party was filling out. Talk, jokes, laughter rose and fell. A favorite song of Alyssa's blared, with an abrupt change of beat. She squealed.

"I think we should dance!"

By one a.m., only a few people were left. Cleo showed up late, in a good mood—she'd finished a new draft of her thesis, earlier than expected, and was about to send it to her advisor and a couple other reviewers. She took Joanie in her arms and slow-danced with her to one of Gus's chiller tunes.

They'd turned off the torchiere, so the dance-floor corner was lit only by candles. Joanie shuffled in the arms of her girl, scented with sandalwood and musk. She nuzzled the smooth flesh of her neck.

At a pause in the music, she said, "Gimme a sec. Gotta hit the bathroom."

"No rush." Cleo drew another coven member up from the couch and got her to dance, not as close.

On the way back from the bathroom, Joanie saw Pete's bedroom door cracked, to a low-pitched but emphatic conversation. "Pete?" She ducked her head in.

Dave and Pete were talking, sitting on the edge of the bed, Gus beside them on the floor.

"Hey," Pete said. "Come in, if you want, and close the door." She did.

Gus leaned against the bed, eyes closed, saying nothing. She wondered if he was drunk, or asleep, or what.

"We were talking about Odin's Hunt and the alt-right scene around them," Pete said. "There's a couple of new groups. They break up and reform as they're infiltrated and as people get thrown in jail. Some of the most notorious offenders are in prison now."

"But we're down a couple of people who were doing some work for us," Dave put in.

"Mike from the coffee shop volunteered," Gus said, eyes still closed. "Might be good. He doesn't go on social media, he's new to town. Alyssa says he's good people."

"He's an idea," Pete said. "I'd like to talk to him further."

"I wonder—I see Josh on campus sometimes," Gus said.

"That guy who beat up the guy in the park?"

"Him. Bet if I took him out and got him drunk, told him I was still sympathetic to the cause, I could get pretty much any information I wanted. They wouldn't share anything strategic with him, but I could get the lay of the land."

Pete and Dave exchanged a look.

"Could work," Dave said.

"There's some obvious pitfalls," Pete added, "but I think you can avoid them."

"Is there anything I can do to help?" Joanie asked.

"Certainly," Dave said. "If you want."

"I'm pretty sure we can figure out something," Pete said. "But I'd like to teach you some self-defense first."

At the very end, all who were left were the two roommates, Alyssa, and Joanie. Alyssa had lost a battle with the whiskey Pete had unearthed, so Gus had put her to bed. Joanie had promised to stay to help clean up in the morning.

Joanie made a sweep for glasses, put what she found by the sink, then went to lie beside Pete.

"Still awake?" He slipped an arm around her. "Did you enjoy it? You looked like you were having fun."

"I did. Thank you for making me throw a party. It was useful to introduce Dave and Gus. I think it drew Gus out of his shell a little."

"It looked like. Are you serious about the self-defense? I think it's a good idea."

"Absolutely."

"As long as when we wrestle sometimes I can lose."

His side moved as he laughed. She slipped down, feeling for his cock.

Chapter 43

$\mathcal{M}$onica set a meeting with Joanie for one p.m. Monday. Joanie knew what it was about.

She'd made up her mind, but she regretted she might lose a chance at friendship with Monica over it. Monica was the one person she connected with at Gunnar Group.

But she wasn't there to make friends. She was there to make money. The raise was a lot more money. She'd deal with whatever questions came with it later.

Beforehand, she took lunch on the roof terrace, in her favorite corner between two potted junipers. It was another clear day, though that wouldn't last. From day to day, Seattle watched for the rains to come.

She'd thrown her Tarot deck in her purse some time ago. The wind had died down from the weekend, so she could set the cards out. She shuffled, hand over hand, considering this work change.

She cut and drew one card, the Tower.

Struck by lightning, attendants falling.

A gut-punch. Also confusing.

Wasn't this whole time the Tower time, as fascism loomed and the climate was destroyed? The Tower meant the fall of the bad guys, right?

A breeze all of a sudden rose, flipping the Tower, threatening to toss it across the terrace. But she caught it. Bundling the cards into her purse, she went in.

◦

Above in the ether, Puabi-Ekur paced back and forth like an angry cat in a cage.

Joanie had sensed the wall of razor-wire, had drawn a card that told her not to take the path offered, and had decided to go forward anyway.

What could they do with this girl?

Perhaps they could ask for help. They recalled they were supposed to do that. They had a new ally—maybe Dea could do something.

On the spirit level, a thought was as good as a wish between two connected spirits. They knew Dea registered the thought.

◦

Joanie took the guest chair as Monica closed her door behind them. Joanie had never seen Monica look so serious, the wings of her red-blonde bob folded behind her ears.

"I'll get right to the point. I understand Don offered you a paraplanner job and a twenty-five percent raise. I can see why that would be attractive. But this self-insurance package of Don's is risky."

Joanie kept her face still. She wasn't surprised. Don had the air of a sleazebag. But wasn't that how you succeeded in finance

—sailing close to the wind? All of capitalism was immoral, at least how it was done.

"Do you know what I mean by risky?"

"Not exactly."

"It means I wonder what our auditors will think of it. It means I've asked Jack to review it in depth."

Jack wouldn't be quick to investigate Don. Don was good for the bottom line.

"Don't let this leave this office, but I wouldn't hitch myself to Don's wagon. I don't know what his future looks like, but he may not be here long. And if he forms his own firm—" She broke off, frowning.

"I understand."

Don was doing something the auditors might find illegal. Once Jack fully reviewed it, he'd lean on Don to shut it down. Don might persuade Jack to ignore it, a hazard in itself. Or, if he didn't and started his own firm, Jack's and Monica's business might not keep Gunnar Group going. Don's own firm might fall apart.

"I hear a but," Monica said.

"To be honest, one of my main motivations here is to pay off my student loans. A pay raise would help me do that. And having a paraplanner title couldn't hurt in the long run."

"If Don ran into problems, I wouldn't want you to get mixed up in that."

So what? Capitalism was piracy. She could be a pirate too.

"I appreciate your concern." It was true. "But I don't see how I can turn down Don's offer."

A strand of heavy red-blonde hair swung forward, and Monica pushed it back again.

"I wasn't going to say this, but I don't trust what Don's doing with you. If he's going to pay you that much, he's either paying you to look the other way, or for something else."

"Such as?"

Monica's hazel eyes met hers, and Joanie knew.

In the hotel meeting room, Mark Walker had given her an assessing look, skimming her figure.

She was here to sweeten the pot, in some way not yet clear.

"I don't think so," Joanie said.

If that came up, she'd call a halt. Unless it were her choice, her game. She'd never had a pimp and never would.

"Maybe I'm wrong."

"We'll see." Joanie stood. "I owe it to myself to take this opportunity."

Monica sat still a moment, staring up at Joanie.

It stung, because she could see Monica's opinion of her falling. But she was here for the money.

"We're done here. Don wanted you to check in with him after we talked."

Joanie half-stalked Don's office, popped in as soon as he was free. Her meeting with him was brief.

"You'll go to three-quarters time with me, a quarter with Monica. We'll get a temp to help while we figure out how to support Monica ongoing. Hopefully, very soon you can come on full-time working with me."

He stood and shook her hand. Then nodded, which was her sign to go away. She did.

As she left, she caught a smirk on his face.

Samhain was usually one of the coven's most intense rituals, and Joanie prepped Pete accordingly. Like the past two, this was a Hekate ritual, though written as more initiatory than earlier ones. They had planned it together with the Silver Branch, and would do it at Nora's house.

That meant carpooling. Joanie's car had been sidelined for a while. Hannah planned to take Alyssa and Gus; Joanie and Pete would catch a ride with them, meeting them at the coffee shop. Cleo had dropped out; she'd gotten thesis comments to address and was fighting a cold.

Hannah had fed them a few tidbits about the ritual. The more Joanie heard, the more she wondered if it had been the right one to invite Pete to. They planned trance work, which could trigger people if it fell the wrong way. Hannah had said Pete could attend, but she was inclined to be an old-school, sink-or-swim kind of witch.

Pete and Joanie met a bit early at the coffee shop, so she filled him in.

Just after dark, the end of October, the sky had gone overcast, with pendulous dark blue clouds and cold light wind. As Joanie entered, rain spat, cold and sudden, sharp. She pulled her jean jacket tight over her black skater dress.

She greeted the barista, whom she knew barely, placed her order, after a few moments collected her Americano and stuffed the tip jar. Pete got a packaged sandwich. He was always hungry.

"Samhain might be a little intense. It's not much like a Christian service."

"What does it involve?"

Joanie gave him a brief rundown of the holiday: a time to honor the unseen, so it was spooky and ominous, but also the witches' new year.

"A bit like the Irish Samhain feast." He'd peeled a crust off his sandwich and rolled it up in a cylinder.

"Yes." Of course, he would know Samhain from Irish mythology. "This one, I don't know the details, but it will be some kind of initiatory thing. Intended to go deep."

"I don't mind. If I'm going to a pagan ritual, I want it to be the real thing. I mean, we've had that cave stuff come up in sex, right? The pagan thread is really present for me. I need to go further."

Coffee scent wafted upward. "Some people work with Hekate as a cave goddess." In Alyssa's vision from the year before, Hekate had brought Alyssa to a cave.

It was a long ride, packed into Hannah's older American car. Pete, the tallest, got the front seat, which made Joanie wistful. She'd wanted to snuggle against him. At the ritual, she'd have little chance.

They took the hairpin turns up to Nora's, dark exurban landscape thinning to farms and forest. Lights twinkled among the fir and cedar, then dwindled. She reached forward, put her hand on Pete's shoulder, and he took it. The ritual lay ahead of them, all darkness, but with his hand in hers it felt like an adventure.

They rattled down the long drive to the hollow that held Nora's house. Around the big, red-boarded, rustic house, circled on three sides by porches, wind susurrated in fir and cedar.

Stepping out of the car, Joanie breathed in the fir-scented air. There was a homecoming here, a sense of earth spirits who loved witches, the feeling of a witch-farm. Jack o' lanterns lined the porch steps, smelling of cooking pumpkin.

Hanging back a little, Pete caught her hand. She let Hannah, Alyssa, and Gus pass. "What?"

He shook his head. His eyes went from one side to the other; his shoulders shuddered.

"I'm happy to be here, but it's intense."

"Social anxiety?"

"More, there's something big here waiting."

A spurt of excitement went through her. Maybe this was Pete's big initiation into witchcraft. Maybe not—Pete had triggers and edges.

She petted his arm and shoulder. "Big how? Big and bad? Big and good?"

He shook his head. "I don't know. Just big."

"You can choose not to take part in the ritual, or take part at your own level. I can talk to the ritualists."

A long look from dark blue eyes, wide, full of pupil.

"Please."

Chapter 44

*a*bout a half-hour before the rite, the last stragglers gathered and the ritualists perfected their setup. Joanie caught Nora as she checked over the living-room altar.

"It'll be intense, but I think positive," Nora said. "The central focus is about working with the Higher Self or inner deity."

"It's just Pete has no experience of pagan ritual, and he has a childhood background with fundamentalist Christianity. It left him pretty spooked about spirituality. My take is he's naturally psychically attuned." She sighed. "It might not have been his best ritual to start."

"Feel free to tell him to opt out whenever, as long as he can do so without disturbing people. We're going to do part in the cabin; he might want to sit by the door. Feel free also to drop out and take care of him."

"I will if I need to."

"I know. You're a good partner." Nora laid her hand on Joanie's arm a moment, then bent to straighten the altar cloth.

Joanie stepped away, not wanted to take more of Nora's time. The word Nora had used made her stop and think.

Was Pete her partner?

It had been lovely so far, but did she want that?

She stepped aside from the thought, went to find him, filled him in on what Nora had said.

A call came from the living room: "Time for preritual discussion."

About twenty people gathered in the living room by the main altar. Black draped most of the surfaces, including the altar and the mantelpiece, where a line of human skulls cast in resin sat. A silver candelabra held the altar candles, and in front of that lay a small cauldron filled with earth. Nearby lay feathers, a lit lamp, and a clay cup of water.

Nora stepped forward. "Hannah and I put together the ritual tonight, and we will be your co-priestesses. I know a few people here haven't done ritual with us before, so I'm going to describe things in some detail. Though not everything—this ritual has a mystery aspect to it."

She discussed how the Silver Branch set up their circle—not as formally as some—and asked for element callers. "We don't work with the elements in specific directions because we believe the elements are in all the directions."

She gestured: "We'll cast the circle in here, all around the property. Much of the ritual will be outdoors. We'll make offerings to ancestors and deities and walk to the cabin, home of the local goddess we call Dea. For ancestors, if you're not at peace with your family of origin, that's not going to affect the ritual. This is about the line of ascended spirits whose energies brought you here—the happy and bright-spirited ones, not angry or hungry ghosts. When Hannah and I put up the circle, we'll specifically shut out negative energies, including as needed family members."

Joanie saw Pete nodding. She thought of his family—angry, hungry ghosts. She squeezed him tight.

"For deities, we will work with Dea and Hekate Soteira, Hekate Savior. We'll also work with the deity that is your Higher Self. We're hoping to set up a stronger connection with our inner deities, so they can lead us along the paths best for ourselves and the world. Any questions?"

She satisfied people on a few points. "Let's break for about ten minutes, then come back here and we can get started."

Pete stood, and Joanie followed.

"That doesn't sound so harsh," she said. "I would guess the main part is a meditation."

"I still feel a sense of foreboding. Maybe it's just me, with my parents and their religion. Did I tell you about the time my grandfather tried to exorcise me?"

"You didn't. That sounds awful."

"He thought I had an unclean spirit inside me."

"If you had an unclean spirit, I'd know by now, I think."

"Baby, I'll show you an unclean spirit." He grabbed her, pulled her in, kissed her deeply. She gave way, letting him, and the ritual preparation dropped away for a few moments to a circle around them two.

It was true, what she'd implied to Nora—their connection was as important to her as ritual. Or in itself it was ritual.

"You say unclean, I say magical," she whispered, as he drew away for breath.

He caught her eyes, and for a moment it was complete connection.

Coven and friends regathered in the darkened living room, amid the flicker of candles. Dark ambient music played. Nora and Hannah cut the circle; ritualists called earth, air, fire, and water.

"Get your coats," Nora said. "We will call deities and ancestors outdoors."

The company assembled and walked out along a dirt path, across the bridge over the brook. Black trees stood against a dark-grey, overcast sky, the air full of tiny points of wet. On the next small rise, a table stood, set as an altar and draped in black, to either side tiki torches for light. Ritualists lit candles and incense coal.

Hannah stepped forward. "I call to us the lady Hekate, Hekate Soteira, World Soul. Great One, from you springs the primordial soul, filling light, fire, ether, and all the world. Great Lady, come to us tonight, support us in this work."

A feeling washed over Joanie, a rushing like wind or water, filling the space with darkness and depth.

Standing next to Pete, she took his hand, squeezed it. His was cold. She stole a glance. His eyes were wide and fixed, but he seemed present.

Hannah lit a massive black candle. Nora stepped forward.

"I call to us the lady Dea, goddess of this place. Dark mother, protector and warrior, ground us and protect us in this rite, we pray you. Come to us now."

The dark, humorous presence of Dea entered, spangled like a starry sky.

"Do you feel that?" she whispered.

"I do. I felt Hekate, too. A lot."

"Hang tight." But she was excited—he felt the energy.

Nora lit a dark-bronze candle encircled with fall leaves.

Another ritualist stepped forward. She circled the group, ringing a silver bell, clear and penetrating.

"I call to us the happy ancestors, those who have gone to the shining places, who look upon us wanting to help and support.

I call also spirits of place and all spirits who want to help with this working."

A dancing, laughing crew, invisible, came on a rising of the breeze, filling the space till it was packed. The ritualist lit a purple candle circled with shiny stones.

Puabi-Ekur watched, sensing Hekate and Dea come in, the troop of spirits fizzing.

An ascending power, a drawing in, such was this time, Samhain. All these energies touched humans more strongly at Samhain. Puabi-Ekur saw them pour through the assembly.

They saw a rising. These witches were strong; they were calling in a change. Puabi-Ekur saw no enemies, felt only support from the goddesses and spirits present.

"Now we will make offerings to Hekate, Dea, and the ancestors, asking for their help."

The line started forward. Along the altar, the attendees moved from one incense burner to the next. Hekate received a blend containing mint and aconite, Dea patchouli with rose, the spirits mugwort and sandalwood.

After offering, at the far end of the black-draped altar, Joanie stood a moment in the combined smoke. It went into her and through her, part lifting, part madness. Behind her, Pete stroked her shoulder.

"I think I'm getting the hang of this," he said. "I'm glad I came."

At the far side of the altar, Nora as priestess of Dea had donned an antlered crown. "Follow me in silence."

They took a path lit by luminaria into the small woods, cedars interspersed with fir and alder. Wet leaf mast lay under their feet. The line shuffled slowly till they reached the small cedar-shake cabin, door engraved with an ivy-twined pentacle.

Inside, a fire burned, flames licking the sooty stove window. "We can all fit if we sit close," Nora said. Joanie held Pete back, so they could take the space by the door.

Hannah took a place on the bed built into the side of the cabin. "Settle in and take a few deep breaths," she said.

Joanie wrapped herself around Pete a little tighter and matched her breaths to his, the easier to meditate and be so close.

"Relax, as completely as possible."

Hannah led them through a grounding and centering, connecting themselves as a tree to the center of the earth, and centering themselves behind and below their navels. Next she led them to connect upward to their chosen star. Then she had them draw in energy and balance between earth and sky.

"Now relax still deeper and follow me to the realm of Hekate World Soul, the better to connect with the deity that is you. Imagine yourself like the World-Tree, and draw up the deep energy of the earth and down the celestial energy of the sky. With each sustaining and releasing cycle, as I count to ten, let yourself fall deeper into trance."

Joanie gave herself to the meditation, letting it take her.

"At the top of the celestial tree is the realm of the World Soul, translucent, edged in blue flames, a layer separating the mortal world from the realm of the everliving. Miraculously, a portal opens, and you step through to the undying realm. You feel yourself grow and change, becoming your true self, the self who is a deity. Become your god-self."

Behind her shut eyelids, Joanie grew into a being of divine nature and inestimable energy. In her arms, Pete let out a gasp and stiffened. But that was far away.

"A celestial mirror appears to show you what you look like."

She saw herself edged in green-white light, emanating power. The tips of her hair stirred like the tails of snakes, emerald green.

"See if your divine self has advice for you."

Pete was restless in her arms, nearly taking her out of trance. She strove to focus.

In a voice like the whispering of dozens of snakes, her god-self said what Puabi-Ekur had told her: her calling was sex work, work for Inanna, with the aim of healing and love.

"Child and daughter of Inanna, child of love," her divine self whispered. "Always and always, child of love."

"See if any symbol, sound, or scent comes to you."

The sounds and scents of an Inanna shrine: rose perfume, sweet smell of sex, gasps and moans.

"Let yourself know if there is any ritual practice you can do to bring your god-self closer."

In her arms, Pete was shaking.

She saw herself lighting a beeswax candle, next to a lit coral-pink Inanna candle, and meditating there.

"Let yourself relax into and become your highest self, your god-self."

Pete leaped to standing. "I am the Horned God!"

Shocked out of trance, she scrambled to her feet.

She had to get him outside.

Chapter 45

Cold night air hit her. Darkness hung above towering fir trees. It was good to be outdoors, away from people and confined space.

She drew him further from the cabin.

"I am the Horned God!"

It echoed from the trees.

An immense energy blazed from him. She shivered, with cold and fear.

Pete the human was still in trance, eyes wide and staring, foreign energy filling him. She could just barely hear Hannah indoors, settling the attendees and attempting to restart the meditation.

Fear started to threaten, but she pushed it down. First things first. She needed to get Pete back to himself.

They hadn't planned for him to embody a god, only do a meditation. If he were going to draw down, become a god in the material world, there were agreements to make and protections to build. Gods didn't understand human limitations—they could be dangerous to carry.

"Come back to the main altar," she said. He let her lead him.

She drew him along the path, among the cedar and fir. Fear brushed her again with dark feathers. A nudged branch released cedar scent. Behind them, the cabin door opened; feet stepped along the path. He trembled, wanting to cut and run.

"Ssh. Stay here, stay calm."

It was Nora. "May I take your other arm, Pete?" He said nothing, and she took it.

Nora would know what to do.

The three of them stepped out of the woods into the open grassy space, paced up to the altar with its candles and tiki torches, into the light.

Nora let go Pete's arm and dropped Dea incense on the still-lit coal in her burner. "Dea, Lady, help us ground this man and bring him back to himself."

The goddess laughed.

To her, the Horned God was Pete—his deepest self.

Joanie sat Pete on the cold, damp grass and knelt down beside him, holding him in her arms.

"Pete, come back. Come back to yourself, your human self."

She sensed also the unfairness, from Dea's point of view: They'd wanted everyone to become their god-selves, then panicked when it happened.

What if Pete never came back?

"I'll give him some food," Nora said. "That should help bring him back into his body. I've got some soup I can heat up. It's potato-leek, all vegan."

"That'll be fine."

Nora headed back toward the house.

Pete leaped up again, shaking off Joanie's constraining hand.

"I am the Horned God! I've come to the call."

She stood, and he stared her in the face.

He grabbed her hand and dragged her toward the unpathed woods, into the underbrush. Stiff with fear, she let him. Darkness, wet, slipping on leaves, whip of small alder saplings as they passed. They lost the light; everything went near-black. He didn't seem to care what lashed him. She was afraid she'd twist her ankle or walk into a tree.

A small clearing opened, a grove of young cedars circling a space padded with flat brown needles. He stopped and turned on her, her wrist still hard-clamped in his hand.

Enough light came from the clouded sky she saw his eyes wide and mad.

In the space of a breath, she saw what would happen.

Her mind did rapid calculations. They'd been waiting for his STI test results to skip condoms, but there was every reason to think they were both fine.

He reached forward and ripped her dress and bra in two. The cloth fell away with her jeans jacket. He pushed her down on the cedar mast, tearing off his black jeans, rending the cloth with inhuman strength. Pale skin flashed, and then he was on her, thrusting at her. Scrabbling, she moved to help him, suddenly slick and dripping with wanting him.

As his cock entered her, she came, an intense orgasm, as if she were being split in two. As if in an explosion, everything went white. Her self fell away.

When she came to, she was lying in the center of the small cedar grove, in near-complete darkness, on cedar bits and her destroyed clothes. He was gone.

She sat up. What if he'd disappeared for good?

But even in near-darkness, his trail was clear. He had blundered into the woods, heedless of the brush, almost a silhouette cut-out like a cartoon.

Shit, shit, shit.

Making her way out of the trees, Joanie met Nora at the wood's edge. Clearly she'd only passed out for a few minutes. They and members of both covens who'd followed Nora out reconnoitered for flashlights and machetes at the house. Nora found Joanie a multicolored patchwork dress, big on her; she tied it up to walk back into the woods.

We have to find him.

Alyssa and Gus had slipped out to help. The rest of Hannah's coven finished the meditation in the cabin.

Back into the woods they traced the new god. Joanie let a couple of Nora's coveners take the lead, one a back-country hiker and the other a trained nurse.

Fuck. This is crazy.

She focused on the task. In darkness, flashlight beams crossed. Drip from trees, wet flat brown maple leaves below, big as plates. Lichen on the trees, bright in the light; darker moss. The trail was obvious, broken through the brush. At the edge of the hollow in which Nora's house sat, at the border of the National Forest, the god had begun to climb.

The searchers stumbled upward, to the scent of fir and sound of hard breathing. The hill was steep.

Then, from above, came the call: "We found him!"

Joanie scrambled up to meet the voice.

Though a god, he was still in human form. A rotten stump had split under him. In his fall, he'd brought down a small dead alder, hitting his head, knocking his human body out.

Nora's nurse covener, purple hair drawn back in a no-nonsense ponytail, felt him over. "Hard to say for sure, but I don't think it's anything more than loss of consciousness. I think we can carry him out of here."

Joanie sat down beside Pete, Alyssa to the other side. His flesh was chilly to her touch.

"You're going to be okay." He didn't stir.

Nora and a couple other coveners doubled back, made a makeshift stretcher out of trimmed saplings and a beach towel, and returned. With Nora, Joanie, Gus, and one of Nora's coveners, each on a corner, they brought him down and out, into the house.

"Take him to the guest bedroom." It was on the first floor; they wouldn't have to carry him upstairs. In the cedar-paneled room, the bed sat covered with a patchwork quilt. They laid him on top of it, throwing a blanket over him.

"We should call an ambulance," the nurse said.

Then Pete moved, and moaned. His eyelids flickered open. "Where am I?"

Joanie sat down on the bed beside him. "You're in Nora's guest bedroom. You got knocked out—a sapling fell on you."

The nurse said, "You almost certainly have a concussion. We should call an ambulance."

"I don't want that. At least not yet. I want to find out what happened." Sitting up, he winced in pain. "I feel as if I got hit by a truck."

Nora scanned the gathered handful. "Let's give Joanie and Pete a little space, shall we?"

She closed the bedroom door behind her.

Quiet fell.

"What happened?"

"Give me a second. This has been crazy."

She let herself take a few deep, long breaths, calming herself. The worst was over.

She told him. He sat a few moments taking it in. Then he let himself fall back onto the quilt.

"You said you came to the call. Does that mean anything to you?"

"I don't remember any of that."

"Hannah says that's not unusual when a god takes over. Though if I'd had any idea this would happen, we would've approached things differently." Joanie herself had never drawn down, but Hannah's coven had a protocol. She stroked his forehead.

"I guess the Celtic heritage holds. The Horned God, huh." He levered himself up again. "Thanks for taking care of me." He kissed her on the cheek.

"I don't think it's a bad idea to have you checked out at the ER. You were out cold at least fifteen minutes."

"If it would make you feel better. But I'd rather get a ride into town—no need to call an ambulance." He was thinking of the expense.

"Do you still feel him in there?"

He closed his eyes.

"I do—I feel like he's waiting. I'm not sure for what." His dark blue eyes reopened and met hers. "He really is me, or I am him. An avatar of the Horned God."

"I can see it."

They stared at each other.

"So what next?" he said.

At least Joanie had gotten a chance to hear from her inner deity what her path should be. His had just flung him into the night—to do something, but what?

"I don't know. I do think we should figure it out so that doesn't happen again the same way. Obviously you want to keep the relationship, and keep the doors open."

"Just not to randomly run into the forest and knock myself out."

"Right." She kissed him gently. "How are you feeling?"

"I have a headache, and I'm kind of scraped up. Otherwise fine."

"We need to get you to the ER. But one thing the meditation gave me was an idea of the direction my inner deity wanted me to take. Did you get anything like that?"

"Maybe? It feels like more of the same: Take down capitalism; start a collective. Though a little bit more about run into the woods and live with the deer, or maybe hunt the deer, than before."

"So deer are your thing?"

"There's a connection there. But all of this is like remembering a dream you've almost lost."

A knock came at the door. "Y'all okay in there?" It was Hannah.

She entered, followed by Alyssa and Gus.

Pete grimaced. "I'm sorry to mess up your meditation."

"I got it goin' again after you left. And it definitely worked for you. That's gratifying. How're you feelin'?" He gave her the rundown. "We're going to leave in a few. Nora wanted you to try these jeans on, since you ripped yours up." She handed him the pair.

"Glad you're feeling better, dude," Gus put in. "You gave us a scare."

"Better now. Or mostly."

"I'll go bring the car around," Hannah said. "I parked a little ways away. Y'all get your stuff together."

They collected in the entryway, sitting on a rough-hewn bench, facing the largest of the jack o' lanterns. By ones, twos, and threes, people came up and asked after Pete. A few folks left, and the entryway cleared.

"I'm curious, if you want to say," Joanie said to Gus and Alyssa, "what deities came up for you?"

"A visionary, a mystic strongly connected to Hekate. No huge surprise, right?"

"How about you, Gus?"

"A hunting god, with connections to Odin and the Wild Hunt." He eyed Pete. "Guess it's no shock we're roommates."

Pete merely grinned.

"When I went hunting with my dad and his friends, I hated it."

"It might be different if you hunted for food in the traditional way," Alyssa said.

"Yeah, I think it was not wanting to hang around with my dad. And feeling for the deer. If we needed the meat, it'd be one thing. My dad was trophy hunting."

A car headlight flashed, signaling Hannah's car had pulled up.

~

Puabi-Ekur watched.

Seeing souls claim their deity status bore attention, but few people would claim their full deity abilities. Pete might be different.

A long time ago, Puabi-Ekur had been Maelan, the lover of Daegal, who was now Gus. Daegal had a strong connection with Woden, the hunter who led the Wild Hunt, which had helped draw Gus in with his lover Max's Hunt.

Here, now, Gus had moved in with this Horned God, deer god to Dea's bear goddess: two strong animal spirits of the Pacific Northwest.

Summoned in ritual, Dea had made the space ready for the Horned God, likely called him—he had come in answer to a call. She'd responded to Puabi-Ekur's request for help by bringing in a god of nature to fight for the Green Path.

Puabi-Ekur sent an inquiry to Dea, but she didn't answer.

Tentatively, carefully, a web or net was being drawn together: a net of connection, something to keep people together against a rising storm. And as part of that, to address their common enemy.

Hannah dropped Joanie and Pete at the ER at ten p.m., where after some waiting a doctor gave Pete a once-over.

"You seem to have a mild concussion. If you have a headache, take acetaminophen. Get plenty of rest, avoid strenuous activities, and don't drive a vehicle or ride a bike for twenty-four hours. Also avoid alcohol."

They caught a Lyft back to Pete's.

"Should I stay over?"

"No strenuous activities, now."

"If activities occur, I will do the work, I promise."

Wrapped around each other, they dreamed, and Puabi-Ekur watched the dream.

Again they entered the Paleolithic cave, flickers of firelight illuminating paintings, figures dancing in the smoke of a fire.

It was a different timeline, not Puabi-Ekur's own with Joanie, yet important.

It connected Joanie and Pete in love, an old love, a procreative love, between man and woman. Here, she was priestess of the Lady of Animals, womb and mother of the world. Here, he was priest of the Lord of Animals, the shaman who wore the drooping pelt and the skull of the deer, the protector of the natural order.

Chapter 46

The following Monday, Joanie found she had her own office. A note on her old desk led her to it, with her name on a plate on the door.

Small, tucked into the larger office's corner, it was not itself a corner office, instead butted up against a pillar. But it was still far better than the cubicle she'd had. Now she had a door she could close. The space barely fit a guest chair, but it was hers. A third of it was window, which today showed drizzle and cranes.

She stopped by Don's office and raised an inquiring eyebrow.

"Your title is paraplanner now," he said, smiling. "You can get your CFP over time—that's just a detail. Your new salary starts as of today, your new duties as well. We've ironed out the details with Walker Nelson. The only thing left is to sign the papers, which will happen Friday. If you don't mind, I'll ask you to take the papers over. Mark Walker will sign for the company."

"Sounds good." Joanie had no idea whether this was usual

or not, but she was inclined to do what Don asked, for twenty-five percent more pay.

The weather continued rain. At home, Cleo had gotten back another round of reviewer comments and was revising. At work, Monica pushed Joanie to tie up the projects they shared before the temp took over. Monica was short about it—a sore loser.

Tuesday night, she and Pete went out to dinner, this time a local Italian place. Small, badly lit, it had plaster walls between walnut-black beams, with a faux grapevine and Italian flags. The service was lax. But the food was decent, for Seattle it was cheap, and it served inexpensive red wine.

"Carafe, please," Pete ordered.

"I thought you were avoiding alcohol."

"For twenty-four hours. I figure if my headache's gone, I should be okay, right?" The flame of their table's candle shone ruddy on his face. She leaned and stroked his cheek.

"Has the god come back?"

"I sense him in the background, but that's all. I keep having the cave dream."

"Me too. Every night since the ritual."

"I think you're right, we should do something with it."

Joanie bit her lip. "You think? I'm just afraid he'll come back in a destructive way. I mean, we can do something, but—"

"No more concussions."

"Right."

With the dark and the cold rain, she'd chosen Caesar salad and then lasagna. "I thought you were vegetarian."

"I am basically, but lasagna is comfort food. I'm sending good energy to the cow."

He laughed. "Does that count?"

"You can't be perfect always. This isn't bad red wine."

"Not for what we pay for it. What should we do about the dreams?"

"We can do it tonight, if you like. Meditate with them, go further with them. Ask the questions we want to ask. If we keep returning there, there's a reason. We can build in a lot of safety."

"Then we should go easy on the wine."

"I suppose."

She still poured herself another glass. It bothered her more than she cared to admit, how short Monica had been with her.

"Do you need dessert?"

"I think so. It was a hard day."

They split a dish of tiramisu.

"I never want to go back to work again."

"I get it. But what brought that on?"

She'd explained switching bosses. Now she went into a little more detail.

"Hold on—do you think this Don guy will get indicted? Because I have to agree with Monica, if I understand what you're saying."

"I agree with Monica too. But the whole thing is reprehensible. I mean, wealth management in itself opposes everything I believe in."

"But if you took the job to keep your future options open, shouldn't you keep your future options open? I mean, what happens if Don is breaking the law?"

"The more they pay me, the sooner I get out."

"Did you do a Tarot reading?"

"The Tarot gave me the Tower." She made a face.

"And?"

"It means the end of a current world, everything falling apart. But it's hard to read the Tower now, because that's what the world looks like in general."

"True that."

Back at Pete's house, she scouted the best place for a circle.

"Maybe in my bedroom, since the dreams come there."

"Makes sense." She went in, lit the candles she'd given him, and looked around the room. A tan comforter, white sheets, one print on the wall. A guy's room, simple.

"Are you okay with Hekate protecting the space? She's more my goddess than yours, but for me she's powerful protection."

"I'm okay with Hekate."

"I can lead a meditation, if you like. But keep it light."

He gave half a smile. "So no gods come in."

"Exactly."

Joanie kicked off her shoes and sat cross-legged on the bed, long black skirt puddling on the comforter. Pete threw himself down next to her, put his arm around her. She could feel him wanting to push her down on the bed and make love to her.

"Let's do the meditation first, or we'll never get to it. But what questions do we want to ask?"

"My main question is: Why do we keep returning there? What are we supposed to get out of it?"

"Okay." Leaning forward, she stroked his face, kissed him. "Get comfortable. Lie down, if you want. If you think you'll fall asleep, sit up."

Pete grabbed a pillow and propped himself against the headboard.

Joanie put up a protective circle and called in Hekate. "Dark Mother, protectress, savior, keep us grounded in this world, in our human forms and expressions."

She led them both into trance, down a long set of stairs. They went out a door and along a path through dark woods to the opening of the cave. She described it as she remembered it, the high walls painted with animals of the hunt, the firelight wavering on the paintings, figures in a circle in the fire's smoke.

As she spoke, she went there.

She asked the question they both had: "O spirits of this place, and Lady Hekate: Why do we come here? What are we supposed to learn?"

In response, one of the figures in the cave turned toward her, took her gently by the arm, drew her into the dance.

She let them both stay in that place a minute, two minutes, enough time to receive whatever answers they would get. Then she walked them back out.

Pete opened his eyes, smiling.

"I think I get it."

She studied his face in candlelight. "What did you see?"

"There was a shaman at the head of the dance. He was wearing a cape and headdress, made of the skull and hide of a deer. He put that on me and told me to lead the dance. And I did. I remembered how."

"You're supposed to become a deer shaman?"

"Something like that. Which is, of course, what the Horned God appearing says too."

"I was supposed to join the dance myself. They led me in."

"It connects to what I've felt for a long time, that I should help form a collective. The dream is telling me that for the collective, the basis is this ancient spirituality."

Joanie nodded slowly. "Okay, I get it."

"Is Hannah teaching a class soon?"

"Not as such. But I think she'd make an exception for a god."

Chapter 47

By luck, Friday afternoon was overcast but with no rain: high, grey clouds, featureless, the sun a hidden smudge. She crossed downtown to the Walker Nelson hotel. She'd worn one of her new business outfits, a fitted black dress with a vine-covered scarf at her neck and a grey blazer. Classic, even conservative, but she liked it, and she knew she looked good.

She went to the same small meeting room, dominated by its Art Deco painting of bathers, with the neutral cream-colored walls, grey drapes, black table. No one was there yet when she arrived.

In her messenger bag, in an embossed folder, she carried the papers—two sets, each signed for Gunnar Group by Don. She drew these out, then helped herself to water.

At five minutes after two, Mark Walker came in. Wavy grey hair, lots of it, blue eyes. Face crinkled in a smile, he stepped forward and shook her hand. "Joan, so good to see you. These must be the papers."

"Yes." She opened the folder, admiring her own manicure

as she did. She'd redone her nails, a conservative neutral polish. She could play the business-girl part. She was going to offer him a pen, but he whipped out his own fountain pen and put his dark, thick, square signature each place it was needed.

"Good, that's done. Now, I'd like you to have lunch with me. I have reservations at the Metropolitan Grill."

This was a high-end Seattle steak place. She thought of the twenty-five percent raise. "My pleasure."

Don had mentioned she could take the rest of the day off after she'd gotten the papers signed—just get them on his desk by the end of the day.

She walked the few blocks to the restaurant beside Mark. A sound hung in the air, an electric buzzing like overhead power lines, or like some kind of giant fly. She ignored it; she wanted to get this right.

As they walked, they traded small talk; he asked about her time at Gunnar Group. They went under a forest-green awning; a doorman opened the door.

From late afternoon, the interior took them into evening: low-lit lamps, dark wood paneling. "Right this way, Mr. Walker."

The hostess took them to a booth, cushioned seats upholstered in green velveteen. He turned to the cocktail menu.

"What do you like to drink?"

She smiled. "I don't drink when I'm on the clock."

"Please join me. It's a milestone for Walker Nelson. Don said he'd be fine if you helped celebrate."

Oh, did he? She sighed inwardly.

"Maybe some rosé." Something light that wouldn't get her too drunk.

"You know what? Let's get some Champagne. I'm excited about this self-insurance scheme. Would you like that?"

She nodded, smiling, playing a role, not quite sure what role to play.

What had Don told this guy—that she came with the contract? She didn't mind being window-dressing. The whole game was corrupt, but she was playing it, and that went with the territory. But if she went back to whoring, it would be her own decision, not some random financial planner's.

The Champagne came. He kept her glass full. She tried not to drink quickly from nervousness. She got a dinner-size Caesar salad; he got a rare steak. "This will probably be my dinner," he explained. "You're not a steak-eater?"

"I lean toward vegetarian, or pescatarian."

"I love fish. I own a seafood restaurant. But I love a good steak too." He cut off a dripping piece, chewed it, then wiped his mouth with his napkin.

"Now, I'm not sure how much maintenance this insurance plan will take on the Gunnar Group end, but I'd love it if you were the face I dealt with. Don's a great guy, but if I have to see someone, I'd like that to be you."

Reaching forward under the table, he patted her knee.

It was a completely ambiguous act. Not appropriate, but something a hearty, entitled man of his generation might do with no explicit sexual intent.

He smoothed his hand up her leg, squeezed it, and let it go.

Less ambiguous, but still deniable.

She folded her knees away from him, out of easy reach.

"I need to check in with Don about that."

"Of course."

She declined dessert. When they parted on the sidewalk, he gave her a big hug, arms enveloping her. He was a tall, muscular man, almost twice her size, animal heat from his body radiating through his suit. The hug knocked her off-balance.

Recovering her footing, she smiled. "Have a great evening, Mark."

She walked back to the office. Downtown lights winked against the growing twilight.

The electric buzzing sounded again. Her emotions were a dark swirl.

She didn't like being pushed around. She'd been abused—she didn't have to take it now.

And yet, before she'd started this job, she'd thought about calling some of her old clients to make extra cash. Mark Walker clearly wanted her. Why not do that with him?

The trouble was, she had no idea what his expectations were. If she shocked him, it could lose her the Gunnar Group job. When she left, she wanted to leave on her own terms.

And she didn't like the uneven playing ground. He had far more power than she did in this situation.

I'm my own woman. I set my own terms.

When she got back, she planned to set the papers on Don's desk and leave, but unexpectedly Don was in his office.

Setting the embossed folder on his desk, she pulled up the guest chair. "Mind if we talk a moment?"

"No problem."

She closed his sliding door and seated herself. The space sounded with a high-pitched buzzing whine, like an electric mosquito. She wondered again if it came from Don's computer.

"I got the signatures, and Mark took me out for a late lunch. I assume from what he said you expected that?"

"It's how he likes to do it."

"He got a little handsy."

Don wrinkled his brow.

"If you want, you don't have to see the man again."

She frowned, listening.

"But I'd think about it, if I were you. All this guy wants is a pretty face on the deal, someone to have lunch or dinner with occasionally. Is that so much to ask? If it greases the wheels—it's business. We all do things for business. I'd rather be taking my son to his basketball game than be here now."

That's a little different.

"If it makes you feel better about it, I'll give you another five-percent raise. This self-insurance plan is going to make us a lot of money."

If she agreed, what was she agreeing to?

As far as she could tell, Don didn't care what Mark asked of her, as long as the deal went through.

If she went back to whoring, she'd do it her way, and she'd get considerably more than was on the table now.

"I'd rather not get groped."

"We can back it off for the time being. The contract's signed. I don't expect a lot of meetings for the next bit."

Ice-blue eyes studied her.

"I do want you on this deal, though."

She could stalk out. But she didn't want to burn her bridges.

"Okay." For now, at least. "I'll let you know if he does something that makes me really uncomfortable."

Don sat back, swinging in his chair a little, so it creaked.

"You do that."

Chapter 48

*E*ver since the Halloween party, whenever Gus was on campus he kept an eye out for Josh, the Odin's Hunt member who last year had jumped a Black guy.

Now he was looking for him, he didn't find him.

Rainy November, grim and overcast, dropped drizzle on the city, sometimes a random downpour. He spent a lot of time on the bus, staring out the window at passing grey buildings, the fog of his breath, wondering what he'd do next.

He'd almost decided on med school. But his grades were adequate, not stellar. Plus, he was a year behind on the process, and he had a few classes he should take still. It might be best to slow down a little, spread his last year out.

At base, he needed to decide if he wanted to be a doctor. Medical school was brutally hard, and if he wasn't in love with it, he wouldn't succeed. Or he could get a med tech job or something, pay off some of his loans.

Stay with Alyssa. They were good together. They were engaged, but they both wanted to see what came next before they took the further step into marriage.

He missed the passion of being with Max. But no passion lasted forever, and Max was crazy. And violent.

And a great top.

He loved Alyssa, but he missed having a guy in his life.

One lunchtime, done with his morning lab class, all these things rattled around his head as he stared out the bus window heading over to Alyssa's. As he stared, he saw a young male student walking down the street, head down against the light rain.

Tall, broad-shouldered, white-blond hair—it was Josh.

As if stung, Gus sat up, pulling the wire to halt the bus.

Josh had turned the corner onto the main drag. Gus scrambled, nearly knocking over some woman in a navy raincoat with her arms full of books.

Taking the corner, he saw Josh a couple blocks down. He slowed to a walk.

His quarry hadn't looked up.

Best to make this seem casual.

Gus stepped up his pace, and when he was close, pulled out his phone, which would make it make sense when he walked into Josh.

A solid hit, shoulder to torso.

"Oh, sorry. Hey—hi!"

Josh stared at him. Then he frowned.

Gus was no longer supposed to exist in his world.

Josh turned to walk the other way.

"Hey, Josh, wait up, I haven't seen you in ages. What's up?"

Gus moved to face him, rubbing his nose as rain dripped on him, radiating friendliness.

Josh frowned and moved to go around him. "Can't talk."

"Don't be like that, dude." Gus once again stood in his way.

"I haven't seen you in months. I never heard, after that fight in the park—what happened?"

Josh stared, scowling, looking like an angry bull. Gus might have been frightened, if he hadn't been focused on this mission for weeks. Also he was faster than Josh.

"I'd love to know what's going on. How about I take you for a beer?"

"Bruni said you betrayed us, Gus."

"He said that to me too. Don't know what he's talking about."

When he put his mind to it, Gus could be a glib liar. He'd had years of practice with his dad.

"Bruni thought you told the police about the Wild Hunt ritual."

Gus had guessed as much, but it was good to have it confirmed. Already, after maybe two minutes, Gus had a lot more information than he'd had. He wasn't going to leave Josh's side till he had it all.

"That's absolutely not true." No shame in lying if it was for the cause. "Come have a beer, I'll tell you my side of it."

"I don't know if that's a good idea, Gus."

"Ah, come on. I mostly want to know what happened after the fight. You don't have to tell me anything you don't want to."

"Okay. Just one beer."

Gus knew a semi-dive bar close by. A block, two blocks, and they pushed their way in through the door.

In the half-darkness, beer signs cast a faint red glow. Gus and Josh sat at a vinyl-topped table, and after a minute a waitress showed up. Gus got an amber ale, Josh an IPA.

"So what happened?"

"You mean, after the fight?" Josh took a mouthful of beer,

then wiped his mouth. "That's good. I've been on a budget, so not much beer lately."

"I feel you, dude. Shall I get a pitcher?"

Unthinkingly, Josh made puppy-dog eyes. Gus waved for the waitress and ordered a pitcher of IPA. He wasn't a huge IPA fan, but it was for the cause. He intended to drink much more slowly than Josh.

Josh told his version. "The police came looking for me. Bruni told me not to say anything without a lawyer. Max got me hooked up. Max was great." He eyed Gus. Gus kept his face stony. "The guy made it through and didn't press charges, so it got dropped."

"That's good. Bruni's not right that I betrayed the Hunt. I'm not part of the Hunt anymore, but I'm not an enemy. How is everyone?"

"Oh, more of the same. We got the roof on the hall. It's too bad Max had to leave, because he was a great worker. But we got it done anyway."

"Have you heard from him?"

"Bruni's been talking to him. I guess he's hanging out with some friends in Austria."

Far-right friends, Gus guessed. "Is Julia still taking part?"

"She is. You know, she's still on your side. She told Bruni she never believed you betrayed us."

"She's right."

"I know she's old and stuff, but she's kind of hot. She doesn't have a boyfriend right now." Josh scanned his face. "The way she talks about you, it's clear she likes you."

Gus still had her email address.

"Have you been down at Odinshof?" The Odin's Hunt land near Yelm.

"We've been clearing a bit more land. Jake wants a bigger

firepit and a few more A-frames. I think he and Bruni want someone to live out there all year long."

Or hide out there.

Josh finished his pint glass, and Gus poured another.

"What about in town? You all going to more protests?"

"I'd like to. Bruni wants to coordinate, he says. We have a lot of new Hunting Pack guys."

Pint by pint, Gus kept poured pale ale into Josh. The dam broke.

"Max might be coming back, around solstice. Bruni wants to do another ritual like that last one, maybe."

"I see."

"They threw that rock through your window."

"I know. I wish you'd tell them I didn't betray them."

"I don't know if they'll believe me." He leaned across, threw a heavy arm around Gus. "But I see it now! You were always my friend."

"It's true." Sort of true.

"I missed you, dude! We should go out and find some niggers to beat up."

Gus glanced around to make sure the waitress hadn't heard that.

"Don't think that's a good idea, Josh. I think Bruni's right about wanting to coordinate."

"You're probably right." Josh subsided, staring forward, breathing heavily.

Time to get this boy home before he started puking on the floor.

"Hey, Josh—we should take off."

"I think I need another beer."

"No—some pretzels or something might help." He caught

the waitress. "You can have them all." As Josh finished them, Gus paid.

"Let's get going." Josh lived at the same nondescript building as before, boxed in among narrow junipers. Once inside, Josh bolted for the bathroom.

Gus thought of the man Josh had attacked the previous year, how he'd beaten the man's head on the sidewalk. He could have killed him. There was no reason to feel guilty for getting Josh drunk.

Chapter 49

"But that's great!" Pete yelped.

"What's great?" Joanie was in their apartment's kitchen, opening a bottle of cheap red she'd brought with her.

"Gus ran into Josh on campus and fed him beer, and he told Gus everything he knew."

Joanie came in with a couple of jam jars of red. She raised her eyebrows at Gus, and he shrugged. She got him a jam jar as well.

"The big bombshell is Max is coming back, and they might replay their last solstice ritual. I'm in the running for their quarry."

"Not if I have anything to say about it," Pete said, leaping up and taking a turn around the room. "I'll get a few of my friends. They try kidnapping you, and they'll regret it."

"They might change their minds, now Josh has told me everything. That's bound to get back to them."

"Not killing people is a good outcome too." Pete flung himself back down.

"Still would be great to catch them in the act," Gus said.

They pondered and sipped. Joanie put on background music and lit the candles.

"Is there any way we can find out what they're planning?" Pete asked.

"The only in I have with them now is Julia. Josh made it plain she's still on my side. But she won't know about the men's rituals—they keep all that separate."

"Really," Joanie said.

"It's their way. I don't defend it. And even if Julia does know something, I'll have to be careful with her."

"Why?" Pete asked.

"With Josh, I don't really care if I lie. He's Mr. Let's Go Beat Up Niggers. With Julia, it's not so clear-cut. I have no idea if she knows what the men of Odin's Hunt get up to. And I like her a lot better. I don't want to lie to her."

"Well, don't lie to her," Joanie said. "There must be some way to avoid revealing you've changed sides."

"Maybe? She's a lot quicker on the uptake than Josh is, and a lot less likely to drink to excess."

"You can withhold information," Pete said. "Remember, if Odin's Hunt doesn't decide to kill you, they might kill someone else. Even if they don't, they're putting on white-supremacist rallies and assaulting people of color. So getting proof about them is good."

Joanie rolled her eyes. She'd been doing her reading. "Proof. You mean for the police? As a good anarcho-communist, can you support going to the police?"

"I don't support the police. But I'd like Bruni and Max to face consequences for Rob's death." He leaned forward. "He was my friend. I can't bring him back, but we can figure out some way to make these fuckers face the music. Whether the police or otherwise. Either way, intel is our friend."

"Okay, I'll look up Julia."

"And sooner rather than later. Josh is going to tell Bruni he told all, and after that information will dry up."

For a couple of weeks, all was quiet on the Walker Nelson Hospitality front.

Joanie didn't know if that was because Don had decided to cover maintenance work on the account, or if they really didn't need anything. She suspected the former. Instead, Don gave her all the other scutwork he had.

Meanwhile, Monica acted as if Joanie didn't exist—walked past her in the hallway, kept silent in the elevator, spoke the minimum to her in meetings. Joanie was now reporting full-time to Don.

It hurt. But she didn't work there to please Monica.

Cleo was making still more thesis revisions, complaining about conflicting feedback. At least once a week, Joanie dragged her out for dinner.

A vegan-only Thai place had opened a few blocks from them, relatively cheap. Painted white, it had family style tables, but if you got there at the right time you could sit in the corner, alone. They split mango salad; Cleo got red curry. She was a three-star girl.

"Nothing from that Mark Walker lately?"

"Nope. I think Don is interposing himself."

"It's one thing that slimeball could do. Still, you're probably going to have to make the call at some point."

Joanie had gotten pad thai, comfort food. "What would you do if you were me?"

"Hmm." Cleo spooned a bit more rice into her curry bowl.

"Well, I'm *not* you. But like you say, it's not that Mark Walker wants you to do something you've never done before. But you don't necessarily want to endanger the day job by shocking him with some straightforward whore proposition. And—if I get you—you don't want to do sex work in a situation where the other person holds all the cards."

"Right."

Cleo picked up her cup of jasmine tea in both hands. "I guess my advice for you—if you're asking for it—sometimes I get in trouble for unasked advice—"

"I'm asking."

"Decide what your boundaries are. How far are you willing to go with this guy, and what does it look like? It sounds like your issues are you want respect and, if it comes to it, to be able to negotiate in clear terms."

"Something like that. I suppose I need to count in I already got a thirty percent raise. My take-home pay is nearly twice what I got at the coffee shop now." Though as a whore, if she'd put her mind to it, she could make two weeks of her current pay in a long weekend.

Cleo shrugged. "Count what you want. It's your life. I know you didn't say you wanted to go straight, but isn't that part of it?"

"I wanted to make better money without the legal hassle. But that's another way of saying the same thing." She twirled a rice noodle on her plate. "If I'm going to play by straight-world rules, I shouldn't have to fuck Mark Walker. And if I have to fuck him, I want my usual rate. In other words, I want to make the call. It's my body."

Cleo reached over, stroked Joanie's hand.

"It is your body. You make the rules. You know I never want any nasty man touching my girlfriend. Nasty man being one she doesn't like. I don't want you ever to feel like a victim."

Joanie brought Cleo's hand up and kissed it. "I love you."

They went back to Cleo's room. She pushed Joanie back among her pillows, Indian patterns in orange, yellow, magenta, with gilt and mirrors, scratchy to Joanie's bare skin. She pumped her pelvis against Joanie's, kissed her, tongue probing. The scent of heated sandalwood rose, with a faint lingering scent of curry. Cleo fished out her red and orange marbled glass dildo, slid off Joanie's jeans, licked and pronged her till she called out, sobbing.

"Turnabout is fair play." Repositioning herself, Joanie licked Cleo, drawing it out, sneaking glances at her face, until she moaned and writhed.

In the long, slow ebb, they returned to their everyday selves.

Yet it was night, the time for confidences.

"If I have one thing I want to do most, that all this is taking away from, is starting the Inanna shrines again."

"I'd like that too. I'd like to do that, even do a temple around it—some kind of organization."

They talked lazily a while, building castles in the air.

"But hold that thought," Cleo said. "I really, really, really cannot focus on anything else till I finish the thesis."

"I understand."

Chapter 50

*I*n the middle of the night, on his laptop, Gus wrote the email.

It took the middle of the night for him to work on it. Because he cared about Julia as a person, even if he'd never seriously thought about pursuing her sexually. Though that wasn't impossible.

And this wasn't about that.

As usual, he'd wound up that night at Alyssa's. She lay asleep beside him, illuminated by the laptop light.

It felt disrespectful to try to set a date with another woman while Alyssa slept next to him. Even if it was a coffee date to fish for information.

He got up, picked up laptop and cord, and went into the living room, finding a place on the couch.

His twitchiness made him wonder: How much of a date did he want with Julia, for real?

He thought back to meeting her, a tall woman with dark braided hair and an hourglass figure in a green kirtle. He'd thought about fucking her. Even Max had noticed his interest.

But this was about intel, to prevent people from being hurt. And to bring Bruni and Max to justice, if they could.

He wrote it pretending it meant nothing. He scanned it for typos, cleaned it up, and hit send.

Chapter 51

The next evening, Joanie had a date with Pete. In honor of the continued cold, rainy weather, he made her vegetable soup.

She stepped off the bus, glancing up to the dark branches of trees against the blue-ink sky. A gust threw raindrops in her face. Her way led under overarching boughs, now mostly bare.

She'd brought a bottle of wine. She'd been drinking a lot of wine lately. The world was dark and lowering, darker than this sky. Who wasn't running to wine, beer, drugs, sex, material goods (if you could afford those)? Cleo buried herself in writing, trying to address at least some race issues on paper, hoping that could help change the world.

Joanie hadn't given up, but some days it felt like a slog.

Pete buzzed her in, to the comforting smell of soup. Gus was out, as usual. She wondered how much it mattered that he'd changed where he lived, since he hadn't really changed where he lived. At least Alyssa had changed apartments.

Pete was in the narrow kitchen, standing over the pot of

soup, stirring and tasting. "Here," he said, by way of greeting, "taste this and tell me what it needs." He offered her a spoon.

"It tastes great to me."

Covering the pot, he took her in his arms. They stood there wordlessly, wrapped in each other's energy.

"How was today?" she asked.

"I'll tell you over dinner." They grabbed bowls and sat on the couch.

After a few mouthfuls, he said, "So this is another week for papers." He didn't do much teaching, more was there for office hours to help students and for grading. "It's kind of amazing how many kids get to college, even through English classes, without being able to write a basic essay. What about you?"

"More of the same. I had to troubleshoot some stuff on the portal."

"Any more on Walker Nelson?"

"Not for now." She stirred her spoon in the bowl, watching bits of carrot and celery circle. He watched her face.

"So?"

"So what would you do, if you were me? You know I approach the question in terms of whoring."

"At least it's an office job. Don't tell me it's more fun to suck old men's dicks, because I don't think it is."

She rolled her eyes. "You haven't worked an office job, have you?" He shook his head. "A job is a job. If I get to set the parameters, if I get to do it as an offering to Inanna, I'd rather suck old men's dicks."

"I'm not putting down sex work."

Expressions flitted across his face. There was still a lot of pain there.

"To a certain extent, we are talking about sex work, just in a different venue," she said. "To turn this around, if I cared about the job, it could be the end of taking it seriously if I sucked this guy's dick."

"But you don't care about this job."

"True." She sipped her wine. "But I do want to be in charge of how I burn my bridges. If I have sex with Mark Walker, it needs to be worth it to me."

Pete nodded, and she continued.

"Assuming I keep the job, to play it straight, I need to be sure I'm never alone with him. Or too close to him. I don't like it, but I make excellent money for an entry-level job."

"What about the other direction? Would you want to go there?"

"Have him set me up? Be my quasi-boyfriend? I don't think so. It's a low-power place, one down. I don't want to be there with this guy. I don't like him. I don't trust him."

"How much would he have to offer you, to have sex with him?"

"If he offered me a million dollars for one night, I'd go for it."

"But realistically? And speaking of intel, how can you find out about this guy? I mean, who knows what he gets up to."

With her former sugar daddy, she'd assumed she could handle anything he did, not realizing he'd dish out more than she expected.

"Point taken. I've done some internet research, but of course anything really shitty he has lawyers to cover up. Beyond that, I guess I can ask Monica. Though I can barely get her to talk to me. I assume she'd say if he was really awful."

She sighed. "But yeah, I should figure out what my boundaries are."

"And not just in terms of actions. In terms of cash. You're

doing this for money. How much money do you need to have, to cash out?"

"I want to pay off my student loans, if I can."

She stared a moment at her jam jar full of dark red wine, a jeweled spot in it from reflected light.

She wanted to change the subject. "We've looked at the cave. But what about the other part, the part where you became a god?"

He grimaced. "Oh, that."

"Start with the cave, then. It's like the cave in Alyssa's vision and her later dream. It makes me think of Nora's goddess, the goddess they call Dea."

"Mmm."

"An antlered god, a horned god. Maybe he's the god of those woods? Or some version of the god that called out the god in you? And to connect the dots, maybe he's connected to Dea, the goddess of the cave? A mate or ally?"

"Maybe. You know more about these things than I do."

"Not much, not at this level." She rubbed her mouth thoughtfully.

Getting up, she walked into his bedroom. She lit the candles, pulled her dress over her head; he came up behind her, unhooking her bra took it off, cupped her breasts. She turned around quickly and kissed him.

They had gone slowly with the sex, not to hit his sore spots. Yet part of the thing that drew her to him was a flickering vulnerability, that encouraged in her not dominance but a cradling, like cupping your hands around a flame to protect it from being blown out.

She unbuckled his belt, unbuttoned his jeans, pushing them down; she gently took his hardening cock in one hand.

Reaching around, she squeezed his ass and slid her finger between his cheeks.

"Do you want this?"

A pause, a breath. "Let's go slow."

"Yes."

She put her harness on. On the bed, he got on hands and knees.

"I'd rather see your face."

He lay down, on his back, pulling his legs up. She watched the changes on his face from moment to moment.

"Yes?"

"Go ahead. I don't want to keep talking."

She settled herself into place, pushed gently, pausing between breath and breath, pausing when he gasped. Feeling for the release, she pushed the head of her silicone cock deeper, rocking. "Touch yourself," she whispered. She wanted to see him come.

He was stroking himself, but his other hand reached outward, and she caught it in hers. It started a circuit. The energy rose, and she responded. He groaned: the spit of white on his stomach, the full-body release. So pretty.

He reciprocated, licking and mouthing her, long and slow; just before she came he inserted himself. They both came again.

Chemistry like fire. You couldn't buy it, you couldn't wish it into existence—either you had it, or you didn't.

"You know—we both have our test results now, right? Want to raw it?" They'd done it once when he was the god, but she wanted to formalize it in words. She had her implant for birth control.

"It would sure save on condoms."

She laughed. "Fucking broke student."

"Cleo doesn't have an opinion?"

"She doesn't own me. We're poly. But she's fine with it."

It wasn't like he was fucking anyone else. She hadn't quizzed him, but by now she would know. Though, who knew, over time he might.

But they wouldn't have this particular flickering, delicate connection.

Chapter 52

*P*uabi-Ekur watched them circling and circling, this pack of half-gods.

Some would fall away from their path, no matter how many nudges the unseen gave. Some wouldn't.

Thanks to these half-gods, they had met Dea. Now this new god, or old god, had arisen, perhaps called by Dea. It was time to find out why.

Now they'd established a connection, it was only a step sideways, and they were there.

To the lady of the hillside, old before she came over the land-bridge, it was obvious. Why had this human come to their god-self, here and now? She wouldn't say she'd helped, but Puabi-Ekur saw that as obvious.

The Horned God, the god of the wild, was also god of hunt and husbandry. Even before he protected flocks, he protected the stock, lest they be overhunted. So too he protected the people.

He was an ally, then, in the fight against the wall of razor wire, against these djinni—the minor Don, the larger bully Mark.

Joanie and Pete decided to talk to Hannah next. She invited them to dinner.

Joanie said, over the phone, "You really don't have to make food for us."

"It's no trouble at all. You're vegetarian, right? I have some spaghetti squash I have to get rid of."

Joanie rolled her eyes. It was as if Hannah could hear her do it.

"I would rather feed it to someone than have it go to waste."

"Okay, thank you. See you at seven."

Cleo eyed her as she hung up.

"Hannah's going to feed you whether you like it or not, eh?"

She pecked Cleo on the cheek, put on her raincoat and headed for Pete's apartment.

She took a fast walk over, swinging by the grocery. It was still November—uninspiring, rainy November. The birches along Pete's street, pale-barked and black-barred, huddled against the rain, all their pretty leaves down, brown wet scraps in the gutters.

Pete buzzed her in. As she came through the door, he waggled a bottle at her.

"I got good bourbon cheap. Like, half-price. Would Hannah want it?"

"Not really her style. Save it for later. I got her some pinot grigio."

They took the bus to Hannah's, not a Lyft, a new pact to save money. Pete wanted Joanie out of Gunnar Group as soon as possible; she did too. She'd drawn up a budget. If she could work there a full year, she could escape with loans paid off.

At the stop, they caught the bus and climbed on. They swayed to the electric moan; Pete leaned against the bus side, under the window. He wrapped his arms around Joanie a moment, pulled her close and kissed her forehead, then let her go.

"Your intuition was right on, about something big coming down that night," she said.

"True that. I had no idea what was coming, and would never have believed it if you'd told me."

"Did you have anything like a hint?"

He shook his head. "When I was a kid I was religious, in my early teens. I used to pray for an hour or more."

"What about?"

He laughed. "I wanted God to take away my desires. All of them."

"What were you desiring?"

"Mostly girls, occasionally boys. People in the middle too. But mostly girls."

"You weren't praying the gay away?"

"Oh, no, I wanted to be an ascetic. My parents had one of those marriages no one could envy."

"You told me about it."

"I'd spend half an hour to an hour, every night, in my room, praying, asking for purity. I literally had calluses on my knees."

"What changed this?"

"What do you expect? Sex. When I was fifteen, I went to Bible camp, and in the space of a couple of weeks, first a guy then a girl seduced me. The guy was one of the lead counselors; he swore me to secrecy. Then a girl and I got canoodling, one night late by the lake. One thing led to another, and the next day she told everyone I was her boyfriend. Daniel was horribly jealous."

She laughed. "Drama at Bible camp. What happened?"

"He had me kicked out of Bible study for being impure. Between the two of them, I basically was under house arrest the rest of Bible camp."

"Harsh."

"It helped sour me on the whole fundamentalist thing, let's just say."

But sometimes, there on his knees by his twin bed with its plaid blanket, he would zone out and see visions. "I saw angels, or at least I thought I did."

"Spirits?"

"I guess? They were encouraging; they tried to help me."

"Spirit guides." Joanie was getting excited. "It's not uncommon to have one."

"What I generally got from them was purity was from within, and to have faith. Which is good advice, though I misinterpreted it at the time. After I ran away, I left all that behind."

"That might be useful to tell Hannah."

In Hannah's dark, dripping yard, the rose on the trellis still had a last couple flowers, tight pale buds that might never open. They knocked and stepped in.

"Joanie, Pete! Gimme some sugar." They hugged her. "Dinner's in the oven. We can wait, or we can eat right away."

Joanie glanced at Pete. Pete was always hungry. "Eat, I guess," Joanie said.

Hannah's tiny wine-red dining room sat at the far end of the railroad kitchen, its oval table clothed in a pattern of harvest cornucopias.

"We can talk while we eat." Hannah passed dishes. "Pete, I

have an idea what brings you here, but I'd like to hear it from you."

"Mmmph." He finished his mouthful, set down his fork. "Well, obviously, I came to Samhain, and I—what Joanie has been calling it is, I drew down a god." He swallowed hard. "I want to know how to deal with it. It feels like a fairly strong call to paganism, and to connect that to my existing desires to create community and, well, reform the world."

Hannah nodded, as if he'd made the right answer.

"Up front I want to teach you a few things about grounding and agreements with spirits. It's a fantastic gift, mind, to be so connected with a god, and at the same time it's good to learn how to run that energy in a way that works for you."

"No more concussions," Joanie put in.

"We can get started tonight if you want to."

Pete visibly relaxed. "That would be great."

After dinner, they descended to the basement ritual room— big, with alcoves, a couple of couches, and a Celtic hanging of a tree of life with branches woven together. They got settled on the couches.

"Y'all know I work with Hekate, an ancient Greek goddess," Hannah said. "The ancient Greeks did a lot of thinking about this stuff. They didn't draw a strong line between, say, spirits of place, of trees or mountains, and the gods. That's what I see, too. And there aren't strong boundaries between all of those and us. It's like spirit possession. You see it, negatively, in scenarios like exorcism."

"Yeah, my grandfather did an exorcism on me at one point," Pete said. "I've always thought that was about my experimenting with bisexuality. But who knows? Maybe he caught a whiff of the Horned God. To him, that would have looked like Satan." He frowned, thinking. "I have to say, the Horned God feels familiar. Joanie and I both dreamed of a Paleolithic cave, and he's got a feel of that."

"Could well be. I think spirit possession is common to all of us. There are multiple religions where we take the god within. Folks think of Vodou, where the lwa inhabit their worshippers. We do that in witchcraft too—take deities within. We generally have people create some boundaries with the deities before they do somethin' like that. It's important to get consent from deities too."

"How does that work?"

"I can lead you through a meditation. But maybe the first thing to do, now you have this new thing in your life, is figure out what you want from this. What do you want your boundaries with the god to be?"

"What kind of thing do you have in mind?"

"Do you want to stay present some or all of the time when the god appears? Do you want some assurances you won't be hurt, physically or otherwise? Do you want to be able to step forward if there's a need in the external world, like if you hear a pot boilin' over on the stove?"

"I get the idea."

"I'll get you some paper and a pen—you can make a list."

Chapter 53

*L*ater that evening, Gus and Alyssa made their way back from their movie. Separately—for a change, Gus decided to stay the night at home.

He had an email to write.

It had taken a while, but Julia had replied to his first short email:

> Sure I'd be open to having coffee. Let me know
> when/where. I can do most weekend days, some
> Tuesday & Thursday nights.

They'd named a Thursday evening; now he was going to set a time and place.

Not Alyssa's coffee shop, obviously. It had to be somewhere he could get to on the bus. Julia lived and worked in Renton, far away. He settled for a coffee shop south of downtown, in the Beacon Hill area.

Alyssa was cool with the idea—why wouldn't she be?

Why wasn't he, entirely?

The next evening, he studied late at the university—he found a table at the library—then hopped the bus to Beacon Hill. The bus deposited him a few blocks from the place. After an industrial side of downtown, he found himself in a residential neighborhood where close-trimmed lawns fronted small houses.

The shop itself was one of these, white with mauve trim, inside simple, with open-format bookcases and small potted plants—clean, airy. He got his usual drip coffee, and settled down to wait. He was early; he'd brought his laptop.

On time, practically to the minute, she entered.

He'd seen her in her Odin's Hunt garb—now, her shapeless under a rain jacket, he hardly recognized her. But then she pushed off her hood, so her long brunette hair fell down.

The place was small; she saw him immediately.

"Gus!" She came over.

He stood. They stared at each other a moment. Julia reached forward, and they shared a half-hug. He managed to bump her breast as he pulled away. She ignored it.

"I'll go get some coffee."

She ordered an elaborate frappé drink, which took a few minutes to make.

It gave him time to regret coming.

It was such a fine line he was walking with her. Or a couple of lines.

Obviously, he wasn't interested in Odin's Hunt anymore, except intel. But he didn't want to tip his hand about that.

And he liked her. He wanted her. But also he didn't want to show that.

Julia got her frappé and sat down. Through the broad windows, afternoon was shading into evening. He glanced outside a moment, the sky a darkening grey.

"It's good to see you," he said.

"Likewise."

"How are things?"

She tilted her head slightly. "Fine. You mean things with Odin's Hunt?"

"Yeah." He took a mouthful of coffee. "I don't know I'm coming back, but I miss the people."

"Bruni's been going around telling everyone you betrayed the Hunt."

He shook his head. "I don't hold with everything they've done, but I don't want anyone hurt or endangered."

"Really?" She studied his face. He kept it blank. He had a lot of experience doing that.

He might make an exception for the men who hurt and endangered other people. But he didn't say that.

"The Hunt goes on, as I'm sure you know." She glanced out the window. "There's new people, new talk. I know you know Max is gone."

"Yes." He stared at his coffee cup, turned it slightly.

"It changes the conversation. I didn't always agree with him, but he kept things on a higher level." She cast her voice lower, not to be heard across the room. "Now it's all nigger this, and nigger that. I'm interested in northern heritage, but... I don't know, I can't help feeling my parents taught me better than that. I've been keeping my mouth shut. But maybe that should change."

"I get where you're coming from. I ran into some of the same things."

"I figured as much." Even more quietly, she continued, "You were there last year, at the men's ritual for the solstice." He nodded. "I gather some shit went down. They were talking about doing the same thing—with you as the target."

His chest tightened uncomfortably. "They have to catch me first."

"Bruni said he saw you at a march, with some Antifa guy."

"I was at a march. I ran into the Antifa guy, who I met, actually, through Max."

Suddenly he was tired of all this subterfuge.

"But I am leaning that way. I love northern ritual, but I don't think it has to go with racism. I just don't agree with that."

She sipped her drink, watching his face.

"I see."

Her gaze was as if she had a knife leveled at his heart.

"I'm starting to think I agree with you."

"Oh?"

"Travis, my ex, he went in for that kind of thing, nigger and so on, and I kept my mouth shut. But I can't help thinking—I grew up in Indiana, a pretty racist state. And yet, my mother would never put up with anything like that. She was outspoken, when it wasn't always easy. She's been gone, five years now. I think about her."

"Right." The opposite was true of his parents—his dad was explicitly racist, his mother implicitly. Maybe his being anti-racist was a way of defying them.

"So you're hanging out with Antifa now?"

She might be on her own fact-finding mission, whatever she volunteered about her mother.

"At the march, I ran into Pete, who I met through Max. We went out and had a drink afterward."

"So you have contacts."

He nodded; so much was obvious.

"Here's the thing. I just can't hold with this racism. And no one's said what happened in so many words, but something bad went down last solstice. It's obvious from the way Bruni and them act."

"You're right."

"I hate to be this person, but... Bruni talks about betrayal." She ran her hand through her hair. "What they're doing is wrong. I feel as if they've betrayed northern heritage. I want to meet your Antifa friends. I want to be a—what do you call it? Mole. Like in spy movies."

"What?"

"I want to keep tabs on Odin's Hunt for your Antifa friends. What the Hunt is doing is wrong."

Gus took a moment to take this in.

Did he fully believe her? How well did he know her?

"Julia, you have to realize, that might be dangerous."

"Believe me, I get that. They're going around looking for Black people to beat up, trans people to beat up." She shook out her hair behind her. "I will be very careful. I have no interest in getting beaten up, or worse. But I feel strongly about this. It's what my mother would want."

This was amazing, if she was telling the truth.

"Okay. I'll find those guys, get a meeting set up." Pete and Dave would know how to quiz her, to make sure she wasn't a double-agent.

Julia sat back in her chair, gaze weighing him. "So tell me, why exactly did you come here to meet me?"

His face went warm. He hoped he wasn't blushing, and if he was she didn't see it.

"To say hi, check up on the Hunt."

"I saw Josh at the book club. He said you went drinking. He said he told you I was single."

He knew he was blushing now.

"Josh isn't the most tactful."

"No. But I'm curious—was that part of the reason?"

Their eyes met. Hers were dark brown, with a ring of amber around the pupil.

"It wasn't not."

She laughed. "That's not a very strong statement."

"You may be single, but I'm poly—polyamorous. I do have a partner. Don't know if that's the kind of thing you want to get involved in."

"You have a serious partner?"

"We're engaged."

"Well, honestly, I'm not sure if I'm in a place to do any serious dating myself. My last breakup, with Travis, was hard. And I have a job and a kid to contend with."

She said this quite seriously, but a smile quirked the corner of her mouth.

"So?" Gus said.

"So let's have an entirely unserious date."

"Date?"

"Booty call. Whatever you want to call it. Is that a possibility?"

Gus grinned at her. "Think we can do that."

Chapter 54

To teach self-defense, Pete took Joanie to the big recreation facility on campus, to a mat room lit flatly by fluorescents, with no windows and a yellow-and-blue mat floor. He talked for a while, then showed her some moves.

She found herself more unwilling than expected. She'd learned early the more she fought physically, the more likely she'd be punished—hit, or locked in the closet. Knowing where the reluctance came from didn't make it easier to set aside.

Pete got Joanie to punch a mat he held up. "Harder than that. No, harder."

She socked it again.

"Put your body into it."

She did, with a satisfying thwack.

The rhythm of it took her, him moving, moving, gaze encouraging. "Again. You're doing great." She pounded at the mat, sometimes glancing, sometimes a solid punch. After a bit, she stopped, out of breath.

"It's more work than I thought."

"You're not really releasing yourself. Ideally, it's easy, even a pleasure. It's a problem a lot of women have—they hold themselves back, from long training."

Puabi-Ekur followed filaments of energy, like a current in water, to the cabin with its corner shrine.

They spoke then to Dea, without speaking—Dea, a goddess of birth and death, worshipped in caves from time immemorial. Puabi-Ekur in comparison was an upstart, young in Dea's timeline, once a human themselves.

Puabi-Ekur had been drawn into this timeline through Clayton's need. Here they'd met Joanie, their one-time consort, a priestess of Inanna and also one of the Lady of the Animals—Dea.

Hovering close stood the Horned God, Lord of Animals. Of course working in Dea's cabin would bring forth the god in Pete, susceptible, inclined, and opened by meditation.

The strands like cords connecting the Horned God to Dea made it clear he was her mate.

Taking leave of Dea, Puabi-Ekur stepped back and back and back, to their own space, curling up in a corner of Joanie's basement-apartment ceiling. They needed to be far from Dea to consider things.

What did it mean, that the Horned God was Dea's mate?

Dea hardly planned to ravish Pete, either as herself or as Nora, her priestess. But she might turn her gaze to Joanie.

A flare of jealousy. They shook off the feeling. Puabi-Ekur's connection to Joanie was of a different kind. Stronger connections on all sides would help.

But what should they do with them? Behind everything lurked the memory of Akkad. No one knew now where that city lay. The gate crowned with lapis-blue, long-horned bulls pulling the king's chariot, had fallen to dust, leaving no trace.

Was there a future for the people they loved?

Chapter 55

Their vision fogged, then cleared, to a strip of red sunset that flared over a lava flow, black and rusty brown. The lava lay beside the ocean, a froth of foam at the waves' edge. Last rays scintillated on the water.

Tiny motes of life danced in the sea. At the edge of the lava flow fuzzed a scrub of vegetation, adapted to air dense with carbon dioxide.

Puabi-Ekur floated, sending their consciousness outward, seeking larger beings, animal or human. They sensed a few animals, far away, though it was hard to tell if they were alive. They sensed many human spirits, no humans in the flesh—none at all.

This future held no human life.

With a growl, the nearest volcano belched smoke.

They backed away, out and out, to the corner of Joanie's ceiling, her present day.

That future was no future.

~

In a form-hugging grey houndstooth suit, under a darkened sky, Joanie walked along an empty street. Polished nails shone burgundy-dark; a gun nestled in a holster at the small of her back.

She reached a matte-silver double door in a shining frame, flanked by two guards in anonymous steel-grey uniforms. The doors showed a large corporate logo, built around a stylized T.

"Your badge, ma'am." She showed a badge. She stepped forward, and the guard lifted a tool and scanned her right eye with it.

His gaze moved to her, expectantly.

With a sigh, she fished a bill from her jacket pocket and gave it to him.

He turned to the double doors, made a complex pass with another tool. The gate snicked open, and she entered.

Tapping in high heels through corridors emblazoned with the corporate logo, she found and took an elevator, followed another hall, caught a second elevator, exited. On the higher floors, the corridors went from brushed metal to wood wainscoting, the occasional overstuffed chair by a table. Here the corporate logo was rarer, dots of subtle shine on the paneling.

She came to a massive oak door reinforced with polished steel. On this she knocked.

A guard in the company uniform opened from within, bowing. Another guard stood to the door's other side, two more at the room's far corners, each with a submachine gun and padded armor. She approached a gigantic desk, carven from a single block of red marble, strewn with papers.

An aged man stared at a laptop. Discreetly to one side stood a wheeled IV pole, from which a tube snaked to his arm. As she closed on him, he raised his head.

"Chairman Tremblay."

He shut the laptop.

"Joanie, so good to see you. There's that business we spoke of. But first, come here."

She stepped around to the front of the desk, half-sat on it, hitching up one leg. Puabi-Ekur saw pale stockings from which garter straps rose. She wore no underwear. She breathed in hard and closed her eyes.

Also closing his eyes, the old man shoved four fingers up her pussy.

She gripped the desk. Her knuckles whitened. Her eyelids fluttered in pain. Anger poured through her—anger at herself, for letting this happen, anger at the old man.

Below that an ocean of sorrow. So much had been lost.

Again, Puabi-Ekur backed away fast, washed out on a wave of sorrow.

Neither of these futures were any future, at least not for humans. Far better was the path Puabi-Ekur had been shown before, to Witch Farm.

How could they make sure their people got there?

Chapter 56

In their living room, Gus and Pete sat over some stout. The room lay half-dark, the floor lamp on.

"Julia volunteered she wanted to help Antifa and go undercover with Odin's Hunt. She wanted to talk to someone. I thought maybe you and Dave. Or whoever you think."

"Are you sure about her?"

"I was hoping you could vet her."

"I hope she understands how potentially dangerous it is."

"She does. Also she confirmed what Josh said. They're going to try to catch me and do the same solstice ritual, this time on me."

Pete stared at him, hand on chin.

"If she's the real thing, we could play this a few ways, depending on how you want to go."

Gus raised an inquiring eyebrow.

"Either way, we need to make sure everyone is safe. You and I both have martial arts training. I'm starting to train Joanie, but she's got a ways to go. What about Alyssa?"

"She's not got any experience, and she doesn't have time or interest."

"So the muscle here is you and me."

"Think Hannah's got a shotgun."

"That's not bad for backup, but you don't want to pull that out right away. Especially with Bruni and that lot. I can dig up some other Antifa folks as well. But what do you want to have happen?"

Gus downed a swallow of stout, turning the question in his mind.

"I'd like to see Bruni and Max behind bars."

"I can see that. But I don't see any virtue in adding them to the prison system, where they'll meet other toxic white supremacists and come out more hardened. That said, I would like to see them not hurt you, or Julia, or random Black and trans folks."

"Right."

"What if we trick them into trying to grab you, and give them the fight of their lives?"

Gus shook his head. "Sounds dangerous for everyone involved. If the police show up, chances are Antifa will go to jail."

"True that." Pete took a thoughtful sip. "And as for catching both Max and Bruni, we can hardly guarantee Max will be at solstice."

"No."

"I think you're right—the best position is the sane, defensive one. That means you and Alyssa stay here now through solstice, and I see if there's one or two Antifa folks willing to help protect Hannah's house."

"Also Hannah may have some tricks up her sleeve, people who might help her out."

Chapter 57

annah planned an orphan's Thanksgiving. Joanie and Pete both begged off going home. Joanie was on tense terms with her mom—a few years ago, her mom's boyfriend had come to Thanksgiving drunk and made lewd remarks at her. Pete only went back every few years, generally when he could avoid his father.

Joanie had a lot of scutwork left the Wednesday before Thanksgiving. Gunnar Group took Friday off to give them a four day weekend, so she stayed late.

Against late twilight, drizzle stitched across her window's glass. When she went for some tea, she saw another office had a light on, Monica's.

Monica was still giving her the cold shoulder, but over time had softened—they saw each other every day, and at a base level liked each other.

She leaned in Monica's doorway.

"Can I ask you something?"

Monica looked up, strands of red-blonde bob tucked behind her ears. Her lips set. "If you like."

She'd open up if Joanie took a particular angle. "I think you might have been right about Don's scheme."

Monica inclined her head.

"Okay." She gestured. "Sit."

Joanie took the cobalt-blue-upholstered guest chair.

"You know Don brought me on mainly to work on the Walker Nelson self-insurance scheme. What do you know about Mark Walker?"

Monica stared. "The *Walker Nelson* insurance scheme? Don told me he was planning that instrument, at least to start, for a different company. Are you sure?"

"Absolutely. We've met with them several times. They signed the contract. Maybe he changed his mind?"

"Maybe." Monica looked as if she'd eaten something rotten. "Sure, I'll tell you what I know about Mark Walker. Shut the door, will you?"

Joanie did, and sat back down. Monica gazed at Joanie, her elbows on her desk, hands steepled against her lips.

"You may know this, but Mark's one of the richer men in town. He's a hotelier, he has a background in construction, he has investments in a lot of other businesses across the area."

She looped a stray red-blonde strand behind her ear again.

"What you probably don't know is, Mark's got some big questions in his past, things you won't find on the internet. His first wife died in a boating accident. He was never formally charged, but he was a suspect in her death. Also, till recently, Mark regularly donated to far-right organizations. Someone must have told him the optics were wrong. They've cleaned up his Wikipedia page. Mark's current wife is Austrian; her family's big in the Freedom Party."

Joanie frowned. "I don't know Austrian politics."

"Right-wing, populist, nationalist. At least historically,

Mark's as close to being a neo-Nazi as you can be and do serious business in Seattle. He would call himself conservative."

A globe of light fell around Monica's desk, casting a gleam on her hair and her polished nails. Her eyes were as somber as Joanie had seen them.

"He's the kind of man, you don't get in his way. He plays hardball. There're rumors he's not above mob-style tactics. I'm surprised Don went after him. And, frankly, I'm shocked he drew you in."

"Well, this is what happened." Joanie told the story of her meetings with Mark Walker. "Now I'm wondering what exactly Don told him, or planned for me."

"Whatever Don is planning, it's not pretty. I thought better of Don than this. I guess you're a kind of honey trap."

Their eyes met.

"Mark Walker said himself, he'd rather deal with me for the face on things than with Don. But how much of a honey trap?"

"Mark's always had girlfriends, and while he's gotten older they've stayed the same age. About your age."

Joanie nodded slowly.

"So far I've been able to draw a line with him. I said something to Don, and since then he hasn't sent me to meet him."

They stared at each other.

"That won't last, will it?"

Chapter 58

The middle of a summer night in Akkad, it wasn't the heat that prevented Ekur from sleeping.

He had rolled out of Eannatum's arms. When he looked, Eannatum's eyes were open too, whites blue against the darkness.

"The drought is coming north through the empire, city by city," Ekur said. It was an easy leap; the cities weren't far apart. Some were visible from one another. "My superiors aren't listening."

"They will in the end."

It was hard to tell if Eannatum's tone was threatening or reassuring.

Returning to Witch Farm after the tree-planting and party, they found the irrigation pump had broken again. Everyone there had tried their hand and admitted defeat.

Cleo gave a half-hearted try herself but also gave up.

"Clayton will be back this weekend. If it can be fixed, he'll fix it. In the meantime, we can carry water."

"Great," Joanie groused. "This is totally what my back was asking for."

"Other suggestions?"

"Motion seconded," Joanie said, half-joking.

"Show of hands?" It was unanimous.

They carried water, in a long, hot early-autumn afternoon, among the green leaves of their cornfield. Seattle hadn't had such heat till the last twenty years. Though from what data was showing, even with worldwide greenhouse-gas emissions having fallen steeply, the climate remained hotter than before.

Many species had died, but the die-offs had slowed. But except in a few well-guarded enclaves, human civilization had not recovered the ease and plenty some had once had. Perhaps it never would, since that had been predicated on practices no one could justify now.

"I miss automation and water from central taps," Joanie said, folding to reach fingers to toes to stretch her back. "Not to mention constant access to hot showers without worrying about how the solar is doing."

"We have control over our own well," Cleo said, sitting on the stone wall beside her. "All in all, I think I'm happier now."

"Those were dark days. It was worse, waiting for the blow to fall."

Tracy had been taking two laps to her one. He paused in front of her, and she made room for him on the wall.

He sat. "You never told me the story of the person who loved Celtic music."

Cleo and Joanie eyed one another.

"I will. But it's more of an evening story."

Chapter 59

The following Monday, at work, Joanie went to Don's office first thing.

She had to quit. She could never make terms with a man like Mark Walker. Cleo and Pete had both made it clear they stood behind her.

But Don wasn't in his office. He rarely got in until ten. Grey daylight fell across his blond wood desk; out the window, scaffolding and concrete blocks rose.

Taking deep breaths to calm herself, Joanie went to get coffee and took it to her own office. She deleted email and went through her folders to see if there were any general business articles she wanted to keep. It was hard to concentrate.

After three-quarters of an hour, she saw a flash of blue shirt-sleeve go by. Jumping up, she headed to Don's office.

When she poked her head in, he grinned.

"Joanie! Good morning." He gestured. "Come sit down."

She did, taking the guest chair. His was upholstered in burnt-orange. The high-pitched mosquito whine she associated with his office was back.

"I think I can guess why you're here. I think there's been a misunderstanding. Monica might have characterized our client to you in a way that's a bit unfair. It's true Mr. Walker has a checkered past, but that's behind him now. I wouldn't work with him otherwise."

Joanie recalled Monica saying, "I thought better of Don than this."

"Certain kinds of thing won't fly in Seattle. I think Mr. Walker has realized that."

Joanie frowned. "Monica told me also you planned to do the self-insurance with another company. At least you told her that."

"Things were going fast and furious there for a while. I did start with a couple other options, but we narrowed it down to Walker Nelson. I tried to keep Monica in the loop, but I may have missed copying her on some emails. All sorted out now."

He grinned, teeth shining. Don had excellent teeth.

"Yeah, no, Walker Nelson had a big reorganization about a year ago. Cleaned house." He swung a little in his chair, then stopped. "Jesus, Joanie, did you really think I wanted to do business with Nazis?"

He stood and grabbed his raincoat off the wall-hanger. "As a matter of fact, I was just going to have coffee with Mark Walker. Why don't you come along?"

"Uh—"

"Monica seemed concerned I was trying to set you up in some way. I'm not. You wanted me to keep Walker away from you. I have."

The ice-blue eyes met hers, and she had to look down. Because he had.

"But come on, make nice, he won't bite. Are you really that much of an angel yourself?"

She looked up again. Their gazes connected, and she saw it. He knew about her past.

Buzzing sounded in the air again. For a moment, she couldn't breathe.

"Maybe not this time. But I need you to be able to be in a room with him. He's one of our biggest clients, and he specifically asked to work with you."

If she quit now, Don or Mark, or both, could blacken her name. She didn't want to lose all her chances at a real-world job at one go.

"Are we good?"

At the very least, she needed to gather more information.

She nodded.

"Now, if you'll excuse me—" He edged past her out the door.

After a few mouthfuls of coffee and a few more calming breaths, Joanie went to Monica's office and leaned in the doorway. Monica glanced up, and her mouth set.

"Come in, sit down, close the door."

There were circles indented under Monica's eyes. Joanie wondered fleetingly how her Thanksgiving had gone.

"Don's convinced me I need to walk back some of the things I said about Mark Walker."

"Do you agree with Don?"

Monica folded her arms.

"He told me some things I didn't know. Mark's wife's family has distanced themselves from the Freedom Party of Austria. And, as he may have told you, Walker Nelson cleaned house. Fired a number of folks, including some of Walker's relations."

"Is the change for real?"

"Who knows where Mark's heart is? But the company is treading the straight and narrow, or close. And, as you said, Gunnar Group has signed the contract with them."

Her face was grim.

"You planned to quit this morning, didn't you?"

"I did."

"Well, don't. Or don't just yet. I'm going to make sure Jack takes another look at that contract. If it shades into illegality, that's a reason to break it. In the meantime, you might as well get paid."

Chapter 60

*I*t wasn't like Gus never thought of it.

Sometimes you met someone, and you were instantly infatuated.

Sometimes you met someone, and the first thing you thought was, hey, cool, I like this person. Then it dawns on you they aren't bad-looking, in their way they're hot.

And they're an option, at least, when you thought they might not be. You thought they didn't like guys, and it turned out they did. Or could. Or had sometimes.

And life brings you closer, and you find out, maybe you're devotees of the same god. Or he is a god, your god.

"Going home for Christmas?" Gus asked Pete.

They saw more of each other, with Alyssa staying at Gus's. In return, one of Pete's Antifa friends stayed in her room at Hannah's most nights—it was a benefit for him, since it was close to his early-morning job.

Tonight, Alyssa had a late shift. Pete had brought home porter. Each with a bottle, he and Gus sat at opposite ends of the leatherette couch, along its back between them the purple and gold crocheted blanket.

"Probably not. If I do go home, it's generally for my mother's birthday in spring. How about you?"

"I spent a lot of time at my parents' house last year. I might go for Christmas Eve. Alyssa's mom is having a holiday brunch, so I might stay here. Alyssa wants to introduce me." Alyssa had reconciled with her mother over the last year.

"Joanie wants me to come to the coven solstice. Apparently it'll be more chill than Samhain. What about your date with Julia?"

Gus waved his hand vaguely. "That's a week from now. Don't know what's going to happen. You don't smoke weed, do you?"

"I do sometimes."

"Now?"

"Sure. Open the window, will you? I don't generally smoke inside, but I don't want to go out in the rain."

"Let me do a few things." To smoke with other people, he liked things to be just right. He lit the torchiere and candles, killed the overhead, put on some ambient Pete liked. Then he retrieved one of his tight-corked weed jars and glass pipe and cracked open the window.

Sitting down again, he loaded a bowl and passed it.

"You're from New York?"

"Not the city, or not to begin with—New York State. How about you?"

"Utah."

"Mormon?"

"Yeah."

Their families weren't that different.

"I was the second kid," Gus said. "My sister Liz, she's the eldest. Smart, different. She fought my parents, finally escaped to the East Coast—we're not in touch. My parents weren't religious the same way as yours. They believe in it, but we finally agreed to disagree."

"My dad didn't make the grade as an evangelist. He's a preacher's kid. Almost worse."

Gus waved the pipe. "Want more?"

"Maybe a little."

"Your grandfather tried to exorcise you?"

"Got the council of elders from his church together to do it."

"Never had to deal with anything like that. What happened?"

"I was about to turn sixteen. They did it in the spare room in my grandfather's house. They were all praying for me, and my grandfather was casting holy water over me. I just started laughing. My grandfather thought that was the demon in me. More praying and holy water—who knew how long it would take? So I started howling and shrieking and flailing my arms, then collapsed like I was unconscious. They got what they wanted, and we were done."

"It sounds fucking traumatic."

"Let's say my grandfather and I were never close."

"What happened after that?"

"My grandfather wanted to know if I repented of my sin. I did, though not for the reasons he wanted. I had clearly done the sin with the wrong person."

Guy took a toke, focusing on the pipe. "You mean the guy or the girl?"

"They were both awful people."

"Hate the sinner, love the sin?"

Pete smirked. "Something like that."

Now or never.

Gus slid over on the couch.

Pete put an arm around him, and they kissed.

Liquid, deep, the feel of the stubble on his cheek, the heavy scent of weed. Pete's hand went to his crotch, fumbled for his zipper.

He'd never thought this would happen.

He had to push himself backward.

"Hate to do this, but I told Alyssa I'd talk to her before I had sex with someone new." Especially with her staying there.

Pete blinked.

"I understand."

Chapter 61

$\mathcal{I}$n the first week of December, toward the end of the day, Don sauntered into Joanie's office and half-sat on her desk.

"We give holiday gifts to our biggest partners. This year, Walker Nelson qualifies. I won't ask you to deliver it yourself, but I hope you won't mind coming with me."

She swallowed hard. "Sure."

She'd taken a look at her finances. She needed to play this game a little longer. She was just beginning to climb out of debt —it'd take another eight months to get free.

"Let's walk that by tomorrow, okay?"

The next morning, she stood in front of the bathroom mirror, studying herself.

She needed something holiday, attractive but not too sexy.

Her wardrobe was still scanty, so she'd gone to the roommates for help. They'd come up with a red and white shirtdress, matched with gold jewelry and her usual pumps.

"Try putting your hair in a ponytail. I have a red bow that will match," a roommate said, and fetched it.

"That helps a lot, thanks."

The dress's owner said, "I usually unbutton one more button at the neck." Their eyes met in the mirror. "Of course it's your call."

Neutral blue eyes checked her over when they met to walk to the hotel.

"You look nice." Don hadn't dressed, particularly, just his usual sport coat and chinos.

He handed her the gift, a basket of gourmet nuts and dried fruit. Its red ribbon matched her dress and the bow in her hair.

The day was overcast, no rain but cold, a knife-edged wind darting around corners. The electric buzzing was up again—she wondered if she were getting tinnitus. Maybe she'd just gotten more sensitive to a particular range of sound.

Maybe it was some kind of sign. But she couldn't worry about that now.

In the hotel lobby, they passed the ceiling-high palms in multicolored pots and the Art Deco bathers. Don directed her through the lobby to the hotel restaurant.

His eyes flicked over to her. "You don't mind having lunch with him, do you?"

"It's fine."

It was a seafood place, accented in tones of blue. The host led them toward the booth where Mark Walker sat. She recognized the full shock of grey hair from across the room. Don slid in across from their client as Joanie set the present in front of him.

"Happy holidays," she said, smiling brightly, and sat next to Don.

"Marvelous." Walker took a quick look. "The nuts will go over well at the office. As has the insurance plan. Don, that's really the best holiday gift you could have given me."

"You're very welcome, Mr. Walker."

"Please call me Mark. You too, Joan. I went ahead and ordered oysters. I hope you like oysters?"

This was directed at Joanie. "I do."

A legendary aphrodisiac. Very old-school. She stopped herself from rolling her eyes.

They got three each. Don slurped his, then looked at his phone. "There's a call I need to make." He met Joanie's eyes, his gaze flat. "I need to head back to the office. Please do stay for lunch."

"All right."

You bastard.

She watched him leave.

"I'm happy you could stay," Mark Walker said.

"I can't stay that long, really."

"You needn't, if you don't want to. But I'd like to treat you to lunch. I asked Don to leave us alone so we could talk one-on-one."

She opened her mouth to speak. He put up his hand.

"I owe you an apology. I gather from Don last time we met I offended you. I'm sorry. Eat lunch with me. They have black cod here today; you should try it."

A nonapology at best, but she nodded.

The waiter reappeared, and Mark ordered for both of them,

getting her the cod. "And maybe some chardonnay? Or some Champagne?"

"Club soda is fine." She wanted to quell the party atmosphere.

They traded chit-chat till the waiter set down their plates.

Mark took a few bites. "Very nice. When Don introduced us and said you would be on the account, I was intrigued. I asked some friends of mine to do some background checking on you."

She glanced sideways but kept eating. Behind him, above the seat, was a glass screen in blues and sea-greens, abstract fish.

"I found out a little bit about your friends. Interestingly enough, we're only one degree of separation apart. Do you know Augustus Masterson? He goes by Gus."

She couldn't keep her reaction off her face, so she ducked, riffling at random through her purse. When she looked up, she'd composed herself.

"Sorry, I thought I heard my phone. I don't know him well."

"Gus and I have a few friends in common." He smiled. "Former friends, on my side, for the most part."

He meant Gus's alt-right friends. What did "for the most part" mean? Was it a threat?

"I found out a little bit about you too."

He left a pause. She met his gaze.

"I don't think you and I are very different, Joan. You're trying to change your life, reach for something better. So am I."

Like Don's, Mark's eyes were blue, but his were ocean-colored, grey-blue.

He meant he'd seen her expunged criminal record. Some judge or prosecutor had done him a favor.

"I haven't shared this information generally, and I won't." Though he'd shared it with Don. "I'd like to keep working with you. In fact, I'd like to see more of you. In view of your background, I wondered if we could come to an arrangement."

The buzzing whine returned.

She took a deep breath, and laughed.

"I thought you were trying reach for something better, and so was I?"

He sat back against the leather seat. "You know, it's funny. If I go to a hotel by the airport, make time with a young lady, leave her a tip, technically that's illegal. If I set my girlfriend up in an apartment, give her an allowance, that's not."

She sipped her club soda.

He was making the proposition she'd wondered about herself—a straight-up financial opportunity. Whoring, of the respectable kind. But, though he'd said he wouldn't use it, he had information he could blackmail her with. If she left this job, she wanted to go on her own terms, not because Don or Mark pushed her out. And she wanted to leave cash in hand.

"What did you have in mind?" The first person to make an offer often loses the negotiation.

"I'd like you to meet me for dinner."

"And you a married man."

He laughed. "The classic line is, my wife doesn't understand me. In fact, my wife understands me very well. Just now, she's in Vienna, helping our niece get ready for her wedding."

A ray of sunlight fell across the blue leather seat. "That's nice."

"She doesn't mind if I have an evening out now and then."

She cut her fish.

"I'd consider dinner."

Saying no to him would only make him pressure her more.

"Dinner would be marvelous." He handed her his phone. "Give me your number, and we can get the ball rolling."

She did. "Now, I'm sorry." She patted her napkin to her lips. "I have to leave. I do apologize."

"I look forward to dinner."

Outside, the overcast had broken to streaks of pale blue sky. The air was colder. She welcomed it, coat open, as if the fresh air would cleanse her, till she was so cold she had to wrap up again.

The buzzing hovered in the background, but the further from the hotel she got, the more it dropped away.

She didn't mind sex work. She liked it, even loved it when she was working for Inanna. But she needed to have the upper hand, or at least equality. That was not something Mark Walker would ever give her.

She was angry at Don, too. Though Don was playing the part she'd expected—the anomaly was when he'd stepped between her and Walker.

In the elevator, she ran into Monica. They ducked their heads at each other in acknowledgement. Back in her office, Joanie hung up her coat. A pale ray of sun fell across her blond wood desk.

The classic response to blackmail was to tell the truth about yourself. The person to tell was Monica, her ally.

Leaping up, she went to find her. But Monica had left on another appointment.

Chapter 62

*I*n Akkad, a half-year had passed, and earliest spring had come. The northern crop of winter wheat was meager. Last summer's southern crop of barley had failed.

At last, Akkad acknowledged the drought.

"Send stores south," the king decreed.

The king went to pray to each of the major gods. People whispered he'd offended them. Ekur was pulled into drought relief. He found it a juggling act getting the city-states to share.

One spring night, he came home well after dark, a torch-bearer lighting his way. He dined with Eannatum in the court-yard on barley soup and beer.

The lamp flames wavered in an eddy of breeze. Ekur turned his chair away from the chill, toward Eannatum.

"The king is praying in the Enlil temple, to protect the country from drought and destruction. He's been praying there a week. He takes his meals there."

Eannatum finished his soup and set the bowl aside. "The country people are saying he shouldn't have declared himself a god. That's what Cook says."

"It's a formality, to show his rank and make the city rulers respect him."

"You don't have to defend the king. It's not as if you know him." Eannatum gazed across the courtyard, into the darkness of the passageway. "We've known about this drought nearly a year. You've brought it to the attention of the administration. But everyone is too interested in maintaining their own livelihood, their own personal place. Not listening to what the land has been telling us."

"The gods have their own plans. Sometimes you can't do much about them. Even if you're the king."

Eannatum gave him a sidelong look. "Yes, but what if we'd started a year ago? What if Sharru had listened? What if the king had listened? The gods have been telling us—in the way they talk, in signs and omens. They can't make us pay attention."

Ekur had no answer for him.

"And you, Ekur—what will you do?"

"I'll do my job. Provide relief for the starving, support the farmers."

"Should we move the children north? We can hire a nanny."

It went without saying Irkalla would find her own path.

"Not yet."

A month into an unusually hot spring, they journeyed to Uruk. The week before, storms had brought strong wind. Scant rain had fallen, but the wind stayed, under an overcast sky.

As they traveled south, Eannatum kept his eyes on the sky. He'd spent more time in the country than Ekur had, at his parents' farm.

"Have head-scarves handy," he told their servant. "And coverings for the donkeys."

In a slow day, no farmers out, their road passed through green-brown fields, many fallow. Wind played at the ground, picking up bits of sand, hurrying tiny columns along the ground, tossing plumes. They watched the horizon.

"There," said Eannatum. A line of tan-brown billowed, clouds expanding against a flat grey sky. Sheets of sand traveled below the billows. They and their servant wrapped their heads with cloth and did the same for the donkeys.

"Should we stop?" Ekur asked.

"If we had a building to shelter in, perhaps a good idea. Not otherwise."

"Should we put up our tent?" They'd left before dawn, to make the trip in a half-day and avoid the worst heat, but they'd brought food and camping supplies just in case.

"Not enough of a shelter. We should keep going. Anything we put up will just collect sand. This kind of walking wall of sand generally only lasts a few minutes."

They kept going, slowly. The gritty wind grew stronger, the air tan-colored, full of stinging sand. Ekur's mouth tasted of dust. He kept hold of the border of Eannatum's robe.

After a few minutes, he tugged it. "I'm afraid we'll get lost. We should stop."

A wall loomed into view, the edge of some farmer's building. "There."

Eannatum hollered to the servant, who'd gone ahead. He came back, wading through the thick air. They hunkered against the wall.

"Stay low. It's possible the wind can carry objects—you don't want to get hit."

The sound of wind rushing came, a ripping sound, rattling

and scraping as objects broke and flew. The tan wall of atmosphere hung dense. Ekur could barely see the donkeys, not three feet away. Sand infiltrated everything, his mouth, the creases in his neck, his crotch.

"You wanted to walk through this?"

"I thought it would pass off faster."

New sand dunes hurried by. Against the wall, their legs, the donkeys' legs, sand piled. The servant muttered a prayer to Enlil, god of the wind. Ekur and Eannatum repeated it.

They sat, sand piling around them, in the monotonous howl and scratch of the laden wind, lulled to a half-sleep like a bad dream.

The falling sand waved like a heavy curtain, weighted with scratching beads. The spirit-moan of the restless wind rose, fell, calling for something, in a half-dream of hidden shapes.

Ekur dozed, almost fell over, wakened by his own movement.

Eannatum said, "Listen."

"What?"

"Silence."

He stood. The other two followed.

Gingerly, they uncovered themselves. The servant went to the donkeys to do the same.

Piles of sand lay everywhere, the road and fields covered with layers of dust and sand, tiny tan dunes. A desert landscape, completely different from before.

"The road was about ten feet this way." Eannatum scrabbled in the sand, pushing it away. "The wall was parallel. Here, I think."

Ekur came forward, peering. "Yes."

"We should come to the nearest irrigation canal in a few minutes. When we find a bridge, that should set us straight."

Early sandstorms meant the drought was worsening.

They found Uruk full of factions; men fought in the beer-halls.

Rather than disturb Irkalla's household, they stayed in their old room above the tavern. They brought the children honey-cakes and took them walking in the public gardens, where gazelles with questioning brown eyes would eat out of your hand, soft lips against your palm. At a movement, they would dart away.

Ekur had planned dinner with the children, Irkalla, and Shulgi, who had moved in. They met at twilight in the house's roof garden, as red stained the horizon. Irkalla had new lamps dyed lapis blue; from them hovered a scent of burning sesame oil. The servant passed them early dates.

"Is it true the Gutians are raiding in the north?" Shulgi asked.

That was the rumor, but Ekur only said, "We've seen nothing beyond the usual border skirmishes."

At dinner, Shulgi told hunting stories with self-depre-cating punchlines. Against his will, Ekur found himself liking him. The children clearly did too. Shulgi hugged them goodnight.

He insisted on sending a torch-bearer to walk Ekur and Eannatum home. "The streets aren't as safe as they were, and you're wearing Akkadian clothes."

They followed the bobbing flame through cobbled streets, turn and turn again. At the tavern, raucous with drinkers, he dropped them.

"I'll get some beer, if you like," Eannatum said.

"It couldn't hurt. Some water too, if you don't mind."

In the dark, to the sound of muffled off-tune singing, they climbed into bed, sharing beer out of the beer-pot.

"It's not my city anymore," Ekur said. "Not the same way."

"You've been away a year. It's partly Irkalla changing the house."

"That and the feel of the city. I didn't like how some of the passers-by looked at us. It's as Shulgi said, they don't like the Akkadian clothes. We were tolerant of the Akkadians, before."

One lamp stood lit on the side table, casting deep shadows. Eannatum caught Ekur's eye.

"Maybe the weather will turn; maybe the drought will end. But what if not? What will we do, Ekur?"

Their eyes met.

"I have family in the mountains," Eannatum said. "They have a vineyard. We could take your silver and go there."

"I have to keep my post, darling. I'm keeping hungry people fed."

"You know the rumors are true. The Gutians will attack if they see us weaken. And we are weakening."

"Perhaps I will be called to serve in the army. I must serve my king."

"Perhaps the drought will break."

"Perhaps."

Chapter 63

*A*lyssa had gone to bed. Gus sat up late with his laptop, writing up a last project's notes for one of his classes.

The floor lamp threw shadows. He'd moved his space heater into the living room—Alyssa was under a pair of quilts and an ancient down comforter.

He finished, checked his work over, clicked the button, sent it. It was A or B work. To celebrate, he padded to the refrigerator and got one of his last winter ales.

Just after midnight, Pete came in. He'd been at Dave's. A week ago, uneventfully, the three of them had debriefed Julia. Odin's Hunt rituals were strictly gendered, so she'd learned nothing about what the men planned for solstice. But Pete and Dave had confirmed Gus's instinct she was sincere in wanting to combat Odin's Hunt's racism.

"Want my last winter ale?" Gus asked.

The idea of his hooking up with Pete had made Alyssa nervous—she knew Pete was more important to him than Julia. But they had solid agreements, and Gus made it clear she should speak up if something bothered her, so she'd agreed it was okay.

Pete grabbed it and threw himself down on the couch next to Gus. They drank in silence a minute.

"What's it like, being a god?"

Pete laughed.

"Honestly, I don't remember much of it."

"Tell what you remember."

"You were there, in Nora's cabin. I followed the meditation. Then—it was like lightning in my head. I don't remember anything till I woke up in Nora's guest room."

"Wow." Gus chewed on this a moment, took a sip of his beer. "What did Hannah teach you?"

"Just to make an agreement. I wrote out a list of things I wanted. Then in meditation she called up the god."

"The Horned God?"

"A form of Horned God. My personal one. And he agreed— that part was easy."

"What wasn't easy?"

"I feel him waiting to reappear. And while he was happy to make an agreement, I also feel he's willing to push its boundaries."

Pete stared at his beer bottle a moment, then emptied it.

"I should go to bed. I have to be up early."

Gus watched his black-jeaned ass till the door shut behind him.

Drip and runnel on the windshield, falling to the pavement. Every winter, it seemed, Seattle got more rain than before.

Gus and Julia met at an Italian place in Julia's neighborhood. She looked great, in a fitted dark-red dress reminiscent of her Odin's Hunt wear. They had pasta and a carafe of the house red. He didn't need to be drunk for this, but a little drunk didn't hurt.

She drove to her low-slung half of a duplex in Renton, a line of junipers in front for a hedge. The neighborhood was rangy and flat. Parked in front of the garage sat a bright yellow Big Wheel trike.

Tonight Julia's kid was with her ex-husband.

She turned the key in the lock, opened the door. The door fell open to darkness.

Here hung sorrow—why was he sad?

It was so far from what he had with Alyssa, her sweet submission that instantly got him hard. Or with Max—that had been fire, liquor, madness. It was even far from the hot possibility of Pete.

He let the thoughts go, shook himself out of the mood.

Crossing the room, she lit a lamp, to show a simple room, couch and chairs, a braided throw carpet. On the walls hung a couple mismatched paintings, he guessed by friends, and a framed photograph of her young son, smiling, with a gap in his teeth.

"You want more wine? I have some syrah."

"Sure."

He sat on her couch, cumbered with a crocheted throw, some velvet pillows. These had cat hair on them, with no cat in evidence—hiding, likely.

She set wine cups on coasters on the table in front of them, sat next to him, took a sip. Her breath sounded in the glass.

Turning to him, she kissed him.

Shy, tentative—she'd put herself out there, but this was hard for her. He kissed back, stroking her hair. She needed him to take control, so as a gift he did.

Standing, he took her hand. She gazed at him under her eyebrows.

He stood her up. "Where's your bedroom?"

It was easier once he did that, but still there hung this sorrow.

A ray of light fell from the other room. On one off-white wall, a space showed where something had been taken down, a paler square on the wall.

How long since her ex had left her?

Kissing her, sitting next to her, he undressed her, button by button. He tipped her back onto the bed. Lovely full breasts, a double handful, pink nipples. She liked when he bit them. A gasp, then a moan.

"Can I leave marks?"

A whisper: "Not where you can see with clothes on."

Slipping down, he inched down her panties, licked her, but she pulled him up.

"Let's just fuck."

He let his animal self take over. Maybe that was what she wanted.

Entrance, the feel of her; deeper, he wanted to go deeper. He threw her legs over his shoulders. She whimpered.

"You okay?"

"Keep going!"

After that she was loud. The fire burned out the cold of sorrow.

Afterward she cried. Feeling awkward and young, he took her head on his shoulder.

"What's wrong?"

She just shook her head.

"You're not over him, are you? Your ex?"

"That's not it. I can't explain."

He let her cry, kissing her forehead.

"Honestly, I don't know what it is. Maybe just release."

"If you're sure you're okay."

"I am."

He stayed the night, which they'd agreed on. She'd be driving north in the morning.

She went to sleep, snoring lightly—he'd been with men who snored worse. He wasn't ready to sleep yet. In the living room, he found his glass of wine, stood in his jeans looking out her window into the street. Streetlight illuminated relentless rain.

This had been worth trying, but he didn't think he'd do it again.

The next week, Julia made a date for a drink with Gus after Odin's Hunt's weekly book club meeting. She found him waiting in their agreed-upon dive bar, red-lit by beer signs, one wall a red-vinyl banquette against exposed brick. She had little to tell. Bruni and Jake the gothi had dropped a few jokes about plans to attack "undesirables," nothing about solstice.

Gus saw her home—she drove them both there, then he planned to leave. She lived on a bus-line, so it wasn't too far out of the way. It let them keep talking a bit.

Streetlight cast a sheen across wet pavements as they drove. The light above her door flashed on as they drove up.

"You want to come in?"

"For a little. I have to get home."

She unlocked the door to the dark house, one light on in the kitchen. The cat rubbed around both their ankles. Julia turned on a lamp.

"Want a glass of wine?"

"Half a glass."

He sat on the couch. She brought two glasses and sat next to him.

He studied her. "For real though, are you okay?"

"I'm fine." She raised an eyebrow. "What brought that on? My crying jag the other night? Sometimes I'm just like that. The world's a weird place right now. My friends, or I thought they were my friends anyway, are turning into full-blown Nazis. Not to mention, my picking you up. For me, that's pretty weird too. Not what I planned when I met you."

Something in her confession changed his mood. "What did you plan when you met me?"

"Nothing. I thought you were a prospect for the Hunt."

He slid closer to her, kissing her on the cheek. "You didn't think, what a hot guy this is, I want to have sex with him?"

A ghost of a smile. "Maybe a little."

"A little." He took the glass out of her hand, set it aside, turned her head toward his, and kissed her. "What about now? Is that still on the table?"

She smiled against his mouth. "Sex? Maybe."

"Let me go down on you this time."

"All right."

∿

In the middle of the night, his phone rang. Julia gave a muffled groan.

It was Alyssa. "I have to take this," he told Julia.

He slipped out of her room, went to the kitchen, and in a fall of streetlight poked his phone. "What is it?" he asked Alyssa.

"I thought you'd want to know. Two men broke in at Hannah's house tonight, into our old bedroom, and tried grabbing Joe, who they thought was you."

"Oh shit!"

Alyssa told the story. Joe had jumped out of bed, yelling; Hakim came running downstairs. Faced by two men, neither of them Gus, the attackers vaulted out the window and ran.

"Did they get video?"

"Yes, though the quality wasn't great. Hannah sent a copy. You couldn't really see the one guy. The other one looked like Bruni."

The police had come and gone.

"Hannah told them about the incident earlier in the year. We're supposed to go in tomorrow. They said nothing was sure, but with the video there's a lot more chance we can make a charge stick."

Gus leaned against the sink. "Wow. How are you? How is Hannah and everyone?"

"Hannah's not thrilled to fix the window again. Otherwise she's fine. Joe wasn't hurt, except for some cuts where he stepped on broken glass. I think he felt vindicated. I'm glad I was at your place."

"Me too."

"Maybe with this, and the earlier break-in, and your statement, they can move on Odin's Hunt. I mean, the video's a step forward."

"Yeah. I should check with my lawyer again." He heard Alyssa yawn. "You go back to bed. Sleep tight."

"I figured they might do that," Julia growled, in the morning. "They didn't say a thing to me about it. I wonder if they trust me."

"They could be working on a need-to-know basis." It was a cold, dripping morning, rain intermixed with sleet. Luckily, he had nothing he had to do today, besides study for a last final. Part of him wanted to curl up on Julia's car seat and sleep. "Anyway, I hope the video helps."

She dropped him off on a rainy corner, and he trudged back to his apartment.

He didn't want to, but he had to: he called his lawyer. By a miracle, he caught her.

"Do you want to come in? Or we can just do this as a phone call." He'd get charged either way.

"A phone call's fine."

Gus filled her in.

"I don't have a lot to tell you," she said. "It's great you got video. Every step is one step closer. They'll look at the video, decide to what extent Bruni can be identified, if they think it will stand up charge him with criminal trespass. On its own, it's a misdemeanor. It's plenty for you and your girlfriend to get a restraining order on him, though, which is what I'd recommend at this point."

It was a small win, he understood that, but still a letdown.

"What about the rest?" He'd made a statement last year about the previous solstice, where he'd seen a man die. But after he talked to a detective, nothing had come of it.

"Same as before. Without hard evidence, you're probably going to get nowhere."

It wasn't like he could come up with a body. Max had gotten rid of that—where and how he had no idea, but Max was thorough.

"Okay."

"Sorry I couldn't give you more. Hey, happy holidays. We only talked a few minutes. I won't charge you."

Chapter 64

Gunnar Group was a small shop, and they closed outright the week between Christmas and New Year's. The weeks before Christmas were insane, getting together quarterly reports and finishing out the year's business.

Added to this, Monica was trying to land a big deal. When she was in the office, she had her door closed, an agreed-on sign not to bother her.

Joanie steeled herself to knock several times. The first, Monica shook her head, pointing—she was on the phone. The second, Monica had to leave immediately. After that, she worked from home a few days. Joanie wanted to catch her in person.

Joanie had gotten several texts from Mark Walker asking to make dinner plans, but she put him off. She needed to play for time.

When Pete asked what was happening, she showed him the texts.

They were having an evening in. Pete had made tacos.

Alyssa and Gus were studying in the university library—mostly Alyssa; Gus had finished his coursework and all but one final.

"Do you have to make plans? You don't want to. Can't you get rid of him?"

"I don't *have* to do anything. But I want to keep this job, and for the time being it's kind of predicated on playing nice with Mark Walker."

"I thought you weren't going to do that."

"Monica asked me to wait to see if we could nullify the Walker Nelson contract. It's a real possibility. And my budget said it would take about a year to pay off my loans. That still seems right, and I'm only five months in. I need to play this out as long as I can."

She thought wistfully of her whoring days, where she'd made several hundred dollars a night.

"At least this year I'll be chill about holiday shopping."

"Except for your nieces."

Her half-sister had twin girls. "They're only seven once."

"Time does generally move in one direction."

She threw shredded cheese at him.

Toward the end of its hours, the mat room at the university gym often lay empty, under its flickering fluorescent lights. Joanie was getting the hang of punching and kicking; she enjoyed ground fighting. Learning how to fall woke memories of little-kid gymnastics.

They finished; Joanie threw a hoodie over her workout gear. Getting home, the hill was a nasty climb on foot, so they splurged on a Lyft.

In the dark back seat, she asked Pete, "Do you want to come

to solstice?" Hannah's coven planned to work with Nora's—Nora had gotten the use of a friend's house in the mountains. Cleo might be there, but the three of them shared space easily.

"Do you want me there?"

"Yes, but only if it works for you."

A cold night: water sparkled in the air, somewhere between liquid and ice. At Pete's, she jumped in the shower. After a few minutes, he joined her there.

They were both tired, it had been a long day, but when she soaped him up—the slickness on his lanky body, on his lovely cock, slippery in her hand.

She rinsed him off and took him in her mouth.

He tried to stop her, wanting to pull her up and pin her to the wall, fuck her, but she held him off. She had considerable oral skills and wanted to show them off.

"You don't have to—oh—unh..."

She finished him.

"I don't have to what?"

"Never mind."

At the end of a winter workday, chill rain sketched on the office windows, Joanie knocked on Monica's office door.

Monica waved her in. "I don't have a lot of time, but go ahead."

Joanie sat in the cushiony arms of the cobalt-blue guest chair.

"We've talked about me and Walker Nelson."

"I talked to Jack, but he hasn't reviewed the contract yet. He's got a pile of reports to finish."

"It's not that. It's the honey pot thing."

Monica frowned and tucked a wing of her red-blonde bob behind one ear. "I'm listening."

"My record is clear now, but at one point I was sentenced for prostitution. I got two years' probation, which I did with no problem. But people in the court system can find these things out. I'm pretty sure from hints Mark Walker dropped he knows about it."

Monica sat back in her chair, hands steepled against her lips.

"Go on."

"He's trying to use that information to make me sleep with him. I'm pretty sure Don knows too. At one point, he basically said he knows I'm no angel. Not quite that blunt, but close."

Monica rocked in her chair a moment, then sat forward with a creak.

"To start, you don't have to do anything you don't want to. Obviously."

Joanie nodded.

"I personally think prostitution should be decriminalized. But whatever I think, your record is supposed to be clear."

"Yes. I want to be able to quit without having Mark or Don blacken my name."

"I understand." Monica glanced across her desk, then stood. "I don't want to talk about this here. I'm mostly done for the evening. Let me buy you a glass of wine."

Collecting their coats, they went a few blocks down to a wine bar Monica liked, hiding under her umbrella against the spitting rain. Holiday lights blinked against the grey streetscape; rainwater rushed in the gutters.

At a small table, above a flickering candle, Monica leaned toward Joanie.

"Don't let those guys win. You should get to keep your job

and not get pushed out. I thought better of Don, but at bottom he's got his eye on the money and doesn't care about collateral damage. You're smart, you're personable, and if you want a job in the financial world, you should have it."

"Well, thanks." It was good to know someone at Gunnar Group was on her side.

"My bet is this deal of Don's is illegal. If we keep going with it, it could shut the company down. Jack needs to take it seriously. I will make him read the contract over Christmas. Please stay at least till then."

In the shadowy space dotted with light, a chalkboard list of specials hung on the wall past Monica's shoulder.

She was right. Why let the assholes win?

If the deal turned out illegal, Jack would shut it down, and any leverage Don had would be moot. With Monica as her ally, she could tell Mark goodbye and stay at Gunnar Group or leave as she liked. In the meantime, she could put Mark off.

"Okay, I'll stay. At least for now."

Monica clinked Joanie's glass with her own.

For solstice, they carpooled, the same party as for Samhain: Hannah, Joanie, Pete, Gus, Alyssa. At the last moment, Cleo opted out. She was working on what she hoped was her final thesis draft, and Hannah gave her a pass.

The car climbed up to the mountains, a long slow rise, a dust of white beginning on the firs, then along the verge beside the highway. Close by the road, snow lay dirty grey, but further on pristine. The dense living forest rose on either side, gorges no one but deer visited.

An electronic road-sign said only chains or four-wheel drive

vehicles for the pass. In slush the consistency of mashed potatoes, the car pulled over.

"I can help," Joanie said. "I've done this before."

Hannah let her. "There's such a thing as too many generals
and not enough soldiers. I'm gonna drink my coffee over here."

Joanie finished. "With the chains on, you just need to drive
slow and listen for them coming off."

"Oh, lord," Hannah said. "I can do it."

"You've driven over halfway," Gus said. "Let me take it from
here."

Hannah navigated, finding the route to the log cabin: a turn
up a narrow road covered with packed snow, another long curve
between towering firs, and they were there.

Nora ushered them in. Simple but big, the cabin's central
room had a riverstone fireplace and high ceilings. Its partial
second floor held a bunkroom with bunks and a couple rooms
with queen-size beds.

Nora had reserved one of the second-floor rooms, as had
Hannah; most of the rest would crash in the main room. They
stashed their belongings.

Outside, Joanie and Pete found a wood-fired sauna, narrow
weathered wood, a stove within, an ample amount of split wood
beside it.

"Do you want to try?" Pete asked.

"I'd love to, actually. Then maybe roll in the snow. I've never
done that."

Chapter 65

"et's take a hike around before it gets dark," Alyssa said.

"Sure," Gus said.

Through a clear, blue-skied day, under brilliant sun, a tang of woodsmoke rose from the cabin and sauna. Through a foot of snow, footprints showed a path up to a loop of hiking trail.

"Let's head up there," Alyssa said, pointing to a nearby shoulder of the mountain. They crunched forward in companionable silence.

"How is it," Alyssa ventured, "being out in the mountains here?"

"How do you mean?"

"Last year about this time, Max was busy throwing you off one of these."

Gus shook his head. "It's not like that. I spent a lot of time in the mountains in Utah."

"Okay."

"Think it would be a lot harder if I was wandering around

the woods around Yelm. Though I might feel different if I came to a ledge."

"Especially if you thought you might fall off?"

"Exactly."

Alyssa took his arm, leaning in close.

"That won't happen."

Did he miss Max? He missed the deep release of being taken, being topped.

He missed Max sometimes.

He missed being with a man.

Chapter 66

That first night, Friday night, was a time for everyone to collect. They shared a loose potluck dinner, lentil stew Nora made, plus additions everyone brought; Joanie's was apple cobbler.

Nora's coven hadn't seen Pete since Samhain. He fielded questions. "No, I'm fine, just a concussion. I did some work with Hannah to set boundaries with the god."

"I was worried about you," said the purple-haired nurse, swinging a backpack to the floor. "Nora said you were fine in the end, but still."

"It's real, the stuff we work with, y'all," Hannah said, coming around a corner.

The nurse peered at Pete, wanting to probe further, but Hannah said, "Let's get you situated." She found them a nook.

A few went to bed early; more stayed up, drinking mulled wine by the fire.

"Should we heat up the sauna?" Alyssa asked. The people who hadn't saunaed earlier left Joanie and Pete alone by the fire.

In the silence, burning wood crackled. Along the main log lay a layer of waving flame, nearest to the wood a hovering electric-blue.

"Is it weird, everyone asking about Samhain?" she asked.

"Not really. Samhain was a call to me to take the pagan stuff seriously and see how it connects to my political stuff. I know some leftists think neopagan spirituality has to be fascist, but that's not so."

"We're pretty left-leaning, though not necessarily all. Cleo was our activist, really, before she started spending twenty-four/seven on her thesis."

"You're ready for her to be done with that."

"I am."

"And yet it gave some room for our relationship to grow."

"That's true. Pete—"

He laid a finger across her lips. "You don't have to say it. I get she's more important to you. She's your primary."

She moved his finger. "That wasn't what I was going to say. Actually the opposite." He'd been holding back; it was for her to speak. "She's not more important. All my relationships are different."

He stared at her. The glowing flames lit his face red.

"I love you, Pete. I'm in love with you. I have been for a while, though I've been slow to put it into words."

His mouth dropped a little open. He took a deep breath, and spoke.

"That's not what I thought you were going to say." He picked up her hand, intertwined his fingers with hers. "You have to know—I love you too."

"Yes," she whispered. "I know."

～

Over morning coffee, Joanie cornered Hannah. She found her in the kitchen—small, its linoleum forty years old, but warm.

"Tell me about this ritual, okay? I want Pete to be safe."

"Nothing to worry about. Main part is celebratory, just a hint of magic at the beginning. No deep meditation, just a chill solstice, a chance for everyone to get up in the snow and have some holiday time that's not about toxic families."

"I get it." Setting aside her coffee, she gave Hannah a hug.

Still, a little later, tucked into a corner of a couch with coffee, she interrogated Pete.

"Are you sure you're going to be okay with this?"

"Fairly sure. I've been doing what Hannah suggested, meditating and concentrating on boundaries."

"You have some reservations, I know."

"That's true, but nothing here is designed to call out the god. Which was the whole point of Samhain. I had a whole conversation with Hannah." He took a sip of the coffee. "That's hot!"

"She just made it."

"Yeah. Ow. But so, how can I find out about pagan ritual without doing pagan ritual? I don't want to go out of my head again, but I do feel called."

"I just want to do the right thing by you."

"I know."

In the short afternoon, in the snowfield behind the house, Nora's coven trampled out a ritual space, pounding in a circle of tiki torches around it.

At the end of twilight, they all gathered outside. The weather had gone overcast; the low sky shook out powder. The torches lit the snowfield, golden with blue shadows.

On a wireless stereo, Nora queued the music, classical, with flutes.

From opposing corners, out stepped the traditional battlers of solstice, the Oak and Holly Kings. Both had stag-horn crowns, one twined with silk oak leaves, the other with real holly.

Joanie glanced at Pete. He was rapt. The horns worried her.

Light and delicate, both dancers women: the effect was more like fey princes than grunting, muscular men. In the light flashed swords. As the two dancers wielded them, Joanie realized they were real. It gave bite to the dance, but the dancers handled them with care. The two passed and passed again, weapons shining.

The Holly King was struck down in a throw of red ribbons, no blood.

The Oak King stood over the fallen one, raised the sword aloft.

The gathering cheered.

Joanie put her hand on Pete's shoulder. He was trembling, started at her touch.

"Are you okay?"

"I'm fine. Just cold."

After a pause, the coven gathered by the fire. Hannah, in red with a black cloak, stepped in front to face them for the preritual discussion.

"The first part is about the darkness and the return of light. I'm going to ask everyone to extinguish lights all over the house and turn off your phones. We want as perfect a darkness as possible."

Everyone scurried to do this. They moved the couches to set the altar in the room's center, then raised the circle.

With all dark, Hannah led a brief meditation: thoughts about the darkness and the loss of light. Then they simply sat, in darkness and silence.

With all the lights out, the structure of the house sat black against the midnight-blue overcast beyond.

Joanie let darkness and silence soak into her.

She'd needed this.

Hannah lit one candle. "We will pass the light sunwise, candle to candle. As the light returns, think of one point of returning light for your life in the coming year."

At summer solstice, Joanie had thought about community. At Thanksgiving, she gave thanks for love and community.

Flame on the wick lit the next wick, and the next. The flame came to Joanie.

More love and community.

She passed the light on to Pete. His eyes went wide.

A party came after, a holiday feast with hot drinks. On solstice proper, next week, Hannah's coven would hold a smaller all-night vigil.

After ritual, Pete was quiet.

"How are you?" Joanie finally asked. He was sitting on the couch, half-watching people play a tabletop game. She sat on the couch arm, leaned and stroked her hand over his buzzcut red hair.

"I'm fine."

"What point did you think of, for the coming year?"

He gave her half a grin. "Now that's telling."

She met his eyes and smiled. He had wished for her, in some way; he had wished for their love.

"But you're okay?"

"Mostly. Though I definitely feel the god. Particularly during the fight of the Oak and Holly Kings."

She'd thought so: those horns.

"I feel him waiting."

"You're making me nervous."

"Maybe you should be. So far he's been willing to be kept on a leash."

Puabi-Ekur watched their charges, Gus and Joanie, here in the arms of the mountains. At least here, now, she was free of the metallic-buzzing djinni.

Still, it was frustrating—for all the presence of ritual, she hadn't checked in with Puabi-Ekur. And she was still flirting with danger.

She was their Joanie, their love of loves. Puabi-Ekur could help her, but she had to ask.

Chapter 67

*I*n Akkad, half a season passed, to autumn—harvest time in the irrigated fields of the southern empire, preparation for sowing winter wheat in the north.

That hot night, Ekur once again worked late. It was getting to be usual. Cook would put something over a low fire and go to bed.

He was trying his best to help hold together the overstretched empire. The drought had taken hold, hard. The agricultural tracts, the fish farms, the orchards of the empire were failing, from one end of the land to the other. The people whispered the gods had turned their backs on them.

He walked home among dark buildings, just a few lamps lit, a dusty wind playing in the street. At his gate, he dismissed the torch-bearer and came into the courtyard.

"There's pea soup," Eannatum said, gesturing to the servant to go get it. They no longer tried to get meat, except on special occasions—it was far too expensive for everyday. "I have some beer here."

"Let me sit down a moment."

They sipped beer from the common pot in silence, at the courtyard table. The servant brought the soup, and Ekur ate greedily.

"They don't feed you in your offices?" They worked in separate administrations now; Eannatum had kept his old job when Ekur moved to drought relief.

"I forget to eat."

"I'm sure you heard about the attacks at Eshnunna. The Gutians."

"It was bound to happen. It's the same hit and run raids stepped up a notch. It hurts the farmers worst—it's unsafe to work in the fields."

"You think you'll rejoin the military?"

Ekur shook his head. "No. The best thing I can do for the king and people is stay where I am." He met Eannatum's eyes. "I was a good general, but I'm better at this. I know you want to go north to your family's vineyard. But I need to help as long as I can."

Eannatum stood up, crossed to pet Ekur's long hair. "You know I'll stay at your side till the mountains fall down. But there will be a time to go to my family. There is a time to work for the people, and there is a time to look after yourself."

"There are also things you cannot escape."

"Let's have a little hope, Ekur."

Chapter 68

The Monday after the solstice ritual, Gus went for his last final. Afterward, he had time to kill. He wanted to give Alyssa space to study. He wandered over to her coffee shop, where everyone knew him by sight. Midafternoon, business was light, so he could take his favorite booth in the corner.

In a break between showers, pale sun cast itself across the wooden table. He got his usual drip coffee, poked around on social media.

A chime announced a text from Julia.

<Big news. They picked up Bruni>

<Can I call you?> He wanted the full story.

<Ok>

Bruni had been picked up for criminal trespass, and Odin's Hunt was trying to make bail.

"Everyone's freaking out. No one thought this would happen."

"And they didn't double-check if I was still living at Hannah's."

With Max gone, the brains of their operation had disappeared.

"I'd be careful till after solstice, even so," Julia said. Odin's Hunt was having their ritual the following weekend.

"Are you going?"

"I'm on the fence. It's a long drive. Alice wants me to help run the kitchen. I might do it for her sake."

"If you possibly can, it'd be useful. But don't put yourself in danger."

"We'll see how I feel. Noah likes running around in the woods with the Hunt kids." Noah was eight.

For Christmas, Alyssa and Gus survived brunch at her mother's. Joanie saw her sister and nieces but was able to avoid the rest of her family.

Just after, Julia and Gus met at the coffee shop on Beacon Hill. The Odin's Hunt solstice had been wet and inconclusive, focused on asking the gods for support. With Max gone, the balance in the Hunt had changed. Jake the gothi had stepped forward as one of the leaders.

"Jake has more common sense than either Max or Bruni," Julia commented. "He doesn't want to pick fights. He just wants to honor the gods and do his thing."

"Yeah." Though Jake had never been a fan of Gus's.

"Bruni still wants to murder you, though."

Gus stared at the glassy black surface of his coffee, a far light reflected in it.

"No new news."

"It hasn't gone away either. The men had their own rituals, and I don't know what they talked about. I'd watch your back."

Chapter 69

*a*s the year turned, the Gutians attacked. No more raids, but full-out war. Every possible man was conscripted. The war council begged, and Ekur became a general again.

The ring tightened as the Gutians claimed the empire. The King of Akkad lost vassal cities one by one. The drought continued.

Every day in the countryside near Akkad city, from his battle-car drawn by onagers, Ekur led his dwindling number of men—many limping, with wounds in various stages of healing, cuts and bruises to broken limbs. They carried the badly wounded back to the city. Ekur had come off light so far, the worst a bound-up slash on his arm. Each battle made its own sandstorm, tan with dust. Eannatum now led another company.

In the morning, Ekur rose in his shadowy tent to the yell of attackers, held off by an outer ring of soldiers. Bone-tired, in pain in a dozen ways, he put on his leather armor-cloak covered with metal discs and grabbed his spear.

Pushing out through the tent-flap, he saw incongruous on the ground a lone severed hand. He kicked it away. The mud was part blood, and everything stank—the battle, the same place for weeks, left piles of rotting bodies. Smoke floated on a bitter wind, a haze half of dust.

In the brown shadow of the main tent, he met his captains. The attack had lulled for now. For several days, they'd defended a hillside. It protected arable land, no longer farmed.

They formed a plan; he strode out to find his chariot and charioteer. His man harnessed the onagers to his battle-car. From it, he led a sortie, yelling the war-cry, falling with his men like hawks on the birds of the plain. Reaching the fray, he leapt from the chariot wielding his spear.

He felled men left and right. His soldiers hit and broke the line of Gutian infantry. When his spear shattered, he unsheathed his sword.

Stabbing, wounding, clash of metal on metal, breaking wood. Dust caked his mouth; pain stung from innumerable cuts. He hacked men down to blood spray, red to his elbows. Dead cast-aside bodies piled like pillows, torn pillows that dripped blood. A man before him lay choking; frothy blood spurted out his mouth, from a lung hit—his charioteer.

But they fought off the attackers. The Gutians fell back; his company took a break.

In his tent, no longer draped in red and blue but simple leather, he found water, washed, cleaned out minor wounds, drank beer. Wiping his mouth, he wondered if he could see Eannatum that night.

A cry: another war band came on. He found his second spear, dispensing with his chariot ran to battle.

As he approached, a wind full of dust half-blinded him. Gutians came through it, brown ghosts. Spears poked from the haze.

One scored a hit, an impact to his midriff. The pain was shocking. He fell.

Running feet—some man stepped on him. He managed to roll into a saltbush, grey-green and prickly. The spear wound in his belly oozed blood.

He passed out.

When he woke, it was night, the chilly wind full of smoke. He lay in cold mud. Pain enveloped him, his body one huge aching wound. It overwhelmed him again, a wave of black.

He was being jostled. He lay on a makeshift stretcher, his carriers making quick time to the city.

"He's awake!"

"Don't worry, my lord, we'll get you to the city!"

He wanted to puke, but he was too weak to reach over the side of the stretcher. He passed out again.

When he woke the third time, they were bringing him into the house he shared with Eannatum. Shadows of palm leaves fluttered and disappeared. The air smelled like dust, with a meaty smell of blood. His side was still dripping.

"Bring him in, put him there. In the courtyard. That's fine. He needn't go upstairs. Here, take this silver. No, take it. You've taken good care of him."

They laid Ekur on a pallet Eannatum had set out. Seeing his eyes were open, Eannatum said, "The doctor's on the way."

"What are you doing here?" Didn't Eannatum have his own company to lead?

"You slept through the retreat. What's left of the army is back in Akkad."

He took Ekur's hand—contact, warm. It had been forever since he'd had that.

"I thought we were winning."

"The Gutians came like flocks of birds, huge numbers. They keep coming."

"Siege?"

"Nothing so formal. They can't surround us, with the river. But we're trapped in the city."

Cook and the maidservants hurried up, Cook wringing her hands.

"What can I do, Lord Eannatum?"

"Bring some beer mixed with clean water, half and half. And some broth. He needs to eat; he needs his strength."

When one of the maids returned with the beer-water, Eannatum said, "I'm afraid this is going to hurt. I have poppy juice if you want it."

"No." He caught Eannatum's hand. "I want to stay awake if I can."

Eannatum kissed his knuckles. "It's probably wise."

Ekur hissed and groaned as he wiped the wound. "It's forming pus. I wish we'd found you sooner."

"I was lucky to be found at all."

The shaven-headed physician entered through the passage-way. "Let me see," he said as the maids took his over-shawl. "You've been cleaning the wound, good."

Eannatum stepped aside, and the doctor examined the wound.

"It's not very deep. It is starting to putrefy. We shall finish cleaning him up, then apply a poultice and dressing."

Eannatum finished work at the doctor's direction. The doctor took a mortar and pestle from his bag, with several packets of dried herbs. He ground these as he chanted incantations, applied them, and tied on a loose dressing.

To Eannatum, he said, "I will give you prayers to chant. Take these herbs and reapply the poultice and dressing twice a day till the wound closes. If anything goes wrong, send for me."

Cook brought a bowl of clear broth. Ekur ate as much as he could, then fell asleep.

~

The next days passed in fever and dreams. Vaguely he sensed he lay in the courtyard—they didn't want to move him.

Sun and shadow, nausea and eternal pain. Eannatum, Cook, maidservants were at his side then gone. They fed him broth and changed his dressing, dosed him with poppy juice when he couldn't sleep.

It made the dreams weirder. They took him to a far place, where he watched like a spirit. A cold wind rustled in dark unknown trees. Perhaps it was some border of the underworld.

Chapter 70

*I*n late December, cold wind soughed in cedar and fir, trees of the land that still haunted the city, in clumps on campus or at the edge of a park. Along this street, maples stood, bare-branched, leaves piled in the gutters in brown masses, wet with rain.

The four of them, Joanie, Pete, Alyssa, and Gus, met at Pete and Gus's apartment for a talk during the lull after Christmas. They shared a pickup dinner—Alyssa had grabbed some pizza. Pete had invited Dave and a couple other Antifa to show up later.

"This is good, Bruni getting taken in," Joanie said through a mouthful of mushroom and pepper pizza. "We're winning."

"The next steps are important," Pete said. "Bruni will be out on bail any time now."

"Just hope we fucked up their solstice plans," Gus said.

"And that Hannah never has to clean up window glass like that again," said Alyssa. "I really appreciate what Joe did, staying over."

She took a big bite, dripping cheese.

"Is there anything we could do for him?"

"Living there did put him closer to his job," Pete said. "He might like an invite next time you throw a party."

"I think Hannah would be down for that."

"What do we do about Bruni?" Joanie asked.

"He's now part of the system, right? It's unlikely, even with the background, the case will go to trial."

"Max'll hook him up with the excellent lawyer he always boasted about," Gus said gloomily.

"Yes. But, as your lawyer pointed out, after this you can get a restraining order," Pete said.

"Only helps if he comes back."

"What I would love to do," Joanie said, "is get in the way of their let's-go-beat-up-marginalized-people plans."

"Then we should show up at one of their marches," Pete said. "They still do them, just not on Capitol Hill."

That first morning, back at work, Joanie found entering the office like a dive into cold water. The receptionist had made coffee, and she poured a cup, went to turn on her computer. Though everyone had taken the week between Christmas and New Year's off, she still had a hundred new emails in her inbox.

One was from Don, about the Walker Nelson account. It brought a sense of dread.

She put off opening that one, turned to the routine ones from the IT guy, most of which she could delete.

Toward the end of an early January evening, Gus got a phone call.

Alyssa had gotten an extension on her last paper and needed to finish before classes started again, so he'd returned to his own place. He'd grabbed a beer, found something to stream on Netflix. Pete had an account he shared.

A call came, from Julia's number, which was unusual. He picked up.

She was crying so much it was hard for her to talk.

"I'm calling you because I don't have anyone else to call—I gave so much of my life to them—"

"What's wrong? What happened?"

She blew her nose and collected herself.

"I went to Odin's Hunt book club, like I've been doing. We meet over at Jake's—his wife's part of it, she and I are buddies. We're reading a book about rune magic. Maybe five of us are sitting there when Bruni comes in. He looks at me and says, 'Get out, you traitor.'"

"What?"

"He looked at me and said, 'Get out, you treacherous bitch.' Josh, bless him, stood up and said, 'Bruni, what are you talking about? She's one of the leaders of the women's auxiliary.' And he said, 'Not any more she's not. She's been sleeping with Gus. She betrayed us. Luckily she doesn't know anything important. Get out!' I collected my stuff, and he said, 'You're banished from Odin's Hunt.' So I went."

She burst into tears again.

"I did so much for them. They were my friends. I don't know what to do now."

"I'm sorry. Sounds awful. Would it help if I came over?"

"No, I just—no, I need someone to talk to."

From the couch, he stared out the window, blank and black.

"Wow. We were so careful—how do you think they found out?"

She sniffled. "It might have been me. I said something offhand to one of the women at solstice I was seeing someone new. Maybe someone saw us—I don't know. Or somehow people put two and two together."

"Josh noticed we liked each other."

"Yeah."

He thought of the rock through his window, the attack Joe had been there for.

"Do you feel safe?"

"I think so. I think—I'm not sure all the Hunt is on Bruni's side."

"Call me, immediately, if you don't feel safe, or if something happens."

"Okay."

She hung up. He sat, phone in his lap, staring at it till it went dark.

Chapter 71

The Gutians destroyed the remaining fields and fish farms. But they couldn't keep Akkadians from drawing water from the river, and some caught fish. Gardens sprang up across Akkad city. From rescued chickens and dairy cows, city people could sometimes buy eggs or cheese. Ekur's cook gave silver for a nest of chicks, so they had their own eggs.

Everyone became farmers. But the river shrank and shrank. The poor begged in the streets. The poorest starved, and the city guards carried them out from the gates in the hours before dawn.

Ekur woke one morning early, the zenith blue and clear. Translucent yellow light poured through the courtyard, flat gold on the leaves of the potted palms, turning the red geraniums to flame.

The pain in his side had receded. Tentatively, he sat up, a little dizzy.

Hearing movement, a maidservant ran in.

"Oh, my, Lord Ekur." She turned and called out, in a ringing voice, "He's awake—Lord Ekur's awake!"

Cook came hurrying in, from the shadowy hallway to the kitchen.

"Oh, I'm so happy to see you sitting up, my lord. Maybe we can get you to your proper bedroom now."

"Where's Eannatum? He can help me upstairs."

"My lord, I don't know." She wrung her hands. "He went to pick up oil and grain yesterday, but he hasn't come back. Now, me and the girls, we can get you up there, get you some nice broth."

He accepted their help. The stairs were almost unmanageable. He rested between each step. A few years ago he'd climbed mountains, east in the Zagros range.

No word came of Eannatum. Ekur held onto hope. Eannatum was a soldier; he'd killed men with spear and sword. But anyone could fall if set upon.

He spent much of the next week in bed. His old supervisor sent asking for help; there was still need to organize relief. But when he tried to do something simple, carrying water for the garden, he got dizzy and collapsed.

The doctor stopped by, looking thin and harried, his beard and pate not well-shaven. His paying patients were the upper classes, but he saw townsfolk in need. "You're healing well. Do not push too hard. You'll only undermine the healing."

"Can I get back to work?" If he couldn't work in administration, maybe he could in the garden.

"Next week, perhaps. Save your strength. You don't want to relapse."

"I've been saying the prayers," Cook put in.

"Those will help. Also, not too much poppy juice."

"Don't worry, I stopped that," Ekur said.

Toward the end of the week, he began his routine again—rising before dawn, splashing his face in lukewarm water, putting on coriander scent, dropping over his head his long administrator's robe.

In a corner of his room, he had a small shrine to Inanna, with a statue he'd brought from Uruk, an image cut of alabaster and painted in bright colors. There each morning he gave beer, praying for Eannatum's return. Still no word had come.

It was hard not to approach these days with a feeling of doom—encircled by the Gutians, the city broken by drought and famine, the dead carried out daily, no one to burn or bury them.

The first morning he returned to the palace, Cook also rose early, in lamplight in the cool-tiled kitchen made him barley porridge and set out weak beer. Water on its own might not be drinkable. He found his wool cloak, wrapped it around him, opened the door to the morning streets.

The stench hit him. Despite being a seasoned soldier, he gagged.

Strewn over the doorstep, in the dust of the street, were body parts.

Here lay a femur, cracked and gnawed. A jawbone. Blood pooled everywhere, painting the step and the doorjamb.

Recognizably human, the wet, broken bones stank of rot.

"My gods," he said. "Get water!"

Cook ran forward, dragging a just-wakened maid. On the doorstep, the girl pulled out of her grasp, moaning.

"What in the gods' name?!" Cook yelped.

"The dogs must have found an unburied body," Ekur said.

A couple of street-dogs lurked at the corner.

Ekur leaped out the door. "Out! Out!"

The dogs ran, still scared of men at that point.

A croaking noise made Ekur pause, hand on the door latch.

"Don't close the door."

Around the corner lay a dirt-paved alley. The voice came from there. Hand to his knife, Ekur approached. Cook and the maids peered out the house door, watching.

Where the shadows fell, a dirty hunched-up figure sat huddled in rags.

"My gods—Eannatum."

Eannatum began to cry.

A scarecrow, gone to skin and bones—he must have lost fifteen pounds. With the help of Cook and the maidservants, Ekur got him inside. "Bring back the pallet," Ekur ordered. They laid Eannatum on it and carried him in.

"Are you hurt?"

"My head got hit. But more I'm starving. Also thirsty." One of the girls ran to get beer and pea soup.

"You need a bath," Cook said. It was true—he stank.

He wolfed his soup, got another bowl. "No more than that," Cook said, afraid he'd hurt himself. He drank the beer more slowly, then lay back upon the pallet. Cook and the maids set up the bath in the courtyard, since he clearly couldn't get upstairs.

The servants left them. Touching him, kissing him, Ekur sat beside the bath to help Eannatum wash, shampooing his lover's long hair. "I was afraid."

The water was already black. He tried to run a comb through his tangles.

"We might have to cut your hair. What happened?"

"A little more beer."

Ekur handed him the small jug.

After a few sips, Eannatum said, "I took silver to buy grain and oil. I knew if I walked around the city I could find better prices. I dressed simply, but down by the river thieves jumped me. They knocked me out cold."

Ekur touched a large lump on his head, bisected by a cut. "Here?"

"Ow. Yes. I was out for a long time. When I woke, I was outside the city. The city watch had brought me out with the dead. I woke up in a pile of bodies."

"My gods." Ekur imagined the dusty wasteland outside the walls, bodies swarming with flies, the stench and blood.

"I crawled away and found brush to hide in. I was close enough to get water from the river. Then I had to get back in the city. I decided to join some people bringing in water." First thing in the morning, armed men from the royal household protected water carriers as they filled jars at the river. Other households' people joined them.

"But it's been two weeks!"

"I was pretty confused at first. I'd had a bad blow to the head. I kept passing out. When I woke up, I was dazed."

"We'll have to get the doctor to check you over."

"Yes. And I had nothing to eat. In a way, I was racing time."

Dropping the comb, Ekur threw his arms around him. "Darling."

"I'm getting you all wet."

Ekur left Eannatum asleep. Outside, the maids had cleaned, and blood and body parts were gone.

As Ekur walked to work, he considered the omen.

His partner had returned from the dead, but in exchange, a

dead man had been laid on his doorstep.

Maybe it was time to leave Akkad.

Being human, he hung on.

Rumors—that the palace denied—held the king was ill.

"He is, isn't he?" Eannatum asked one night at dinner. They had turnips, boiled eggs, and cress salad, all from their court-yard. Eannatum enjoyed working the garden.

They both went to their palace posts, but there was less and less to do. They no longer were paid.

It had been months since Ekur had seen his children. Part of him expected never to see them again. Part of him still had hope.

Tonight, they sat to one side of the courtyard, a lamp throwing shadows—only one, to save oil. The night wind whispered, lifting and dropping dust.

Perhaps Enlil, king of the wind, had been offended. Or perhaps the gods had gotten bored, decided to put away these playthings and try the mountain-people, the Gutians. Court propaganda said they looked like monkeys, but Ekur—who'd seen them across a line of spears—hadn't noticed that.

"Yes, the king is ill."

Even before this rumor, he'd been in seclusion for months, spending days in prayer at different temples. He seemed to have given up on war. But someone had to drive the Gutians back. Then the people of Akkad city could rebuild the great farms, or at least deal with drought and famine.

Even with the countryside so dangerous, Ekur considered Eannatum's plan—to go north to his family's vineyards, far up in the hills, where his cousins made a small army. Their secret was they'd intermarried with Gutians. Most of the time, this side of the family was regarded as a disgrace, but now it might be a gods-send.

The king died, and the palace shut down. For a month, courtiers performed the ritual lamentations, days of fasting as all the women wailed and tore their hair. The main burial rituals took seven days. In the great royal tomb of his fathers, the king's space was fitted with gold and silver, weapons, wares, food. Wives and attendants went with him, ritually killed—though with all the disorder, certain servants marked for death disappeared.

Then the first claimant declared himself king.

In later years, people asked Ekur: What was it like, the fall of Akkad?

They expected him to tell it as a story, and he did. But until you turned that corner, you didn't realize your city would fall. You didn't see beforehand the gate three stories tall, its crown still lapis-blue, topped with long-horned bulls and a crowned king, with its bronze-nailed doors fallen open in the dirt.

You didn't see that last sight, till you did.

"If we wait much longer, we'll have spent all the silver," Eannatum said.

It took something resembling an argument to force the decision, because even now Ekur was loath to leave Akkad. It had become his city. He had given his life to its people.

But now there was no more need for their services in the administration.

"Leaving is better than dying here," Eannatum said.

Cook and the maids were distraught, but they saw the need. If the Gutians overran the city, it was unlikely they'd be killed, but high-ranking men would be. Ekur left them with silver. They also kept the chickens and garden. They might be more lucky than he and Eannatum.

He had no way to contact Irkalla. He knew she'd fall on her feet. He had to trust her to protect the children.

The guards almost never left the city now. Prisoners manned the gates. Wild dogs roamed the streets at night. A pack could kill two men together.

To leave the city was not forbidden—it was only near-certain death.

Eannatum spoke a little Gutian. He had taught Ekur some —"Hello," "Thank you," "Our cousins live in the Zagros mountains." They would go with only what they could carry—the donkeys had long ago become meat.

In the darkness before dawn, they dressed themselves in mountain clothes, overlaid with cloaks the color of dust. They had silver sewn into their kilts. Their packs held flatbread with a little last dried meat and fruit; they had knives in their boots.

Cook fed them a last meal, barley gruel.

"Goodbye, my lords," she said, crying, hugging them both, and gave them a packet of honey-cakes—she must have been hoarding the honey.

Outside, a dust storm the previous afternoon had left tiny orange-tan dunes piled everywhere. But the sky was clear translucent blue. A good day to start a long walk.

Chapter 72

ou wanted to face down the neo-Nazis. Here's your march." Cleo sent Joanie the link on her phone.

They'd met for lunch near Joanie's work, at an Indian place. Pale sun fell across white tablecloths topped with glass, winking from the edge of condiment bowls. Cleo had at last finished a final draft of her thesis, including bibliography, and handed it off.

A coalition of Black Lives Matter groups planned a march for Martin Luther King Day, led by a group of Black feminists, some of whom Cleo knew from her department. There would be a Blue Lives Matter counter-march in support of the police —likely by the neo-Nazis.

"I'll go," Joanie said. "It's important. But I know Pete and Gus want to face down Odin's Hunt in particular. For them it's personal." She didn't trust them to avoid violence.

"The counter-march is being arranged by the Washington State Patriots, the same group that did that summer protest. I'm guessing Odin's Hunt will be there. Especially since they like to beat up Black people."

Joanie had ordered samosas, but they felt heavy for her current stomach. She pushed one with her fork, so it skated on her plate.

"I'm afraid for those guys," she said. "Particularly Pete."

Cleo cocked her head. She looked radiant, having gotten enough sleep for more than a week. She wore a green and yellow headscarf whose colors made her skin glow.

"Why Pete? It's Gus they're gunning for."

"Pete has gotten so—I don't know. I told you about Samhain. I see the god in him, like a stag."

Cleo snagged one of her samosas. "Doesn't sound so bad."

"A stag who wants to fight."

Don called Joanie into his office. "Come in, shut the door."

She took the burnt-orange guest chair, glanced through the window at grey city under rain.

She'd gotten the paraplanner title because she was supposed to run the Walker Nelson account day to day. She'd taken the numbers side, but whether she'd pick up the client-facing business had been hanging fire since before the holidays.

So far, she'd put dinner with Mark Walker off. She hadn't caught Monica yet to ask whether Jack had reviewed the contract.

"I'm going to keep this short. All jobs, even good jobs, come with parts you don't like. They call it work for a reason."

"I know."

"I need to give last quarter's results to Walker Nelson. Mark Walker wants to talk over them at lunch. He asked me to bring you. I will probably leave early, like I did before."

She nodded.

"He says he asked you to socialize with him."

"He asked me to dinner."

"The company would really like to keep this account. Going to dinner is not out of bounds, with a good client. Has he been inappropriate with you?"

Yes, but not how Don meant.

In a few days, the whole thing might go away.

"No."

Was dinner such a high price?

"I'll go," she said.

Let's have this deal blow up.

She'd been spending nights with Cleo, but Cleo's advisor had asked her over for dinner. "It's basically an evening meeting, with food—we're going to talk shop. Besides, that boy probably wants to see you."

The Seattle winter got dark at four-thirty. Facing wind-carried drizzle, Joanie sloshed across the University District. Rain splashed from gutters as cars passed.

Pete buzzed her in, met her with a hug. She loved Cleo, loved sex with her, but this had something different. With Pete, she was still falling. Beautiful and frightening.

He'd made soup from mushroom broth with added veggies. "I just have stout, no wine. Sorry."

"No problem." They ate then snuggled, listening to some new music he'd gotten—new old music, sessions from a classic Irish band from the nineteen-fifties.

She put off telling him about work, because she knew what he was going to say, which was just what Cleo had said.

"Joanie. You know you don't need to stay there."

"I've been there less than half a year. I want to be out of debt. Or at least more out of debt. Monica thinks she can stop the deal."

"Sure. But if not—this guy's an old dog, the worst kind of capitalist. He threatened to blackmail you. He's used to getting what he wants, and he's not going to back down. You don't trust him, and you shouldn't."

"You're right, I don't."

If the deal stuck, she had to go. She took a big mouthful of stout, sighing into her glass.

"I wanted to try regular employment in my field. All I've done is meet the exact person who could dig up the skeletons in my closet."

"I feel you on that one. I've had to come out to people when I really didn't want to. Luckily, in leftist academia, a lot of people don't care."

"Monica doesn't care, but she's not the only person at the shop. Still, I think she could protect me."

"If the deal blows up."

"Anyway, I want at least another month, two if I can. I really need more savings. Maybe you don't know what it's like to grow up with money uncertain all the time, but I do." And it wasn't just money, but the world's whole future—having cash in hand was bound to help.

Pete wrapped his arms around her. "Okay. I hear you."

"It's my decision, Pete."

"It is."

❧

The next day, at lunchtime, Joanie and Don walked across downtown. Sunbreaks alternated with white-and-grey clouds, a brief spatter of rain. She tightened her raincoat against the wet wind.

They paused at a light. She hadn't heard the electronic buzzing for a month—maybe something like it, in Don's office —but now it came back, high-pitched, like the sound of a thousand manic flies.

Glancing to one side, she saw in the shadow of a building a man hunkered with a backpack. At first glance, he could have been a visitor.

Not when you caught his gaze. His eyes were sea-blue, almost the same color as Don's. Or Mark's. But this man's eyes were bottomless and lost.

Had she seen this man the first time they walked to a Walker Nelson meeting? An omen, if she needed one—a victim of heedless capitalism. Pete had been homeless a while.

The stoplight changed. She had to keep up with Don.

Entering the hotel, they passed the ceiling-high palms, the painted bathers. In the second-floor meeting room, with its neutral beige walls and grey table, they found the financial manager and Mark Walker.

Mark stood, shook Don's hand, then smiling, shook Joanie's.

Don caught him up. "I have entire confidence. The setup's a little unusual, but this approach has been used successfully by a number of other companies."

Mark and his financial manager looked through the papers, called out a few points. Then Mark stood.

"Don, Joan, won't you join me for lunch?" he asked. The financial manager begged off.

"Maybe an appetizer," Don said. "Joanie, you'll accompany us, right?"

They went back to the hotel's seafood place, found a booth, dark teal leather. A ray of sun cast fish shapes from the glass screen behind their booth. Joanie sat by Don, across from Mark.

"Care to split an appetizer?" Mark asked. He ordered fried calamari for the table. Joanie ordered shrimp cocktail.

The food came quickly, which was good; it was an effort to maintain conversation. Don, if possible, was more neutral than ever. He finished his tea; he'd refused lunch.

"Sorry to leave," he said, smiling. "I love good seafood."

"Another time." Then Mark and Joanie were alone.

Mark made small talk. He'd gone to Austria for his niece's wedding. "They're serious about Christmas there."

Finishing his fish, he took a sip of water.

"Well, Joanie? You know I'd still like to see you."

Hanging in the air, as if he'd said it: He'd been patient, and now he wanted dinner, or dinner plus.

She met his sea-blue eyes.

Dinner plus had always been off the table—he'd only push her around.

Between now and the time she set dinner, she needed to talk to Monica and find out what was going on.

If Gunnar Group kept the contract, she'd leave. If Gunnar Group ended the contract, she had no reason to see Mark. Either way, no dinner.

She took her phone out.

"When's good?" she asked.

She set a date a couple weeks out, ample time to catch Monica.

Cleo and Joanie lay in Cleo's bedroom, entangled among her pillows: spangled for show, silk and cotton for snuggling.

"I'm glad you're getting some kind of closure with all this. I'm glad too your boy Pete agrees with me. I know you want more money, but you really don't have to stay at this particular sorry-ass job."

Joanie stared at the tented sari above her, orange and purple, glittering with golden threads.

"It's kind of frustrating, though. My life work is for Inanna. I *am* a whore, a sacred whore. I was thinking about calling some old clients before I got this job."

"You have an agreement worked out with your old clients. This guy's low-key blackmailing you. Not good client material."

"True."

"See how this contract thing goes, but honestly, I think you're better out of there. Monica's the only decent human being you've met there, to hear you talk about it."

Joanie sighed. "It's true. Really I just need to quit, take back the barista job, and get moving with the Inanna shrines. I had a list of people to help drawn up before I started work, and then I just sat on it. I can get my accounting degree later."

Cleo petted her hair. "I think you're right. Compared to a lot of us—compared to *me*—you have hardly any student debt."

"That's true."

"If the shrines are your true path in life, I feel like the doors will open, you know?" She patted Joanie's ass. "Sure, shake your money maker. But do it the way you want."

Chapter 73

School started, Gus's second-to-last quarter at the university, though he was considering pushing some classes into summer. Cold rain, short days, early nights. Alyssa had moved back to Hannah's, and he spent most nights there, but not every night.

One night, he was almost asleep when his phone rang. Bleary, he sat up, checked the number calling.

Julia.

He'd gotten a few texts from her since they'd last spoken. Odin's Hunt had showered her with online abuse, with alt-right trolls in the mix. "Die you ugly cunt" was average. She'd suspended her social media. She'd fielded dozens of nasty emails, name-calling and death threats.

He'd offered support, but she mostly wanted reassurance.

Now he answered. "What's up?"

"Okay, I'm getting scared. Last week, I told you they left a nasty note in my mailbox. Just now, someone drove by the house and shot a gun in the air. By the time I got up, they were driving off. I didn't recognize the car."

Gus heaved a sigh.

"They're escalating. I'm a woman alone, with a kid."

"Does your ex know what's going on?"

"He does. He thinks I'm stupid to get mixed up with you and get caught."

"I think you should get out of there, go somewhere they don't know where to track you. Sooner rather than later. Is Noah with you?"

"He's at his dad's."

"I think they've probably shot their wad tonight, but I would get out. You can camp here if you like." He'd kept Pete apprised of the situation, and Pete would approve.

"Come over tonight?"

"Sure, if you want to."

"I just don't know. What I want to do is get in bed and pull the covers over my head."

"I understand, but you want to stay ahead of these guys. They're already sending death threats and shooting off guns. You know what happened to me. I'd get out if I could."

"I get it. I don't think I want to come tonight. I need to plan a little. God, I never expected this."

None of us thinks it will happen to us, until it does.

"What are you going to do tonight to make sure you stay safe?"

"I'm decent friends with my neighbor. If I asked her, she or her husband could come over tonight. Or I could stay there."

"Please do that. And then, please think about moving. You really are welcome to stay here while you figure things out."

Chapter 74

 he day of the march dawned with a cold drizzle. Joanie woke up yawning, snuggled against her girlfriend's back.

She padded downstairs to make coffee. After she brought Cleo some, she showered and found warm clothes, leggings under jeans and a black sweatshirt. She filled the small cloth backpack she had for protests: water bottle, ID, bus pass, forty dollars in bills, a quart of milk to counter the effects of tear gas or pepper spray.

She had a sense of hovering doom, but she had that all the time now.

She'd taken the day off work, a paid vacation day. She wouldn't miss the job when she left, but she'd miss paid vacation.

Back upstairs, she found Cleo dressed. The group of them were going to meet at the coffee shop and bus downtown together. The rally didn't start till one p.m.

"Let me take you to breakfast," Joanie said. She'd be back to broke soon enough.

At their favorite diner, they found an old-style red-Formica-topped table, slurped up bottomless coffee and scrambled eggs. But breakfast didn't cheer Joanie up.

When they got to the coffee shop, Pete was a jolt of energy.

Glowing in a white t-shirt with a black anarchist A, he wore a black hoodie, his black bandana now down around his neck. His close-trimmed hair shone red as if on fire.

Joanie squeezed Cleo's hand, then crossed to the booth where he sat with Gus and Alyssa. Standing, he embraced her.

An arc of energy burst into her, a shock, not a surface one, one that went to her bones.

It's the god in him.

"Are you okay?" she whispered, close to his ear.

"I'm fine."

"Are you Pete?"

He pulled back, raising an eyebrow.

"As much as ever, nowadays, I think."

This wasn't a good answer, but it also wasn't the time to talk about it.

Westlake Park lay at the heart of downtown, a triangular corner paved in red brick and concrete. They were early. People were collecting. A small number of police stood around the periphery, nothing like the proportion at the July march. A mixed group of people propped up a sign: "Black Lives Matter. Hold Police Accountable. End Racism. Economic Justice."

A couple of guys maneuvered a podium into place, and a woman in a Black Lives Matter t-shirt set up a microphone. Feedback squealed. She warmed the crowd up: "Are you ready to shout? Let me hear you!"

"We care—we're aware!"

"White silence is violence!"

The park was beginning to fill—fifty or more people there for Black Lives Matter. The first speaker, a Black woman minister who'd helped put together the protest, was followed by a second, a socialist. As she began, Pete grabbed Joanie's arm and gestured with his chin.

Bruni stood a half-block away, broad-shouldered in an Odin's Hunt t-shirt. By him gathered a few other Odin's Hunt followers. Some milling near them had protested in July: a bulked-up white man with a chestnut beard, a dark-skinned guy with wraparound sunglasses. One held a homemade "Blue Lives Matter" sign. Maybe ten people stood in their group.

A couple shouted, interrupting the speaker: "No communism in Seattle!" "Blue lives matter!"

Stepping up, the black t-shirt woman turned up the mic. After a moment, the speaker continued.

The speeches finished. The first woman yelled to the crowd: "Are you ready to march?" A drizzle started, and Joanie pulled up her hood. The crowd at last moved.

"I want to get up front," Cleo said. "My girl Kiara is up there, and I want to say hi." Kiara worked at a nonprofit that supported Black Lives Matter and environmental groups. Cleo might apply there after she got her master's.

Joanie scrunched up her face. "You go on ahead."

Cleo eyed her sideways. "Okay." Cleo wanted Joanie to come too, be introduced as her girlfriend, but Joanie was getting wet and suddenly was in no mood. Her hovering unease had intensified.

Pete took her elbow, and Alyssa and Gus hung back too.

"Are you okay?"

"Not in the mood for this."

"We can peel off now if you want."

"It's just a mood."

He gave her a quick kiss on the cheek. "We'll be done soon." He still hummed with energy.

The route wasn't long, eight blocks to the Federal Courthouse. The march strung out along the street, maybe a hundred people now.

Chants began, raised, ended, in waves. "We care, we're aware!"

"When Black lives are under attack, what do we do? Stand up, fight back!"

"Blue lives matter!" popped up but was drowned out.

They circled the courthouse, whose red-brick steps gave onto a pavement, to either side green front yard. People gathered; a few sat on the steps. Some still chanted: "Stand up, fight back!" The group thinned. The police had disappeared.

Joanie had lost sight of her girlfriend. "I want to wait for Cleo."

"We can do that," Pete said. Joanie texted Cleo they were in front of the courthouse.

Gus said, "I don't see Bruni and them anymore."

He and Pete traded a glance. They'd expected some kind of menace from Odin's Hunt. Maybe given the large turnout, the Hunt had turned tail.

Cleo texted back: <Kiara wants to show off her web project. Meet you at home.>

Fleetingly, Joanie was jealous. She let it go.

"No need to wait for Cleo."

"Let's walk across and catch a bus to the U District," Pete said.

After a couple blocks, Joanie stopped him. "Give me a

second." Her sneaker was untied. She leaned up against a light pole. Pete stood beside her, almost vibrating.

"This way's faster." Alyssa and Gus went ahead, aiming for an alley across the street.

Gus shouted, "Hey!"

Alyssa screamed.

An unfamiliar voice yelled, "We got him!"

In a narrow alley, between concrete walls, Bruni and the red-bearded guy had Gus down. They were kicking him.

Pete was ahead, running. Leaping in, he almost flew.

Joanie ran after, scouting the alley sides for potential weapons. From a dumpster, a cardboard tube jutted out. She grabbed it, tugged. It was stuck.

Alyssa shrieked. Joanie turned.

Light blazing from him, golden-red, Pete picked up the chestnut-bearded guy and threw him.

That isn't possible.

He landed, skidding to a stop against the wall.

Pete spun to face Bruni. His punch to Bruni's chin landed so hard Bruni flew three feet.

Gus scrambled up. "We gotta go."

Taking a running step, Pete picked Bruni up by his shirt, punched him again.

Dropping the tube, Joanie ran forward. "Pete, no!"

Bruni was down. Pete was on him, punching him in the face.

Joanie threw herself forward and grabbed Pete's shoulder. "Pete, stop, you'll kill him."

He turned toward her, mouth and eyes wide open, as if to scream.

Seeing her, something in him focused.

"We have to go," she said.

He stood, shaking his head as if shaking something off.

Below him, Bruni lay, face a mass of blood, moaning.

"Let's go," Gus said behind them.

"Yes." She took Pete's arm. "Come with us. Walk fast, don't run."

Blood had splashed across his white t-shirt.

"Zip your hoodie."

Alyssa wiped Gus's face with her sleeve. He had a cut above one eye. In her bag, Joanie found tissues, handed him one.

"Keep pressure on it."

At the bus stop, luckily they didn't have long to wait. They got on, found seats.

Pete hadn't said a word since they left the alley.

"You okay?"

"What?" He shook his head again, as if to clear it. "I guess."

She saw the shimmer of the god.

Chapter 75

he bus wobbled and groaned, making its way to the
U District.

"That was over the top," Alyssa said.

"Sorry," Gus said.

"It wasn't you." Raising her voice, Alyssa said, "How if Gus
and I go back to my place tonight? I think we need an evening
off people." She glared at Pete.

Joanie glanced over.

Alyssa hadn't seen what she'd seen, the golden-red light.

Best to leave it for now.

They split up. She walked Pete home from the bus stop. The
rain had cleared; a pale spot in the sky showed the sun. Pete still
looked dazed.

At the apartment, he fumbled with the key. Taking it, she
opened the door and led him upstairs.

"I'm worried about you. Let's get you cleaned up. Take a
shower with me." He had some surface cuts, and they both were
sweaty, their hair dank.

In the white tile bathroom, she pulled aside the shower

curtain, started the water, hot. They dropped their clothes and climbed in.

The shower woke him. Again he shook his head as if to clear it, and rolled his shoulders.

"Oh, Joanie," he whispered, "where would I be without you?"

She laughed. "Less clean."

He put her hand on his cock. At her touch, he hardened.

"Let's dry off," she said.

Dried, she took his hand and drew him into the bedroom, thinking vaguely sex might be healing.

She lit the candles, lay down with him on the bed, holding him in her arms.

His shoulders heaved, and he gave a sob.

"What is it? Pete?"

She drew back to look at his face, but he shook his head. She let him cry, holding him.

After a bit, he grew hard against her leg.

Without words, she opened her legs, rolling on her back, and he thrust himself inside her.

She sat up, cross-legged in his lap, scissor-fashion, rocking. Almost she saw horns rising from his head. A rutting stag, her love, her lover.

Gently rocking, she became the goddess, with her own glowing powers: tamer of wild men, not to control them but to give self-control.

"My love, my love." He bit her, hard, on the shoulder, but it was like massage. They rocked, holding each other.

The room filled with a golden glow, orgasm like an avalanche of light.

∾

Midevening, Joanie woke with a start.

Pete lay beside her, still asleep, breathing heavily, just short of a snore.

She realized what had wakened her, the chime of a text. It was from Gus.

<Checking in. Is Pete OK?>

<I think so. He's asleep.>

She threw on her hoodie, wandered into the kitchen, opened and was perusing the interior of the fridge when movement sounded in the bedroom.

She found Pete sitting on the side of the bed, bleary-eyed but more himself.

"How are you?"

"I've got a massive headache. Also I'm sticky. I fell asleep in a lake of come."

She laughed and got him some ibuprofen. "Change the sheets?"

"Sure."

Pete pulled off the current ones, grabbed new; they put them on together.

As he folded a corner, Pete said, "I'm a little unclear what happened at the march. It's dreamlike."

"You think the god was there?"

"I think so."

She described what happened. Done tucking sheets, they sat; he let himself fall back onto clean cotton.

"I think Bruni will probably be okay," she said, "but you did a number on him. You think he'll go to the police?"

"If he does, we have several witnesses who can say I was defending my friend."

"Still, it's not ideal."

"No. It goes past defending someone, if I act like that."

"I don't like that the god keeps taking you over. We should talk to Hannah again."

The following day, she went in to the office. Getting a cup of coffee, she went looking for Monica.

Monica's office was dark, blank windows looking out over a drizzly winter day. One of the administrative assistants saw her peek in.

"Oh, you weren't here yesterday. Monica had a family emergency."

"Oh no! What's wrong?"

The girl's face twisted in worry. "Her mom's real sick, heart trouble. She flew to California to be with her. It's hard to say how long she'll have to stay."

"I'm sorry."

"We're getting together some money to send a card and flowers—you want to join us? Talk to Cherie."

Joanie nodded, numb.

A couple of days later, midmorning, she got a call from Pete.

"It looks like Bruni went to the police."

"Oh yeah?" Getting up, she shut the door of her office and sat down again. Rain speckled the window.

"Some policemen showed up at my door early and wanted to talk to me. I gave them the usual spiel. I'm a white boy, so after I said I wouldn't talk without a lawyer, they went away."

"Do you have a lawyer?"

"I have some contacts."

"Shit."

"I don't think we need to worry yet. Next they have to get an arrest warrant. Since this is hardly their top priority, that'll take a few days. And no one took video of that fight. At least, I don't think they did."

"No, I don't think so either."

"Yeah, I don't think this will go anywhere."

"Do you want me to come over tonight?"

"Sure."

That night, as Joanie came in, Gus and Pete were talking across loud Celtic music. Alyssa sipped seltzer next to Gus.

"I can hook you up with my lawyer. I think pretty highly of her."

"I might take you up on that."

Seeing Joanie, Pete took her under his arm. "Hey, question for you," he said. "We talked about that guy Mark Walker having alt-right connections, and we thought it might be Max."

"Yeah." She'd talked it over with Gus and Pete. Gus had pointed out Max was in Austria, just as Mark's wife's family was.

"I wonder if that's where the Hunt's getting their money, from Mark and friends? It costs money to get lawyered up."

"Have they lawyered up?"

"I'm guessing so. It's not like Odin's Hunt to go to the police over a fistfight. My guess is they're getting money and advice."

Maybe they were talking to Max.

Pete turned to Gus. "Hey, before I forget, I meant to ask you —what do you think of this stout?" He handed Gus his beer bottle.

As the two talked beer, Joanie took Alyssa aside into the small kitchen.

"You thought Pete was out of control, the other day, at the march."

"He was, don't you think?"

"I'm going to take him back to Hannah."

"Do you think that's enough? He almost killed Bruni."

"It's a kind of berserker rage. I think it's connected to his experience at Samhain. I think talking to Hannah again is the next step."

"Okay." Alyssa glanced at the two guys taste-testing beer. "But what if he's not drawing down? What if he's just crazy?"

"That's why we have counseling and psychiatrists and drugs."

As if those would work to exorcise a god.

Next evening she spent by herself, in her room, which was set off by a dark-rose brocade curtain from the rest of the Firebird House basement. Across her windows, a trellised grapevine twisted, barely visible against darkness. She lit her coral-pink candle for Inanna.

At Samhain, she'd been told to keep a shrine for her goddess-self. She'd gotten and anointed a beeswax candle; she lit that too.

Her days had been broken up with two lovers. She hadn't paid as much devotion as she'd wanted to.

But with Pete, she'd felt the goddess she'd connected to at Samhain, the atmosphere of an Inanna shrine, glowing soft pink, the cries of humans making love.

She called that goddess forth.

Yes, there was doom everywhere. But there was a way through.

The Sumerians had come through hard times, drought,

disease, famine, war. But Inanna had lived, morphing into Ishtar, still worshipped now.

And she, Joanie, had a calling with Inanna.

In her mind, Joanie saw her path forward as a golden thread.

~

To see their girl connect with the goddess that was herself—for Puabi-Ekur, a star of happiness burst.

But the golden path she and her friends followed was fragile.

At a thought, Puabi-Ekur went up, and up, out, then dove back in, to commune with Dea, keeping an eye on Pete.

The most fragile point was Pete.

~

"I'll just do something simple for dinner," Hannah told Joanie over the phone. "You bring dessert."

"You don't need to feed us."

"You're sayin' words, but I'm not hearin' them."

Hannah loved coconut cream pie, and on her way home Joanie stopped by a bakery. A bit battered, the pie box accompanied her and Pete on the bus, through dark streets, past rose leaves shining with rain on the arbor.

They entered to the scent of food. In the narrow kitchen, Hannah was putting on finishing touches. She inspected the pie.

"My favorite. Y'all mind setting the table?"

Hannah had roasted the chicken with Cajun seasoning, collard greens and cornbread on the side.

"Hannah, this is amazing," Pete said. "The chicken's perfect."

After pie, in the ritual room downstairs, Hannah sat down by a table in one of the alcoves. On a nearby ledge sat a statue of three-formed Hekate, dark and shining, its patina like bronze. Joanie told her about the march and Bruni.

"That god's getting to be a little too much for you, huh?"

"I'm starting to get scared."

"That can happen to anyone, but particularly since you jumped in without any training. I'd say for now, back off entirely. No meditation, nothing. Just stay in the here and now, grounded and present. If you feel the god trying to get at you, do something that brings you back, like eating or sleeping. Meanwhile, Joanie can do some work to propitiate the god, make it clear y'all are still cool with the Horned One, just taking a break."

"Like a relationship," Joanie said. "Just taking a step back for a bit."

"Exactly. Then, you and I can work together to get you back into meditating with your deity. I think this relationship is important, for you and for the world. But we need you healthy and happy in the world too."

"I can do that," Pete said.

"I can talk to the Horned God," Joanie said. "I'll make him an altar in my room."

Puabi-Ekur watched, off in the woods with Dea.

Green and brown, ancient, coiled like a snake, she kept her counsel.

The Horned God was her consort of old. But Dea must

know, as Puabi-Ekur did, how attached human beings were to their little lives.

After Joanie put out the magical call, items for the Horned God's altar appeared. Stopping by the coffee shop, Joanie learned a friend was moving had to get rid of tchotchkes, one a tiny ceramic figurine of a rearing stag. She had it with her, the easier to get rid of it. "Cute, isn't it? But it's bound to break in the move."

Joanie snatched it up.

Cleo gave her a big green candle, and the winter wind brought into Firebird House's narrow yard a fall of fir twigs to put at the altar's base.

She put a tiny altar next to Inanna's. Lighting the candle, into darkness she said, "Horned One, forest god, guide and protector, please look after Pete. Be gentle to him. Our devotion remains with you." As an afterthought, she added, "And please extend your protection to myself."

Chapter 76

*G*us decided to push a couple of his classes out to summer. Statistics and genetics was plenty for this quarter. He was hunkered in his dark room reading, just the desk lamp on, when he got a call.

"This is it," Julia said. "I've got to move."

"What happened?"

"They threatened me when I was with my kid."

He pushed himself away from his desk, leaning back in his chair. "Are you okay?"

"I'm fine, I just need to talk."

"Sure."

"It was time to take Noah to his dad's for the weekend. I'm about to go, and I look out and see two men by my car. No one I know, both wearing bandanas for masks. So I called my neighbor, and he came around back and walked me and Noah out to the car. It was tense. My neighbor was like, 'I'm going to have to ask you boys to leave, or we'll all just sit here till the police arrive.' Meanwhile, I took their pictures on my phone, and pictures of the cars around. Finally they cleared out, but one of them said, 'We'll be back. For you and for him.' And they pointed at Noah."

"That sounds scary. Can you come here?"

"Do you really want me to?"

Julia had stuck her neck out for him, and the least he could do was protect her.

"Of course I do."

"It won't make problems with your girlfriend?"

"No." Alyssa knew the score.

"Okay. I have a bag packed, and I told my ex I was going to a friend's. I didn't say who. He used to be in Odin's Hunt, and I don't entirely trust him."

In about forty-five minutes, she arrived—hair mussed, in a baggy sweatshirt. When he put his arms around her, she was trembling. She started crying, and he kissed her tears.

"Oh, Gus. I guess this was always going to happen."

"Maybe. I'm sorry."

"I thought they were really my friends."

"People change. I was about to go to bed. I can sleep on the couch."

"No, please, stay with me. I could use the comfort."

He slept with his arms around her, wondering how his life had gotten so complicated.

Chapter 77

*M*onica stayed in California a week, then two. Don made sure her clients were covered. From day to day, Joanie expected to see her back.

She wanted to talk about the contract in person. She didn't want to ask Jack. Doing that might mess with Monica's plans.

Joanie's dinner date with Mark Walker came up, on a February night just shy of Valentine's, eight p.m. downtown. He was mysterious about where.

"You don't have to go," Cleo said, over coffee at the coffee shop the day before. Joanie had gotten her usual cappuccino. Cleo's thesis had been approved, and she'd let herself celebrate with a mocha. "You can say no, Monica or no Monica."

"Eh, it's just dinner."

Cleo looked at her under her eyebrows.

"Why are you bothering with this guy? You don't owe him shit. Put him off."

"I've already put him off. If I don't go tonight, he'll drop the bomb, and everything will come out sideways. I can still get what I want, and I mean to do that."

Cleo gave her a jaundiced look. "I have a bad feeling about this."

"It's just dinner. It'll be fine. I'll be pleasant, maybe give him a kiss. I'll string him along just a little bit more till Monica gets back."

"Are you certain this will work?"

"There will be waiters and various other human beings. I can stab him with a fork if I have to."

Pete took a different tack.

<You're worried, aren't you?>

<Yes>

<It's downtown, right? I can be in distance of a call, if you need me.>

Maybe this was ridiculous. She was a grown adult. She'd been taking his self-defense lessons. But it felt good someone wanted to take care of her. Cleo did too, but with Cleo that often took the form of second-guessing her.

<OK>

And after a moment: <Thank you. <3 >

Chapter 78

The night of the dinner date, she worked late at the office. She changed into a cocktail dress after everyone had gone. A little black dress, with a modest scoop neckline and a skirt to her knees. She wore black pumps with low heels, and good-girl pearls.

Over the dress, under her raincoat, she wore a black bolero jacket with a lace overlay that matched. She'd found it thrifting. She liked it because it had an inner pocket for her phone.

Dressed, she sat back down at her desk. She had plenty to do—she'd taken admin work for a few other of Don's clients. But she found it hard to concentrate.

Finally, not having heard from Mark, she texted him—she couldn't meet him if she didn't know where.

<Hi, Mark! Where did you want to meet?>

<Why don't you meet me at the hotel? The penthouse has a bar; let's meet there.>

She hadn't seen anything at the hotel about this penthouse bar. But whatever—she just wanted to get this over with.

A cold, rainy Seattle evening, dark blue clotted clouds hung over it. Rather than spend twenty minutes crossing downtown, she called a Lyft, then regretted it because it ran late and she sat in her office fidgeting.

She walked in past the potted palms.

At the elevators, she pressed P for penthouse. Going up, she studied the elevator interior panels, grey-stained wood, light-bulbs recessed in the elevator ceiling.

She was close to hyperventilating.

The electronic buzzing came up in her head, always present as she approached Mark.

It's just dinner.

Stepping out of the elevator, she found herself at the door of the penthouse suite.

"The penthouse has a bar," he'd said. She'd assumed a retail bar—maybe he'd meant her to. Likely there was a wet bar in the suite.

He'd heard the elevator and opened the door, stood in front of her. He wore a blue oxford shirt, dress pants—less formal than she'd ever seen him. She caught a scent of cologne, subtle, mint with woody undertones.

"Come in."

She froze.

She wanted to keep her job. Maybe she could talk him around.

She went in.

A big room, with a blue rug, its walls beige and neutral, it held another painting of bathers. A few feet away lay a king bed, with white sheets and a cream coverlet, its pile of fluffy white pillows immaculate.

"I ordered Champagne."

He gestured to a small table by the cream-colored couch,

where a Champagne bucket held a green bottle. He walked over, poured a flute full, brought it to her.

Insensibly, she took it.

She took a few deep breaths, trying to calm herself.

"I thought you said dinner."

"We can have dinner. They'll bring anything you want from the restaurant up here. Special order, if you like."

"I don't want to special order. I want to eat out." Her voice sounded like a petulant child's, but at least she spoke. She wanted out—out of the room, where she could get away.

His gaze drilled into her.

"Joanie, I thought you understood me."

She set her glass down on the table, a little awkward even in the lowest of heels. "I thought there was a bar up here. I wasn't thinking you meant the penthouse suite. I don't want to have dinner here." With each sentence, she backed toward the exit.

He moved between her and the door. "Joanie, I thought you wanted this."

He thought he had her trapped.

She needed to play for time.

"Oh, all right. But I do want a nice dinner." Leaning forward, she gave him the lightest possible kiss on the cheek. She slipped off her raincoat and folded it over a chair. "Mind if I use the ladies'?"

"Not at all."

In the bathroom, she locked the door. Slipping her phone out of her bolero pocket, she turned on the water in the sink and called Pete.

He picked up immediately.

"It's not good. I'm at the hotel he owns, the one I told you about. He said to meet him in the penthouse bar, but I got here, and he meant the penthouse suite. Me, him, room service, and a big king bed."

"Have you ordered room service yet?"

"No."

"Text me something, anything, when you do, and I'll be in the room in fifteen minutes."

"Okay, done." She made a kissing sound. "I love you."

"I love you too, sweetheart."

She took a few deep breaths.

Turning off the water, she slipped out of the bathroom, smiling her best whore smile.

"I'm happy you decided to meet me."

Taking her by the shoulders, he kissed her full on the mouth, slipping her his tongue. She endured it.

"Let's have dinner." Stepping away, she found the menu on the table, scanned it. "Do you want some oysters?"

While he was on the phone ordering, she moved to stand behind him, and texted Pete: <now>

Fifteen minutes, and she'd be free.

In the meantime, she inched toward the door. Maybe she could make a run for it.

He caught her movement out of the side of his eye. "On the phone?"

"Just wanted to turn it off."

Setting down the room receiver, Mark again moved between her and the door.

She hadn't focused on how big he was. More than six feet tall, broad shouldered. He probably weighed twice what she did.

She needed to play for time.

"Looks like there's a balcony!" She went to part the curtains at the end of the big room. Opening the door, she stepped out into the wet air.

It had stopped raining. The clouds had wisped to shreds; a waxing half-moon shone down, a gleam of hope.

Selene, Luna, Moon-Goddess, I ask your aid. Hekate, Horned God, Inanna, if you ever loved me, hear me now.

Puabi-Ekur.

It was a nexus point, a place where fates change.

All was in place to save their girl and defeat this djinn Mark. Puabi-Ekur had smoothed the way. Dea hovered nearby, supporting her consort, the Horned God.

Mark came up behind Joanie. He took her waist in both hands in proprietary fashion, then with one hand stroked her ass. Going lower, he slipped his fingers between her legs, slid them up along her inner thigh, began caressing her through her panties.

"I've been thinking about you all day," he said in a low voice.

"How nice," she said, flatly.

As he saw it, she had no protection. Don wouldn't stand up for her. If she tried fighting him legally, her background would hurt her. He had all the lawyers money could buy.

She stepped away. "Let's have some Champagne."

She found her glass on the table, settled herself not on the couch but on a nubbly beige chair, smiling sweetly.

He stood in front of her. "You're such a beautiful girl."

"That's nice." She smiled up at him, still seated.

"I want you to feel how excited I am." He moved close to her chair, looming over her.

A power play. She hated bullies.

"I'm sorry, can I just have a moment?" Leaping up, she ran to the bathroom, leaving her empty Champagne glass. Making the door, she locked it behind her.

She pulled her phone out of her bolero pocket, looked at the time.

Eleven minutes had passed.

Four more, or less, and Pete would be there.

She took her lipstick out of the bolero pocket, and slowly, languorously made up her lips. Red, like blood.

She wanted to kill Mark. With a knife—a knife would be satisfying. She wanted to stab him again and again.

"Joanie, come out."

"In a moment."

She owed him nothing.

With no haste, she washed her hands and opened the door.

Facing her stood a tall man, square-shouldered, mane of grey hair now rough. She stared at him, frowning, letting her displeasure show.

He ignored it.

"I want you, Joanie." He took her hand and put it to his crotch. Under loose cloth, his penis was hard.

She didn't move her hand, but she didn't rub, either, just stared unblinking into his eyes, pure defiance.

"So hot," he said. Taking her by her wrists, he threw her on the bed.

He leaped on top, holding her down, kissing her face, grinding against her. She let it happen.

Come on, Pete.

Still pinning one of her wrists, he slid his other hand under her neckline and fondled her breasts. Most of his weight lay on her. She had a hard time breathing.

A knock at the door. "Room service."

Pete's voice.

Thank the gods.

Mark jumped up. She rolled off the bed and stood, hair messy, lipstick smudged, shaking in fear and anger.

Mark stepped over, unlocked the door, opened it.

There was Pete, all six feet of him, in a black hoodie, black t-shirt, black jeans. Hood back, buzzcut hair blazing red, golden-red aura around him.

He had no room service cart.

"You're not—"

"No, I'm not." Pete took one big step into the room and glanced at her, saw her mussed state. His mouth set. "Joanie's coming with me." She scurried to stand beside him in the narrow entryway. "But before that—"

He took two steps toward Mark and hit him in the face, knocking him down.

Oh, shit.

Mark bounced back up again.

"Fuck you, you little shit bastard. You're not getting away with this." Taking Pete by both sides of his hoodie, he head-butted him full in the face.

Pete dropped, falling toward the table—not hitting it.

Mark leaped on top of him and punched him.

Grabbing her Champagne glass, Joanie tossed it at Mark's head—not trying to shatter it, more to distract him.

It did. He glanced at her, angrily. Pete jumped up. Around him flared the red-gold aura of the Horned God.

"You disrespected my girlfriend," he said. Grabbing Mark, he threw him across the room.

"Stop this," she hissed. "Let's go." But she might as well have been talking to the wall.

Mark leaped to standing. "Fuck you, punk!"

They threw themselves on each other, struggling, fell to the ground wrestling. The electronic buzzing Joanie associated with Mark returned, loud.

She grabbed the Champagne bottle. If she could get a good angle, she could drop Mark and they could get out of there.

Rolling, pushing, punching—Mark was in good shape and hung in.

But Pete had the strength of a god.

Ripping away, he leaped to standing, swung his leg to kick with his steel-toed boot. But Mark, full of adrenaline, jumped up, threw himself on Pete, and knocked him out the door onto the balcony.

She crept close, closer. They wrestled on the cement balcony floor. Pete again dragged himself up, pulled Mark with him, and propped against the balcony railing punched Mark in the face. Mark threw a roundhouse at him.

Momentum threw Pete backward. He grabbed Mark to steady himself. Mark head-butted him, hard.

They went over the railing.

a man's scream. Mark's.

Something awful was in it, a tone Joanie had never heard before—a primal fear of death.

She ran for the balcony, made it just as they hit, thud and thud again.

Twelve floors down, on the sidewalk, two bodies lay—tiny broken dolls, limbs at odd angles.

She took a deep breath in.

I can't freak out or cry. I have to deal.

She called 9-1-1, grabbed her things, and took the elevator down.

Outside the hotel in the cold night, the policewoman—she was glad it was a woman—walked her through every detail. It took a long time.

"I was going to meet him for dinner, and he met me here. I'd expected dinner at a restaurant. I was scared, so I called my boyfriend. He came up to get me, and they started fighting."

The moon had gone in, a wet wind, no rain.

The authorities cleared the area and cordoned off the block with yellow tape. They'd taken the bodies away in an ambulance, but both men were dead.

That scream—Mark had known he would die.

Pete had made no sound.

She thought of Mark's wife. Whatever arrangement they had, she didn't deserve this.

After about a half-hour, Cleo showed up, hovering outside the police tape. By about eleven, the police released Joanie, and Cleo took her home.

"Sleep with me tonight," Cleo said.

"I don't know if I can sleep."

"I don't care."

She lay in Cleo's arms under the spangled hangings. After a while, from her breathing, she could tell Cleo was asleep.

Joanie was frozen. She kept hearing the last scream, seeing the broken bodies.

She woke in the middle of the night, crying.

She moved to get up, not to wake Cleo, but Cleo was awake.

"Oh, baby. Come here."

She let Cleo take her in her arms.

"My sweet girl. How are we going to get through this?"

Joanie only cried.

"We'll figure it out."

In the morning, first light pale and dripping, Cleo took control. She called Gus, asking Gus if he knew how to get a hold of Dave. They agreed Dave could get the word out to friends. She called Hannah briefly, to let her know and to ask advice— Hannah had dealt with deaths before.

Joanie sat naked on the bed, watching her.

"Now all that's started. His body's going to be at the hospital. The next of kin can pick it up. Who's his next of kin?"

"Probably his parents."

"Do you need to see him again?"

Joanie burst into tears.

"Okay, let's not talk about that. But there's one more thing you need to do this morning, and that's call in to work."

Joanie pulled herself together, sniffling, wiped her eyes.

"I should talk to Monica if she's back. She's been about to come back for a week."

"Are you quitting?"

"I can't imagine otherwise."

She wanted to collapse. She wanted just to sit on her bed rocking, for days, weeks, years. Whatever it took. But the world hadn't stopped.

The first couple of times, she got Monica's voicemail. The third time, just before she tried someone else, she got through.

"Hi, this is Monica."

"This is Joanie." She didn't know how to do this. Monica had her own trouble too. "Did you hear the news?"

"What news?"

"About Mark Walker."

"We found out he—wait, what? Did you have something to do with it?"

Joanie dragged her hand through her hair. She'd gotten into her bathrobe, at least—progress. "Yes. He said he wanted to have dinner. He tricked me into meeting him at his hotel's penthouse. I was frightened and called my boyfriend. They fought, and they both fell off the balcony."

A god threw them off the balcony. But she couldn't say that.

"How awful. I'm so sorry. You should take the day, whatever you need."

"Monica, I think I need to quit."

Silence, as Monica processed.

"Okay."

"I'm really sorry to do this to you, especially right now. But I just can't come back."

"Okay. I won't ask you to do the two weeks. This is crazy. But take a few days first. Take your vacation, whatever you have on the books."

"I don't care about that."

"Every few days of pay count when you're just starting out."

Monica was right, and she was looking out for her.

"Thank you."

"I'll tell Don. Let me know when you're coming in to get your things. I'd like to be there." She wanted to keep Don away from Joanie.

That night, Cleo asked Joanie to sleep in her bedroom again.

"I can't. I'm keeping you awake."

"I don't care. You're my girl. I want to take care of you."

"Cleo, don't. You need your sleep." Cleo rolled her eyes, but Joanie held fast.

She loved that Cleo wanted to support her, but she needed to be alone.

So she was alone that night, in the cold basement. In the windy night, the transition between winter and spring, the grapevine rattled against the basement windows.

She couldn't sleep.

Mark's scream haunted her. As he fell, he'd known he would die.

He was a shitty person, but death was so—final.

And Pete, Pete.

After a while, she sat up, sheets and blankets bundled around her.

How could you do this to me? she thought, at her gods.

It wasn't Inanna who'd taken him. Sitting next to her Inanna candle was the other candle, for the god.

Asshole.

Wrapping herself up warmly, she grounded and lit the Horned God's candle.

"All right, motherfucker. What the fuck did you do that for?"

Maybe it was being three-quarters asleep and out of her mind with grief, but she got an answer.

The warmth of the god rose, a deep animal warmth, a sexual warmth. It was hard to keep her anger, but she held onto it.

What came to her then was wordless, tactile feelings and emotions, yet she could follow. A sense of coming from a great warm depth, to a narrow, chilly space: incarnation. Being abruptly awakened, thrust out into the world, as the Horned One had been at Samhain.

The narrowness, the embodiment—gods don't know how to

drive human bodies. And anger, at her being preyed upon. Outsized, as a god is angry.

"Joanie?"

She started.

"Pete?"

"Yes."

I'm just lying to myself.

"It's me," he said. The warmth grew stronger, as if he was holding her. "I love you so much. I miss you."

"How, why?"

"The god brought me here. Don't be angry—it isn't his fault."

"How is it not? He took you over. He made you fight."

"No, fighting was my choice. The god made me powerful, so I could accomplish what I wanted. But I started it."

"But did you want to kill him?"

"Yes. The god granted me my wish."

"But, Pete—it was a stupid wish." She leaped from the bed, pacing. "You shouldn't have wished it. You had a whole life to live. Now you're dead."

"I am, Joanie, but it's not what you think. It's amazing. I can see so much. I can fly! Watch for what happens after this. I think you'll be pleased."

"But, Pete—how can I be? I love you. I want you back."

"Oh, Joanie."

The feeling of being wrapped in his arms intensified, as if a length of warm scarf had been tied around her.

"I love you too."

Wordlessly, it sank into her body. He was dead. Gone. It could not be undone.

She sobbed, sorrow pouring from her.

His presence stayed till she fell asleep.

Puabi-Ekur watched Dea, green and dark, lady of caves in her bear-aspect.

Had she called Pete to herself, to die?

But this thought brought a swirl of energy, a growl. Dea had been with humans for many lives. She knew now not to ask for sacrifice.

Pete had wanted murder. He'd called death to himself. And yet flung by the god, he'd made ripples.

Perhaps an entire malign fate had disappeared.

Chapter 80

The landlord gave Gus notice to vacate—he had fifteen days. Alyssa offered to let him move back in. Julia had found a place in Renton.

She and Gus traded moving help. She had an entire half-duplex to deal with, and a lot of her things went into storage.

After their last trip, they reconnoitered once more at their coffee shop, white with mauve trim, with its open-format bookcases and potted succulents.

"How are you doing?" Julia asked him.

Mostly he was weary. He'd made it clear at the beginning the visit could only be coffee.

"I'm okay. I mean, I miss Pete, obviously. He introduced me to Antifa. I'm grateful for that."

"I'm really sorry." She put her hand over his on the table.

She filled him in on her side—she'd been talking to Jake's wife, who was no fan of Bruni's.

"On the criminal trespass charges, Bruni's lawyer talked him into a plea bargain. He's on two years probation. While that's on his record, he should lie low."

Gus fidgeted with his coffee cup. "Is he smart enough to do that?"

"Who's to say? I think Odin's Hunt will leave you alone for now."

"Maybe."

Pete's parents showed up while Gus packed, collecting his few pans, plates, and pieces of silverware from the kitchen.

The key turned in the lock, and a man in a tan trench coat entered; next followed a woman, also trench-coated, with a flowered scarf. They looked East Coast. The man had Pete's height. Though her hair had gone white, the woman had faded freckles. Pete had gotten his coloring from her.

"Hey," Gus said, and then inanely, because the man stood glaring, "can I help you?"

"Who are you?"

"Pete's roommate, or was." He held out his hand to shake. The man ignored it.

"We're here to get Pete's stuff," the man said.

They stared at each other.

"Can you point out what's what?" the man said impatiently.

The woman stepped forward. "Now, George, the young man's probably distraught."

This jogged a reminder. "I'm sorry for your loss."

The man gave a tiny nod.

"Pretty much everything left is Pete's," Gus said. "I'm just grabbing my kitchen things." He pointed to Pete's room. "That one's Pete's."

The two moved in the direction of Pete's room.

"Hey," Gus said, "while you're here—"

Pete's mother stopped.

"Yes?"

"You going to have a memorial service? Pete had a lot of friends."

Her exactly painted orange-red mouth pinched tight.

"We're taking the body back home. We'll have a small memorial there."

She disappeared into Pete's room.

Chapter 81

a few days later, Joanie went in to her old office to pick up her things.

In a sunbreak, she approached a dream skyscraper, steel and windows shining with reflected light. Up the elevator, she went to reception, its wall cobalt blue.

She remembered how excited she'd been to start—ambivalent, yes, but excited.

Now she was numb, moving as if underwater. She could afford no sidetracks; if she sidetracked, she stopped dead in place, like someone catatonic.

Monica met her in reception, and they went to Joanie's office, against its big, white pillar. It sat bright with glaring sun from its huge window. Closed for days, it was hot and stuffy.

She didn't have much: a coffee cup, a plant she'd gotten as a gift, some pictures of her nieces. Monica found her a box. She packed as Monica watched.

"You about done?" Monica asked, when she stopped.

"Just let me take one more pass." She stood by the desk, eyes roaming the room.

"I'm going to the bathroom. Be right back."

Thirty seconds, and Don appeared at the door—sport coat and chinos, blue eyes narrowed.

He drew the door shut behind him. The sun made his eyes chips of sky.

"I guess this is goodbye, huh?"

"Yeah. I just can't stay here."

"So your boyfriend killed Mark Walker."

"Uh—they fought."

He closed in, six inches away from her.

"We had a deal, you and me. I gave you everything you asked for. But you didn't keep your end of the bargain."

"If you think—"

"Now the whole thing's going to fall apart. Best deal I ever made in my life. And you had to screw it up."

They stared at each other.

What could she say?

"I—"

The door flew open. Monica stepped in. "Don, what are you doing? Get out of here."

One last look of blue fire, and Don stalked out.

Monica shut the door behind him and turned to Joanie.

"He's been insane since all this went down."

Half-sitting on the desk, she glanced out the glass door to check who was there.

Leaning forward, she said, "His insurance scheme is going to get audited now, since Walker Nelson is going to have to restructure. I'm pretty sure it's illegal. Which means Don's going down."

She sat back and took a deep breath.

"That means Gunnar Group is going down. Jack's name is

on that thing too. Nine months, tops, we close the doors. I'm job-hunting."

"Really."

"It's the way of this business. It's hard to make real money in a large shop, but in small shops, you're in danger of people like Don."

Not only had Pete and the god taken down Mark, but also the whole financial group.

"I think that's it," Joanie said, looking around.

Monica slipped off the desk and gave her a hug. "Best of luck. Let me know if you need a reference. And let's have a drink sometime."

Time had stopped, and every day was like the next, grey inside and out, sodden earth and steady rain.

Joanie needed a job. An opening had come at the coffee shop. She needed to take it.

She gave herself a deadline, two weeks of full-on grieving. A deadline was ridiculous, but she needed something to make sure it wasn't forever.

Gus had let her take one of Pete's old, sweaty black t-shirts from the laundry pile. She kept it in a plastic bag. She didn't take it out much, because it made her cry.

With Cleo's help, she slowly mended.

Just one thing stuck out from this grey, slow time. An email reached her from an anonymized source:

We know your boyfriend killed Mark Walker.

It was what Don had said. But the email didn't feel like Don. Her guess was Don was out scrambling for his next job.

The email went on:

Your boyfriend killed Mark Walker because you told
him to.

She blocked the address, and no more mail like that came, but it gave her a cold trickle down the neck.

A few days later, she had to go in to the coffee shop to fill out employment papers. She rendezvoused there with Gus and Pete's friend Dave, for their take on it.

Wan light fell across the blond wood tables. She got a cappuccino while she waited.

They showed up together—they'd bonded over the last bit. She showed the mail to them.

"The mail was sent through an anonymous proxy. So we can't tell from the mail itself," Dave said. "Who would do this?"

"I don't think it's Don," she said. "He was angry, but my guess is, right now he's running around looking for his next gig. He's not going to bother with me."

"Who else knows and cares?" Dave asked.

Joanie and Gus gazed at each other a moment.

"I can't help wondering if it's the Austrian connection," Gus said.

"The Austrian connection?" Dave asked.

"Pete speculated about this," Joanie said. "We know Max is in Austria. We also know Mark's wife's family is Austrian. Mark said he and Gus had a friend in common, and we think it might be Max."

They glanced at each other.

"This was a week ago, and nothing before or since?" Dave asked.

Joanie nodded.

"I think all we can do is wait for the next move."

The hall lay almost dark, just a few candles lit. A spotlight pointed at the podium, and Celtic music played. Nearly a hundred people had collected: Antifa, people from the university, witch friends.

Hannah and Nora had pulled together a celebration of life, nondenominational since many of Pete's friends were atheist. Everyone could give eulogies. Joanie both wanted to and didn't want to speak.

One after another, people stood and told memories, vignettes, stories. In the end, she read a poem, though she finished it crying. Then there was no one left to speak.

Hannah came forward and took the mic. "Thanks, everyone, for the beautiful words. Before we close, I wanted to give Pete a couple minutes of silence. There's candles here, up by the podium, if you want to light them, to carry your prayers or thoughts. Or you can take a candle and light it at home."

Joanie stepped up, lit her tealight, set it on the table garlanded with pine and early daffodils.

For the first few days, she'd felt him constantly. It had gotten less, but now he rushed in.

I'll always love you. All my life.

Chapter 82

She started at the coffee shop again, with a weird sense of déjà vu.

That first day, putting her hair up in a ponytail, tying on her apron, pulling coffee, smiling at customers—it was strange. She'd been here a year ago.

Still, things had changed. When the owner gave her back her manager position, he made it clear he wanted her to stay. He hinted she might over time move to general manager, take the reins of the business. Her degree and business background helped, also her many months of hard work.

The world around them had changed as well. And she had changed. She'd paid down her student debt. She'd also learned something: she wasn't meant for the corporate world. She'd dealt with her share of corporate titans, or would-be corporate titans, as a whore, and now in the financial industry. She didn't like the unequal playing field.

The golden thread of her life pointed toward the Inanna shrines. Get the accounting degree eventually—money wasn't going anywhere; trade predated capitalism. But find a way out of "normal life"; whore for the goddess, maybe run the coffee shop. She might check in too with Nora, her tiny house and witch-farm projects, herbs and herbal tinctures. Create the community Joanie had imagined at summer solstice.

At least Pete's death had nudged her that direction. She wasn't going to let him sacrifice himself and then fall right back into the corporate trap he'd saved her from.

It gave her a new determination to get on with things.

The Horned God had sacrificed himself, again—the deer god gave himself that people might live, a pattern old as the Paleolithic yet still alive. Now Dea was leading Pete across the planes to join the mighty dead.

Puabi-Ekur floated up, up, up, to the wave of green-golden light, the plane of becoming. They saw also part of its result, the web of being, the golden weaving of interactions of everything on earth.

The drought had cursed Akkad the same way the path of fire menaced Joanie and her friends. But now Joanie was stronger on her green-gold path. Pete had exploded into the ether, changing her forever.

In some way, small on this plane, larger elsewhere, the whirling maelstrom of cold metal had retreated, beaten back by the red-gold flame of the Horned God. The change reverberated across the golden web.

Chapter 83

*a*gainst the sunrise, the sky to the east palest pink, a stand of oaks rose silhouetted at the top of the hill. Nearer, rows of grapevines stood on props, one after the other, orderly, in the mist of early morning.

Ekur and Eannatum got there as the rest of the harvesters collected.

In the grape fields of the foothills, workers were always needed. Eannatum's family had been happy to take them on. Now harvest had come, and all hands spent the long days in hot sun, steady work. A quick look to see if the grapes were healthy, a snip with the wine shears, a toss into the basket, then you moved on.

At the harvest celebration, the families roasted goat and drank wine from earlier vintages. Eannatum managed to snag a wine jar. After a time, he and Ekur came away from the communal fire to their hut at the edge of the small village.

He lit a few of the lamps, which they'd set around a rough-mown courtyard. Some of Eannatum's cousins laughed at their city ways, but they kept lighting the lamps.

Eannatum filled for them each a crude pottery cup. Back in Akkad, Cook would have spurned such pottery.

Ekur raised a toast. "To the lady Inanna, and to Geshti-nanna, heavenly grapevine, lady of wine." He poured some out, then drank. Eannatum did also.

Sometimes they got news of Akkad. Four kings had ruled in four years. The Gutians kept raiding, with destruction, plague, and death. Ekur sent tablets to Irkalla when villagers went west to sell wine. So far he'd heard nothing in return.

Tonight, by the glinting lamps, being alive with a little wine in him had to be enough.

At least as Ekur they had come to this resting place. With Joanie, Puabi-Ekur could do better, lead her to Witch Farm and make it bloom into a paradise.

Chapter 84

*a*t the end of the day when they hand-irrigated Witch Farm, everyone was exhausted. As they collected in the kitchen, someone suggested something simple, maybe lentil soup. A couple of the younger folk, still relatively fresh, volunteered to cook.

"I'll wash dishes," Joanie said.

They ate and washed up as the sky darkened, a rare night with no clouds, stars against a clear dark like silk. They found their way to the outdoor firepit.

Cleo brought a couple tiny cups and the last of a bottle of lavender tincture. Tracy built and lit the fire.

"You going to play tonight?" Joanie asked him.

"Maybe. I wanted to hear your story, about the person who loved Celtic music."

Cleo glanced over at Joanie. "How would you tell this story?"

She looked into the flames, stirring the coals with a stick.

"Once upon a time, there was a man who was a god."

About the Author

Mary Trepanier writes fantasy, horror, and erotica. You can find her short stories in the *Blood in the Rain* anthologies of vampire erotica, among others. For more of *Tales of the End Times*, check out *The Queen of Heaven's Daughter and The Deer Stalker*.

Join my mailing list by clicking THIS LINK and be the first to learn about the second volume in the *Tales of the End Times* series.

Tumblr : https://marytrepanier.tumblr.com/

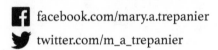

facebook.com/mary.a.trepanier

twitter.com/m_a_trepanier

9 781947 234321